BUCKSKIN DOUBLE:

RIFLE RIVER

GUNSTOCK

ROY LeBeau

LEISURE BOOKS NEW YORK CITY

A LEISURE BOOK®

October 2006

Published by

Dorchester Publishing Co., Inc.
200 Madison Avenue
New York, NY 10016

ISBN 0-8439-2375-X

Visit us on the web at www.dorchesterpub.com.

CATHOUSE TERROR

It came from next door.

Lee was already standing beside the bedstead with the Colt in his hand and cocked before the second scream came.

The two women lay frozen on the bed.

The scream rang out again; not the furious yell of a drunken whore. It was a shriek of terror. Lee had heard a girl scream like that before, in Old Mexico. Her throat had been cut a moment later.

He started around the bed without thinking—then he thought. And stopped. He was in this valley to make a home—not more trouble.

Then he heard the clatter of boots on the stairs, coming up fast. The girl started to scream again, just out in the hall, but the cry was cut short.

Phyllis was lying in the bed as white as the sheets. She was crying without making a sound. The Indian girl was stroking her hair to comfort her.

There was a shout out in the hall—Lee couldn't make out the words—then some kind of swift scuffle, and the sudden, cracking blast of a shotgun.

It sounded like a stick of dynamite going off just outside the door. Phyllis screamed and covered her face with her hands.

RIFLE RIVER

PROLOGUE

In the early 1880's, throughout the whole West, perhaps only a dozen men were known as truly supreme gunfighters—the deadly best of the thousands of tough, gunwise frontiersmen who made their livings by violence: manhunters, Indian fighters, lawmen and bandits. The names of these top guns were known to everyone, and one of the most infamous was Buckskin Frank Leslie.

Gambler, killer-for-hire, ladies' man and mad dog—he had been called them all. Friend to Doc Holliday and the Earps, deadly enemy of the Texan killers, Ben Thompson and Clay Allison, Buckskin Frank Leslie had killed twenty-seven men with knife and gun by the time he was thirty. Doc Holliday called him "the fastest gun I ever saw."

Then one night in a savage, booming trail town, the legend of Frank Leslie came to an end. In a blaze of gunfire, provoked by Leslie himself in a drunken rage, a young girl was accidently shot to death by a terrified tinhorn gambler. The girl, a young dance hall singer, had loved Frank Leslie. And he had loved her.

Within hours of the girl's funeral, Buckskin Frank Leslie had ridden out of town. And out of history. He was never heard of again.

CHAPTER ONE

Fred Lee reined the big dun in and sat back easy in the saddle to take a long look down Rifle River. The narrow, brawling mountain stream raced straight down the mountain slopes to the broad green valley beyond On the skyline, the *cordillera* of the Rockies rose granite-gray and snow-peak white against the clear vacant blue of the Montana sky.

It was a perfect spring day. The kind of day when most men are happy to be alive.

The big dun, catching the scent of spring grass from the rich valley below, snorted and shook its head shifting under Lee's calming hand.

Lee was a man in his thirties, lean, wire muscled, a shade under six feet tall. His face, high cheekboned almost gaunt, was sunburned into a deep mahogany scored by squint and weather lines about the dark, gray eyes and thin, drawn lips.

He might have been a ranch foreman, or small ranch owner, judging by his fine horse and neat woolen trousers, tooled leather boots, and pale gray Stetson. He wore a Colt .45 Peacemaker, as many of those men did. But his rig was a little different from most. The .45's barrel had been cut down short, to about five inches, and he wore his gun rather high, the walnut butt at his right hipbone, the barrel slanting down and in across the crease of his thigh, almost to his groin. It looked a little odd, but handy.

The only decoration Lee wore was a silver watch chain, and a very handsome fringed vest, decorated along its stitching with tiny turquoise beads. It looked like fine Indian work.

The vest was buckskin.

Lee pulled one foot out of a stirrup, leaned back, and crossed his leg over the saddle bow. He reached into his vest pocket and extracted the fair butt of a black cheroot. He'd smoked most of the cigar that morning.

He struck a lucifer against his saddle, lit up, and sat the dun relaxed as any kid cowpoker, taking a long, long look at the valley below.

It was a pretty big stretch, maybe sixteen or eighteen miles long from where he sat out to the sudden steep foothills rising fast into the Rockies. And about eight or nine miles wide. A big stretch. And probably cold as Belaam's Balls, come winter!

It might become a man's home, a valley like this. Cree Valley, it was called. And it looked good. It looked rich as Greenback Heaven.

Even from this distance, Lee could make out the buildings and smoke of three or four ranches. And he could see the town plain. It sat down square in the middle of the valley, just at the place where the river took its first bend. Up to there, Lee saw that the river did indeed run straight as a rifle shot, but right at the town it took its first bend, and then broke into two branches.

Lee could follow one branch curving off to the left and out of sight beyond a distant hill. The other branch ran on out into the valley's distance. It gleamed like silver under the morning sun.

Lee couldn't make out the number of buildings in the town; it looked to be quite a few. "A fair-sized town," he remembered McGee having said. He'd been leaning on the bar in the Alten House in Helena at the time. "A

9

fair-sized town, Mr. Lee," McGee repeated, "in one of the most goddamned beauties of a valley you ever saw! Now, I warn you, the winters are pure refined pissers up there! But your northern ranchers are a sight smarter than your scrubcattle southerners. Up there, the men put up hay for their beasts instead of leaving them in the snow to scratch or starve! There're no fools up in Cree valley." He'd given Lee a shrewd glance. "But I won't say they're all perfectly peaceful men, either . . ."

"I'm intending to mind my own business wherever I go," Lee had replied.

"So I'm sure you are," said McGee. "Still, it's only fair you should know that there's some of the same small-ranch and big-ranch trouble you find everywhere now." He heaved a sigh and took a big bite of his beef sandwich. "There's a little trouble in every paradise," he'd mumbled through the meat. Some bits of beef fat clung to his ginger whiskers. "No heaven without it."

Lee ground the cigar stub out on the sole of his boot, sat up, and slid his boot toe back into the stirrup. He touched the horse with his spurs, and the big dun, happy to be moving, took off down the long slope in easy swinging strides, single-footing fast along the broken ground beside the steep river bank.

It was a long way down to the valley floor, perhaps a one- or two- thousand-foot drop; it would take most of the day to reach it. And Lee had a stop to make along the way.

Early in the afternoon, after a cold meal of jerky and one of last night's campfire-baked potatoes, Lee pulled the dun up at the edge of a small meadow. Across a stretch of high buffalo grass, the river ran wide over a series of broad rock shelves, bubbling and brawling in the bright mountain sunlight, but running shallow over the stones.

Lee tugged a folded sheet of paper from his vest pocket and unfolded it across his saddle bow.

It was a rough map of the valley and surrounding range. One small section of those hundreds of square miles was outlined in heavy ink. Lee traced it carefully with his finger, looked across the river again, then folded the map and put it away.

He spurred the big horse out across the meadow, breasting through the tall grass to the edge of the river's shallow rapids, on into the racing current without a pause, the dun lunging out into the foaming rapids, plunging and high-stepping through the low, swirling water, its hoofs slipping and clattering on the wet rock shelves drenched with spray.

The dun reached the far bank and lunged up into the thin beech scrub that lined the stream. Lee pulled his Stetson low over his eyes and bent in the saddle as the whippy branches lashed back at him.

"Hold up a little, dammit!" He gathered the reins and slowed the big horse down. The dun's sire had been a Morgan, the dam, some Texan's cross of a mustang Barb and Louisiana Thoroughbred. It made for a restless, shifty horse; but a strong one, and fast enough to win some country races, if Lee had still been interested in that.

He rode cross-country for almost an hour by the big silver hunter on his watch chain. Then he saw the house lower down on the long, gentle mountain slope.

He was still at least a thousand feet above the valley, but the house and some outbuildings rested in a little hollow of their own, overlooking the final, slow fall of the mountainside into Cree Valley.

Two low ridges guarded the ranch buildings on either side, and both ridges were rich with thickly clustered beech and pine.

Lee rode on down.

A few hundred yards out, he saw a man walk out from behind a shed, carrying a sack of something over his shoulder. It looked like feed or seed.

11

Lee could see a twinkle of steel. The man had a pistol stuck in the belt of his pants. He was walking on his way, doing his work. Either he hadn't seen Lee coming down the near side of the ridge or he was pretending so.

Lee stretched back for the Henry carbine in its saddle boot and lifted it out. He didn't care for the Henry much; its short cartridges were short-ranged as well. If he were going to stay in this mountain country, he would need more gun.

The man had seen him now. He'd let the sack down and was standing by the corral fence, waiting.

He was an old man, sixty at least, had a big gray beard, like old Saint Nick, and rusty, tore-up, old cowboy clothes and split boots. He was also bowlegged to a considerable degree.

Lee rode right down to him.

The pistol was a Colt .38 Parrot grip. Clean and oiled.

The old man kept his hands away from it.

"My name's Tim Bupp!" the old man yelled to him. "What the hell is yours?"

Lee waited until he was upon him. He kept the old man in the corner of his eye and watched the windows of the house.

"There's nobody up there, Mr. Nosy!" the old man said. "And I would like to know your name . . ."

"My name's Lee."

"Named after that fancy general, I suppose." The old man was eyeing the dun.

"No, I wasn't."

"Well, whoever, you don't belong on this land, mister! This is the property of the Chicago Union and Development Corporation. And I'm the caretaker, signed on and paid."

"That's all right," said Lee. "Why don't you get a horse saddled and come on down to town with me?"

"Where did you get that horse? It looks to me like

he's got a funny-lookin' back." The old man jerked up his head. "And what the hell do you mean come to town with you?"

"I own this ranch now," Lee said. "And the horse is short one of his backbones; he's part Barb."

"That's it . . . that's it," the old man said, and he slowly walked around the dun, looking it over. "Some horse," he said. He went back to where he'd been standing and bent down to pick up the feed sack. "Shit," he said. "So you bought this ranch, did you? Well, that's bad news for me, if true!"

He walked off with the feed sack, and Lee rode the dun along beside him.

"Why bad news?" said Lee.

"Because I'm too old to be a cowpoker, that's why. And I can't cook worth a damn."

"Is there a woman in town who can cook?"

"Hell yes, and so what?" Bupp dumped the feed out into a trough under the corral fence rails.

"Then you work for her for a few days until you learn something of simple cooking from her—and I'll hire you on."

They both watched the horses come up to the trough to nuzzle the feed. There were two good *grulla* mares, one in foal, and a strong old cob, too slow for working cattle.

"Where are the ranch horses? Where's the cavvy?"

"Sold off," Bupp said. "All sold off when the cattle were." He watched to make sure the pregnant mare was eating well. "These are mine."

"Well, when that cob's fed up, saddle him. I want to get into town and do some business."

When Bupp led the cob off to the stable to saddle him, Lee rode slowly around through the cluster of ranch buildings, getting the feel of the place. The sheds were old, but in good enough shape; the barn was almost new, and bigger than most ranch barns that Lee had seen. Probably for that winter hay. And all the buildings were built solid of heavy, fat, split logs, with fieldstone foundations. They looked crouched down into the ground, braced for a storm—or for a rough mountain winter.

He looked at the house last. He rode the dun up to one of the side windows, bent in the saddle, and peered in. It was dim inside the house. Most of the windows had been left shuttered. The rooms, low-ceilinged and whitewashed, were clean and bare of all but a few pieces of rough furniture: rawhide chairs and a long rawhide sofa too, with feedsack cushions. There was also a long pine-plank table with pine-slat chairs set around it. The room was intended for some sort of parlor; and in fact the whole house was bigger, with more rooms—at least four—than most ranch houses boasted. Lee had known men who owned whole counties, who had started running their empires from a one-room, dirt-floor shanty no more than eight feet by eight and not six feet high at the roof, either. This was a pretty fancy setup and would look odd with just a lone man living in it.

Lee slid the Henry into its saddle scabbard. The house was certainly empty.

He heard the cob's heavy hoofs thumping up behind him.

"Why the hell don't you get down and go in? It's your damned house, isn't it?"

Without answering the old man, Lee turned the dun down the path worn alongside the corral. It looked to lead off down to the valley.

Past the meadows, over the thick green of the ridge woods, he could see the afternoon sun low over the hills to the east. Night would come fast to a valley set this deep.

Bupp kept his peace for the first few miles of their riding, jogging along beside Lee on his stocky cob, occasionally moving ahead on a new lead when the path thinned away under the spring grass. Lee was content to follow him, marking the landscape as they went, so that he'd know how to go the next time.

At a broad meadow, Bupp pulled up and pointed off to the right and broke his silence.

"There's your bad luck over there, Mr. Lee." He said it with a certain satisfaction.

"That so?"

"That it is. Over there, just past that meadow, is your line. And on the other side is Fishhook."

"Is what?"

"Fishhook! Mr. Ashton's place. Everything past there to the mountains is all his. Ashton owns every damn square foot by legal deed, bought and paid for!"

"I won't bother him," Lee said, "if he doesn't bother me."

Bupp turned in his saddle to look back at Lee.

"Doesn't bother you, huh? You talk more like a sport than a cowman, Mr. Lee!"

"I've done some gambling," Lee said.

"You better have," Bupp said, and he spurred the cob on down the trail. "Because you're gambling now, that's for sure!"

They reached the valley an hour later and were combing their way through a thick patch of scrub. Rifle River had curved down the mountain to run beside the narrow trail for a little way, and the scrub growth had taken heart from the flood of water and grown thick enough so that even the dun had to shove and lunge his way through.

"We've got to clear this out down here, burn it out, maybe, or we'll lose some colts."

"Are you planning to raise horses?" Bupp said, and he gave Lee a quick, sidelong glance.

"Yes, I am. Mountain appaloosas, if I can settle a good-enough stud on the place . . ."

"No cows?"

"No," Lee said, guarding his face against a low branch. "I don't know cattle well enough."

Bupp rode along for a few minutes, muttering at the dwarf birch that tripped their horses and tugged at their shirts as they rode through.

"Listen," he said. "Mrs. Boltwith runs the hotel in town, though Christ knows it's not much of a hotel. A road inn is more like it! But she is a fair cook; nobody in town will say she isn't."

He didn't say anything more for a while. They were almost out of the scrub. Lee could see the river water flashing in the sunlight through the last of the brush in front of them.

"Well," said Bupp, "I suppose she'd teach me some cooking, if I was to wash up and swamp for her for a week or two."

"Then you'd have a job with me," Lee said to him. They rode out of the brush, Bupp leading.

A shot cracked past Lee's head and flicked the old man's shirt sleeve as it went on its way.

"Jesus Christ!"

Bupp kicked the spurs to his cob, and took off out into the river meadow at a stiff gallop. It was the wrong thing to do. Any man shooting at them had to be concealed in the scrub they'd just worked through. Out in the open, old Bupp would be dead meat.

Lee hauled the big dun up on his hind legs, turned him, and spurred him back into the tangle of dwarf willow and birch. The big horse squealed at the rake of the spurs and lunged and heaved its way back into the brush like a steam locomotive. It was the kind of fast, rough going the dun was made for.

Lee ignored the willow branches lashing across his face and reached back for the Henry. The light rifle was fine for this close work. Lee felt his heart pounding as the dun battered through the scrub; he'd always hated rifle fights. He worried for years that some man who

16

wanted to kill him would be wise enough, some day, to come after him with a rifle and catch him well out in open country where only long-distance shooting would matter and nothing else.

But this wasn't such a long distance, after all.

Lee rode the bucketing dun like a sailor on a skiff in a stormy sea, watching the willow thickets ahead for the heaving motion that would betray a horse plowing through them, trying to get away. The shooter wouldn't have expected this kind of charge.

For a few moments, Lee thought he might have misjudged his direction and faulted on calculating the angle the bullet had come from. Then he saw the brush shudder and bend suddenly a hundred yards before him. In front, and a little to the left.

The shooter was running.

Lee steadied himself on the galloping dun, eared back the hammer on the Henry, then raised up in the stirrups, and began to shoot, ignoring the branches whipping at him.

He levered the Henry as fast as he could, cracking out the whole magazine into the low center of the heaving clump of brush in front of him.

It was scattergun shooting, nothing to be proud of; and it was a horse-shooting too. There was no use shooting for the rider in that green flurry of scrub.

And he missed—or thought he had.

Then a branch kicked back not thirty yards ahead of the dun's nose, and Lee saw a black and white spotted horse's leg—a pinto—and then the animal's muzzle as it reared up out of the brush.

It was hit hard; blood was pouring from its mouth.

Lee kicked the dun on in, driving it down on the thrashing pinto, searching the brush for the rider.

He dropped the Henry, swung off the dun, and dove into the scrub, falling and rolling into the thick greenery, the small branches catching at him, splintering

17

and breaking as he rolled.

No rider showed.

Lee rolled to his feet and lunged past a low, dwarf birch near where the pinto lay. It was in plain sight now, kicking and thrashing. Lee hadn't drawn his gun; he never had to draw his gun to make it more handy.

The dun was bucking and snorting away. Lee could hear the brush crashing under its hoofs a few yards further on.

Then he saw the rider.

The shooter.

He was standing, past the downed pinto, hanging on to a bent box elder as if he were hurt. Dirty canvas pants, dirty brown homespun shirt. No gun showing.

Lee considered killing him, and would have, except there was no gun showing.

He walked over toward the man, watching his footing amid the tangle of branches and bush roots. The pinto was dying, coughing out great blurts of bright-red, foamy blood. One of the Henry rounds had caught it in the lungs.

"Turn around, you son-of-a-bitch!"

The man started to turn, then stumbled, tripped on something, and fell over on his face.

Lee thought he must have shot the son-of-a-bitch, after all.

"Oh, Mr. Lee!" It was Bupp, calling through the brush. The old man's voice was quavering, scared.

Lee walked to the fallen man. As he did, the man stirred. Lee strode over, kicked him in the side of the head, and set his boot down hard onto the man's right arm.

It was an Indian. A young one, a boy maybe fifteen or sixteen years old. Tall, skinny, and ugly as sin.

The boy lay back under Lee's boot, staring up at him, blinking his eyes, still stunned by the kick.

He was a really ugly boy. His face was blackened by

18

the sun and dirt and pitted by old smallpox scars. His eyes were Indian-black and slanted as a Chinaman's. He had a big, broken nose like one of General Miles's pack camels.

Lee looked around for the boy's rifle and couldn't find it in the underbrush. Suddenly, the Indian turned under his boot, and Lee stepped back to kick him again. The boy began to vomit, heaving and spewing his guts out into the branches and leaves beside him.

Lee smelled the sour stink of whiskey from the vomit, and stood watching while the boy threw it up, groaning and gasping for breath.

A drunk Indian. And a boy at that.

"Mr. Lee?" Lee heard the old man kicking his cob into the brush toward him.

"Over here!"

"Did you get him?" Lee heard the cob stumble over a root.

"I got something, Mr. Bupp!"

Bupp rode the cob through the scrub into the small clearing the pinto had made in its death throes.

"Why you little red-nigger bastard!" Bupp said, staring down at the boy. His face was still pale with fright over his frizzy gray beard.

"Do you know him?" Lee asked, watching the boy still gagging, retching on an empty stomach now.

"Hell, yes, I know him! That's Tom Cooke. The son-of-a-bitch worked for me for two years, and this is the thanks I get, a goddamned bushwack murder!"

The old man was shaking like a leaf.

Lee left the boy and walked around the little clearing, looking for the rifle.

"I had to let the bastard go because the company wouldn't pay extra for his keep. Hell, they don't pay me enough to stay alive, as it is!" Bupp leaned down to shake his fist at the Indian. "And this is what you do, is it, you little son-of-a-bitch!"

19

Lee found the rifle under a broken birch sapling. It was an old Spencer with a split stock.

He walked back to where the Indian boy was lying.

"Is that so?" he asked him. "You were aiming to kill Mr. Bupp here?"

"Yes," the boy said, spitting some phlegm out and lying back in the brush. He looked sick. "Bupp made me go from the place . . ." He spoke good Mission English, and his voice was as deep as a man's.

"I didn't have the goddamned money to pay you, you dirty pissant!"

The Indian boy tried to sit up. He was still drunk. His eyes rolled and he slumped back into the brush.

"And that was a month ago, too!" Bupp continued. "This little bastard has been plotting to murder me!"

"What would the sheriff of this county do to him?" Lee asked, "if we took him in?"

"The sheriff wouldn't do shit! He's in Caswell, anyway, and that's forty miles away. But the town marshal will sure as shit hang his ass. He don't like Indians, anyway—and especially not a Blackfoot."

"You do what you want," the Indian boy said. And he lay back and closed his eyes.

"Now, how do you like that?" said Bupp. "The little red bastard damn near kills us and just don't give a shit!"

"It's not that easy, boy," Lee said to the young Indian.

"You giving him to the marshal?"

"No," Lee said, "I'm not. Lend me your belt."

"Say what?"

"Your belt."

The old man stripped off his wide leather belt and leaned off the cob to hand it to Lee.

The Blackfoot boy had sat up.

"You don't hit me with that!"

"Yes, I am," said Lee. "I'm going to beat the hell out of you."

CHAPTER TWO

The young Blackfoot raised his arms to ward off the blow as Lee stepped up to him, the heavy belt swinging. When the heavy leather struck him, the boy kicked out, trying to catch Lee in the knee.

It did no good. Lee kicked the boy's foot aside and brought the belt down again and again, lashing the boy as if he'd been a vicious horse, the belt leather cracking home like a coachman's whip.

The Blackfoot tried to roll away, scramble to his feet, anything to escape the searing fire of that hissing length of half-tanned rawhide. But Lee kept after him, kicking his feet out from under him when he tried to get up, swinging the heavy belt down with all his strength.

The Blackfoot was tough, but he was only a boy, and drunk. The pain finally became too great for him, and he lay huddled in the brush, vainly trying to protect himself with his raised hands as the belt sliced into his skin, leaving long, scarlet welts where it struck. His homespun shirt was torn to strips by the leather, stained with blood where the belt had cut deep. The boy's face was a mask of pain. But he didn't cry. The heavy crack of leather striking flesh sounded through the surrounding scrub.

"Mr. . . . say, Mr. Lee . . ." Tim Bupp shifted uneasily on the cob. "Don't you think he's had enough now?" he said, raising his voice above the hiss and snap of the belt.

Lee struck the boy three more times, grunting with the effort, the leather slashing into the boy's back when he turned on his belly, writhing from the pain.

Then Lee straightened up and tossed the belt to Bupp, its leather spattered with blood.

He reached down, gripped the boy's shoulder, and turned him over.

The Blackfoot was pale under the dirt on his face, and his narrow black eyes were brimming with unshed tears. He looked sober enough now.

"Listen to me, boy," Lee said. "You tried to kill a man—murder him from cover—and you got a good beating for trying it! Now, there's just two things you can do: you can get out of this valley and stay out of it or, if you want, you can come back to work at the ranch."

"Mr. Lee owns the River now, Tom." Bupp sounded sorry to see the boy hurt. "He can hire you back."

The boy said nothing. He lay staring up at the two of them.

Lee whistled for his dun, picked up the old Spencer, and walked off into the scrub to bring the animal in.

"Why don't you do that, Tom," Bupp said. "You know that man could take you to Marshal Phipps if he wanted to; and what the hell would happen to you then?"

Lee rode his dun back into the little clearing.

"I'll see you up at the ranch, Tom Cooke," he said. "You can walk up there by morning." He turned the dun to spur away. "I'll see you there tomorrow—or I'd better not see you anywhere!"

"You do that, now, Tom," Bupp said, as he turned the cob to follow. "That man just gave you a break, as well as a goddamned good beating you deserved, you pup!"

The boy said nothing. He lay still, listening, as the riders prodded their horses away through the brush.

When the scrub was quiet again, except for the gentle sighing of wind combing softly through the willows, Tom Cooke sat up and held his face in his hands and began to cry.

"I thought this was Cree country," Lee said, when the old man caught up with him. They were leading out across river meadows, striking along the stream's course for the trail to town.

"It is," Bupp said, bouncing a little to the cob's rough jog. "Young Tom there is the last of the Mohicans—the last of the Blackfoot around here, anyway. And those Crees don't like him any better than white people do."

"Why did he stay here then?"

"Hell, his ma's buried here! She was a whore at Rebecca's. Or a laundry girl, anyway. She was damn near as ugly as Tom is. He sure is an ugly Indian!"

"Here." Lee swung the boy's old Spencer off his saddlebow and handed it across to the old man. "You can give it to him if he shows up on the place."

"Oh, I don't know if he'll show up." The old man hesitated. "You gave him a real larrupin'."

Lee didn't say anything to answer him, and they rode in silence for a while. The valley branch of Rifle River ran clear as fine glass off to their right. It looked like good swimming water. Good fishing water, too. Good for everything.

"No," the old man said. "I don't think he'll show back at the ranch."

"Then he'd better not show at all," said Lee. "Anywhere in this valley."

Bupp glanced over at him, but said nothing.

It was after dark when they reached the town.

They'd stopped just once, to water and rest the horses, and Bupp had asked if he could try the dun out. Lee had let him, and the old man had done quite well, sticking for a good while before the dun had suddenly

23

sunfished and dumped him. The old man had hobbled around, cursing, "You fuckin' reprobate, you!" until he felt better. The dun had dropped him hard.

Lee pulled up on a little rise just to the south of town and sat quiet for a few moments looking it over.

Cree was a fair-sized settlement, pretty easy to see under a rising moon, its windows shining yellow with lantern light. There were about thirty buildings—log and shingle or dressed planks—and three or four of them were substantial, two-story affairs. And there was a scattering of shacks on the outskirts, one just below the rise.

There were people in the streets down there, and some fair action too, by the sound of it. Lee heard a piano and a concertina playing somewhere else and women laughing.

"It's bigger than I thought."

"Oh, there's about one or two thousand going in and out most times. Cowpokers, mostly, from Fishhook or Bent Iron or one of the small spreads. And some lumberjacks too from the logging camp over the mountain."

"A lumber camp? Where do they raft their wood?"

"There's a lake over there—about a two-day ride—and they got a train spur out to Helena. Just a one-horse line."

"Could that line take stock as well?"

Bupp threw him one of his sly glances, his eyes gleaming in the moonlight.

"I'm glad to hear a man that can ask a smart question! The answer is yes, the line will take stock into Helena for you. But it costs."

"Let's go," Lee said, and he heeled the dun into a trot.

For a Friday night, the town was full of life.

The main street was dirt, with a careless layer of rock and gravel strewn across it, and it was fairly crowded with supply wagons and buggies and tied horses.

The raised plank sidewalks on both sides of the street were thronged with cowboys marching along arm in arm, shouting and laughing, already drunk. There were a few women walking with them, fat, ugly girls, for the most part, as drunk as the cowmen.

Lee saw only a few lumberjacks. Big men with full beards, wearing blanket jackets and heavy, hobnailed boots. He noticed that they and the cowmen stayed out of each other's way.

Lee felt good being in a town again. It had been three weeks since Helena, six weeks since Denver. And that had been a sad time, anyway, except for buying the ranch. It was never a pleasure saying goodbye to a friend.

"There's Mrs. Boltwith's," the old man said, pointing to a small two-story building standing beside what looked like a bank.

"Where would I find the land office?" Lee asked, raising his voice as four cowboys stumbled past them in the street, singing "*Lorena*."

"In the bank," Bupp said, nodding at the brick building. "And, say, Mr. Lee, I could use some kind of an advance on my wages if you could see your way clear . . ."

The dun was shifting restlessly, not liking the crowds.

"Let's get out of this," Lee said, and he turned the dun to a hitching rail in front of the bank building.

They crowded the horses in beside a weary row of cow ponies and tied off the reins.

They stood on the high plank sidewalk while Lee dug his purse out of his vest pocket, counted out five silver dollars, and put them in Bupp's hand.

"That's five out of your month's thirty," Lee said, and Bupp nodded and sighed.

"Listen," he said. "What do you want me to learn to cook, Mr. Lee?"

"Eggs, bacon, biscuits, steak, potatoes, and pie."

"Oh, my God Almighty! It'll take me a year to learn all that!"

"And stew, too. You learn those things, I'll have no complaint."

"I should think to hell you wouldn't! Pie too?"

"Any kind you can."

Two fat men, who looked like sharpers or cattle buyers, jostled them as they went by, arguing about the price of something. —Yearlings. Cattle buyers.

"I'll do my damnedest, but I don't know." Bupp wandered away toward Mrs. Boltwith's. "Pie . . ." he muttered.

Lee walked down the sidewalk to the double door of the bank. It was a heavy door, banded with iron, and there was a small barred rifle slit high up on the right side. It was more like a jail door than a bank door. The town of Cree must see some lively times.

Lee looked for some sign saying when the land office would be open, but there was no sign at all. He tried the door; it was open.

The place was empty except for a pimpled kid wearing a clerk's eyeshade. The kid was perched on a high stool behind an oak desk, writing in a ledger. The oil lamp hanging over his head threw shadows around the empty counters and tellers' cages.

"What do you want, mister? Banking hours are from eight to six . . ."

"What time does the land office open?"

A door opened behind the clerk.

"Banking hours," a man's voice said. He stood framed in the doorway, outlined by the lamplight behind him. "You have a transaction to register, mister?"

"You the land agent?" Lee asked.

"I am."

26

"I've bought a ranch in the valley. I want to get the title registered."

"Have you, by God!" the man said. "Well, it's after closing, but what the hell. Come on in."

Lee walked back into the office and found the man already sitting at a rolltop desk, looking up at him. He leaned forward to offer his hand.

"Bill Calthrop, Mr.—?"

"Lee, Frederick Lee."

"Well now, what property is it that you've bought, Mr. Lee?" Calthrop was a big, beefy man, with shaggy black hair and thick eyebrows that ran in a straight black bar over his nose. His eyes were brown and small, watchful, like a bear's.

"River Ranch," Lee said.

Calthrop didn't say anything for a moment. He sat staring at Lee as if he hadn't heard what he'd said. Then he leaned forward.

"You say River Ranch?"

"That's right."

Calthrop pursed his lips, considering.

"Well, well, that's some news, all right. May I ask who you bought the ranch from?"

"Phillip McGee, in Helena."

"Phillip McGee. Let me see the papers, please."

Lee pulled the long oilcloth envelope from his shirt and handed it over to the land agent.

"Sit down—please sit down, Mr. Lee. I've forgotten my manners." He unfolded the papers and checked through them. He sorted them out onto his desktop and then slowly read them through.

"Jumpin' Jesus Christ . . ." he muttered.

"Is there any problem, Mr. Calthrop?"

The land agent looked up at Lee with a sigh. He slowly folded the papers, put them to one side, and dug into one of his desk drawers for a stack of registration forms.

"There is no problem with the sale, Mr. Lee. It looks

legal, all right. You paid $27,500 for the property?"

"Yes."

"Well," he sighed again, "you weren't taken on the price; that's fair enough . . ."

"Then where's the difficulty, Mr. Calthrop?"

The land agent paused in filling out his forms.

"The difficulty, Mr. Lee, the possible difficulty is that someone else was intending to buy that land for himself. In fact, that somebody else had already sent a hard offer to the Chicago Union people for it!"

"How is that my business?"

"It isn't, really. You just had the luck to run into McGee in Helena and were able to close the deal with their agent right there. It was lucky for you, I think." Calthrop didn't look as if he thought it was lucky.

"Nothing wrong with the property?"

"Oh, hell no, nothing wrong with that property! You've got good buildings up there—better than average, I'd say—and you've got three thousand acres of prime land to go with them. Of course, its not a big ranch as stocklands go, but still prime land . . ."

"So?" Lee sat relaxed, watching the land agent's face. The agent had something more to say.

"The thing is, Mr. Lee, that your place is called River Ranch because it straddles the north branch of Rifle River, right on up to the falls . . ."

Lee said nothing, just sat, listening.

"Well, dammit, you see you control that river! You own the water rights on it! Hell, if you decided to dam it up—well, there's not a damn thing the other ranchers could do about it—legally, anyway."

Lee sat forward a little, his dark gray eyes looking almost black in the lamplight.

"And what about the previous owner? Anybody scared over him having the water rights?"

"Well, no. But Thompkins was an old man. All his family was gone or dead and buried. He was a gentle man. He wasn't about to make trouble for anybody And everybody knew it . . ."

"And how did the Chicago people get the property then?"

"Thompkins owed money in Chicago. He'd gambled on the corn exchange, the old fool, and those boys took him and took title to the ranch after he died."

Lee stood up. The agent, like most land agents, was quite a talker.

"I'm obliged for the news. What do I owe you for the registration?"

Calthrop stood up with him, handing the papers back across the desk.

"That'll be $15.00. And I want you to know, Mr. Lee, that you should be able to work that water rights business out with your neighbors. They're a good set of men, by and large."

Lee took the deed copies and registration, slid them back into the envelope, and tucked them into his shirt

"A couple more things," he said.

"Yes?" Calthrop led him to the office door.

"First, who was the man who tried to buy the place?"

Calthrop hesitated. Lee stood silent, looking at him

"I—it was Ashton, I believe. He owns the Fishhook Ranch. The line runs down your east boundary, Mr. Lee."

Lee nodded.

"And one more thing," he said to the agent. "I don't want you to talk of my business to other men, the way you've spoken of their's to me."

The big land agent flushed scarlet, looked as though he were going to say something, then didn't.

When Lee held out his hand, the agent took it without a word, then turned, walked back into his office, and shut the door.

The pimply clerk was still scribbling away on his high stool.

"Say, boy . . ."

He looked up.

"Tell me where I can find the cleanest bed and the best supper in town."

The clerk thought a minute, considering, sucking on the tip of his pen.

"Now, the best place to sleep is over at Mrs. Boltwith's hotel. And she's a good cook, too. Or you could try the Arcady. They do a good dinner . . ." He smiled slyly. "And they got the prettiest girls in town, too."

Lee strolled down from the bank building to Mrs. Boltwith's. Some men, they looked like hostlers and dry-goods clerks, were sitting out on the steps in the dark, smoking pipes and cigars and watching the occasional bunch of drovers go singing by.

Lee climbed up the steps past them and went through the whitewashed front door. The lobby of the little hotel was only a desk and an old bench set beside a steep, narrow flight of stairs. It was empty. Lee could smell meat pan-frying in the kitchen in back.

He walked on down the hall.

"It's got to be dry!" a woman's voice—a big woman, by the sound of her—rang out. "Dry!"

"All right, all right!" That was Tim Bupp. It sounded as though the old man was getting his first cooking lesson.

"Now, what in the world do you want?" A big, horsy, ugly woman with cold light-gray eyes turned to stare at Lee when he walked into the long kitchen. A pan of breaded steaks was sizzling on the broad black range.

"If you want a room, Abel will check you in out front, and if you want dinner, you're too late!"

"Hello, Mr. Lee," Bupp said.

"Oh," said the big woman. "You're the fella that

30

dropped this old fool in on me! Well, I'm damned if he can cut enough firewood to make it worth my while to teach him a thing!"

She had a harsh Kansas accent. Lee had heard it many times before. And she had a rough way of speaking, too. Lee had the feeling she'd seen darker days; she had that hard, grim air about her. A right old whore gone straight.

"Then put him to scrubbing pots as well," Lee said. And he walked to the kitchen table and sat down.

"Meanwhile, Mrs. Boltwith, I'll try one of those steaks he's done, by way of an experiment . . ."

For a moment, the big woman seemed near to exploding with anger. Then she paused and gave Lee a hard, searching look.

"Who the hell are you?" she said.

"A new landowner in the valley, Mrs. Boltwith. And a hungry one."

She gave him another slow, examining look, then grunted a grudging acceptance.

"Feed him," she said to Bupp. "And for the Lord's sake, next time dry a steak before you sear it!" And she stomped out of the kitchen.

"You sure have given me holy hell to go through, Mr. Lee," Bupp said, tinkering and clinking at the stove. He was dabbing at the frying steaks with a long-handled fork. "That old dragon's a pure pain in the ass—and no salve for it!"

"The steak's done, Bupp. And you can just call me Lee. The 'mister' isn't necessary. And by the way, you could take the horses over to the livery. Tonight."

"All right, all right." The old man was looking hot and harassed. He gingerly forked up one of the sputtering steaks, flopped it down onto a chipped platter, and brought it over to Lee, holding the plate in both hands like a new father with his first baby.

The steak was as tough as whang leather.

Lee was half through it, and chewing hard, when the horsy head of Mrs. Boltwith appeared around the kitchen door.

"Tough, ain't it?" she said, with some satisfaction.

"Not bad," said Lee.

"Not bad!" she laughed a hoarse, rumbling laugh. "I'll bet!"

"Tasty though?" old Bupp said hopefully.

"Tasty as horseshit," Mrs. Boltwith chuckled. She appeared to have a rough sense of humor. "As for you, Mr. Lee, if you want a room, you got one: 2-E, second-floor back." She pulled her head out of the doorway and was gone.

"Damned old dragon," Bupp said.

After the steak and a cup of Bupp's coffee—which was better than the steak—Lee had had a wedge of Mrs. Boltwith's peach pie. A tough old piece she might well be, but she could cook. Then he'd strolled out of the hotel, past the smokers on the steps—they'd stared at him, curious, as he went by—and out on down the street.

The Arcady was the biggest saloon on the strip, and it looked to be doing a land-office business. Lee took a slow stroll around the building, working the last of the trail cramps out of his butt and legs. He checked the back door and stairs. It was an old habit he had. It often helped to know the back way out, particularly in a place where there was heavy action.

When Lee climbed the front steps and pushed his way through the batwing doors, he was jostled hard by three lumberjacks coming out. The place was packed, heavy with the shouting and uproar of a jammed crowd of men and women, the broad, low-ceilinged room thick with the smells of spilled whiskey, stale sweat, vomit, beer and cheap perfume.

Lee stepped aside from the doorway and stood looking the place over.

There was a piano player and a man with a military drum pounding out some tune from the back, the music lost in the yells and arguments, the clatter and stomp of boots on the hardwood floor, as dozens of couples danced and whirled in the center of the room, knocking into each other, shoving each other aside as they spun around and around.

The faro tables were along the left side of the room. There were poker tables, too, further back. The bar ran down the right.

As Lee watched, two girls headed up the rough-sawn staircase at the back, each with a drunken jack on her arm. A bully stopped them on the landing, took the two bucks from the men, and pointed them to one of the corridor rooms beyond.

It was a prosperous place, as rich as any in Dodge City or Ft. Smith. Lee was impressed. And he saw that it was the lumbermen who kept the extra suckers coming in. The cowpokers alone wouldn't have been enough to support all this action. It was a first-class joint.

He didn't see anybody he knew.

Lee shoved his way toward the bar, found a place, and squeezed into it. The bartender picked him out right away.

"What'll it be?"

"Martini."

The bartender didn't blink an eye. He stepped over to his wet-bar, dipped up the ice, slid in the gin, dropped the vermouth in after it, and did a nice easy shake.

Lee knew it would be good before he got it; it confirmed what he'd already seen. Most cowtown bartenders couldn't make any kind of mixed drink—let alone a fancy cocktail—and if they tried, they ruined them. But this was a damned good Waldorf martini.

"Make me another one." The bartender heard him

and nodded while heading three beers down to some jacks twenty feet further down the bar. A real professional.

Lee finished his second drink, paid up—four bits each—and felt the gin settle in his belly. It mixed well with Mrs. Boltwith's peach pie. Then he left the bar and moved through the crowd toward the back of the room. There was another bully with a Greener shotgun leaning against the stair rail, watching the dancers.

Lee saw two girls, flushed and sweaty from dancing, standing off together, talking. They were holding hands.

He walked up to them to get a better look.

One was an older woman in her early forties. A beauty once, probably, and still not bad. She had a long jaw, and big blue-green eyes. Certainly a beauty—once. When she turned to look at Lee, she was still talking to the girl with her. Several of her front teeth were missing from her lower jaw.

The girl with her was a younger piece—half Indian by the look of her,—with a dark, broad face, big nose, and narrow black eyes. She had a squint in her left eye, not bad, but bad enough to keep her from being pretty. She had wide, heavy hips, and short stocky legs in high-laced, red-leather boots.

She looked as round and ready as a mare in season.

"How much are you charging, handsome?" Lee asked her.

The older woman made a face and turned away, letting go of the girl's hand. They were sweethearts, no doubt.

"I cost house rate," the half-breed said. "Two bucks for quarter, five for hour." She looked him over—from boots to trousers, from belt to gun to vest, from shirt to hat. It was a quick, squint-eyed glance, and she missed nothing.

Lee saw her glance down to his left boot again. She

34

was a very sharp whore. She'd seen the long, slight bulge in the boot leather where the six-inch toothpick he carried was sheathed. A sharp whore.

Lee made up his mind.

"I'll go for you both. Seven each for the hour."

The older woman made a disgusted noise, and the young girl said, "Not enough."

Lee shrugged and turned away.

They let him get a few steps, till they saw he meant it. Then they came after him and said all right.

CHAPTER THREE

Lee handed his fourteen dollars to the bully on the stair landing, a thick-necked thug in a cheap black suit, and followed the two women up the steps to the narrow corridor running the length of the building's back wall.

The women stopped at a pine plank door with the number twelve stenciled across it in white paint, opened it, and gestured Lee in.

He stepped in fast, his glance cutting through the room, checking for hide-holes, trick closets, trap-doors—all the stunts that grifters used. But the room looked clean, a small whitewashed bedroom with a few doodads, a long mirror, and a red-shaded oil lamp on a table beside the double brass bed.

A nice, hometown whorehouse with nothing shady. Except the mirror, maybe.

"This room all right by you, mister?" The older woman looked impatient to get down to business.

"Don't hustle me, sister. We've got a nice hour to do." Lee smiled at them. "Now, why don't you ring down for a bottle of champagne and tell the bartender to go easy on the gas." He wanted to see where the bell-pull was.

It was behind the thin yellow curtain drawn over the room's single window. The half-breed girl stepped over, found the cord, and gave it three short pulls. Signal for service. One sharp yank probably meant trouble.

Lee took off his clothes, hanging his vest and shirt over the top of the long mirror, draping them down to cover the glass.

"I don't like putting on a show for jerkers," he said. He noticed the quick flick of a look the two women exchanged. The mirror had been a two-way trick, a courtesy and pleasure for regular customers with the gazing inclination.

"Get your clothes off, ladies."

"It's extra if we take everything off, mister," the older one said.

"No, it isn't," Lee said, still smiling. "Are you two looking for trouble with me?" He was standing naked, with his gunbelt and purse in his hand. Still smiling, but the smile looked a little strange. His eyes were as cold as gray ice.

Lee had always liked to get value for what he paid.

The older one lowered her eyes, biting her lip nervously. "No, we're not . . ."

"Come on then, pretty," Lee said to her. The smile was warm again. "I'm not rough . . ."

The older whore sighed and started to take off her clothes, and the half-breed did too. Lee crossed to the wall side of the brass bed and draped his gunbelt over the knob on the bedpost—just to keep the Colt handy. He dropped the purse on the table. In plain sight.

Then he stretched out on the bed—and a nice soft feather bed it was—and watched the two women undress.

They'd gotten down to their corsets, when there was a knock on the door. The Indian girl went to open it, and Lee saw a fat old Indian woman in a greasy buckskin dress waiting there for the order.

"Champagne, Grace, and tell Harry easy on gas."

She'd remembered. A sharp whore.

Then they finished undressing.

The Indian girl was short and thick through the body,

37

with round, fat, full thighs running up into a butt like a soft, shining pair of brown balloons. Not much hair on her Jane, it was sparse, like most Indian women. A sweet round belly on her and full, hard-thrusting tits with nipples dark as plums. Lee could smell her across the room, his nose sharpened by weeks out on the trail away from city stinks.

She smelled smoky—rich and smoky—and dark. She smelled like campfire ashes after a rain. His cock came up full, just lying there, smelling her, and looking at her.

The girl must like him, or something about him, anyway—maybe the seven bucks—because she smiled shyly as he looked at her.

When Lee glanced over at the other whore, he chuckled out loud, because she was staring at the Indian girl as hard as he was—maybe harder. Her blue eyes were bright, looking at the girl.

Sweethearts, sure enough.

"She's beautiful, isn't she?" Lee said to the older one. He said it nicely, with nothing ugly in his voice.

The woman flushed and didn't say anything. She was something of a beauty herself. Tall, rangy as a hard-run deer, her stone-white skin was very smooth, but marked a little here and there with the slight scars, the soft puckering, and faint blue veins that a woman's body gathers in years of work, and babies, and fucking.

Lee never disliked those marks on a woman. They were what life had done to her, going along; nothing wrong with them. He liked the long legs she had, and the fine, narrow bones in her feet. Her cunt was furred with a thick coat of light brown hair, like an otter's belly.

Lee could smell her, too. Perfume, something like the smell of violets. And sweat, just a touch of sweat. She smelled just fine.

"But you're a beauty too, aren't you, darling?" She

38

gave him a grudging smile. "You think between us we can make your pretty dark-eyed girl here happy?"

She blushed at that. It was surprising how shy some whores were about some things.

Lee held out his hands. "Come on, come on over here, sweethearts." The Indian girl came romping and giggling over to the bed, bounced on it, her big breasts shaking. She reached out to give Lee's cock a friendly squeeze.

She had a soft, hot little hand.

Lee gathered her in in a hug. It was odd how few men took the time to give women a little cuddling, when there wasn't much that a woman liked more. He squeezed the plump Indian girl till she grunted with pleasure, and he reached up to pull the older woman into bed with them.

He felt how awkward she was in his arms, probably upset at having her Sappho-loving talked about.

Lee turned her, cradled her in his arms like a newborn colt, and kissed her on the ear. Then he nibbled on her earlobe, making hungry sounds. She giggled and struggled to get away—but not too hard.

"What's your name, beautiful?" he asked, still nibbling.

"Phyllis . . ."

"It suits you. An elegant name . . ."

"Oh, God. A lover boy," she said, but was not displeased.

There was a knock on the door.

The Indian girl rolled out of bed to answer it. It was the old woman again with the champagne and three glasses.

The girl came back to the bed with it. "That is ten dollar," she said.

Lee reached for his purse. "Here. Eight bucks for the champagne and one buck for the old lady."

The girl hesitated, then shrugged and went back to the

door to give the old woman the money.

Phyllis giggled in Lee's ear. "You do know the game, sugar! You're a sport, aren't you? You been to see the elephant!"

"I've seen it, and I've painted it, and I've left it with child!" Lee said, and he leaned over to kiss the Indian girl's nipples.

He'd learned long ago not to try to fool whores about being green. They didn't fool—and they didn't like the try.

Lee left the girl's breasts for a moment and caught Phyllis's head and drew it down so that he could whisper in her ear.

"And what's your pretty's name, Phyllis?"

Phyllis nuzzled into his throat, nipping and licking at him there. "Her name's Sarah Talltree . . ."

"So," Lee reached down to cup the woman's Jane and run his finger gently up and down her soft crease there, "so what does she like, hmmm?"

The Indian girl was cuddled against his side, while he stroked the cheek of her butt. She was wonderfully soft. He slid his fingers down into the crack of her ass. She was even softer there—and moist.

Lee put his tongue into Phyllis's ear blew gently into it, and said, "Tell me, sweetheart, what does she like? What would make her happy?"

"Oh, God," Phyllis murmured. He had managed to spread her and ease a finger up into her. "That's dirty talk . . ."

"What does she like?" He thrust another finger up into her and turned and turned his wrist back and forth. She was oiling, getting wetter and wetter. Now he could smell her cunt, the odor mingling with the violet perfume. A sea smell, like a dish of fresh oysters served beside a restaurant garden.

"She likes . . ." Phyllis started to whisper in Lee's ear. "She likes . . ." Then she began to giggle.

40

"What you say, Phyllis?" asked the Indian girl, looking annoyed.

"I'm just—I'm just telling him what you—you like!" And she collapsed across Lee's chest in a gale of giggles. She sounded more like a schoolgirl than a whore.

"Oh, Phyllis, you bad!" the Indian girl pouted.

"She likes to—to have her bottom licked!" And Phyllis went off in shrieks of laughter, her face as red as a beet.

Lee laughed along with her and rolled her over on top of the Indian.

"Then do it," he said. But she was embarrassed and shook her head. "Come on, sweetheart," Lee whispered in her ear. He gently gripped the back of her neck and guided her face down to the soft rounds of the half-breed's ass.

Phyllis resisted, struggling against him—but not much.

Lee pushed her face firmly deep into the crease of the girl's buttocks, holding her there, and, with his other hand, he stroked the Indian girl's long, strong back, soothing her like a fractious horse.

He felt the women's resistence a few moments more. Then the tension slowly went out of the smooth muscles of the girl's back, replaced by a kind of movement, a slight rhythmic motion.

He glanced down. Phyllis lay quiet, her face still pressed against the girl's ass. Her head was moving, slowly nodding, burrowing deeper into the girl's soft crotch. Lee saw her jaw move, working as she licked at the girl there.

He leaned over the Indian girl, gripped the cheeks of her ass, and gently spread them apart, opening her up so that the older woman could get at her.

Now he could see what she was doing, see the slim pink tongue sliding down into the girl's dark cunt, licking at it like a cat. She then went slowly back up to

41

the small brown bud of the girl's ass. She lapped at it wetly. Phyllis was groaning with pleasure from what she was doing. The Indian girl lay silent, her eyes shut, only moving a little, sometimes arching her back under the delicate probing of the woman's tongue.

Lee took his hands from the girl's big soft buttocks and got up on his hands and knees to slide behind the two of them. As he did, Phyllis reached up herself to force the girl's ass-cheeks wide apart again. She seemed to bite into the girl, groaning, burying her face in her. Lee saw her throat work as she sucked the girl's ass hard.

He was up on his knees behind the woman now, and he reached down and lifted her hips high in the air. He searched with his fingers, found her cunt running with juice in the tangle of her fur, propped the end of his cock up to her hole, set himself, and shoved it up her all the way.

She moaned into the girl's meat as the cock went into her, but she didn't stop what she was doing. She grunted as Lee drove it into her again.

Her pale back was slippery, running with sweat, as Lee worked on her. He ran his hands down to her small, dangling breasts, and gently squeezed and tugged at her nipples. He had thought it was the Indian girl he had wanted, but there was more to Phyllis, more person there to fuck with . . .

She struggled under him, bucking back up into his cock as he drove it into her, faster now. She was soaking wet there. It made a liquid, sucking sound each time he shoved it in—and she was at the girl all the time, her mouth working and lapping at her.

And the girl came, silently, suddenly heaving up under them, twisting, reaching back with both hands to clutch Phyllis' hair, to pull her deeper in. The girl's legs kicked out to the side in spasms of pleasure. Lee felt himself coming too, felt the semen surging up. He slid his hands down Phyllis's wet flanks to the long slim muscles of her thighs. He rode her like a mare.

She screamed into the girl's trembling softness, and he came and came and came into her, as if he were coming into both of them at once. It was so good that it hurt. He gritted his teeth with the pleasure of it.

And then it was over, ebbing away . . .

Lee sagged down across both women, getting his arms around them, hugging them to him. The smells of sweat and perfume, semen, and the salty fish-smell of well-used cunt—all mingled together.

A few minutes later, Lee was propped up on pillows between the two women, drinking down a glass of champagne. As champagne goes, it wasn't much—just thin wine with bubbles blown into it from a bartender's gas-charger—and it had warmed up considerably waiting for them to get to it. But it tasted damn good nonetheless.

"You're a bad man," Phyllis said to him, murmuring cosily as she cuddled into his right shoulder.

"No," Lee said, "I'm not, not any more."

"You are very bad," said the half-breed from his other side. She bent down and bit him on the shoulder—not lightly, either. She had strong white teeth.

So Lee had two contented whores with him. Only a fool became sentimental about whores; but it was a sad man who couldn't play the fool, at least sometimes.

He sighed and wriggled out from in between them.

"Where's the pot?"

"Under the bed," Phyllis said.

Lee reached under, got the chamber pot out, and turned his back to the women to take a piss.

"A real gent," Phyllis giggled to the half-breed, who giggled back.

Lee finished his pee, gave his cock a flip for the last drop, and stooped to slide the pot back under the bed.

It was right then that the girl began to scream.

It came from next door.

Lee was already standing beside the bedstead with the Colt in his hand and cocked before the second scream came.

The two women lay frozen on the bed.

The scream rang out again; not the furious yell of a drunken whore. It was a shriek of terror. Lee had heard a girl scream like that before in Old Mexico. Her throat had been cut a moment later.

He started around the bed without thinking—then he thought. And stopped. He was in this valley to make a home—not more trouble.

Then he heard the clatter of boots on the stairs, coming up fast. The girl started to scream again, just out in the hall, but the cry was cut short.

Phyllis was lying in the bed as white as the sheets. She was crying without making a sound. The Indian girl was stroking her hair to comfort her.

There was a shout out in the hall. Lee couldn't make out the words. He heard some kind of swift scuffle and then the sudden, cracking blast of a shotgun.

It sounded like a stick of dynamite going off just outside the door. Phyllis screamed and covered her face with her hands.

Lee jumped to his clothes and started jamming them on as fast as he could. There was going to be trouble in the damn place, top to bottom. No use being naked in it.

He buttoned up his pants, shoved his shirt tails in, and shrugged into his vest. Then back across the bed and into his socks and boots. He scooped his purse off the bedside table, stuck it into the pocket of his vest, buckled his gunbelt on, and bent to give the weeping Phyllis a quick kiss on the cheek.

"Don't worry, sweety. Whatever, it's all over."

He headed for the door. The sooner he was out of the

Arcady and back in Mrs. Boltwith's hotel, the happier he'd be. He'd already scouted the back way out, thank God.

He stepped into the corridor—and there was trouble, right there. Trouble in a haze of left-over gunsmoke.

The bully-boy, the beefy one who'd been on the stair landing, was lying half propped up against the opposite wall. He appeared to be dying. The right side of his face was broken in as if he'd been struck with a blacksmith's maul. There was not much blood at all, which somehow made the injury look worse. Just that bashed-in wound. His right eye looked to be broken by the same blow. The shotgun was on the floor beside him. He'd been too slow with it.

Lee heard the girl again, her voice crying from downstairs from the big front room. She seemed to be begging, pleading about something. She sounded very young, no more than a kid.

He knew it was a mistake when he did it. He knew damn well he shouldn't. *Knew it damn well.*

He walked to the head of the front stairs, to the landing. Then he started down the steps.

For a few moments, nobody looked up at him.

They were looking at something else.

A young girl wearing a whore's shift and red boots lay sprawled on the splintered wood of the dance floor, blood running from her nose and mouth.

The whole crowd of people had fallen back to the edges of the big room, packed along the walls and in among the faro tables, watching in dead silence.

The girl cried out and tried to crawl away, but she couldn't. A man had hold of her wrist.

A bad one.

A very bad one.

Lee was surprised. It was true that almost any town or county had its hardcases, some of them considerably tough, too. And it was also true that Cree appeared to be a nice little boomtown for the lumbermen working up in the mountains, and so might draw some badmen to it.

But this one seemed like something special.

He looked deformed at first, his short, thick legs as squat as a dwarf's, his hands broad, hairy paddles of bone and muscle. But he wasn't misshappen; only the immense width of his shoulders made him look it. He was dressed like a cattleman, except for a narrow-brimmed plug hat. He held the girl's arm with his left hand.

The girl's thin white wrist seemed to disappear in that massive grip.

Lee had stopped on the tenth step down from the landing: it put him above and about fifteen feet from them. There was still nothing that said he had to butt in. The man was facing away, looking around at the crowd. Lee could tell where he was looking by the lowered eyes around the room. The other bully was not to be seen; he'd skedaddled fast.

The man yanked at the girl's arm, dragging her a few feet along the floor. She shrieked with the pain from her twisted wrist and, weeping, tried to hit out at him.

"Don't you make me angry now, girlie!" He had a high, rather sweet voice, like an Irish tenor's.

He hauled her up to her feet.

"Don't you want to be with old Mickey, now?"

"Please help me!" she screamed, to the people standing round.

"Jesus!" said a woman's voice. "Where in hell is Phipps?"

The man started toward the front door, hauling the struggling girl along.

"Where do you think you're going, fatty?"

The words had come out of Lee's mouth despite himself.

You fucking fool, he thought. Now you've ruined everything.

46

The man in the plug hat seemed surprised. He slowly turned back to look up the stairs at Lee as if he weren't sure that Lee had been speaking to him.

"That's right, fatty; it's you I was talking to . . ." In all the way now.

A huge, round head rolled back on those massive shoulders, getting a good look up at Lee. His eyes were very blue, the wide, innocent blue eyes of a child. They looked strange, staring out of that murderous face. The man looked like a vicious dog, a huge bulldog with brutal, meaty jowls.

He carried a big old Colt dragoon .44 for a right-hand cross-draw. It looked slow, but Lee had known big men who were fast, and fast cross-draws, too.

"You was talkin' to me, wasn't you?" he said in that high, sweet voice, some Irish accent still in it. A city man, originally, Lee thought. A thug out of Hell's Kitchen, or maybe Chicago.

"Let the girl go," Lee said. "Just let her go, and walk away . . ."

"Oh, sure," the man said. "Why not?"

And he smiled an oddly charming smile, for all his brutal ugliness, and let go of the girl and reached for his gun.

He was very fast.

Extraordinarily fast for his size; he must have been a dreadful opponent in a fist fight.

The huge hand snapped across his broad belly to the Dragoon's butt. The gun was coming out in a blur.

Very fast.

Lee drew and shot him in the chest.

The man staggered back a swift step, his round face frowning, preoccupied. The dragoon was sweeping up, coming level.

Lee shot him again, firing through a haze of gunsmoke. Center chest, an inch or two to the right of the first slug.

The man's plug hat fell off; he had short red hair. He

staggered left for a step or two, still trying to level the dragoon.

Lee stepped sideways to clear himself of the smoke, being careful not to trip on the steps. He shot the man again.

His childlike eyes wide in agony, the big man stumbled and fell to one knee. The dragoon went off with a loud, flat bang, and Lee heard the bullet slam into the saloon's back wall.

The man heaved himself up and lurched forward, the big pistol wavering in his hand. But he couldn't seem to see Lee; he stumbled again, and went crashing into a faro table, knocking it over on its side. On his hands and knees now, he thrashed and struggled in the tangle of table legs and chairs, dying, his boots scraping and kicking along the rough flooring.

The blood was running out in a wide puddle around him. He was still heaving and rolling in it, but less and less.

For the first time, Lee heard the women screaming and the shouts of the men. All the light and color and noise of the place came rushing back in on him.

Now you've done it. Now you've done it, sure as hell . . .

"Mister, allow me to congratulate you!" Some jackass of a drummer in a yellow suit. Whores had gathered around the young girl now, lifting her up off the floor, cooing to her and taking her up the stairs. Lee glimpsed her face as they went up past him. It was dead white, blank with shock.

People were crowding all around him now. That damn drummer and a lot of others, all shouting and yelling in his face.

He needed to be alone for a minute. You always need that when you've had a faceoff with a man and killed him. Lee had the odd thought that the man in the plug hat had probably been a rough prankster when he

48

was in good humor, an amusing man to get drunk with—sometimes.

He always had these thoughts about people when he'd killed them. And thinking that way always made the killings worse.

He had to get outside the noisy hole!

But as he pushed his way through the crowd, heading for the batwing doors, they were suddenly shoved open, and a tall man with long blond hair down to his shoulders stepped into the saloon. He looked flushed from running, and there was a long-barreled Remington .44 in his left hand. Another revolver was tucked into the left side of his wide sash.

For an instant—just for an instant—Lee thought it was Bill Hickok.

Then he saw that it wasn't. This man looked like Bill, and wore his guns Hickok's way, but he was younger and not as tall.

The man wore a long cream-linen frock coat, hanging open. There was a badge pinned on the left lapel.

The marshal had eyes the color of water, and they picked Lee out of the crowd with no trouble at all. Men were all around him now, busy telling the lawman the tale of the shooting, wanting some small part in it. But he sliced through the crowd right toward Lee, the Remington swinging easily at his side.

Another one, Lee thought wearily. Two fast guns in a little town like this . . .

A tall, well-dressed woman, who looked like a lady, had come through the batwings behind the marshal, and Lee could see her now, struggling through the crowd after him. She looked familiar; Lee wondered if he'd ever seen her before.

"What's your name?" The marshal had a deep voice for a slim man. He was standing in front of Lee, but not too close. The Remington was still in his hand, hanging idly at his side.

It was a nice trick, that. You held a bare gun in your hand, but held it down, casually, out of action. Then, if there was trouble, and knowing your man's eye would be on *that* pistol, you simply drew and shot him with the other.

One of Hickok's tricks.

"I said, what's your name?"

"Frederick Lee, Marshal." Lee stammered a little, trying his damnedest to look like a nervous citizen who'd just gotten damn lucky. "I don't even know why he did it! He just drew on me just like that, and all I did was ask him to leave that poor girl alone!"

"You outdrew Mick Slawson face-to-face?" Those water-pale eyes drilled into Lee's. "Mister, if you did, then you're either a fool for luck or you're a very quick gun." He looked as if he'd decided which.

CHAPTER FOUR

The tall woman had made her way to them by that time. She seemed worried that there might be more trouble.

"Tod . . Tod, is everything all right?" She gave Lee a quick glance. "I heard this man has killed Slawson . . ."

"He sure as hell did!" a lumberjack standing near them said. "He blew his buttons off! And Slawson drew first on him, too . . ."

"You sure of that?" the marshal said to him.

"Hell, yes, it was fair and square." And two other men, listening, agreed that it sure as hell had been fair and square.

"Well, you stick around here for a while, just the same," the marshal said to Lee.

"Not for long. I've got a place to look after . . ."

"What place?"

"I've bought the River Ranch, up in the hills." It would be interesting to see if money talked with the marshal.

It did.

The cold, water-pale eyes swung back to Lee and stared at him for a moment. "Well, all right . . . but I want to talk to you before you leave here."

"Now, Tod," the tall woman said, "Mr.—"

"Lee."

"Mr. Lee has just done us a favor, killing that damn

51

animal—Slawson was certainly a rustler—and I'm just going to take Mr. Lee backstairs out of this crowd . . ."

The marshal slowly nodded, then turned and followed one of the lumberjacks through the crowd toward Slawson's body. Everyone in the room was either gathered there or piled up at the bar celebrating. A killing like this, with no bystanders hurt, was always good for business.

"Oh dear," the tall woman said to Lee, "I should never have left the place on a Friday night . . . If you'd just follow me, Mr. Lee, I'll get you out of this."

She led the way through the crowd and around the stairwell to a narrow, green-painted door. There was a short hallway, then another door. The woman paused to dig a key out of her reticule. She was very tall for a woman, almost as tall as Lee; and she was a looker, a brunette with clear, pale skin, and light green eyes. She dressed like a lady, but wasn't one. Apparently, she owned the Arcady, or had a share in it.

And there was something familiar about her. Lee wasn't certain he'd seen her before. Maybe it had been some girl who just looked like her.

She'd gotten the door open, and Lee followed her inside. It was a heavy door; when it was shut behind them, the noise from the barroom dimmed to a dull murmur.

It was a sitting room, with another door probably leading to a bedroom. And it was furnished in fine taste, as rich as any Chicago hotel suite, with big horsehair sofas and chairs, a walnut dining table, and a rolltop desk with a big oil lamp hung over it. Everything was all fringed and gussied up. A class roost.

She sighed, taking off her net gloves. "I'll get you a drink, Mr. Lee. What's your pleasure?" She reached up to turn the oil lamp brighter.

"Straight rye will be all right."

"All right." She went across the room to a small

cabinet and took out a bottle and two glasses. "God knows, I could use one myself." She turned to look at him. "Please sit down, Mr. Lee."

Lee sat on one of the sofas, leaning back into the soft upholstery, watching her. She was a handsome woman, and maybe the marshal's sweetheart, judging from the way she'd come hurrying over to him when he'd faced Lee.

She brought the glasses of rye over to the sofa, handed one to Lee, and sat down with a rustle of silk skirts in an armchair across from him.

"Mr. Phipps and I were having dinner with some friends when we heard of the trouble."

Lee nodded. Phipps . . . Tod Phipps. Now, he had heard of that name. But where?

"Mr. Phipps had always expected trouble from Slawson. This wasn't the first time that man started something." She sipped her drink, and Lee noticed that her slim white fingers were gripping the glass hard. "Mr. Phipps could have handled the matter himself, of course, if he'd been in the place. Mr. Phipps was a deputy to Wild Bill Hickok, you know."

Tod Phipps! Christ. He'd heard that name, all right. One of Hickok's hardcases—and Hickok could pick them! It didn't mean that the man was a fine shooter, of course, but it did mean he'd killed a few. Hickok never used raw help. This fellow must have headed for greener pastures when Hickok took off for the Dakotas.

There was a soft knock at the door.

The woman started to get up, then paused for a second, giving Lee an odd glance. Then she smiled at him politely and went to the door.

It was the old Indian woman. She said something. The tall woman bent down to hear her, then answered.

"All right, tell her I'll be up in a few minutes. And tell Dolores to go get the doctor if she wants."

The woman closed the door and then came back over

to the sofa. She was still holding her drink.

"I'm sorry about that. The girl he injured is still upset . . ." She sat back down in the armchair and took a sip of her rye. "I haven't introduced myself, have I? I'm Rebecca Chase, Mr. Lee."

The name meant nothing to him.

"So you've bought the River Ranch?" She gave him that odd, quick glance again. "Well, it's certainly a beautiful property. I declare, I quite envy you, having a place like that so pretty." She leaned forward to put her drink down on a small table. "Though you certainly have gotten a rough welcome to Cree." She laughed and shook her head. "The wild West . . ."

She glanced across at him once more and suddenly stopped laughing. Her face went pale as a plaster mask.

"Oh, Jesus Christ," she said, staring at him.

"What's the matter?" Lee said. He felt his muscles tense.

"Oh, my God. You're Buckskin Frank Leslie!"

She didn't have a chance to say anything more.

Lee didn't even know how he had gotten there. Suddenly, he was standing over her, his hand clamped across her mouth. The razor-edged Arkansas toothpick was out, the bright splinter of steel lying across her throat.

He had her head forced way back across the back of the armchair. He laid the steel into the taut snow-white skin of her throat.

Everything was clear in his mind. One hard, deep slice and her head would be damn near off. Then a quick jump to the side, so the blood wouldn't spatter on his clothes, and then another jump to the door and out.

It would cost him the ranch. All that money gone. But they'd never find him. A drifter named Lee, a gunfight, and a knifing—just another of those killers the frontier threw up from time to time.

He looked down to get the cut just right—and saw her eyes.

There was nothing in them but terror. The brute, dumb terror of an animal about to be slaughtered. Nothing human left in those eyes at all. Nothing of a pretty woman living a rich life full of chance and pleasure.

The terror made her eyes ugly as an ugly doll's eyes—dirty green glass.

He started to cut. Just started. The faintest quick line of bright scarlet beaded under the blade.

Then he pulled the knife away and stood back.

For a long time she didn't move. She sat there with her head still held back, her eyes staring at him blindly.

She didn't open her mouth. She didn't make a sound.

Lee bent to slide the knife back into his boot.

"You're a very lucky woman, Rebecca."

She started, as if his voice had wakened her, and slowly sat up.

She tried to say something, but had to stop and clear her throat. "I'm sorry . . . I'm sorry, Mr. . . . Lee."

"Where the hell did you know me from?"

"From . . . from . . . Fort Grant." She tried to smile. "I just noticed. I wasn't sure at first . . . You always wore that mustache . . . and that short beard." Her color was coming back now. She knew he wasn't going to kill her. Not right now, anyway.

"Who were you with?"

She knew what he meant. "I was one of Florence Maynard's girls." She tried to laugh. "You remember old Florence . . ."

Now he remembered her. Becky Chase. She'd been a tall, thin girl. Nervous, with a stutter when she talked. They'd called her Pissy, or something like that, because she was always running out back to the jakes.

Well, Rebecca had changed a lot over the years. A heavy madame now, looking like a lady. And a businesswoman too, if she had a piece of the action in the Arcady.

"There's blood on your neck."

She gasped and put her hand up to her throat. When she looked at it, there was a drop of blood on her palm. She suddenly turned so pale, Lee thought she might faint. It had all come back to her, how close she had come to dying.

She fumbled for a handkerchief, a little scrap of lace, and walked unsteadily over to an oval mirror across the room. She stood there, dabbing at the slight cut, pressing the handkerchief to it. She was still very pale.

"And what's Phipps to you, Rebecca?" Lee asked. He settled himself back down on the sofa and watched her face reflected in the mirror.

He saw her start to lie, her eyes narrowing as she thought. Then she glanced into the mirror and saw him watching her.

"I love him," she said, pressing the little handkerchief to her throat. "I love him." She stared at Lee in the mirror, her eyes desperate.

"I have nothing against Phipps," Lee said. She looked away from him. "I have no quarrel with the man. In fact, I don't want to do a damn thing but raise horses and mind my own business . . ."

She walked back over to the armchair. She was looking better now, not so pale, and there was only a faint mark of dried blood where the blade edge had touched her throat.

She picked her drink up off the small table and drank it straight down.

"I won't tell anybody," she said, standing in front of Lee, clutching the empty glass. "I swear on my mother I won't tell anybody."

"Not a soul," Lee said. And he finished his own drink and stood up. "Because if you do, I'll finish cutting your throat for you. And I'll gun that fancy man of yours into dead meat . . ."

"I won't, I won't."

Lee walked over to the door. She turned to watch him go.

"Frank . . . *Lee*, I was sorry to hear about Rosilie . . ."

He looked back at her. She flinched.

"Don't mention her name; don't mention my name." He reached for the doorknob. "Never. And never to your loverboy, if you want to keep him."

"All right . . . all right. I never will, I swear."

He walked out and closed the door behind him.

Phipps stopped him just outside the staircase door. The crowd had calmed down now. Everybody was lined up at the bar with their drinks and their stories of how close they'd been and what they'd seen when the guns went off.

Mickey Slawson was up on a faro table. His body was covered with a canvas tarpaulin. A fat old half-breed with a straggly mustache was mopping the floor, his mop foaming pink in the pool of blood and soapy water.

The wild West.

"Lee," Phipps said in that deep voice, "from what I'm told, it was a fair-enough fight, and I don't intend to arrest you for the killing." He looked as though he was doing Lee a considerable favor. "On the other hand, I don't like killings in my town. I have enough trouble with the drunks shooting up the place just for the hell of it!"

"I'm not looking for trouble, Marshal," Lee said, looking as peaceful ás he could.

Phipps didn't look quite convinced. He'd heard about Slawson's drawing first, and he must have taken a good look at the body, too, and seen the three bullet holes in the chest. He would have been able to cover all of them with the palm of his hand.

Lee wished to hell that Slawson had given him time enough for head shooting. It would have been easy enough, then, to have put that one slug into his brains and to have claimed it as just dumb luck.

But not now. And the marshal was worried about him.

"I'm a horse rancher, Mr. Phipps, not a gunman. I'm a good hand with a pistol, but I don't like to use it. And, tell you the truth, that fellow was pretty drunk."

It seemed to help. The long-haired lawman gave Lee a long, considering glance, then nodded and walked away.

Lee got the hell out of there. On the way out he turned down four offers of drinks and shrugged off five backslappers and congratulators.

He stepped out through the batwings into the sweet night air. It was dark and cool and restful, even with the cowboys still trailing up and down the sidewalks, shouting to their friends.

Lee felt the knot inside him slowly begin to ease. It seemed as though the whole damned last hour in there had just been a nightmare, a bad dream.

But it hadn't been. It had been dead real. Ask Mickey Slawson.

And now he had that damn madame onto him. How long would she keep her mouth shut? Asking about Rosilie, the bitch. When she asked about Rosilie, he'd been sorry he *hadn't* cut her throat. And he would have before, if her eyes hadn't looked so bad. It would have been like cutting a corpse's throat.

He crossed the dirt street over to Mrs. Boltwith's. As he walked, he noticed several people watching him, nudging each other.

Trouble already. He was a marked man. And only a few fucking hours in the damn town . . .

The men were gone from Mrs. Boltwith's steps. They had better things to do. There was nobody behind the small hotel desk. Lee reached back behind it, to the rack of keys, and lifted down number 223. Then he turned and started up the narrow stairs. He was in no mood to talk to Bupp or anybody else.

Upstairs, he unlocked the door to his room, stepped inside, and relocked it. He scratched a lucifer and lit the small oil lamp sitting on top of the battered dresser beside the bed. The room was tiny, but it was freshly whitewashed and clean. The bed linen and thin cotten towels looked as if they were freshly washed. It seemed that Mrs. Boltwith kept a good house.

Lee sat wearily on the edge of the bed and hauled off his boots. Then he stood and stripped off the rest of his clothes, draping them over the back of the kitchen chair by the bed. Then he slipped the Colt out of its holster, shucked the three spent shells out onto the bed, and reloaded the pistol from the rounds held in his gunbelt. He hung the holstered Colt over the chair's back, pulled the bed covers down, and slid into bed. The sheets felt cool against his skin.

For a while, Lee lay staring up at the slowly coiling pattern the oil-lamp flame threw against the ceiling. Then he raised up in bed, lifted the lamp down from the dresser, and blew out the flame.

Now only a faint light filtered through the white curtains drawn across the small room's single window. Only a little noise came through from the back alley below—a dog barking in the distance, a cowboy singing down a side street.

Lee tried to stay awake, at least until he had a chance to think it all out, to work out what the killing would mean to him. Why the hell couldn't that fool of an Irishman have kept his hands to himself? And why the hell did that little whore make such a goddamn noise about it?

And what the hell was he supposed to do about Rebecca Chase and that pretty-boy killer of hers? Wouldn't it be better now if she were dead and he already halfway out of this damn valley on the dun?

He slept.

And dreamt of Doc Holliday. Poor Doc . . . lying in a narrow white bed in a narrow white room in Denver. A sanitarium, they called it. Death house was more like it.

Holliday had been his old self—except for being so small and thin. But he had never been a big man. When Lee had walked into the room, Holliday had called out, "Draw, you son-of-a-bitch!" and had yanked a bottle of Old Overholt out from under the sheets.

They had talked for two hours. About a lot of years. Wyatt, and the brothers, and the Clanton people out in Arizona. Doc was still regretful about not having fought Johnny Ringo that day in Tombstone.

"Come out and fight me, you bony bastard!" Ringo had called. And Doc had called back, "I'm your huckleberry!" and would have done it too, if Earp hadn't stopped him.

"I regret that, Frank," Doc had said, turning his head to cough some blood into a towel. "I regret that a lot."

They'd talked about that. In his dream, Lee seemed to be sitting in Doc's room again, watching him cough his lungs out into that towel and telling him all about having to kill the Irishman. "Slawson . . Slawson? I don't know any Slawson," Doc said in his dream. "How did he carry it, straight? Shoulder-rig? Cross-draw?"

But in Lee's dream, Doc was definite about how good it was that he hadn't killed Rebecca. "Shit she's just a twist, isn't she?" he'd said. "A judy, a nun? Hell, Frank, a man can't start killing women, or there's no hope for him, no hope at all! And a whore is the most helpless thing there is. A man can't kill a whore. Except by accident, the way Johnny Deuce killed your Rosilie . . ."

Lee awoke with a heave, fumbling for his gun. The sweat was pouring off him in the dark.

"Doc, you son-of-a-bitch," he said.

Then he remembered that Holliday was dead. Dead three weeks ago. The attendant who had told Lee he was gone had said that Doc died laughing—a rare way to go in that place—and had said only, "This is funny. . ." and then died.

"Doc, you son-of-a-bitch," Lee said into the room's darkness. "You poor son-of-a-bitch . . ."

It was a bright, sunny morning.

The sun flooded in through the single window and lit up the little whitewashed room like theater limelights.

Lee turned his head, groaning into the pillow, and tried to go back to sleep. He might have done it too, if somebody hadn't started pounding on the door.

"Mr. Lee, if you want any breakfast, you better get down to the kitchen!"

It was Mrs. Boltwith. She apparently didn't approve of people sleeping late.

"All right," Lee called out. "All right."

He rolled over onto his back and lay still a few moments remembering last night, the fight at the Arcady and Rebecca Chase.

Well, it was done. No chance of his being just another rancher come into the valley now. Not with Phipps hanging around. Still, he could let slip some of the truth to cover him. Nothing like a little truth to cover a big lie. He could let them know about Mexico, if it came to that. About the man who worked for Don Ignacio, who earned his living down below Matamoros with his gun, and who also bought Mexican horses cheap, then drove

61

them north to sell in Texas . . .

That man had already been known as Frederick Lee. It would explain where he got the money for the ranch well enough—and the gun skill, too, if it came to that. Montana was a long way from old Mexico; and after all, the story was true.

It just wasn't complete.

But Phipps should be satisfied: a below-the-border gunman makes some money horse trading and then starts fresh up in the States. Not wanted for anything either. Not in Montana.

It should do, and would do, if Rebecca kept her mouth shut. If she didn't keep her mouth shut, then that would be the end of a new life in Cree Valley. Once the word went out, every tinhorn and killer in three states would be coming to Cree to have a look at Buckskin Frank Leslie. And maybe take a shot at him, too, if they felt lucky—or got drunk enough.

That would be bad enough; it would make him a marked man, a man with no choice but to go back into the sporting life, back to the professional gambling, pimping, and killing.

But there was worse. If word got out who he was and where he was, the Texans would come looking for him. Ben Thompson for one, Wes Hardin for another. He'd killed one's brother, the other's friend. And neither Thompson nor Hardin were the forgiving kind.

Lee swung his feet out of bed and reached down for his socks. He could use a bath; he still had the trail dirt on him.

As he dressed, Lee considered the possibility that one of the Texans—or one of their friends, like Texas Jack Omahundro or Clay Allison—might show up one day. What then?

Omahundro he was sure he could take. He'd seen the man in a fight. He had been brave as a rooster—and a very poor shot. He'd tried for a man with four shots, just across a dance floor, and only hit him twice. And at that, the man had been able to get up and walk away. Nothing special there.

Allison was a different kettle of fish. Lee had seen him sober—and drunk. Sober, Allison had been a tall, handsome, courteous rancher. A prosperous rancher with a fine family. A gentleman—or as close to it as Texan ranchers got.

But that was Clay Allison sober. Drunk he was a different man. Lee had seen him drunk, just once, in Waco. Allison had looked and acted more like a devil than a man. And, as careful as Lee had been with him, it certainly would have come to shooting if Allison hadn't suddenly started to pick on someone else, a local lawyer and land agent named Bob Brice.

It had been a grim scene: Allison, staggering drunk, spitting out filthy insults about Brice and his wife, about his young daughters, all the time waiting, waiting for the poor man to try for his gun.

And Brice had had no choice in the end. It was either draw or pack up his family and get out of town. He had tried to back off, to talk his way out of it, but Allison had just laughed and said, "Crawl then, Brice, you daughter-fucker you. Crawl out of here on your hands and knees or I'll kill you where you stand . . ."

Poor Brice had gone for his gun. And made a good try at it, too. He'd actually gotten a shot off after Allison had already put two slugs in him. But Allison had put the next three into the poor man as well. He'd shot him to pieces; literally shot his guts out.

It had been simple murder. But no Waco lawman had come near the Seguaro when they'd heard who'd done the shooting. It was very simple. Even if five or six deputies had come after him, Allison, drunk, would have been happy to take them on—and would sure as hell have killed two or three before they got him.

The Waco lawmen had just passed it up as a fair

63

fight, and Lee and Allison, meeting the next day, had parted cordially. Allison hadn't referred to the killing—may not even have remembered doing it.

And if Clay Allison and Buckskin Frank Leslie were to face off, what then?

Lee wasn't sure. He might have Allison just a little shaded in speed. Just a little. But that difference meant next to nothing. A Jekyll-and-Hyde maniac like Allison wouldn't be stopped by a first bullet. No, he'd have to knock Allison down with the first two or three and hope the lead coming back at him wouldn't be fatal.

And Allison, for all his madness, wasn't the gun that either Thompson or Hardin were. Lee had no illusions when it came to those two. Thompson was a better show than he was, it was just that simple. And Hardin was faster. Hell, Hardin was faster than anybody. Either one of them might very well kill him cold . . .

Lee shrugged into his vest and buckled on his gunbelt. He'd have to clean the piece this morning, should have done it last night.

The hotel kitchen—also, apparently, used as the hotel diningroom—was bright with morning sunlight. Lee had met two men in the hall. He'd seen them on the hotel steps the night before, and they had brushed past him with a muttered, "Good morning," and averted eyes. He'd become the terror of the town of Cree overnight. "Good morning," he answered as sweet as pie, but they'd already hurried on their way.

"About time!" said Mrs. Boltwith; she wasn't so easily impressed. And she was even uglier in the daylight than she had been by oil lamp the night before. Nonetheless, she was done up in a fine, blue polka-dot house dress and big, starched white apron. The very figure of a respectable boarding-house keeper.

And the apron was still white, because Tim Bupp was

doing all the work. He must have already cooked breakfast for the other guests, because he was splashing and stirring at a stack of dishes in a big galvanized tub of soap and hot water. No question, Mrs. Boltwith was getting her cooking lessons paid for.

"Well, there you are!" Bupp said to Lee. "And I suppose you want me to just stop what I'm doing and fix you a breakfast—and it damn near about noon!"

"Yes, you will," said Mrs. Boltwith. "Mr. Lee is a hotel guest. You fix him some ham and eggs and biscuits and potatoes and coffee. And this time don't burn the ham; pigs don't grow on trees!"

Lee was beginning to like Mrs. Boltwith.

"And then you refill that tub so he can take a bath. He's got dirt on his butt and blood on his hands." She sniffed. "Even if poor Mickey did need killing something fierce . . ." And she bustled out of the kitchen with a rustle of skirts and apron.

Bupp sighed. "Well, dammit, just let me finish these damn dishes." He glanced sideways at Lee. "I don't know if I'd want a cooking job, if it's going to mean taking all this abuse . . ." He started hauling the platters out of the tub and cleaning them with a greasy towel. "Of course, one thing I will say," he glanced over at Lee again, "it ain't likely to be a *boring* job."

CHAPTER FIVE

The ham was burned, but just a little. The eggs were fine sunnyside up, but with the whites firm, just the way Lee liked them.

"Good eggs," he said to Bupp, through a mouthful of them.

Bupp just snorted, but seemed pleased, nonetheless.

"Tell me, Tim. What's the lay of the land in Cree? I've met Phipps, and you told me about Ashton. Do they run things? Or is there somebody else?"

Bupp grunted and hauled the tub to the kitchen door, then he swung the door open, heaved, and dumped the dishwater out into the yard. He dragged the big tub back into the kitchen, set it under the sink pump, and started working the pump handle, filling it with cold water for Lee's bath.

When the tub was half full, he stopped pumping. Then he set two big kettles on the stove to heat water for the bath.

When that was done, he pulled a chair up to the table, rolled a cigarette, and gave Lee a tutorial look.

"Listen," he said. "Phipps and Ashton do sort of run things around here, but it's not so simple." He paused for a moment, to watch Lee butter a biscuit. "What do you think about those biscuits?"

"They're kind of wet in the middle, but not bad."

"Wet in the middle, huh? I took 'em out too soon . . ."

"You were saying about Phipps and Ashton?"

Bupp took a deep draw on his cigarette. "It's like this: Phipps has the town, see, and Ashton runs the valley. Phipps is marshal, to start with, and beside that, he's the fastest gun around. He sure as hell is, now that Slawson's dead." He peered at Lee through a cloud of cigarette smoke. "Unless we figure you in . . ."

"Don't figure me in," said Lee.

"How's the coffee?"

"The coffee's just fine. You make good coffee, Bupp. Now, go on with what you were saying."

"Well, Phipps runs the town. He and that lady hooker of his own the Arcady and the Timber Lodge too. And Phipps has a hand in just about everything else in Cree. Has ever since he shot Matt Riboneaux. Riboneaux used to be the big cheese in Cree, but that was a couple of years ago."

"And Ashton?"

"Well now, Ashton's a horse of a different color. For one thing, he's an Englishman."

Lee wasn't surprised. The English had moved in on the cattle business in a big way in the '70s, and they had the capital to make themselves felt. Usually, though, they sent men to run the ranches for them. They seldom ran the ranches themselves.

"He own Fishhook, or just run it?"

"Hell, he owns it lock, stock, and barrel, and every acre under true deed! Ashton's rich. He's some English lord's nephew or something, and he's slicker'n grease, too."

"Ashton and Phipps get along?"

"Well now, I wouldn't say they get along. They just stay out of each other's hair, that's all." He leaned back in the kitchen chair, puffing on his cigarette, happy to be playing wiseman. "But, you know, Phipps just ain't in Ashton's class, gun or not. Ashton's rich, for one thing. And, for another, because he's rich he can hire any guns he wants. And he's got friends in Helena, too.

Big friends."

"So Phipps runs the town?"

"Yeah, but *only* the town."

"What about the town council? The mayor?"

"No mayor. They got a town council. But, hell, those shopkeepers are happy with things just as they are! Phipps don't cut a slice of their cake. He leaves them alone. And with all the lumber money coming into town this past two years, they're happy as clams!"

"A lot of lumber money, huh?"

"You bet! Hell, they're building half the mining camps in Montana out of those mountains back there! Butte and all the rest. There's a damn fortune in it, and those lumberjacks got no place to spend their bucks but Cree!"

"And that's it, Phipps and Ashton?"

Bupp pulled Lee's egg-stained breakfast plate over and stubbed his cigarette out in it. "Well," he said, "there are the farmers and small ranchers, but you pretty much took care of them last night."

"What do you mean?"

"Hell, I mean you shot Mick Slawson, is what I mean! He was a cruel bastard. And him and his boys probably did most of the cow stealing in these parts. But he was the only gun the small ranchers and farmers had. He never bothered their stock, and he wasn't scared of Phipps—or of Ashton, either."

One of the kettles started singing on the stove, and Bupp got up to pour the steaming water into the tub. When he emptied the second kettle into the bath, the tub was nearly full.

"Come on and take your bath. May as well, or we'll have that old dragon in here to throw you in it. And me, too, if I don't look out!"

Lee rode out of town two hours later.

It was past noon, and the dun was shifty, rested by a

night's stabling, and full of timothy and oats. Lee's saddlebags bulged with sandwiches, a side of the breakfast ham, and a dozen apples. Mrs. Boltwith didn't have much faith in a man's feeding himself all alone out on a ranch.

He was wearing new clothes, too. Denim pants and a blue flannel shirt, socks and underwear. Mrs. Boltwith had come into the kitchen while Lee was helpless in the bathtub and had taken his clothes out back to the laundry shed. Bupp had to go over to the mercantile and get him new duds, top to bottom.

It was a perfect day, with sunlight flaming down through the clear mountain air, bringing the distant peaks into glittering relief. It looked like the backdrop at a theater show, bright and light and perfect.

He thought of Rosilie for a moment. She would have loved this valley, the soft greenness of it, the towering mountains looming all around. "A fairy-tale place, Frank . . ."

That's what she would have said, if she were riding along beside him, riding on her little pinto mare, turning now to smile at him.

Lee jerked himself erect in the saddle and struck the spurs to the dun. The big horse bucked with surprise, squealed, and took off up the trail at a hard gallop, crow-hopping stumps and brush along the way. Lee had a lot to do just staying on him, and, after a half-mile run, he slowly reined the big gelding in, soothing him, patting the sweat-streaked withers, talking to him.

It was no good imagining what couldn't be. No good thinking about it.

He guided the dun up along the trail, keeping his eyes peeled. Bupp had said that the Crees still sometimes knocked a lone rider in the head if they could catch him careless. And there were Slawson's men, too. They wouldn't have taken kindly to him putting their boss under the dirt. And they might decide to do something about it.

It was early evening when he rode up into the high meadows. The shadows of the great pines stretched in broad black bars across the trail, and Lee could see flocks of birds wheeling up from the valley below into the red-gold sunset.

The dun was pacing steadily up the slopes, breaking into a trot where the high grass grew thick as prairie grass in Kansas. At the horse's hoof falls, clouds of insects came whirring up, clicking and buzzing off to disappear into the deep carpet of green again, a few yards away.

It was prime horse country. Not perfect for flat racers, maybe, might put too much muscle on the legs. But for cow work, or that new quarter-racing, or just for fine riding stock, it was prime horse country.

The sun was almost down now, dropping fast below the distant peaks to the west. Lee reined in and turned in the saddle to watch. Down in the valley, the land was filled with shadow, brimming with it like a dark green cup. As Lee watched, the darkness rose swiftly toward him as the sun sank out of sight, climbing up his backtrail like an incoming tide off the Presidio in San Francisco.

He'd be getting to the ranch in darkness.

More than an hour later, he rode over the east ridge. The ranch buildings lay below, dark and silent, barely visible by starlight. The moon was still down behind the mountains. There was a night wind breezing through the pines along the ridge. The rich smell swept over Lee as he sat the weary dun in the cool, enveloping dark.

Lee sat up there quite a while, looking over his land. His land. And, by the time the moon was up, shedding a bright silvery wash over the ranch and surrounding hills, the valley far below, he had made his decision.

He was staying. He would have to take his chances

with Rebecca Chase.

He was staying, because Rosilie would have wanted him to.

Lee sat up in the saddle, gathered the reins, and started to spur the dun down the long ridge to the ranch. Then he froze, his head cocked, listening.

"Tom Cooke," he said. "Come out here in the light."

For a long moment there was no movement, no sound but the wind in the pines. Then, from the border of the woods a few yards to Lee's left, a shadow detached itself from other shadows, and the young Indian walked silently out into the moonlight.

Lee looked down at the boy for a moment. The Blackfoot's scarred, big-nosed face was as blank as stone.

"You come to work for me?"

The boy shrugged, not answering.

"Are there deer in these hills, boy?"

Tom Cooke nodded and put his hands up beside his ears in the sign for mule deer.

Lee reached down beside his saddle and untied a thong. Then he slid the Blackfoot's old Spencer out from a keeper strap, balanced it in his hands for a moment, then lightly tossed it over into the boy's arms. Tom Cooke cradled his rifle, staring at Lee without expression, his narrow black eyes glittering in the moonlight. Then, without a word, he turned and walked away into the shadows of the pines.

Lee didn't turn to watch him go. He touched the dun with his spurs and rode off down the ridge to the ranch.

The front door to the ranch house was secured by a large, rusty padlock. Bupp had given Lee the key, but even so, it took a few minutes to work the old lock open.

Lee stepped into the house and walked carefully through the darkness to a table in the parlor. He remembered seeing an oil lamp on it from the day before. He found the lamp, scratched a lucifer on the seat of his pants, and lit the wick and turned it up full. The room bloomed into golden light.

His home.

Lee stood looking around at the rough furniture, the tanned cowhide stretched across the floor as a carpet before the big fieldstone fireplace, the heavy adze-cut timbers of the roof and walls. Then he lifted the lamp and carried it through the other rooms, which were: a bedroom almost as big as the parlor, with a double bed and firm horsehair mattress covered against dust by an old calico spread; an office for ranch business, with a shaved-pine desk and cracked-leather swivel chair; and a long kitchen that ran the width of the back of the house, complete as could be, with a pump sink and a big, grease-blackened range stacked with pots and pans. A table was there big enough to sit a dozen cowhands.

Lee walked out through the back door, carrying the lamp to light his way, and walked down the path to the outhouse.

Standing there, in the rough-sawn cedar privy, Lee sighed and took a long, relieving piss.

Home.

He went back around the front, unhitched the dun, and led it over to the corral. Then he unsaddled it and went down to the barn for feed. There were a few sacks stored up against one wall, and he put down the lantern and hauled one out. Then he lugged it out to the corral and spilled a measure into the trough for the dun and Bupp's two mares. He pumped them some fresh water, too.

He carried his saddlebags and the Henry back into the house. He didn't need the lamplight outside anymore. The moonlight was bright enough to throw his shadow along the ground before him. And he went back to the kitchen and dumped the cured ham, apples, and two left-over sandwiches on the table.

He sat eating the sandwiches in the oil lamp's yellow glow, thinking of the work to be done on the place. Sandburg would be coming in in a couple of days with the horses: the big appaloosa stud named Shokan and nine mares, pure Nez Perce appaloosa every one. And three of the mares would be trailing colts. The foundation stock for the finest mountain horses in the world.

They had cost Lee almost as much as the ranch itself, and even then, he wouldn't have been able to buy them if Bud Lowns hadn't put in a good word for him with the Nez Perce. Those Indians owed Lowns a lot, and they knew it. There were maybe three or four really honest Indian agents in the whole of the West. Lowns was one.

And there was still money to be spent: tack for the horses, tools for nailing fencing, cash for Bupp and Tom Cooke, and Sandburg and his son. And feed. And food: flour, salt, bacon, coffee, corn meal—if he could get it—and a few young beeves for beef. Beans, work-clothes, ammunition—a hell of a lot of goods. It would take most of the rest of his cash just to get set up right, and if he wasn't careful how he spent it, he might have to sell one of the colts off, or even a mare, just to pay his store bills.

And he'd have to get Bupp to put in a kitchen garden, too. Knowing Bupp, it was going to be a chore; he probably didn't know any more about gardening than he did about cooking.

Lee finished the sandwiches, put the ham and apples up in the zinc-lined foodbox, and carried the lamp into the bedroom. He'd have to buy some more lamps, too, and oil, and a good shotgun. A Greener twelve gauge might come in handy for bird-shooting or whatever . . .

No question, all that was going to take most of his money. And he was determined not to play any poker in

73

Cree. A professional just can't play poker with men who are amateurs at the game—not if he wants to be accepted as a friend.

Lee propped the Henry in a corner and draped his gunbelt over the bedpost. Then he pulled off his boots and undressed. He blew out the lamp, peeled back the calico spread, and slid into the big bed, stretching out on the rough mattress cover with a grunt of satisfaction.

Sheets. He would have to buy sheets, too. And blankets.

And no poker.

The square life had its disadvantages.

When Lee walked out of the ranch house at dawn, he found Tom Cooke sitting on his haunches under a larch sapling in the front yard. He was whittling on a stick with an old Barlow knife.

A young mule deer buck hung, dressed out and cooling, from the crossbeam supporting the ranch house's narrow front porch.

"Nice buck."

The young Blackfoot grunted.

"We'll have some fresh venison steaks tonight for supper. Be nice if we could hang him for another day, but all I've got is enough ham for dinner."

Lee strolled down the ranch house steps, took an apple out of his pocket, and handed it to the boy.

"Now listen, Tom," he said. "I can pay you $25 a month, at least to start—and God knows when I'll ever be able to pay you more. You'd bunk in the bunkhouse with old Tim and a couple of men I'll have coming in." He sighed. "And I guess I'll go for a pony for you to work off. You do mount the right side and ride single rein?" He suspected the boy did. Most Indians were brought up to ride that way, and it played hell with the average white-trained cowpony.

For the first time since the boy had took the shot at him and Bupp, Lee saw a change of expression on his face. He looked surprised, and he almost smiled. It was the pony, of course. Lee remembered the boy's old pinto going down with the Henry slug through him. That must have hit the boy as hard as the belt.

"Now, come along with me. I want to get those sheds cleared out today. And if we hump it hard enough, we can get it done."

They humped it hard enough.

The Indian boy was a hard worker and no fool. Lee never had to tell him anything twice. In fact, he had a hard time keeping up. Playing gun for old Don Ignacio had been the cause of action aplenty, but not much hard work. And even on his horse drives into Texas, he'd had two or three *vaqueros* along to help out.

But this was no romantic gun and horse work. It was just fetch and carry—and a lot of it. The sheds hadn't been touched since the old man's death, and they were piled full of every kind of scrap, busted tools, split and knotholed lumber, field mice, horn beetles, grass snakes, and coils of rusty barbed wire.

Lee and Tom Cooke stacked the lumber off to one side. It might come in handy fixing rail fences. The rest of the scrap they heaped on a bare patch beyond the corral and burned. But Lee made Tom Cooke recoil the old barbed wire. They could bury it later. Not that he had anything against it. For cows it was fine. But around fine horses, it was no use at all, just a danger.

He and Tom worked and sweated out considerable till afternoon. By that time, they had the two big sheds cleared and neat. The barn was already in fair shape, so that left them with the bunkhouse still to do.

"Tom," Lee said, "let's go eat up that cured ham."

The boy seemed surprised when Lee motioned him in through the kitchen door. It seemed that most people in the valley preferred their Indians kept out of doors.

"Pump us some water, Tom."

Lee got the ham and the last of the apples out of the foodbox and put them on the table with a couple of tin plates. He hadn't found any forks or spoons in the place, and assumed the old man had used some good family silver, and it had gone with the Chicago people's selloff. More stuff to buy, but damn sure not sterling silver!

He and Tom Cooke sat down, hauled out their jack-knives, and went at the ham like wolves. It was slice off a chunk of ham, gobble it down, take a long, cold drink of well water, and slice off another chunk of ham. Between them, they went through three pounds of meat, and then they scraped the bone.

Lee lit up one of his cigar stubs, offered another to Tom Cooke (who made a face and shook his head), and led the way out into the yard for a smoke-around walk-around before they went back to work.

A few minutes later, coming around the corner of the house, Lee saw the Indian boy crouched down in some brush out past the sheds. The damn fool was going to take a crap out there.

"Hey, damn it, Tom!" Lee yelled at him. "Get your red ass into that privy!" The boy hesitated, then pulled his pants up, and came trotting out of the brush.

"Listen, boy. You don't have to go shitting in the woods on this ranch, you understand? You go crap where everybody else does!" The locals must not like Indians in their privies, either, he thought.

Lee had never understood what people hated so much about Indians. Most of the ones he had known were pretty decent people. It was true that he'd killed a few, but that had been fair enough. They'd been trying to kill him at the time. It was true, too, that Indians sometimes treated white women and kids very cruelly. But Lee had known white men to do every bit as bad to little children, and with less excuse than the Indians had.

On the other hand, he'd never bought all that "Lo, the poor Indian" stuff that some of those church people from the East handed out. Most tribes he knew had been happily killing their Indian enemies before the whites ever showed up and had been pretty quick to enjoy the same exercise with the whites. They'd just lost, that's all. Lost for good; that was the sad part of it.

He finished his cigar stub and was just turning to call Tom back to work when he caught it. Just a flicker of movement on the ridgeline a mile away.

Lee wished to God he'd bought a good long-shooting rifle while he was in town! He'd damn sure intended to, and now he maybe was going to regret not doing it!

It was a horseman—at least one—just topping the rise of the eastern ridge. Coming right on for the ranch as bold as paint. Too far still to make out anything about him, he might be one of Slawson's friends come to call.

Lee turned his head to shout for Tom Cooke, then shut his mouth and nodded. The young Blackfoot was standing just behind him, staring at the on-coming rider. The Spencer was cradled in his arms.

A minute later, they saw that it was a woman.

She was riding sidesaddle, and they could see a feather in her hat.

Tom Cooke drifted away with his rifle, and Lee dug out another piece of cigar and set himself to wait. The woman was taking her time, keeping her horse at a steady canter. She was coming down through the ridge scrub now, the horse taking the rough ground in stride. Lee noticed the horse, too. It was a tall, rangy animal, looked well-bred, perhaps a hunter.

The woman had seen him standing there, must have noticed him some time back; but it was only now, almost in hailing distance, that she lifted her quirt with a casual wave to him. He touched the brim of his hat to reply, tossed down the cigar butt, and stood, arms crossed, waiting until she rode up to him. It was fairly certain she hadn't come as a revengeful friend of Mickey Slawson.

She rode up to him and reined the hunter in. It was a hunter, a thoroughbred by the look of it.

"Mr. Lee?"

Her voice was British, low and crisp, a lady's voice. And her looks matched it. She was a silver blond, and slim and neat as a sapling willow. She was wearing a velvet green riding dress that must have cost half a year of a working man's wages. Her eyes were a soft and guarded gray.

Lee swept off his Stetson and made her a low, graceful bow.

"Yes, ma'am. And may I be of some assistance to you?"

The girl seemed surprised. She must have expected some horny-handed rancher with a plug in his jaw, not a handsome man with experience in manners appropriate to San Francisco's opera-and-champagne-cocktail set.

"Well . . ."

"Perhaps you'd be kind enough to join me on the house porch for a few moments, to rest from your ride, and allow this handsome hunter to cool out for a bit?"

"Well . . . Yes, Mr. Lee. I believe that I will."

Lee lifted his hand to help her. She took it and slid neatly down from the sidesaddle. Her hand was slim and cool and strong.

"My name is India Ashton, Mr. Lee."

"Ma'am."

Lee led her horse into the corral, and they walked up to the house together. India Ashton was tall, only a few inches shorter than Lee.

"I understand you're my neighbor, Mrs. Ashton."

"Yes, I am. But it's *Miss* Ashton, Mr. Lee. Nigel Ashton is my brother."

There was a battered rocker on the front porch, and Lee guided her to it.

"If you'd like to rest here, ma'am, I'll fetch you a glass of cold water. I regret that's all that River Ranch can offer at the present. I haven't gotten in supplies as yet."

"Water would be very welcome, Mr. Lee," she said.

When Lee brought the cup of water out to her, he found India Ashton rocking slowly back and forth in the creaking chair, looking out over the meadows below the house and, in the distance, the soft, varied green of Cree Valley.

She smiled up at him, took the water, and sipped it slowly.

"You have a very beautiful property here, Mr. Lee."

"Yes," Lee said, leaning against the porch rail and looking down at her. "It's a very pretty place and, I hope, will be a profitable one as well."

"My brother's experience is that the cattle business is a very difficult one in which to be certain of profits . . ."

Lee smiled. "I'll be raising horses, Miss Ashton, although I'm sure that doesn't make profit any more certain."

"And I believe you have the river on your property, do you not?"

"Yes, I do." And damn well you know it, Lee thought. The lady had come on a little fishing expedition. Fishing from Fishhook. Lee wondered if her brother had put her up to it.

"The river is very beautiful, and, of course, it will give you assured water for your stock . . ."

"Yes, it does."

She sighed and put the cup down on the top of the porch rail.

"So pretty," she murmured, looking out over the meadows. "And I suppose you could dam the river up, if you chose, and even make a private lake of it . . ."

Lee repressed a smile.

"Miss Ashton," he said. "You may tell your brother that I have no intention of diverting Rifle River, or stopping the flow, or of keeping my neighbors from water for any reason. You may also tell him, that if he has any matters to discuss with me, he is welcome to come and do so in person."

India Ashton blushed a faint pink, and her gray eyes sparkled with anger.

"I had no intention—"

Her furious glance met Lee's smile, and her blush deepened. She stood up and shook out the skirts of her riding habit.

"Thank you for your hospitality, Mr. Lee," she said with icy courtesy. "But I don't wish to intrude on you further . . ."

Her back as straight as a soldier's, she marched down off the porch and across the yard to the corral. Lee had to stretch his legs to keep up with her.

"Oh, you're always welcome to River Ranch, Miss Ashton, but I hope next time it will be a social call, not business. It's so uncomfortable, confusing the two . . ."

It made her too angry to answer him. Those beautifully carved lips were compressed into a thin, indignant, pink line.

Lee led the tall hunter out to her. She waited in silent fury as he came around to reach down, cup her small high-buttoned boot in his hand, and toss her lightly up into the saddle.

She sat glaring down at him as if she would have liked to cut him across the face with her riding crop.

Lee reached up his hand to her with a smile.

"Friends, Miss Ashton?"

"I should prefer to say *neighbors*, Mr. Lee!"

And she wrenched the hunter's head around, spurred him sharply, and flew off at a neat hand gallop, heading east toward the ridge. She rode very well, easy in the saddle as only a lifetime rider could be. She didn't look back.

A lady, Lee thought. The genuine article, and a rare piece to boot, if you could handle her. He wondered if she had been sent by her brother to find out what he planned for the river, or if this little expedition had been her own idea.

"She ride good, don't she?"

Tom Cooke was back, without the Spencer.

"Damn good," Lee said. "Now, let's get back to work."

CHAPTER SIX

Next day, at noon, while Lee and Tom Cooke were rigging Bupp's two mares with pack saddles for a trip to Cree for supplies, they heard hoofbeats descending the west ridge.

They turned and saw a faint cloud of dust rising through the pines.

"Lot of horses . . ."

Tom Cooke was right. It took a lot of horses to raise dust in this green country.

Lee thought he knew who it was, but he strode to the dun and slid the Henry out of its scabbard just in case.

In a few moments, they could see metal sparkling in the sunlight, reflecting off neck-rein chains and bits, saddle conchos and cartridge belts. And a moment later, a small herd of horses, with two armed riders alongside, came trotting down the ridge.

Appaloosas.

There was no mistaking the odd dark and white markings, the spotted rumps. Sandburg and his boy, Jake, had made the drive up from Colorado—and right on time.

"My horses, Tom," Lee said. He was proud of those light-stepping Nez Perce beauties. The finest mountain horses in the world; only pure Arabs could beat them for staying power, and then only on the flat.

Lee saw that Sandburg's boy was lead-trailing two

remounts, both sorrels, carrying their outfits and personal goods. The River Ranch was starting to "horse up."

The herd was close enough now for Lee to make out Shokan, easily trotting well ahead of the mares, the big stud's white, black-spotted coat shining in the bright sunlight.

"A big-boss horse," Tom Cooke said, watching the stud come in.

"The best," Lee said.

All the appaloosas looked in good shape, trim and lively, the colts sprinting alongside their mothers as full of beans as if they hadn't just finished a three-hundred mile drive.

Ole Sandburg had seen Lee by the corral, and now he turned his horse's head and rode down to him, leaving his boy, Jake, to chivvy the appaloosas into the fenced meadow above the ranch buildings.

Sandburg was a tall, bald, mournful-looking man, rail-thin in his dusty Levi's and battered Stetson. His boy, Jake, was his spitting image and equally sad and silent. They were good hands with horses, though, and Lee had been lucky to hire them when the horse ranch they worked on had been sold to a local cowman for graze.

Now they were his men, and damned good men at that. They weren't interested in much else than working with horses and father and son had been working together for so many years that they had come to resemble each other.

"Mr. Lee." Sandburg leaned down from the saddle to shake his hand.

"Ole."

Sandburg's pale blue gaze flickered over to Tom Cooke, but he didn't offer to shake hands with the Indian.

"Horses look good, Ole," Lee said. "Any trouble?"

"They're in good shape," Sandburg said. "No trouble, except the stud tried to bring in a couple of wild mustang mares. We had to keep hazing them ladies off despite him."

"The colts come through the drive okay?"

"Hell, Mr. Lee, those damn colts are as full of vinegar as when they started. You want to come on over and look at 'em?"

"I'd like to, Ole, but Tom Cooke and I are heading into town for supplies, and I want to get that done. Anything you need while we're going?"

Sandburg shook his head. "Some plug tobacco is all I can think of, special."

"Okay," Lee said. "And this here's Tom Cooke; he'll be working with us on the place."

Sandburg nodded to the young Blackfoot.

"And one thing, Ole, you and Jake keep your eyes open up here. I had to shoot a man in town, I'm sorry to say, and he had some friends who weren't above a little rustling, or so I hear."

Sandburg sighed and nodded, looking over the ranchland and the solid log-and-stone buildings. "Trouble." He sighed again. "Well, Mr. Lee. I will say you have you a pretty place here; worth some trouble, I guess."

Lee mounted the dun and waved to Jake Sandburg, who was still chivvying the appaloosas up into the top pasture.

"Hey-hooo! Jake!"

Sandburg's boy waved back at Lee, and then had to spur his sorrel to turn a couple of appaloosa mares who'd decided to make for the west ridge.

"Move on in to the bunkhouse, Ole," Lee said. "We'll be back early tomorrow. And there's a side of venison hanging off the porch. Cut yourselves some of that."

Sandburg nodded, "Okay," and turned his horse to go help his son with the herd.

Lee sat his saddle a moment longer, watching the appaloosas gallop and frisk in the high pasture's lush grass. He would have been happy to spend the day up there, watching them, and maybe feeding some lump sugar to the mares. But, hell, he didn't have any sugar—or anything else, either.

"Let's go, Tom." He reined the dun down toward the distant valley and heard the hoofbeats of the pack horses behind him, as Tom Cooke led them into line.

A fine horse ranch. And fine horses on it now.

Mr. Lee was doing all right.

On his first trip down to Cree, Lee had set himself to remembering the trail, and he'd done a good job, even with all the excitement of Tom Cooke's shooting at them. Today, he didn't get lost more than twice. Once in the trees, going down, and then once more, when they were over the river.

Each time, just before he was ready to admit he was lost, Lee would hear a grunt from Tom Cooke behind him and would turn to see the boy pointing off in the direction they should be heading.

They made good time, although Lee stopped once to take a piss and rest the horses. He also picked and ate about a quart of blackberries along the banks of Rifle River. The berries were big and shiny black, tight and sweet, with juice as a young girl. Tom Cooke ate his share, too, and by the time they both were finished, the blackberry brambles had scratched them up more than a little.

Even so, it was still sun-high when they saw Cree. The town, which had been so lively at night, looked sound asleep in the late-afternoon sunlight. Only a few farm wagons rolled down main street, bringing the loads of spring fodder for the livery and stock yard to the south of town.

Lee pulled the dun up at the edge of town and reached down to check the Colt, easing it in the holster. It was possible that Rebecca Chase had spilled the beans to Phipps, had let him know who Lee was . . .

But she hadn't. Or if she had, Phipps had decided to butt out of the matter. No one troubled them as they rode in. Lee and Tom Cooke tied off the pack horses in front of a sign that read: DRY GOODS AND SUPPLY—W. KIMBLE PROP. Lee climbed up onto the high loading platform and walked into the store's cool darkness.

The big store smelled of sacks of feed, oiled leather, gun oil, hard cheese, cloth goods, pickles, and fresh-sawn lumber. It was a pleasant, rich, comforting smell. Comforting if you had money in your jeans.

A tall, dark, cadaverous man stepped out of the shadows to meet Lee. He had a long, sad face and was wearing a white apron that hung down to his ankles.

"Yes, sir? Can I help you to something?"

"Yes, you can. My name's Fred Lee. I've bought the River Ranch, and I'm in need of quite a sum of supplies."

"Oh, yes, oh, yes . . ." The bony shopkeeper nodded. "I'd heard that land had been bought. And you'd certainly need some goods. I understand those Chicago people just about cleaned that place out. You're lucky they didn't sell the ranch house for lumber!" He laughed a high-pitched, squeaky laugh.

"I've got a list," Lee said.

"Okay . . . okay!" The shopkeeper rubbed his hands. "Let's get to it!" He held out his right hand for Lee to shake. "I'm Walter Kimble, by the way."

"Fred Lee."

"Oh, yes. Now Mr. Lee, let's see that list . . ."

It was a long list, and it took a long time to pick out

the goods, stack them, and shift them out to the pack horses. Tom Cooke bundled them up and strapped the loads to the horses' backs.

"I'll tell you, Mr. Lee," Kimble said. "You're going to need a buckboard for this feed you got written down here. It's going to be too much of a load for your horses."

"I know it. Would you have a notion of a buckboard for sale in town?" It would mean unloading the horses and repacking the buckboard. It would also mean spending the night in town.

"Oh, yes indeed I would," Kimble said, his cheery voice coming oddly from that long, lugubrious face. "Matter of fact, *I've* got a buckboard I could let you have cheap enough, very cheap indeed." He shook his head. "Matter of fact, you'd be unwise to buy a new wagon, seeing that there's no proper road up to your place. Any vehicle you buy's bound to get shook to pieces getting up there and surely won't last much more than a year, if it even lasts that!"

"And what would you ask for this old second-hand buckboard, Mr. Kimble?"

Kimble laughed. "Well, she's more like third or fourth hand, Mr. Lee, but she still goes." He stood musing for a moment, his hand cupping his lantern jaw. "I suppose I'd have to ask $25.00 for her . . ."

"Throw in a set of harnesses, Mr. Kimble, and I might buy it," Lee said, enjoying bargaining with the man.

"Oh, but not *new* harnesses, Mr. Lee!"

"But serviceable, Mr. Kimble."

The tall shopkeeper sighed, stroking his chin. "Oh, very well, a set of serviceable harnesses." He gave Lee a shrewd glance. "And what about horses to draw it, Mr. Lee?" Mr. Kimble was apparently the town horse trader as well.

Lee sighed. Ranching looked to be a damned expensive operation. And he still had a good Sharps rifle to dicker for. A mountain rifle.

It was dusk when they were done.

The sagging buckboard had all it could do to stand up under the sacks of oats and hard grain, heavy tools, rolls of hemp rope and harness leather, wash tubs, and kegs of spikes and nails.

The harness horses that Lee had bought were better animals than he had expected. Kimble had, with the best will in the world, tried to foist off a pair of half-blind and all-galled old wheezers on him, but had proved pleasant and philosophical when he saw that Lee knew horses.

"Oh, I see that you're a knowing man and a considerable judge," he'd said, and laughed his high-pitched laugh and offered a fair price for two fair harness horses.

Lee'd been hungry for supper by that time, and so had Tom Cooke. So Lee'd led the way over to Mrs. Boltwith's. It was early for supper, but the usual crowd of clerks and harness drummers was gathered on Mrs. Boltwith's front steps and porch, waiting for the call to come eat.

These men glanced at Lee as he walked up the steps, but none of them said anything to him. Probably afraid of some terrible temper and a quick gunshot. Lee had felt that fear from most men for many years. He had gotten used to it, and finally had ignored it. It bothered him now, though. He didn't want that sort of feeling around him anymore.

He looked back down the steps for Tom Cooke, and saw that the Blackfoot was going the other way, heading around to the back of the house. The poor kid knew his place, no doubt about it, and it must make him mad as hell.

Lee walked through the front door and past the small registration desk—which he had not seen anybody use yet—and headed down the hall to the kitchen. He might as well see what old Bupp was fixing up for supper.

But he hesitated at the kitchen door. Tim Bupp was cooking, all right, and standing at the big kitchen range, cursing and stirring a kettle or something that smelled like Irish stew. Mrs. Boltwith was in the kitchen, too, sitting at the table, knitting at an object the color of fresh mustard greens. Lee assumed it was a muffler, or maybe a long, narrow sweater of some kind.

There was a girl sitting at the table, too.

She was a thin girl—skinny really—with dark eyes and a fairly big nose. She was dressed in light blue calico, or what looked like calico to Lee, and was really a nice-looking girl, even with that big nose. Her skin was very white.

"Well, now, come on in, Mr. Lee," Mrs. Boltwith said, and she gave him a dignified nod. "Beatrice, this here's Mr. Lee."

The thin girl turned to look up at Lee, and her eyes widened as if there was something special about him.

"Mr. Lee, this is Beatrice Morgan, a very sweet girl and a good friend of mine . . ."

"How do you do, ma'am?" Lee said.

"So there you are," said Tim Bupp. "And come to have some of this stew, I suppose—and serve you right!" Tim didn't seem pleased with his cooking.

"There's nothing the matter with that stew, Mr. Bupp," said Mrs. Boltwith. And, to Lee, "Mr. Bupp apparently never heard tell of pepper, Mr. Lee."

"Well, there's too damn much of it in this here stew, I'll tell you that!" said Bupp. "She put all that pepper in my stew without so much as a by-your-leave!"

His stew. It appeared that cooking was taking hold of Mr. Bupp.

The girl, meanwhile, had been staring at Lee without

89

saying a word to him. But when he hung his Stetson on the back of one of the kitchen chairs and sat down, she spoke up.

"I—I believe that I owe you a great deal of thanks, Mr. Lee . . ."

Lee looked across the table into those pretty brown eyes. She looked very sincere, but he didn't know what the hell the young lady was taking about.

"Ma'am?"

She blushed like a bride. "You . . . I understand that you are the man who . . . fought Mr. Slawson."

Now what the hell was all this about? "Yes, ma'am?" Lee asked.

"Well . . . you saved me from . . . from . . ."

Jumping Jesus Christ! It was the little whore the Irishman was dragging around the floor! He hadn't recognized her.

"Now, now," said Lee. The damn girl was so lady-like, he found himself still talking to her as if she was some decent town girl. "It was just one of those things that happens, miss, nothing for you to fret about . . ."

"Well, I do want to thank you." She held out her hand to him across the table. "It was very brave of you . . ."

Lee reached out and took her hand, feeling like a damn fool. It was a small, thin hand and very cool.

Lee shook her hand, then let it go.

"Don't think about it anymore, miss . . . uh, honey . . . It's over and done with."

"Hello, Tom Cooke," said Mrs. Boltwith. The young Blackfoot was standing at the kitchen door. "Come on in and sit down."

Tom came into the kitchen, but he didn't sit down. He went over to the range and stood leaning against the wall, watching Bupp stir the stew.

"Beatrice has been working for Rebecca Chase for almost a year," said Mrs. Boltwith. "And she don't care for it more than half!"

"Oh, Rebecca's friendly . . ." the thin girl said. She looked at Lee as she said it, her brown eyes steady, looking as if she asked him, yes, I'm a whore, and it surprised you, didn't it?

"She may be friendly enough," said Mrs. Boltwith. "But friendly is as friendly does, and she doesn't take care of her girls! Why, didn't she run Suzy Williams off when she was poxed up? In my day, a woman who'd run off a sick girl like that would have had a bad name for five years, and that's flat!"

So Lee'd been right. Mrs. Boltwith had been in the gay life. And more important, she knew—or felt—that Lee had been as well, or she wouldn't be talking so plain about it.

The thin girl was still looking at Lee in that odd, defiant way, as though daring him to judge her for what she was—or Mrs. Boltwith for what she'd been.

Lee had run whores himself for a couple of years in Dodge City, but he'd never made the mistake of thinking that he really knew what was on a whore's mind—or on any woman's mind, come to that.

Women would whore, same as a man would do anything, if they had to for food and shelter. But when that reason was past, the cause of a woman's whoring got very complicated. Hatred of their daddies was a big reason—hatred of themselves. And Lee had known some girls who simply loved the life—the excitement, the continual change, the free talk and the free ways that decent women could never know. And the fucking, too; no use saying that many women didn't love it as much as men.

"Do they call you Bee?" he asked the girl, smiling.

She blushed again. A blushing little whore. "No, they call me Beatrice. My folks used to call me Bee."

Bee. James's wife had been called Bee. Lee had met them once in New Orleans. Jesse James had been a quiet sort of man, with big farmer's hands. Nothing special about him at all. Frank James had struck Lee as the smarter brother. And Bee James had been a pretty little lady. Very dainty. They'd all had lunch at the Garvey House when the prize fight was over, and Jesse had said, "Sullivan's getting old." The Jameses were calling themselves Mr. and Mrs. Martin while they were in Louisiana. Doc Porteous had brought Lee to that lunch as a surprise. Quite a surprise — and a damn good lunch.

"Bee's a pretty name," Lee said to the girl.

"Well," Bupp said from the stove, "this over-peppered Irish stew is ready to eat. As ready as it'll ever be!"

Mrs. Boltwith had been right. There was nothing the matter with the stew; it had been peppered just enough.

Bupp had served it out to the four of them. Tom Cooke had eaten his standing against the wall—even though Mrs. Boltwith had asked him again to sit down with them—and Lee had been happy to take seconds.

Then, it had been time for the boarders to come in for their supper. "You'll want your same room, Mr. Lee?" Mrs. Boltwith had asked. Lee'd seemed to have become prime with her for some reason. Tom Cooke was invited to bunk it out back with Bupp.

So, after the stew and a piece of apple pie with their coffee, they'd cleared out for the rest of the paying customers. And Lee decided to ask Beatrice Morgan out for a walk. It was dark enough outside now, so that no one would remark that a respectable rancher, new to the valley, had taken a whore out for a stroll.

It was a moonlit night, almost light enough, Lee thought, for them to have made it back to the ranch traveling through the night. The girl knew the town better than he did, so Lee let her guide him down a narrow side street and out to the edge of town.

She didn't have much to say, so Lee did the talking. It

was pleasant enough; it had been a long time since he had gone walking in the moonlight with a girl. He was surprised how pleasant it was.

"So, you've been in Cree a year, Miss Morgan?"

"About that," she said.

"It's a pretty place, this valley, with all the green and the mountains. But I imagine it'll get sort of fierce in the winter . . ."

"It does get cold, yes."

Lee saw that she didn't know how to get on with him now, and was acting as shy as the respected town girl he was treating her like. He stopped and took hold of her slender arm and turned her toward him.

"Listen, Miss Morgan, I don't give a damn if you're whoring. It's a job like any other; better than some I've done, worse than some, too. It doesn't make you any less a nice girl as far as I'm concerned . . . or any more a nice girl, either."

She was standing, looking up at him in the moonlight, her dark eyes shadowed. He couldn't tell what she was thinking.

"So don't stay so stiff with me; I won't hurt you."

"All right . . . Lee?"

"That's right, you call me Lee . . . and I'll call you Bee."

She smiled, and when he took her hand, she let him hold it. They walked along like that for a while. Lee could hear the soft, busy sound of Rifle River passing over some rapids under the trees a little way away. A cool breeze had come up, and he thought he felt the girl tremble.

"You cold, Bee?"

She shook her head, and they walked along a little farther in silence.

"You know," she said suddenly, "Marshal Phipps beat a man up last night."

"Did he?"

"Yes." She hesitated. "It was a lumberjack. A man named Boyd. Marshal Phipps beat him badly. Sarah was downstairs then—Sarah's a friend of mine—and she saw it."

"Well," Lee said. "Keeping the peace isn't always a pretty job." He couldn't make out what was bothering her, she must have seen plenty of the rough house in the Arcady.

She glanced up at him.

"Sarah said it seemed that Marshal Phipps wanted to kill Boyd, that he was trying to force a shooting on him . . ."

"I see." And so he did. Phipps apparently felt he had some ground to make up as the town of Cree's hardcase. Bad luck for Boyd. A man like Phipps would take any ordinary working man—even a big, tough working man—apart as quick as a jeweler would a two-dollar watch.

It might mean more trouble. Trouble with Phipps if he felt his reputation injured by Lee's killing the Irishman. What nonsense it all was.

"Marshal Phipps is . . . a temperamental man," she said.

Now there was a high-falutin' word: *temperamental*. Not one your usual flat-back whore would use. Beatrice Morgan must have been raised up to be something better than she was.

"I'll bet that he is . . ." The silly little split-tail was worried for him. It made Lee feel uncomfortable. This whole damn walk in the moonlight was making him feel uncomfortable now.

It was too damn personal a thing, this worrying about him. Lee didn't like to be pushed this way, by some girl who was getting ahead of herself.

Hell, he didn't even know the little bitch.

"Let's head back," he said. And he didn't say anything more to her until they were back at Mrs. Boltwith's.

There, at the kitchen door, she held out her hand for him to shake it.

"I've got to go to work," she said awkwardly, and blushed in the moonlight. "Goodnight, Mr. Lee. And thank you very much for standing up for me the way you did . . ." She knew he had turned angry at her for some reason, but she didn't know what it was.

"Goodbye," he said and went inside.

Mrs. Boltwith and Tim Bupp were sitting at the kitchen table, smoking cigarettes. When Lee came in, Mrs. Boltwith looked up with that wise, inquiring look women have when they've been matchmaking.

"Cup of coffee, Mr. Lee?" she asked.

"No," he said shortly. "I'm going to bed." The old cow had matched him up with a big-nose whore. Some honor there!

He was up before dawn. He came downstairs with his saddlebags, while Bupp was just stoking the stove.

"Coffee'll be awhile," Bupp said. "It's a might damn early for breakfast!"

"I don't want any," Lee said. "Tom out back?"

"Yeah, he's up. Getting me some wood."

Lee went to the door. "Tim, I probably won't be in town for a while. When you get learned up on your cooking, just come on out to the ranch. I'll expect you in another week or so."

Bupp glanced at Lee's face, started to say something, then changed his mind. Instead, he sighed.

"Well, now . . . those pies. I just don't know. Stew's one thing, but those pies . . . they take a hell of a lot of learning."

"A week, Bupp," Lee said and walked out the door.

An hour later, Lee and Tom Cooke were up on the flats above the town, with the sun rising like a golden ball of fire in the east, the first of the morning's heat striking the dew-soaked grass, burning it off in streamers of mist. It was a beautiful day. Lee turned in his saddle to check the lashings on the horse packs. Behind them, he could see Tom Cooke on the buckboard. Kimble had been right. The high country would be no country for buckboards.

Tom Cooke had asked to drive the wagon, and since the boy hadn't asked Lee for anything before, he couldn't very well refuse. And it was working out all right. The Blackfoot must have driven horses before; he was doing well enough.

It would be good to get back up to the ranch. Out of that damn town. Killers and women, the pleasures of towns. Of course, he'd made a damn fool of himself with that girl. She was just trying for something more than she had at the Arcady. It wasn't her fault that Lee had another woman on his mind—and always would. And maybe it wasn't like that, anyway. Maybe she was just a soft-hearted girl.

It was surely a damn beautiful day. Lee could see the mountain peaks as clear and sharp as if they were only a mile away. They looked like a huge rip-saw blade, shining with snow and ice.

The ride went very well, until they reached the river ford. Then the buckboard jammed its right rear wheel between a couple of boulders in the shallows.

It was near to noon now and hot, so Lee didn't mind as much as he might have tying the horses to a stand of willows on the bank, taking off his boots, and wading out into the cool water to help Tom Cooke heave the wagon free. It was a real nice problem. Either they managed to hoist the loaded buckboard up high enough to free the wheel, or they'd have to unload the whole damn thing to lighten it. And if they unloaded it, they'd have to carry a lot of heavy sacks of feed, sacks that couldn't be wet without ruining them.

So they both set their backs to the wagon hard, to give it the best lift they had in them. They'd heaved a couple of times, and the wheel hadn't budged from between those big rocks. Tom Cooke straightened up and touched Lee on the arm.

"Somebody," he'd said, his head cocked, listening.

Then Lee heard it over the soft, tumbling sound of the shallow rapids.

A man was shouting.

And off to the west, Lee could see a little cloud of dust. Somebody was riding their way, coming fast through the brush and dwarf willow.

Lee and Tom Cooke left the buckboard and splashed through the shallows to the horses.

They'd just gotten their rifles out and cocked when the rider came bucketing out onto the river bank.

It was Ole Sandburg, and there was blood running down his face.

He reined in his lathered sorrel, and then started yelling.

"Mr. Lee! They stole your horses, Mr. Lee! They took 'em up to the woods! Jake's after 'em, though. My boy's after the sons-of-bitches!"

CHAPTER SEVEN

There was nothing like trouble to put juice in a man.

Lee and Tom Cooke bent and got their shoulders under the buckboard, then heaved with all their strength. The wagon lurched and slowly rose free. They shoved together, pushing it clear of the rocks. Then, Tom Cooke jumped up onto the seat and drove the team across the shallow riffle and up onto the river bank.

Lee came splashing out after him, found his boots, and sat on the bank to jam them on.

"How did it happen, Ole?"

Sandburg swung off his tired horse.

"We'd taken the herd up into those pine woods over the ridge, to loose them out on the west range there, Mr. Lee. And the bastards jumped us right there. Maybe three of them, maybe four!"

His long face flushed with anger, and he reached up to touch the bloody graze on his cheek.

"Hadn't been for this, we'd have done all right. It knocked me off my horse—out cold. And Jake thought I was killed. By the time I come too, the sons-of-bitches had their start."

"And Jake's trailing them?" Lee climbed up into the dun's saddle.

"You bet he is. And my boy'll damn sure slow 'em up, you can bet on that!"

Lee didn't feel surprised by the rustling. It seemed

98

inevitable that some kind of trouble had to come to the ranch.

And to him.

First Slawson. Now this. It had to be either Slawson's rustler friends, or Ashton making his first move to control the river.

Well, either way, it was going to cost them. It was going to cost them a great deal. If he had to fight to be let alone, then by God he'd fight!

"Listen to me," Lee said to Sandburg and Tom Cooke. "And do just what I tell you. Pull the buckboard back into the brush, unharness the team, and picket them out to graze. Then take the pack horses back there, unload them, and each of you pick one out and saddle it. Ole, your horse is worn out; I want both of you mounted as fresh as we can."

Sandburg opened his mouth to argue, looked at Lee, and changed his mind. Tom Cooke was already leading the wagon team off into the dwarf willows lining the river bank.

"Then, when you're mounted, follow me as fast as you can go," Lee continued. "I'll be heading up for the river falls—those rapids just down from the pass. If they're taking my stock out of the valley, that's the way they'll have to go."

Ole Sandburg didn't argue at this either, or ask Lee to wait till all three of them could ride together. He was thinking about his boy Jake up there alone.

Lee reined the dun around without another word, and spurred the big gelding into a run, heading up the steep meadow trails to the ranch. He could feel the reserves of power in the dun as the horse took the slope at an easy, floating gallop. Even so, he'd have to ease the gelding soon; it was a long climb to go.

Jake Sandburg. So much like his father, they were damn near twins. Except Jake still had his hair. Jake Sandburg was fifteen years old, and he was up on the mountain with three or four men who'd kill him quicker than spit. Up on the mountain after Lee's horses.

Lee hoped to God the boy managed to slow the rustlers down. And he hoped to God the boy didn't get killed doing it.

He reached behind the saddle to make certain the .50 caliber Sharps was secure in the scabbard. He'd known men to lose their rifles that way on a wild run. Kimble had made him a good price for that rifle and a hundred rounds to go with it. It seemed he was going to find use for them before dark.

He guided the dun up past a grove of larch and then reined him down to a canter, moving fast through deep grass across a wide pasture.

Still a long way to go.

Ole and Tom Cooke should be well on their way by now, coming up fast behind him.

There was a way Jake might hold them. At the rapids. If he could ride around the rustlers—beat them to the ford—then he might be able to keep them from crossing. Then they'd have to get over the white water under Jake's rifle—tough enough for just themselves— a whole lot tougher with a horse herd.

If Jake had thought of it.

And if he'd gotten there before them.

Lee urged the dun up into a gallop again. He had to catch up before dark, either way, or kiss the appaloosas goodbye.

He made it with perhaps half an hour to spare.

The sunset shadows were long on the mountain slope when Lee coaxed the lathered gelding out of the last stand of lodgepole pine below the falls of Rifle River.

The white water foamed past him as he rode the west bank up toward the thunder of the falls. He stood high in the stirrups, the big Sharps cradled in his arms as he searched the fields along the river in the soft, golden evening light.

Nothing.

Not a sign of them.

For a moment, Lee felt sick to his stomach. He'd been a fool. The rustlers must have doubled back down across the valley, maybe all the way to the lumber camps, deciding not to take a chance of cutting out the fast way . . .

Then he saw them.

The appaloosas first. The big stud hobbled to a birch sapling. The mares and colts shifting nervously around him as the stallion sidestepped, trying to free himself from the unfamiliar restraints. The big horse might lose his temper, might cripple himself trying to kick free . . .

Then Lee saw the men—two of them, at least. They were both belly down behind a huge birch log, each of them with Winchesters aimed out over the rapids.

Jake Sandburg had beaten them to the river.

Even as he reined the weary dun in and slid out of the saddle with the Sharps in his hand, Lee heard the crack of shots—first one, then another. The boy must be up in the rocks over there.

As the two rustlers returned the fire, resting their rifles on the big log, taking their time, Lee let go of the dun's reins and began to ease carefully through the scattered birches toward the riflemen.

The other men—one or two more at least—where the hell were they?

They had to be higher up, trying to get across to flank the boy. Trying to cross above the falls.

And they could do it. The river ran fast up there, but shallow. A steep, rocky climb. Too steep for horses. But men could do it.

Lee hoped that Jake had thought of that, too.

He was almost clear of the trees, almost out in the open. He could see the riflemen clearly now; they were laughing and joking with each other as they crouched behind the log, getting ready to fire again. They didn't look worried at all. And why should they? They probably thought they'd killed Ole when they'd seen him fall. They knew there was only one man on the other side of the river.

And sure as hell their friends had already gone across to kill him.

There wasn't time to wait for Ole and Tom Cooke.

Lee knelt beside the birch and cocked the Sharps. It would be about a three-hundred-fifty yard shot. A long shot for most rifles. Not for the Sharps.

He thumbed up the leaf-sight, notched it at 350, then settled the rifle butt into his shoulder.

He drew a low, fine bead, low center on the lower back of the man nearest to him. He was a thin man, in worn denim, laughing at something his friend had just said.

Lee took a breath, let a little of it out, and squeezed the trigger.

The rifle butt slammed back into his shoulder at the blast of the shot. It hurt like a hard punch in a saloon fight. Lee rolled out to the right to clear the smoke, opened the action and reloaded, and came up on his elbow to shoot again.

The thin man was lying still beside the log; the other man was shooting back. Lee saw the quick bright flash from the Winchester muzzle. Then another. The man was fast with that piece. Then, just as Lee set himself to fire, the rustler jumped to his feet and dove over the huge log to cover on the other side. Lee almost chanced a snap-shot, then didn't.

A moment later the man's pale face was over the edge of the fallen birch, and the Winchester with him. He fired twice, taking his time. Lee heard the slugs humming into the woods a yard or two to the left. Too much range for the carbine.

Lee steadied the long barrel of the Sharps, lining the fine sights on that distant little patch of white face that just showed over the log's rough-barked bulk.

This time he was ready for the big rifle's recoil.

When the smoke cleared, the man was gone. No face and no Winchester appeared over the top of the log.

It could have been a near miss; the man could have ducked down. He could be waiting for Lee to step out into the open.

Lee didn't have the time to play it careful.

He reloaded the Sharps, got to his feet, and started walking through the high grass toward the log. It looked like a long 350 yards.

He kept his eye on the log as he walked, ready to snapshoot and hit the ground if the man came up shooting. Lee was damn glad he'd been too young for the war; this was the sort of thing the soldiers must have had to do: walk across a wide field not knowing whether or not a gun was waiting on the other side.

By the time he got across the field, Lee was sweating. The first man he had shot was dead. The .50-caliber slug had smashed his spine.

There was no sound, no movement behind the log.

Lee took up the slack on the Sharp's trigger and stepped around the end of the log.

The man was as dead as his friend. The bullet had struck him in the forehead and torn the top of his head off. The skull was like a fresh-emptied can of red paint; the brains had been blown out of it.

It was a bad sight to see.

Lee had always hated fighting with rifles. He wasn't that good with them to start with, and even when you won, it didn't seem right; it seemed cowardly to stand off and kill a man the way you would a buffalo or deer, without even looking in his eyes.

Then he heard something.

Like a hawk hunting, some cry like that.

A scream.

He reloaded the Sharps on the run, making for the river bank as fast as he could go, jumping the fallen timber, bulling straight through the tangled brush, leaving his hat behind in the scrub. Just as he made the river bank, he heard the scream again.

It was Jake Sandburg.

Lee charged out into the rapids of the ford, stepping high over the foaming riffles, splashing through, sliding, slipping, jumping from rock to rock.

The first shot came at him when he was more than half way across. Pistol shot. And a miss.

He kept running, ducking, plowing through the shallow water. A second shot came closer; he heard the deep hum as the bullet went past his head. Close enough.

He made the bank and scrambled up it, hanging onto the Sharps with one hand, grabbing at reeds and willow branches with the other.

The third shot clipped some bark from a sapling just beside his face. Good pistol shooting.

But not good enough.

Lee felt the calm coming over him, the odd feeling that he usually had in a fight; the feeling that he was moving very slowly, and other people moving even slower. Everything looked clear and bright when he felt like that. It was as if he could see everything that happened for miles. And everything happened very slowly.

He lunged up through the thickets, found the first of the big, rough boulders that edged the river over there, and began to climb.

There were shouts from back across the river. Lee could hear them faintly over the seething shuttle of the rapids. Sandburg and Tom Cooke had come up. It was all right. He wouldn't need them.

Lee reached a wide ledge, climbed up onto it, and

found that there was a clear way up into the top of the rock formation. The jumble of brush-grown boulders here was like the ruins of some ancient city. Close and dark-shadowed.

He bent and put the Sharps down. No 300 yard shots up here.

He didn't trouble to draw his Colt. It wasn't necessary. He walked up the rough ledge path into the shadow of the rocks.

Nothing for a moment. Lee stopped to listen. Nothing but the rush of the river far below. Some little sounds of squirrels or chipmunks.

Then he heard a boot heel grate on the stone some distance above him.

A swift shadow stretched across the rocks further up the ledge. A tall man in a stovepipe hat and long white duster stepped out into the open. He was smiling down at Lee, as if he was pleased to see him. He had a Russian model Smith and Wesson in his hand.

"You're an uninvited guest . . ." the man called down to Lee, smiling. He was a good-looking man, with a big cavalry mustache. "I'm afraid that—"

Lee drew and shot the man twice, just above his belt.

It was painful to see the man's face. To see the shock and the humiliation as he realized he had been killed so quickly, from such a distance, while he still had something to say. Before he even had a chance to fight. He looked as though it was all a mistake, as though it should be done over again in order to get it right.

The bullets—coming one, two—had shoved him back hard, like a bully's push, and the man couldn't recover his balance. He fell into the side of a boulder and gripped the rock with one hand to hold himself up. With the other hand, he raised the Smith and Wesson and tried to aim it at Lee.

It was all too late. Too late and too slow.

Lee shot him once more, through the upper chest,

hitting him in the heart as the man stood turned to the side. The man's stovepipe hat flew off, and he fell back onto the stones of the ledge, struggling and kicking as if he were trying to swim his way up from death.

Lee went by him at a run, ducked through a kind of broken arch of stone, and found Jake Sandburg lying in the sunshine.

His throat was cut.

A man was lying stretched out along the sloping top of a boulder to Lee's left, facing away, peering down over the edge.

"Hey, Tom," the man called. "Did—"

He heard Lee's step and jerked his head around to stare at him, eyes wide in surprise. He had a long-barreled .45 in his right hand. But it was a long way to turn and bring it around to bear on Lee. Too long a way.

The man was a cowboy, and pretty old—in his forties, anyway—with a little potbelly and short, bowed legs.

"Oh, my God," he said. "Please don't kill me, mister."

He loosened his grip on the .45, and it clattered onto the stone. The man was staring into Lee's eyes, frozen, as if, if he didn't blink, Lee wouldn't shoot him. "Oh, please, oh, please, oh, please," he said. "Don't do this . . .don't *do* it!" When he'd said that, he didn't say anything more.

After a few moments, Lee heard bootsteps on the rocks below, and right after that Tom Cooke and Ole Sandburg came ducking through the stone archway with rifles in their hands.

When Sandburg saw his boy lying dead there in a bright puddle of blood, it was a bad time.

They hanged the potbellied cowboy from a willow tree down beside the river.

"Oh, you won't get away with this," he said, when

Tom Cooke had gone across the river and come back with a lasso to hang the cowboy with.

"Oh, you won't get away with this," he said. His face was red, and he was weeping. "Mr. Ashton will make you sorry for this . . . if you do this to me . . ."

"You Mickey Slawson's friend," Tom Cooke said to him.

"Well I'm working for Mr. Ashton now, you dirty red nigger!" He was staring at the loop of rope in Tom Cooke's hand. "Don't you put that thing on me," he said. His nose was running like a crying child's. He looked around for a moment as if he'd forgotten what was going to happen to him.

"I wouldn't be in your boots, mister," he said to Lee. "I wouldn't be in your boots for any money in the world. That was Tom Small you shot back there. And God help you when his brother finds out."

Lee wasn't too surprised. The man in the stovepipe hat hadn't seemed like a cowpoker. So he'd been George Small's brother. That was who the cowboy must be talking about. More trouble.

"God help you, that's all I've got to say," the cowboy said.

Tom Cooke had finished making the knot.

"I didn't kill that boy," the cowboy said. "I never killed anybody. Not in my whole life long."

Lee took the rope, threw the bitter end of it up across a thick willow branch, and went up to the cowboy to fit the loop around his neck.

"I never hurt those horses either," the cowboy said. "Those are some of the finest stock I ever saw. Real pretty horses. I'd never hurt a horse like that. I drove 'em as careful as you would yourself . . ."

Lee stepped back from him, took up the slack in the lasso, got a grip on the rope, and doubled it over his fist.

"You aren't going to do this," the cowboy said. He'd stopped crying. He looked Lee straight in the eye, a man looking at another man. "I'll be all right. You're not going to do this."

Lee planted his bootheels in the soft dirt of the river bank, set himself, and hauled back on the rope as hard as he could.

Sandburg yelled something and grabbed hold too, pulling with all his strength. And Tom Cooke picked up the bitter end, put it over his shoulder, and pulled along with them.

The cowboy rose up off the ground in a slow swinging surge, staring as he went up into the air. It was as if so far he thought everything was all right, just a surprise to be swung up into the air like that. He was only a few feet off the ground.

Then he tried to breathe and couldn't. His face got very red, dark red, and he kicked and heaved himself and spun in slow circles at the end of the rope. After the first few times he kicked, he stopped moving and just hung there staring up into the willow. His eyes were red with blood where the little vessels in them had broken.

Tom Cooke had tied the rope end off on a sapling larch. The three of them had nothing to do but watch.

The cowboy hung still like that for a few moments, then he started to kick again, but more slowly, pulling his knees up high, almost to his chest, and then kicking down, first with one foot, then the other. Very slowly, spinning a little from the twist of the rope.

Then the hanged man stopped doing that, and Lee could smell the odor of shit coming from him. There was a black stain growing on the seat of his pants.

"That's it, that's the finish of the son-of-a-bitch!" Sandburg said. "You smell what he did in his pants?"

"All right," Lee said. He felt tired of the whole thing. "Let's go bury your boy, Ole . . ."

None of them had much to say when they had Jake

Sandburg's hole dug beside Rifle River. They'd dug it with their sheath knives and a split stick across on the west bank, away from the hanged man, and they'd wrapped the boy in a blanket.

Ole picked him up and put him in the grave without wanting any help from Lee or the Blackfoot. Then he took his saddle canteen and filled it at the river, and put that in with the boy.

Lee didn't know if that was something religious, maybe Lutheran, or whether Ole had slipped with grief. Tom Cooke seemed to think it was natural enough, though.

"Oh, my God . . ." Sandburg said. "Oh, my God." Then he couldn't seem to think of anything more to say. He stood looking down at young Jake lying there wrapped in the blanket without saying anything else.

"All right, Ole," Lee said. "You go and catch up the horses. We'll take care of things here." He took Sandburg by the arm and gave him a little push. "Go on, I said . . ."

And Sandburg turned and walked away with his head down, like a man thinking hard.

And that I'd bet you are, Lee thought, watching him go. You poor son-of-a-bitch . . . was thinking just what Lee had thought after Rosilie was killed, and what Tom Cooke after his mama died. They were alone, all alone now.

Lee and Tom Cooke kicked the dirt back in the grave and then got stones from the river bank to cover it with, to keep the coyotes and wolves from digging the boy up. They heaped up quite a number of them.

"And them?" said Tom Cooke when they'd finished, gesturing with his head across the river.

"Let them lie and hang and rot on both sides of the river," Lee said. And he turned and walked away to the meadow, where Ole Sandburg was standing with the saddle horses. He'd unhobbled the stud, and Shokan

109

was pacing and trotting around the grassy field, nickering and nipping at his mares, the big appaloosa's spotted white hide rippling over his muscles as he moved.

There's a handsome sight, Lee thought. There's a creature on this mountain that isn't unhappy at all . . .

"Let's mount and move," he said. "I want to be home by dark."

It looked to be a pretty evening.

Lee rode a little ahead, and Tom Cooke and Sandburg rode back with the cavvy, keeping the stud and the mares moving down the mountain.

Lee looked back to make sure the colts weren't tiring. The rustlers must have pushed the horse herd hard. But they were lively as June bugs, racing each other around the herd, prancing up to the mares to nuzzle at their teats and then tossing their heads and trotting away to play again.

He saw a little filly, racing after a colt a month older than she was—and catching him. Fast, and so pretty. Lee thought he might call her Lightning Bug.

When they got down to the east ridge, it was nearly dark. Sandburg and Tom Cooke eased away from the appaloosas and let the herd spread out into the fields above the ranch buildings.

Sandburg rode on down to the ranch without saying anything, but Tom Cooke came up to Lee for orders.

"Nothing more tonight," Lee said. "Go on down and get something to eat. And try and see if Sandburg will have something."

Tom Cooke nodded and started to turn away, but Lee called after him, "Do you know what that old cowboy's name was?"

"His name Charley."

"Charley what?"

The young Blackfoot shrugged and turned his horse away.

"Well," Lee said angrily to the empty air. "Well, I'll kill any man who tries to take what's mine . . ."

CHAPTER EIGHT

The next week they worked at putting up the long rough-plank fences for the horse pastures. It was dawn-to-dark work, and it sweated some of the badness of Jake's death out of them.

Ole Sandburg had started the week with nothing to say, either to Lee or to Tom Cooke, but splitting the planks out of raw timber, dragging them down to the pastures, setting the posts, and finally nailing the horizontals straight and true, gradually worked the sorrow and the silence out of him. By the end of the week, Ole could talk about Jake, and was telling Lee about what a brave little boy he'd been, up on a horse when he was only five, and running stock into a corral like a Mex *vaquero*.

The week had done them all good. And no trouble about the supplies. Tom Cooke had ridden down the morning after the fight to bring the wagon up and had found it undisturbed, the pack horses safe, but restless, tugging at their tethers to reach fresh grass. So the supplies all came up, but even so, they ran short of nails. Lee sent Ole down to town for them at the end of the week and wrote a note for him to take to the marshal when he got there.

Lee wrote Phipps only a few lines telling him what had happened. He mentioned the names of two of the rustlers, the only ones that Lee knew: Charley and Tom Small.

Lee'd been thinking about George Small during the week. Tom's older brother, the cowboy had said. Well, he had to be pretty old by now. From what Lee remembered hearing, George Small had been a bad man on the Missouri border before the war. That would make the man at least fifty by now, maybe older. A ring-tail terror in his day, he must be a little slower by now, though. A little smarter, too, it could be.

And it could be that he wouldn't give a good damn what had happened to his little brother, that cutthroat son-of-a-bitch.

And it could be that he would.

And Ashton would be certain to let him know his brother was dead, when Phipps told him what had happened to his men.

The afternoon of the day he'd sent Ole Sandburg to town, Lee rode out over the east ridge to have a look at his borderline with Fishhook. If Ashton was hunting trouble that hard that he'd send rustlers and a killer out to take Lee's stock, then it was just as well that Lee saw how the land lay between them.

He'd taken a hunk of deer meat and a pocket full of store crackers with him when he rode. They'd have to get some steers on the place soon for beef. Once he'd ridden over the ridge, and down through the trees, he drew the dun up under a clump of beech trees, swung out of the saddle, tied the big gelding off, and sat with his back against a tree trunk, his canteen in his lap, for a little country lunch.

The venison was tough and chewy, but it had the sweetness of wild meat, the tang and sharpness to it. Lee wished he'd brought some salt with him, just a pinch, but there was salt on the crackers, and he made do. Some cheese would have been nice, too. He reminded himself to buy some store cheese when next he went down to Cree. Hell, no reason he shouldn't buy a full ten-pound round of that sharp yellow cheese that stuck to the roof of your mouth first, then stuck to your ribs.

He was chewing a mouthful of crackers and looking out over the rolling, broken, open land that lay beneath him, when he saw the horseman.

A man in a plaid shirt, riding what looked like a good little chestnut mare. Cutting back and forth through the brush in the low places down there, coming Lee's way. No way to tell who it was from this distance, even if Lee had known any of the people around there . . .

The rider was heading on for River Ranch land.

And he was coming careful.

Lee took a long drink out of his canteen, and then stood up, brushing the cracker crumbs off his pants. The horseman was out of sight for a moment now, riding along the bottom of a scrub-larch draw.

Lee loosed the dun and swung up into the saddle, leaning back to check that the Sharps was riding safe in its scabbard. He spurred the dun off to the right, to cut the horseman's path at the edge of the mountain woods.

He held the gelding down to an easy canter; the stranger still had a good way to go. The thought of George Small crossed his mind, but this man was younger. He rode like a young man, limber and light in the saddle.

Lee rode along, just below the ridgeline. He didn't think the man could have seen him before, and he didn't intend for the man to see him now. And if he hadn't been on the ridge this afternoon? Then the horseman would have come down on them, down the ridge to the ranch buildings, and they wouldn't have known it until he started shooting. It was a disadvantage, that way, trying to run a ranch with three men hired—two men, now that Jake was dead, and not counting Tim Bupp. There weren't enough men to circuit ride the land.

Lee was into the woods now, and he bent forward on the dun's withers to keep the beech limbs from knocking him out of the saddle. He broke out into a small clearing, then spurred the gelding on into the woods again. The trees were more scattered here, and Lee lifted the dun into a lope. The wind was blowing from the east, and the trespasser hopefully wouldn't be able to hear the hoofbeats.

When he broke out of the woods a second time, Lee found himself on a small rise overlooking the steep reverse slope of the ridge. He reined the gelding in and scanned the country below.

Nothing.

He was just turning the dun's head to ride further down the ridge when he caught a flicker of movement off to the left. The rider's mare just stepping down into a wooden draw. Lee glimpsed just the touch of blue from the man's shirt, the look of a broad-brimmed straw hat—and he was gone.

It was working out just fine. That nice steep draw would bring the horseman up onto the slope into deep brush; he wouldn't see shit for a hundred yards.

It was a chance for Lee to take the man alive. No dead rustler to write to Phipps about, no cowboy to have to hang, but a *live* man to take to Butte or Helena to testify. And to put some hot spurs to Ashton. This was far enough north for Lee to take the chance on being recognized. There wouldn't be many Rebecca Chases waiting around the federal judge's courtroom up there . . .

Lee spurred the dun on, driving the big horse deep into the brush, bending low over the saddle so that his Stetson took most of the whipping from the limber branches.

When the gelding's hoofs clattered on the rocky shelving of the draw, Lee reined him in and leaned forward over the horse's neck to gently grip his soft nose and quiet him. He didn't want any nickering to warn the on-coming rider.

The dun sidled restlessly for a moment and then eased, only shaking his head a little under Lee's restraining hand.

For a few minutes, there was almost no sound at all in the woods, except for the chatter and scurry of a pair of red squirrels running through the tangle of larch and mountain willow. When the squirrels were gone, there was only the murmur of the wind gently combing through the brush.

Then Lee heard the horse coming, the slight crush and snap of scrub twigs under its hoofs. Yes, a mare for sure, to be moving so lightly.

The horse and rider were still off to his left and a little below him. Still climbing up through the draw.

Lee closed his eyes for a moment, trying to remember exactly what the horseman had looked like when he'd had that long look at him, riding far in the distance. Young. And slight. A revolver worn high up on his right hip. Maybe a .38. And a Winchester, likely a Winchester, in a front saddleboot.

The mare was closer now.

Lee'd known a man once who'd carried his pistol high on the right like that. But that sure as hell wasn't this man. Pace had been a big man, bony as Abe Lincoln. And still was, as far as Lee knew; he hadn't heard of the Texas gunman being shot in the back yet. Which was about the only way anybody was going to kill Frank Pace.

No, this was a much smaller man, and Lee didn't know him. But he rode in a way that seemed familiar . . .

The horseman was up out of the draw. The dun shifted nervously under Lee as the other horse came on—no more than forty feet away now.

Thirty.

Twenty. The rider would be passing only a dozen feet in front of Lee, unseen in the thick greenery.

Lee let him get just abreast. Then he kicked spurs to the dun.

The big horse erupted out of the foliage like a bat out of hell. As they smashed free of the brush, Lee was already shaking his boots free of the stirrups. As the dun thundered down on the rearing, terrified chestnut mare, Lee left the saddle in a long, driving dive to pile into the rider.

He struck the man hard enough to knock him clear out of the saddle. They fell together in a tangled heap into the scrub. Lee held the man away with his left hand—must be only a boy, not very strong—and went for his boot knife with the other. But, boy or not, the man was kicking hard, trying to get free of Lee's grip. Lee remembered that .38 and lunged again as the knife came free into his hand, piling on top of the man, driving him back down into the brush, staying on top of him, trying to pin him with his knees.

Then he was on him. He had his knees biting into the man's arms, pinning him good. And he had his fingers in the man's hair, yanking his head back to set the knife blade at his throat.

"Now, you little son—"

India Ashton lay beneath him, pale as death, her blue eyes wide with terror.

For a moment, Lee stayed crouched over her, frozen, the knife blade still held to her throat. Then he cursed and rolled away, got to his feet, slid the knife back into his boot, staring down at her.

India Ashton lay in the crushed foilage looking up at him, still pale with shock. The straw hat had been torn from her head, and the long, golden-white hair had fallen loose, swirling in the greenery around her shoulders, bright as sunlight. Her man's plaid shirt had been ripped leaving a slim, ivory-pale shoulder bare to the world.

Suddenly, recovering, the girl struggled to sit up, glaring at Lee.

"How—how *dare* you. You tried to kill me!"

117

Lee reached down a hand to help her up, but she slapped it aside and clambered to her feet without his help.

"I'm very sorry, Miss Ashton. I didn't recognize you."

"And do you go around the country attacking people you don't recognize, Mr. Lee?" The lovely, aristocratic face was pink with rage. Her hands trembled as she tried to pat her hair back into some kind of order, then brushed futilely at the twigs and leaves covering her denim pants. She tugged the torn shirt over her bare shoulder.

"Strange men who come onto my land through the woods, I do," Lee said. He knew his own face was red; he'd made a prime fool of himself, and there were no two ways about it. His quarrel with Ashton now looked like it might become a personal matter, with the man's sister being handled this way. For an instant, Lee's blood chilled at the thought that he might have used his gun and not been close enough to see what he'd done until it was too late. The thought made him feel a little sick.

"Well . . . I think that you are a rough, loutish fool, Mr. Lee!" She was looking around for her mare. "And you have frightened off Sally—and maybe hurt her!"

"I'll go catch up with your mare." India Ashton was a beauty, no doubt about it, and she had her share of guts, too. Most well-bred women would be in a faint or hysterics at being handled so roughly.

"I'll find her, *I'll* find her, Mr. Lee. I don't want your help . . ."

Lee tried to calm her down. "Now, please listen, Miss Ashton, we've—we've had some trouble up here . . ."

She turned as cold as ice and bent down to pick up her hat. "I'm sure I'm not interested in your difficulties at River Ranch, Mr. Lee. Now, if you will just catch my mare, I can be on my way. I can tell you, though, that

118

the men of this country don't approve of bullies attacking women who are riding alone and minding their own business.''

"And what was your business up here, Miss Ashton?'' Lee said. "This ridge is a roundabout way of getting to the ranch house, if you were coming visiting.''

"I was not 'coming visiting,' '' she said, with a toss of her head. "I—I was out looking for a friend.'' She bit her lip and looked around through the brush, searching for her mare.

"Come on,'' Lee said and took her arm. "We'll find the mare. I don't think she was hurt.''

She looked down with a grimace of distaste, then pulled her arm away from his hand. "I'd prefer that you kept your hands to yourself, Mr. Lee.''

"All right.'' Lee gritted his teeth to keep his temper. After all, it had been his damn stupid mistake. He was lucky he hadn't hurt her. "Follow me, then. Chances are she's with my dun, and he's not much of a strayer.''

Lee led the way out of the thickets into a small clearing and stood looking for the horses as the girl kicked her way out of the brush behind him.

"They're probably further down.''

When she said nothing, Lee started off into the woods, heading downslope of the ridge. The dun would likely be grazing in the first lush patch of bear grass it came to. It was rough going for a man on foot, the land being tangled with scrub and broken and scarred by run-off water and lightning fires. Lee went on his way and didn't offer to help the girl when she stumbled into thorn patches or over fallen timber.

It was the damnedest thing. To have been so foolish as to take her for a boy, anyway. And after seeing her twice, even at a distance, he sure as hell should have known better. And he'd even recognized the way she rode. He remembered thinking that just before he'd jumped her.

"Would you mind not going so fast?"

She still sounded mad as hell. Probably ashamed of having been so frightened when he'd knocked her off her horse. She must have thought him stark crazy . . .

He stepped over a fallen larch log and stood waiting for her to catch up. She didn't look quite the perfect lady now, tugging her way through a patch of wild blackberry. Lee had seen whores wearing pants, of course, and some tough old ranch wives wore them too in order to do their chores. But this was the first time he'd seen a pair on a lady. Maybe getting wrestled off her horse would teach her to stick to dresses and side-saddles.

When she climbed over the log to join him, she was panting from her effort and had to stand for a moment to catch her breath.

"You said you were out looking for a friend?"

She gave Lee an odd sidewise glance. "Yes . . . yes, I was. A—a guest at Fishhook. He rode out with some of our men some days ago to gather stock. But they should all have been back by now."

"A man?"

She flushed. "Yes. A friend of my brother. A business acquaintance—if it is any affair of yours!" She was getting angry again.

Lee started to turn away. There hadn't been any stray dude wandering the range that he'd seen. Suddenly, he stopped. There was no reason for it, no reason to be so sure. But he *knew*.

"What was this man's name?"

He could see she was puzzled by his tone, the look in his face. She flushed again.

"The gentleman's name is Thomas Small," she said.

She had started to walk on down the slope when Lee reached out and gripped her arm.

"Oh, how dare—"

Lee had her by both arms now.

"You said Tom Small?"

"Yes, I did . . ." She stared up at him, frightened, puzzled by the look on his face.

"He meant something to you, Miss Ashton?"

"He . . ." Her face reddened. "Mr. Small is a . . . a friend."

Of course. Lee remembered the tall man, the handsome, smiling face with the dashing cavalry mustache. Smiling. "You're an uninvited guest," the man had called to him just before Lee'd killed him.

"Now, will you take your hands off—"

"He's dead," Lee said.

For a moment, she didn't seem to understand, didn't seem to hear. "Let me loose, damn you! What did you say?" Her eyes widened. Her voice was shaking.

"I said, your friend is dead." And if she'd loved the cutthroat son-of-a-bitch, so much the worse for her.

India Ashton sagged suddenly in his hands, almost falling to her knees. "No, no, no," she said, rapidly, over and over. "You're mistaken . . . you're mistaken."

She straightened suddenly and pulled away from him.

"What are you saying?" Tears were in her eyes now, tears of rage. "You fool! You don't know what you're talking about! You don't even know him!"

And what the hell could he say to that? The news hadn't reached Fishhook yet.

"He was shot . . ." Lee said.

"Shot? Shot? What are you talking about?" She looked wildly around, as if she were trapped in a nightmare. "Nobody would shoot Tom . . ."

Lee cursed Ashton for keeping a handsome killer in his house for his own sister to stumble over.

"He and the men with him . . . they stole some of my horses . . ."

The girl looked up at him as if he'd gone crazy, as if he were speaking some foreign language she couldn't understand.

"They stole my horses and they killed a boy." No

121

need to tell her it was handsome Tom who'd cut poor Jake Sandburg's throat.

"You—oh, you dirty, dirty liar!" she screamed at Lee. She backed away from him, shaking her head.

Lee held out his hand to her and spoke softly, trying to calm her. "Small was a gunman, Miss Ashton, a killer. I'm sorry."

"Shot?" she said, staring at him. Now she believed it.

"I'm afraid so." Lee hoped to God she'd calmed down. She must have been head over heels in love with that bastard.

"How was he killed?" she said. "How was he shot?"

"He and those cowboys came up here and drove off my stock . . ."

She was staring at him, her eyes as wide as a child's.

"A man of mine—a kid named Jake Sandburg—followed them over to the river. He held them at the ford."

She didn't say anything. Just stood there, watching Lee talk.

"They killed the boy. Then, when we came up, there was a fight. That's when Small was killed." How the hell could he make something like this easier? "I sent word down to the marshal and, well, I'm sorry."

"You killed him, didn't you?" she said, in an odd, dead voice. "You killed him, didn't you, Mr. Lee?"

Christ.

"He . . . he came at me with a gun in his hand, Miss Ash—"

He saw her move, but he couldn't believe it. With a quick, awkward clawing of her hand, she had reached down to her hip to draw her .38 pistol on him.

He had just time to see how funny it all was: Buckskin Frank Leslie drawn on and shot dead by a pretty English lady. In the next instant, he moved. There was no drawing against her; better to be killed than do that. He would have to get his hands on that gun before she had time for a shot.

The .38 was out now and starting to level; she'd have time for a first shot before he reached her.

The gun went off in his face. He felt a blaze of pain along his ribs, and he had her, had his hand on the gun, twisting, tearing it out of her grasp. He got it, and he turned, still holding her by the wrist as she spat and struck at him. He threw the revolver away into the brush.

Then he glanced down at his side. The bullet had drilled through the material of his shirt and burned across his ribs. A slow, slight stain of blood was marking the faded cotton.

Suddenly, Lee felt a rush of fury. The stupid bitch had almost killed him. If she'd had time for another shot, she probably would have! And all for a cutthroat killer, a child killer.

He swung his other hand hard into the girl's raging, contorted face. The blow sent her staggering, and he deliberately hit her again. She fell, and they went down together into the thick meadow grass, she scratching at him, trying to bite his forearm as he held her pinned down.

Lee raised his open hand again.

"Stop it! Stop it, God damn you, or I'll beat the hell out of you."

She subsided, panting, glaring up at him like a trapped animal.

"Now, you listen to me," Lee ground out, "you spoiled bitch! That grinning bastard Small was the one that killed my man. He cut the throat of a boy fifteen years old! And then the bastard came at me with a gun in his hand. Did I kill him? Hell, lady, I shot the living shit out of him!"

"You're lying." She was starting to weep, struggling to get out from under him.

He never knew why he did it. Why he started. Maybe it was her crying like that. Maybe the feeling of her held so close.

He bent down and kissed her mouth.

She convulsed under him desperately. Lee found himself gripping her hard, bearing her down into the grass, kissing her soft mouth with a kind of murderous hunger.

She tried to twist away, to bite at his lips; but he paid no attention, though she bit him till his lips bled. He clamped his mouth to hers as if his life depended on it, kissing, sucking, loving her.

And his hands were on her now, pulling, tearing at her plaid shirt, ripping it open, yanking down the soft cloth of her undershirt to expose her small breasts. And his hands were on them, gripping the delicate white flesh.

She screamed, pushing at him, trying to shove him away, but Lee bent lower to suckle at the soft, pouting pink nipples, biting at them, licking them.

She groaned as he turned and held her to him as he unbuckled her pants belt and reached down to pull the material down over her hips. She tried to kick out at him, but the cloth was down at her ankles now, binding her, leaving her thrashing helplessly under him as he slid his hand to her groin.

She screamed again. "Oh, please don't . . . oh, please!" He touched her, gently cupping her in his hand, the downy chevron of her sex, white blond against the snow-white of her skin.

Lee forced his fingers into her, thrusting into her roughly, feeling the warm moistness close around them. He drove his hand against her hard, the damp, soft petals of her sex against his palm.

She gasped and suddenly lay still, not struggling against him anymore.

Lee thought she had finished, but she hadn't. She lay looking up at him, her face blank, pale with shock. Lee tried to make himself stop. He knew he should. He knew he'd already done enough, more than enough to deserve hanging . . . like that poor old bastard of a cowboy. Poor Charley. And he was no goddamned better!

But he couldn't. He couldn't stop himself. She was there. And he was there. And now, she was naked against him . . .

He reached down and unbuckled his trousers, kicked them down. He was hard as iron; so hard that it hurt him.

"Ah, Christ," he said, and lifted up, placed the swollen head of his cock against her softness, her dampness.

"Ah, Christ." He thrust into her. Pushing, pushing at first, against the soft fur, her small cleft. Then into her, in a steady, hot slippery thrust. In. In all the way.

She was tight in there. Wet, and hot, and tight. It felt as though a whore was sucking on him, sucking hard on the whole length of him.

The girl was no virgin. He remembered the smiling killer standing high on the ledge above him. "Uninvited guest . . ." the words echoed in his mind.

Then Lee thought of nothing.

He began driving into her. Driving into her so hard that he felt her slight body shaking from the thrusts. She was grunting a little as he fucked her, grunting each time he sank deep into her.

Lee groaned with pleasure. It was sweet. Sweet . . .

She gasped when he went into her harder and deeper. He ground his cock into her, twisting his body, driving into her as if he were trying to nail her to the ground.

She cried out and reached up to twist her fingers in his hair, to tug, to push his head away; he felt her slim bare legs writhe against his naked thighs. And he kept at her—in and out, in and out. He could feel her warm breath panting against his throat. There were wet sounds coming from between them now. He could smell the delicate salt smell of her sex as it began to run with wet.

Suddenly, she let go of his hair, stopped trying to

push him away. Lee felt her hands clutching at his shoulders. She made a hoarse groaning sound, and he felt her legs thrash and kick against him.

"Oh, Tom!" she screamed. And he looked down and saw her weeping wildly, her head turning from side to side as he thrust into her. "Oh, ohhh . . . Tommy . . . Tommy!"

An uninvited guest.

She bucked under him, the long, slender white legs thrust high in the air, straining up, her feet arched in an agony of pleasure. She was soaking now, her cunt made a sucking sound as he fucked into her.

Then it came. It came for him first. It seemed to come pouring out of him in a flood, as if his back was breaking from the pleasure of it. He called out and shot into her, spurt after spurt. It never seemed to stop.

And she writhed and heaved against him with astonishing strength, and drew up her knees and moaned as if she were giving birth, her face and small white breasts flushing deep pink as she came. She stared blindly up into Lee's eyes, groaning softly in ecstasy.

"I'm sorry," Lee said, as she sat silent in the grass, trying to button her torn shirt around her. "There's no forgiving what I did . . .

He walked down into the meadow, searching.

After a few minutes, he came back to her. He had her .38 in his hand. She was standing now, brushing the grass from her trousers.

"Here." He handed the weapon to her. "Go ahead and use it, if you want."

He stood there, waiting.

But the girl just put the gun back in its holster. Then she looked at him, and it was a grim look.

"Not for me," she said, and shook her head. "For Tom. It's for Tom Small that I'm going to see you dead."

And she walked past him, down the meadow slope, to find her mare.

CHAPTER NINE

For the next three days, Lee tried to get it out of his mind, tried to forget what he'd done. It wasn't easy. He'd never thought of himself as a hardcase, as the kind of man who'd do any damn thing he pleased.

He'd thought—he'd hoped—that he was a better man than that. A man, not a dog. Well, now it looked like maybe that wasn't so. It seemed that there was still a lot of Frank Leslie left in Mr. Lee, and a badness, a cruelty, that had nothing to do with being forced into a fight or having to fight or hurt someone to save himself. No excuse for this last thing. No excuse.

And now, if India told her brother what he'd done, it would be a killing matter sure—and a killing with dirt on it. Forgetting the rustling, young Jake's death, he'd be shooting Ashton down for defending his sister, for going up against the man who'd raped her. A dirty killing.

Lee found himself hoping the girl would be too ashamed, after all, to tell Ashton what had happened between them. And that very hope was cowardly.

For the first time since Rosilie had died, Lee felt glad that there was something about him that she would never know. That was the worst feeling of all. It was as if he had spoiled her memory, spoiled it in a way that all the casual girls he had taken since her death couldn't. Rosilie would never have grudged him any kind of love;

but what he'd done to that grief-crazed girl had nothing to do with that. Nothing to do with love at all.

He threw himself into his ranch work, driving himself from first light to pitch dark; fencing, cutting timber and firewood, mucking out the old stables clear down to fresh mountain clay—and working with the horses.

Those were the best times, the times that gave him peace, that helped him best to forget that afternoon in the bear grass with India Ashton.

They were working out the colts, starting to halter train them, get them used to being led, to being held gently on a long rope. It was delicate work. The same intelligence and spirit that made the appaloosas so valuable as mounts in rough, dangerous country made them very tender to train. A beating, even a quick cut with a rope's end—even a harsh word at the wrong time—and the lively, lean-limbed little colts would balk and shy, losing their trust in the noisy, tobacco-smelling men who held them prisoners at the end of thirty feet of hemp.

In a way, treating the little soft-eyed colts with gentleness, coaxing them, stroking them into obedience, seemed to make up, somehow, for the cruel way he'd manhandled the girl on that damned afternoon.

So Lee worked himself into exhaustion, and he trained the little horses. And he waited for the hour when Nigel Ashton would come riding over the ridge, coming to kill the man who'd raped his sister.

Three days went by, and no horsemen came riding over the ridge—none but Sandburg and Tim Bupp, coming back from town.

Lee was glad to see the old man; it was good to have him back on the place. Bupp, although full of complaints about Mrs. Boltwith's tyranny and foolishness, was now almighty proud of his cooking, and indeed could make a fair steak, a good stew (though a little short of pepper), and a reasonable, if somewhat watery, dried-apple pie. He was still pretty weak on eggs; it seemed hard for him to keep his mind on them early in the morning, and they were usually tough enough to need some knife work to really subdue them.

Still, it was good to have the old man on the place. He got on well with Sandburg. One day, out of the blue, he said to the Swede, "I sure am damn sorry, Ole, I never got to meet that boy of yours. I hear that boy was something prime!"

Lee was working on a fenceline nearby, and when he heard what Bupp said, he paused, expecting trouble. But all that Sandburg did was sigh sadly and nod.

"He was the best boy ever in the world," he said.

And that was that.

For four more days, Lee and the others worked the main range. Then it was time to ride circuit. Lee felt like doing it himself; it would mean another week, maybe two, out in the rough, far from meeting any other people for any reason. It was a hard temptation for him. Too much of a temptation. He decided to send Sandburg and Tom Cooke out; Bupp could handle the home chores while they rode the circuit. And Lee would go into town.

There was no use ducking it. After almost two weeks, Ashton had not come riding to revenge the deaths of his paid rustlers or his sister's rape. If Lee met the man in town, then he met him—and the devil take the hindmost.

Dawn on a Thursday morning, Lee had a long talk with Tom Cooke, Sandburg and Bupp. He trusted them now; any one of the three was as good a hand, as good a friend, as a man might find or make in a few weeks in a strange country.

They were to ride careful and well armed. Lee knew that Ashton, who must have his own reasons for not bucking Lee directly, would not have forgotten or for-given the deaths of his men. Lee was now certain that India hadn't told her brother what had happened to her.

Tom Cooke and Sandburg were to ride together, even if that cost them time in covering the ground. And if they found Fishhook stock on River range, they were to just drift it back over the line. Lee had no patience with killing animals for people's quarrels.

"And, Tim," he said to Bupp, "you keep a carbine handy while you work around the place. One way or another, sooner or later, there'll be trouble coming."

"Now, that's nice stuff to hear," Bupp said. "I suppose I'm supposed to sleep real good after hearing that stuff!"

"Just sleep light," Lee said.

Lee swung up on the gelding and left the three of them standing in the ranch house yard looking after him. It made him feel peculiar to know they were so dependent on him. It made him uncomfortable. It was one of the uncomfortable things about bossing a property: having men bound to you. It meant he had to think about them all the time, in whatever he did. Just as he was thinking now about what might happen if Ashton sent some more people onto the land to rustle.

If that happened, he was sure to lose a man whichever way it went. Tom Cooke? Sandburg? Old Bupp? And if he did, what the hell would that man be dying for? Some big-name gunman's second chance? Frank Leslie's new life? Why should one of those good men die for that?

It made Lee uncomfortable just thinking about it. He tried to put it out of his mind, but it went hard. There would have been just about time for a telegram to get to Missouri, or wherever Tom Small's big brother was holed up, to tell him to come gunning. Ashton must have sent that wire; he'd have been a damn fool not to. And if he had, and George Small came riding up to the ranch in the next two or three days, Lee wouldn't be there. No sirree. The new owner of the River Ranch would be sitting on his ass in Cree, waiting for a crate of horse medicine and a bank draft from Nogales, Old Mexico.

The Don's last payment, overdue but welcome. And damned well earned, too, since Lee had taken a .44-.40 slug in the muscle of his leg keeping the old bandit alive.

If Small came to the ranch while Lee was gone, he'd kill all three of those men. Cooke and Sandburg had guts enough, and probably so did old Bupp. But that wouldn't help them against a man like Small, even if he was past his prime. A normal man, even a brave one who might have killed a man or two, just couldn't stand against a shootist like George Small, even if he was getting old. Small must have done—a hundred men in his day, and maybe half of those in face-to-face fights.

An ordinary man would have no chance against him. No chance against someone who'd done a hundred killings and remembered how each one had gone. A man so familiar with killing, with death, that the most desperate fight was like an old friend—that familiar and comfortable.

No. If George Small came to Cree Valley, God send him to town and not out to River Ranch.

The dun was a little overworked from day after day of hard labor, though Lee had tried to spare him and used the remuda horses when he could. Truth was, they could use another few good cutters on the place. And he hadn't yet done what he promised and got a nice pinto for Tom Cooke to keep. That had to be done, too. But one thing: they sure as hell weren't going to work the appaloosas until they were ready for it, and that wouldn't be for a few months, anyway. The mares could do with a little riding, maybe. Tom Cooke was too rough, but old Bupp had good hands.

Cree looked empty in daylight when Lee drew the dun

132

up in the rise outside of town. It would be another day and night befor the wagons full of lumberjacks came rumbling in from the northern mountains. The Fishhook and Bent Iron men rode in from the valley.

Lee cantered the dun down through the town, across the alley behind the general store, and out into main street. There was nothing there that afternoon but a dusty line of buggies at the store and a couple more rigs tethered up by Martin's Yarn, Dress & Knits store. Lee wondered how it was that Kimble hadn't been able to get his hands on that store; he owned just about every other mercantile in town. Martin—male or female— must be a pretty tough customer, commercially speaking.

As Lee rode by, he bent in the saddle to look into the display window. There were three or four women in the place, shopping, and a squat, frog-looking man with a measuring tape across his shoulders was waiting on them. Mr. Martin. And he looked tough enough to give old Kimble a hard time.

It made Lee feel good to think of Cree as his home town now, with all the storekeepers and businessmen, saloon people and whores, ostlers and stablemen, drummers, lawyers, lumbermen—all of them his neighbors in a way. All of them people he might know for years now. Maybe for the rest of his life.

It was what people meant by the word home. A home town.

If Ashton let him alone. If Rebecca Chase kept her mouth shut. If . . .

A farm family came rumbling down the graveled street in a big overloaded wagon. A tall, rawboned man with a worn, lined face. His small, work-worn wife. Three kids—no, four kids; one had just been rooting around down in the wagonload of vegetables. There was a hard life. Lee didn't see how a man, a family, could bear it, farming up so high in the mountain country.

133

What the hell could they grow so high, with the winters as cold and long as they must be? Cabbages, it looked like from the wagonload. Cabbages and cauliflowers. To work your heart out to raise cabbages and cauliflowers! It struck him that farming was the strangest way of life of them all.

He reined the dun over to the front of Mrs. Boltwith's hotel, swung out of the saddle with a grunt of fatigue, and tied off the reins at the hitching post.

For a change, the steps were clear; the ostlers must be at the stables, the harness drummers and whiskey drummers out on their rounds. Nobody to stare at the man who'd killed Mickey Slawson.

The man who'd raped India Ashton . . .

Mrs. Boltwith was seated at the little hotel desk just under the foot of the stairs. Her bulk made the desk look even smaller. Mrs. Boltwith was in yellow print today, looking like a lady schoolteacher with her spectacles. She looked up when Lee came through the front door and gave him a cool greeting nod.

"Mr. Lee."

"Any room in the inn, Mrs. Boltwith?"

She nodded again.

Mrs. Boltwith was definitely angry about something, and it couldn't be losing Bupp's help in her kitchen.

She led the way up the narrow stairs.

"How long are you going to be staying, Mr. Lee?"

"Probably three days. I'm waiting for a bank draft."

She stopped at the end of the first-floor hallway, at the door to the small room Lee had slept in before, and silently handed him the key.

Might as well meet it head on.

"Is anything troubling you, Mrs. Boltwith?"

She gave Lee a hard look. "Now that you ask, Mr. Lee, yes, there is something troubling me." She hesitated for a moment, then cleared her throat. "I just don't think . . . I just don't think much of a grown man

134

that will mistreat a woman."

Lee felt sick to his stomach. He had thought—hell, he had hoped—that India Ashton hadn't told anybody about what had happened. And it looked as though a hope was all that it was.

"When I introduce a friend of mine," Mrs. Boltwith continued, "to a person I consider a gentleman, I expect that person to *act* like a gentleman and not be discourteous and rude to as nice a young girl as ever drew breath."

For a moment Lee didn't know what the hell she was talking about. Then, with a rush of relief, he realized the old dragon wasn't meaning India Ashton at all; she was talking about that little whore, Beatrice. He'd been pretty short with her, he remembered. And that's what had the old hen's tail feathers in a fluff.

"Beatrice Morgan," Mrs. Boltwith continued, "is a nice girl."

"I'm sure you're right, ma'am," Lee said. "I guess I was a little short with her, a little rude . . ."

"Yes, you were. And Beatrice assumed it was because of her trade . . ."

"Now, Mrs. Boltwith, you know it was no such thing," Lee said. "I've been around enough to know better than that." He turned to unlock his door. "But if I upset her, I'll be glad to apologize."

Mrs. Boltwith appeared satisfied with that and gave Lee a pleasant horse-faced smile as he stepped into his room.

Lee tossed his saddlebags down on the bed and went to the washstand, splashed some water from the big china pitcher into the bowl, and washed his hands and face, wetting his hair and combing it back with his fingers. He looked up into the mirror over the stand. No San Francisco dandy there; no gunman or pimp, either. This man looked like a worried, weather-worn, money-short horse rancher. And, by God, that was no lie.

He brushed some of the trail dust from his buckskin jacket, eased his gunbelt on his hips, gave his dusty boots a quick wipe with his bandanna—no dandy, now, for sure!—and left the room, locking the door behind him.

Mrs. Boltwith wasn't behind the desk at the bottom of the stairs, and the front steps were still clear of stable hands and drummers. Lee went down the steps, out across the high boardwalk, and down to the dusty street. The gravel they laid on the road kept a lot of the dust down, but not all of it.

He walked diagonally across the street toward the Arcady. A cold beer would go down very well. They should have their beer on ice, this close to the mountains. And while he was at it, he'd give Rebecca Chase a little look-in, just to remind her to keep her mouth shut concerning that vanished gunman, Buckskin Frank Leslie. A reminder never hurt.

As he went up the steps to the Arcady's swinging doors, Lee noticed a row of cow ponies tied along the rail outside. There was a very nice roan gelding among them. Damn near a thoroughbred, by the look of him.

It registered on him just too late who the hell that thoroughbred belonged to.

Too late. He was already through the doors.

The big bar room was almost empty. It looked as though Cree was a serious working town not heavy on afternoon drinking, at all.

Almost empty.

Not quite.

Six cowboys were lined up along the far end of the bar. A relief barman was serving them beers in ice-frosted mugs.

Standing at the head of the line was another man. Not a cowboy. Not by a long shot. He was bigger than the other men, for one thing—damn near six and a half feet, Lee thought—and he was burly as a bear. But there was more to him than that. The man was a foreigner for sure. His hair was carrot red, and he wore a broad, curling beard the same bright ginger shade. He was wearing a moleskin jacket and a white, stiff-collar shirt, a curl-brim derby, and a pair of riding breeches and long-top English boots.

There was only one man it could be, and Lee was mortified to feel himself ashamed to face him. It was India's brother, Nigel Ashton.

Then Lee remembered Jake Sandburg lying dead with a cut throat—by this man's allowance for sure, if not his direct orders—and he felt less ashamed. This foreign son-of-a-bitch was no better than any other man, and worse than most.

The cowboys had looked up when Lee came in, and the big, red-headed Englishman had looked up too. He had small, bright blue eyes. Then they went back to their beers. They hadn't recognized him. No reason they should; they hadn't seen him before.

Lee was just starting to think he might have his beer and get out of the Arcady without trouble, when he saw the relief barmen lean over and say something, softly, to one of the cowboys at the far end of the bar. The cowboy looked quickly back over at Lee then, and he knew the jig was up on that. He'd have to remember to have a word with the barman about that loose tongue of his.

He saw the news being quietly passed down the line of cowpokers to the boss. When the Englishman got the word, he stood still for a moment, then he slowly put his beer down an the bar and turned his head to stare at Lee.

The Englishman looked down the bar at Lee, as if Lee were a mongrel dog taking a shit right there on the bar-room floor. It was a long, cold, contemptuous look, perfected, Lee supposed, on generations of serfs and commoners.

Lee gave the big man a friendly smile, nodded in the

137

nicest way, as if they were old pals from way back, and tapped on the bar for service.

The barman came drifting down to him, looking a little concerned.

"A tall beer—cold," Lee said.

He kept his eyes on the barman while he drew the beer, and, at the same time, kept his eyes on the Englishman and his men in the mirror behind the bar. The Englishman wasn't armed, unless he kept a Derringer in a back pocket, and none of the cowboys looked to be a fast gun. It was true that sometimes a cowpoker got very sudden with his Colts, but that was rare. Practicing took too much cash for ammunition when a man only earned forty dollars a month.

That didn't mean, of course, that the six cow punchers couldn't shoot him to rags, if they all set in to do it together. He would be able to kill two or three, but he'd still go down for sure.

It didn't worry him. Not many had the nerve for that kind of slaughter.

The barman brought his beer and set it down carefully on the bar in front of him. He started to turn away, when Lee reached out and gently took his arm, to hold him.

"You know," Lee said to the man with a pleasant smile, "you have a very big mouth, friend."

The barman, a tall man with a cast to his right eye, seemed about to say something rough in return. Then he looked at Lee's face and changed his mind.

"I—I guess I was out of line, pointing you out, Mr. Lee." There was a line of sweatbeads across his forehead. "I sure am sorry about it . . ."

Lee let him stand there for a moment, sweating. It gave him no pleasure to frighten a man who was so plainly not a fighting man. But sometimes it was the only way for people to learn.

"Don't do anything like that again," Lee said. "I'm

138

surprised a good bartender would quack like that, to any damn fool across your bar . . ."

The barman wiped his forehead with his bar rag. "Well, I sure won't do it again."

Lee nodded, and the barman eased away back down the bar. Lee saw one of the cowboys lean over to speak to him as the bartender went by, but the man just ducked his head and kept going. He went all the way around the end of the bar and through a door there. The supply room, Lee thought. He marked the door in his mind, just in case of trouble. He'd known shy men before, insulted or angry for some reason, wait until other men started trouble and then suddenly decide to join in. So Lee kept the barman in mind.

He raised his beer mug and took a long, slow swallow. It was damn good beer, home brewed, he supposed, or maybe freighted in from Butte, though it seemed a hell of a long haul. Damned good and ice cold. He took another long pull, feeling the smooth, cold, burning pleasure of the beer in his throat. When he finished this one, by God, he'd have a couple more, if that shy bartender ever came back behind the bar.

"Looks like this fella has scared off old Bill."

True enough. It was the opening note of the waltz. A dance Lee had heard many times before. He threw his head back to finish the beer and took a good look in the bar mirror as he did. None of them had moved up there; the Englishman was closest, maybe twenty feet to Lee's left. The cowboys were still lined up on the other side of their boss. None of them had cleared room for drawing and shooting.

So it was to be just talk for a while yet.

"I'd say this citizen must be real rough." Another cowboy. "Ain't he the one killed that Irishman while he was drunk?"

"Must have been. I'd say bartenders are more in this pilgrim's line."

Any time now one of them would step away from the bar and stroll down to Lee's end to chivvy him close up. It was a problem. If he stood it and just put down his two bits and left the place, it would only mean postponing trouble. On the other hand, to flat out kill the cowboy, and maybe a friend of his, too, would be bound to set Lee as a quick gunman in the mind of every man in Cree. It was something he didn't want. He didn't want that ever 'again.

A problem.

The Englishman solved that problem for him.

"That's enough," he said to his men. He had a high, tenor voice, with that fancy Oxford accent most rich Englishmen had—at least most of the rich ones that came out West talked like that. It was a high-pitched, funny kind of voice, and a funny way of talking, but there was a cold toughness to it. Those generations of serfs and poor people must have jumped pretty quick when they heard it.

It shut the cowboys up, for sure. Nobody argued with him; there wasn't a peep out of them. Mr. Nigel Ashton ran what sea captains called a tight ship: it was useful to know.

Lee put his beer mug down and turned to go. What the hell, he'd have his seconds and thirds of beer another time. Leave well enough alone.

"Just a second, sir."

Lee didn't have to glance back to know who was talking—and who to.

He turned to see the Englishman standing away from the bar, his legs set wide apart, his small blue eyes drilling into Lee's.

"Yes?"

"I have a bone to pick with you, Mr. Lee. That is your name?"

"It's my name."

"Then I say I have a bone to pick with you concernng the murder of four of my men.''

Lee felt the same rush of relief he'd known at Mrs. Boltwith's. India Ashton hadn't told her brother what he'd done.

Maybe it was that feeling that helped Lee keep his temper.

''Murder? And what does the local law have to say about that, Ashton?'' No ''Mister'' for this arrogant son-of-a-bitch.

The big man's face reddened over the carroty ruff of his beard. ''Whatever Mr. Phipp's opinion, *Lee*, my opinion is that you and your people committed murder.''

Lee took a deep breath.

''Now, you listen to me,'' he said. ''Your four men, and one of them a well-known killer''—the big Englishman's eyes narrowed at that—''came riding onto my place, onto my land, and drove off all of my appaloosas! They ran them clear up to the river, and they would have crossed them too, but for a boy that worked for me catching up to them and stopping them getting the herd across.''

Ashton started to say something, but Lee talked right over him.

''And that fine killer of yours, that Tom Small, he killed that boy. Fifteen years old! And that man cut his throat.'' Lee got angrier and angrier as he spoke about it; it seemed to make the whole thing fresh in his mind. ''And did I kill those men? Why, you can just bet your English ass I killed them! I shot 'em and hung 'em, and was damn glad to do it!''

The big man's face was red as fire now. It nearly matched his beard.

''And I say,'' retorted Ashton,'' *I* say, that you, sir, are a damned liar! And that my men, if they had anything to do with your horses at all, were simply checking their brands to find whether they weren't Mr.

141

Allenson's stock! His ranch is only thirty miles from the valley, and he also runs a few of those Indian ponies."

Now, Lee wasn't angry at all. The time for that was past.

"Ashton, you're the liar. And a coward to boot! You sent those men to run off my stock and steal it; you didn't have the sand to come yourself. You're a liar, a coward, and a thief."

And by God, that should tear it.

And it did.

Ashton stood frozen, his face gone as white as it had been red. Lee doubted that he had been spoken to so hard in his life—and he didn't look likely to bear it.

"All right, you mouthy son-of-a-bitch!" A young cowboy had stepped away from the bar, his hand hovering over his pistol butt. He was just a kid, with a thin work-worn face framed by wispy blond sideburns.

Lee didn't want to have to kill him.

"No, Franklin," Ashton said, without turning around. "I'll handle this." He stared Lee up and down a moment more. "I wonder," he said. "I wonder if you're any sort of a man without that revolver strapped to your side?"

It suited Lee. Right down to the ground. Better a fist fight than a killing.

"Man enough to knock you on your ass, English-.nan. "

"That, by God, we shall soon see," Ashton said. And he strode over to a nearby table, shrugged out of his riding jacket, stripped off his stiff shirt collar, and began rolling up his shirt sleeves. He seemed pleased the way things had worked out.

"We'll fight out back," he said to Lee, curtly. His sleeves were up now, his arms bare. They were massively muscled, red furred—the arms of a blacksmith. Lee had heard that some English gentlemen fancied themselves fist fighters, even trained with professionals. It was possible Ashton was that kind; he had the muscles for it.

"Hold your gun, Lee?"

The voice had come from behind him. Lee turned and saw Tod Phipps standing by the swinging doors, smiling at him. He'd come in very quietly; the doors hadn't squeaked at all. Still, Lee cursed himself for his carelessness in standing with his back to the door. If there had been gun play with Ashton's cowboys, Phipps would have had him cold.

Phipps held out his hand, grinning. It seemed that everyone was happy about this coming fight. And it was natural that Phipps would be. Either way it came out, he couldn't lose. Either the high and mighty Nigel Ashton got a beating or the new fast gun in town got thrashed. Either way, good for Tod Phipps.

Lee unbuckled his gunbelt and handed it to the marshal.

"The knife, too?" A big smile then.

Lee reached down, slid the toothpick out of his boot, and handed it over.

"Don't worry," Phipps said. "I'll see fair play."

Lee wasn't so sure that he would, and he wasn't so sure now that this fist fighting was such a good idea. Not that he couldn't beat Ashton. That wasn't the trouble. He'd beaten and kicked stronger and harder men than Ashton down. The trouble was that he was unarmed. Unarmed against Ashton and his men, and unarmed before Phipps, which might be worse.

Well, he'd made his choice when he'd taken the big Englishman up on his challange. The hand was full dealt now, and he'd have to play it out.

Lee walked out through the Arcady's back hall, along with Ashton's men, following the Englishman's broad back. A big man, and no mistake. He'd have to hit him fast and hard and get the boot into him the instant he was down. Kick a kneecap off him to start, maybe . . .

The cowboys seemed almost friendly to Lee now,

winking at him and nudging each other as they crowded out through the back door into a broad, sunny alley. Their sharp-toed boots kicked up little dust devils as they trotted out into the sunlight, making a wide circle. They were mostly young boys, with a few busted-up old rannies among them. They were all grinning and shifting nervously, waiting for the fight to start. It wasn't so often that a couple of ranch owners, rich men as far as the cowboys were concerned, would square off for a knock down and drag out. It made a kind of holiday.

"Go it, Mr. Ashton!" "Git—git—git on him!"

Lee shucked his buckskin jacket and draped it over the Arcady's back hitching rail. Then he rolled his shirt sleeves up. Ashton had already walked to the center of the circle of men and stood waiting. Lee noticed he was standing so the sun would be slanting into Lee's eyes.

"Good luck," Phipps said to him. He didn't seem to mean it.

As Lee stepped into the circle, he heard women talking just above him. Looking up, he saw that some of the whores had come out onto a little second-story balcony to watch. They were giggling nervously, staring down at the men crowded into the alley, at Ashton and Lee standing, facing each other in the afternoon sunlight.

"You do know the Marquess of Queensbury's rules, Lee?" Ashton said.

Bad news. And Lee should have figured it. Of course Ashton would fight by gentlemen's rules. And that meant no kicking, no gouging.

It meant trouble. Lee would either have to speak up, now, for fighting like a gutter rat, or he'd have to box like a gent, and very likely get his head knocked off. He didn't have to glance around to know that Phipps was grinning at him.

The hand was dealt. He'd wanted land and respectability; now he'd have to earn it.

Lee nodded. "We'll fight Queensbury's rules."

And no sooner had he said it than he heard Phipps's voice call out, "Time!" and Ashton was on him with a fast straight jab and a right cross to follow. For a big man, he was very quick.

The right caught Lee in the mouth and knocked him flat.

CHAPTER TEN

He wasn't hurt, but he was sure as hell down. Lee didn't try to jump up, to show that Ashton hadn't hurt him. Instead, he got up slow, shaking his head. The cowboys were yelling like Indians, stomping up and down in the dust.

"You put that pilgrim away!" "Hand it to him, Mr. Ashton!" they yelled.

Lee saw Ashton peering at him closely as he straightened up, measuring how he'd weathered the blow. The whores on the balcony above were murmuring like doves in a dovecote.

Lee pretended to lose his temper and rushed in at the Englishman, throwing his punches wild and pulling them, too. The big man blocked them fast, brushing them aside, moving and ducking. It was like striking at a moving tree. Even when one of his punches landed, Lee saw that the Englishman didn't even blink.

And out of that flurry, the big man struck a right upper cut into Lee's gut that would have doubled him up and out of the fight if it had hit him square.

Lee backed off, still playing weak and flustered.

The Englishman seemed satisfied. He smiled a little to himself and began to move after Lee as steady and certain as a rockslide. Lee kept on backing around the circle of yelling ranch hands, letting the red-bearded rancher come on.

And come on he did. The Englishman was an easy mover, moving to one side or the other, but he was fastest coming at you. Lee backed and backed, playing a little shy and watching the big man's style. No question but he'd learned from a professional. It wasn't that he hit hard; plenty of men who never studied boxing hit hard as a mule kicked. It was the way he covered up, moving with his chin tucked down into his shoulder, his left well up.

The cowboys were calling for Lee to show some sand. They had him figured for scared from that fast knockdown. Lee hoped that Ashton believed the same.

Lee pulled back one more time, backpedaling across the circle, looking as sorry as he could. He caught a glimpse of Tod Phipps out of the corner of his eye. Phipps looked pleased enough with the way the fight was going.

Just as Lee reached the circle of cowboys, Ashton suddenly strode out after him, lunging across the dusty ring to swing hard with a wide right hand. He swung at Lee's head hard enough so that Lee heard the fist whiffle past his ear like an Indian arrow.

Lee stepped in under the blow, twisted his body as if he were throwing a baseball pitch, and hit Ashton flush on the nose with his left fist as hard as he could hit.

It hurt him.

The big man's head snapped back and the small blue eyes widened as the pain of the blow struck him. The cowboys yelped with surprise. But whoever the English fighter had been who'd taught Ashton, he'd taught him well. He'd taught him what to do when a punch hurt him.

Ashton didn't move back and he didn't rush. He stayed where he was, set himself, and punched. He went for Lee's body again, going to double him up, striking with an uppercut and a hard hook up into the ribs without a pause between them.

Lee slid away, shifted back to stand square, and hit Ashton in the left eye twice. He came within an ace of putting the thumb in then, but remembered just in time and kept the blow clean.

There must have been a little hesitation there, though, just for a fraction of a second. It was enough for Ashton to club him across the temple with a quick swinging blow that made his ears hum.

Lee slid away. Another like that might have put him down.

And he was moving across the circle again, thinking hard as he could what he might do to put the big man away. He surprised him, and he stung him. But he hadn't put him down.

Ashton was coming after him again. A bright line of blood was running from his nose, his eyes clear and eager—except for the left, which was swelling across the lid.

He tried for Lee with a long jab. It looked rather slow coming in. The jab tagged Lee on the point of his shoulder, and it hurt as if someone had rapped him with a heavy stick.

Lee hit the big man with his right. Digging deep into the man's gut, it was like striking into a feed sack. Ashton just grunted and kept coming.

Then Tod Phipps called time.

A fat young cowboy, couldn't have been more than sixteen, made a knee for Lee to sit on to catch his breath.

"Mister," the boy said, "you're doing good just to be alive."

Lee couldn't much disagree with him. He sat, a little bent over, taking in as much air as he could manage. He saw Tod Phipps standing across the circle talking to Ashton and laughing. Phipps had picked the winner.

As the seconds of rest ticked away, Lee glanced up at the Arcady's balcony to see how the soiled doves were

148

enjoying the fight and looked straight into the eyes of Beatrice Morgan. The thin girl was all done up as a right good whore, but her face was pale under the rouge and mascara. She'd looked upset just as Lee glanced up, but when their eyes met, the girl forced a bright smile and held her small fist up with a rakish, encouraging air, as if he were whipping the pudding out of that poor Englishman.

It gave Lee an odd feeling for her to do that.

And Tod Phipps called, "Time."

He sounded like a happy man.

Lee got up off the cowboy's knee, went out to Ashton, and hit him fairly on the jaw. Ashton punched straight out in return, caught Lee in the neck, and forced him back into the screeching cowboys, bulling him, punching into him up close.

Lee resisted a damnable urge to knee the big man in the nuts, and then just managed to twist and fight his way back out into the circle. But it cost him: Ashton had gotten in a hard punch to Lee's ribs. It felt as though one was cracked, judging from the pain when Lee took a deep breath.

And the Englishman was still coming.

Lee ducked a short punch to his face and rode out another one that thumped into the side of his head.

It was simple: Lee hadn't yet seen a way to hurt Ashton, but Ashton was making considerable progress in hurting Lee. Much more of this and the big man was bound to get a flush punch home and put Lee down hard. After that, it would just be a beating for as long as Lee could stand up under it.

Get doing or go under. It was as simple as that.

The next time Ashton moved in punching, Lee hit him in the left eye again. Hit him twice, then struck him in the gut. But the body punch was just to keep Ashton from realizing what Lee was after.

Lee was going to blind him.

If he could. If he stayed lucky—and on his feet.

He almost made it.

He hit Ashton in the eye once more, a good hard punch that hurt the big man. He hit the man alongside the head as well.

Then, as he was backing across the circle, measuring the Englishman for more punishment to that left eye, something happened.

Lee never knew what punch the big man caught him with.

Suddenly, without knowing how he got there, Lee was on his hands and knees in the dust.

The cowboys were jumping around screeching, and Lee could hear the women yelling high up over his head.

He hoped Beatrice Morgan hadn't stayed to watch this.

Lee didn't know if he was on his hands and knees on the way to getting up or on his way down into the dirt. There was only one way to find out. He got a foot under him, then two, and tried to stand up. He was feeling a little sick to his stomach.

Then, while he was still trying to stand up, he heard Phipps counting.

"Six . . . seven . . ."

Lee got to his feet. His face was numb. All the faces around the circle were drifting slowly to the side wherever he looked at them. Ashton had knocked him silly.

And the Englishman was coming to finish the job.

Lee sensed rather than saw the bulk of the man moving over the trampled circle towards him. He forced himself to move, to move away until he could think clearly again.

Ashton tagged him a hard punch to the side, anyway. It was the side with the hurt rib, and the sharp pain seemed to help wake him up.

Lee caught his breath and felt his legs well under him

again. He began to fight back.

He stood up to the Englishman when he came in again, took a hard punch to the chest, and hit the big rancher in the right eye.

Ashton swung back, but Lee managed to duck the blow and hit the Englishman again. Again in the right eye.

Ashton now knew what he was about, and Lee saw him raise his guard to protect his face from those punches. But Lee didn't care. He struck at the big man's face anyway, once, and twice, then again. The last punch went through Ashton's guard and hit his left eye. The swollen lid began to bleed.

Ashton stepped back to collect himself, to get his left well up. It was the first step back he had taken in the fight.

Lee jumped after him and struck out left and right as fast as he could. The big man brushed most of the punches off, but one struck his right eye. He shook his head like a bull toubled with flies, jabbed Lee sharply, and swung a roundhouse right at him that just missed.

Tom Phipps called time.

"Well, you're doing the smart thing out there, but you started too late," the fat young cowboy said as Lee sat gasping on his knee. Right then Lee would have given a good deal to see the fat cowboy out there in that circle.

"I guess you want me to shut up," the fat young cowboy said, and Lee nodded and took a deep breath, trying to set that cracked rib somehow so it wouldn't hurt him so bad.

He glanced up at the balcony. Beatrice Morgan was looking at him. He didn't know why he did it, but he smiled and raised his fist to her the way she had done to him. Everyone there must have seen him do it, making up to an Arcady whore.

"Time!" called Tod Phipps.

"Well, pardon me," Lee said to the fat cowboy. "I have to get to work." He stood up and went out to meet Nigel Ashton.

Ashton's eyes looked better. One of his men had been washing them with cold beer. The big man was as fresh and strong as ever. He struck out at Lee like a grizzly bear and hit him on the shoulder and high on the cheekbone. The last one was a jolting punch, and Lee moved back and around the circle, waiting for his head to clear from it.

Then he moved to meet Ashton again and hit him a very hard punch on the left eye. Ashton made a quick face from the pain, and the eye started to look bad right away. Some cowboy in the crowd said, "Uh-ohhh."

Ashton rushed Lee then, and Lee hit out at the Englishman's face as hard as he could, punching short, sharp punches at the big man's eyes.

Ashton hit Lee an uppercut into the belly that took his breath away. And Lee just let his breath go, figuring it would come back sometime, and took the chance to reach out and hit the big man in the right eye. It was looking almost as bad as the left one, and the Englishman was squinting to see through it.

Lee felt better and better. He hurt like hell, and Ashton was still likely to knock him cold, but he found himself enjoying the fight. Everything looked nice and clear now, and moved slowly and clearly, the way it did when he fought with a gun. It was a pleasant feeling.

Lee smiled at Ashton, and the Englishman came in and knocked him into the ring of cowboys watching the fight. Lee spun away from them and hit the big man in the side as he rushed in, hitting him in the short ribs as if he were chopping wood. Then he jumped back into the center of the ring and waited for the Englishman to come back.

When Ashton came back, Lee jabbed at his eyes. When the big rancher brought up his guard, Lee made a feint to the man's belly, then swung overhand and caught him in the eye as the Englishman's guard came down.

Ashton grunted and swung a right. Lee hit him in the left eye and blood spattered from it.

"Uh-ohhh." It was the same cowboy as before.

Ashton was beginning to make panting sounds, as if being hit in the eyes and hurt that particular way was making him tired.

Some cowboys had stopped yelling. It was now quiet enough so that Lee could hear his feet and Ashton's as they scuffled through the alley dust.

He feinted another punch at Ashton's eyes and saw the Englishman wince a little.

Lee was feeling better and better.

Ashton came on the same as ever, trying not to hold his guard up too high to only protect his eyes. The big man had some sand, and the man who'd taught him had known his business.

Lee hit the Englishman in the jaw. Ashton didn't heed it.

Lee hit him in the jaw again, laying the punch with all his strength.

Ashton's guard came down to cover—had to come down to cover—and Lee hit him in the eye. Blood spattered across his face.

No sound came from the cowboys now, not even when the big man hit Lee in the chest hard and hurt him. He struck at Lee again with a clever left hook and sent him staggering sideways. But Lee came back straight away and jabbed Ashton in the right eye. That eye wasn't bleeding yet, but it didn't look good.

Suddenly the Englishman lunged at Lee, bearing down with his great weight, striking down as if he were driving fence posts with a sledge hammer.

For a moment Lee thought he was done. The man was just too damn big. But he remembered what he was

153

about and struck up into the Englishman's face with both fists, punching up into those bleeding eyes.

"Time!" called Tod Phipps. "Time!"

"Well, this is the best fist fight that I ever saw," the fat young cowboy said when Lee came staggering over to sit with a grunt on his bent knee.

Lee was worried about his hands. He couldn't feel them anymore. They didn't even hurt. He wasn't worried about the fight, they'd do for that, all right. But he hoped that no bones were broken. It was hard in a bare-knuckle fight like this not to break some bone in your hand if you were punching at a man's head. And he was certainly doing that. A broken bone in his hand would be very serious, especially in his right hand. Lee could draw and shoot quite fast with his left hand, but he missed as often as he hit with it. It could be trouble.

Tod Phipps strode out to the center of the circle, looking mighty neat and cool in his woven jacket. He had had somebody go get him a cold beer from inside, and he took a sip from it and called, "Time!"

Lee jumped up and walked out into the circle to meet Ashton coming in. Ashton punched Lee hard in the face, and that punch hurt Lee's head from front to back. It was a sharp pain that seemed to cut straight back from his forehead.

The Englishman's left eye looked like a broken plum, and blood was running down from it onto his cheek. He was blind on that side.

Lee stepped around to the big man's left, into that blind spot, and hit him on the ear as hard as he could. Ashton staggered and tried to turn to see Lee and swing at him, but Lee keep moving off around to the side, keeping in the blind spot, and hit the Englishman twice more across the side of the head.

Ashton staggered from the blows, then recovered himself, and spun fast to find Lee with his good eye and hit him.

154

When he turned, Lee struck at his right eye, missed with his first punch, then struck again and hit it. The Englishman grunted with pain, stepped into Lee, hit him in the body, and missed his face with another punch. They were both missing punches now, and Lee wondered if he'd ever manage to hit Ashton hard enough, to beat him.

He feigned a move to the big man's blind side, to his left. When Ashton turned to protect himself, Lee swung a hard punch at his face and hit him in the eye.

"Damn . . . damn!" one of the cowboys said. The rest of them made no sound at all. The women up on the balcony were quiet too. Lee could hear Ashton's hoarse breathing, his gasps for breath. The Englishman's red beard was stained and stringy with blood. His right eye was almost closed now, as well.

If I shut that damn eye, then I've won the fight, Lee thought. He could hardly remember what fight he was thinking about, he was so tired.

But he still felt fine.

Ashton spit and gritted his teeth and reached for Lee, punching at him twice. One punch hit Lee's side, and the other one, more of a push than a punch, hit the side of his mouth. Lee felt a tooth cut into his lip.

It's time to finish all this, Lee thought. If I can.

Lee stepped back away from the big rancher and stood for a moment sizing him up.

Ashton snorted and came for him again, swinging slow, pawing punches at him. Lee stepped back again. The Englishman had plenty of fight left and more strength than Lee.

Lee took a deep breath, stepped into the big man, brought up his hand with a short punch, and then hit him twice in the right eye as hard as he could hit.

Ashton went staggering back, two or three long steps, and Lee was right after him. As the big man tried to get his balance, to get set, Lee hit him in the face again.

Ashton seemed to stumble and fell down to one knee.

As Lee waited, the big Englishman struggled up to his feet again, the flesh of his eyes puffed black and broken, his face splotched and stained with blood.

There wasn't a sound from anyone in the alley.

No sound at all but the Englishman's harsh breathing and Lee's.

Lee felt dizzy, as if he could float away.

He swung his fist back as far as it would go and took a little skipping step. With a hoarse grunt he threw that fist into Nigel Ashton's face just as fast as it would go.

The blow landed with a sound like a dropped feed sack. Blood flew from the Englishman's face. He pitched forward into Lee. He tried to clutch at Lee's clothes, couldn't hold on, and fell out full length into the dust.

"Don't get up," Lee said to the man. "Don't get up."

But he didn't know what he would do if the man did get up. All the pleasure of the fight was gone: it had been hard work. Lee felt tired to death.

Nigel Ashton lay still in the dust for a moment, then he slowly drew his legs up and dug his hands into the alley dirt. His broad back bowed, and his arms trembled as he tried to push himself up so that he was sitting.

"Oh, dear heavens," one of the women said above them.

"Oh, shit," said one of the cowboys.

The big Englishman groaned aloud. He heaved and shoved himself so that he was sitting up. He sat staring around him, looking for Lee, and he reached up and wiped his eyes with his fingers, trying to wipe the blood from his eyes so that he could see.

Lee bent over before he thought and put his hand on the man's shoulder.

"The fight's over, Ashton," he said. His own voice

sounded strange to him. "It was a good fight."

The big man reached up a fumbling hand, felt for Lee's wrist, and held it. Lee thought the man was trying to pull himself up, but couldn't. He just sat there with his hand on Lee's wrist, and then he let go of it.

"Holy jumping Jesus!" one of the cowboys said.

Lee turned and walked through the crowd and on into the Arcady's back entrance. It was cool in there. It was so shadowy in the hall that he felt dizzy for a minute.

When he woke, the first thing he felt was something cool touching his hand. Then it burned.

A hoarse voice said, "Get it in there good and soak it all around."

Lee opened his eyes to a cool, quiet, dark room. An ugly, froggy little man was standing over the bed, looking at him. He was a familiar looking man.

Beatrice Morgan was holding Lee's right hand, dabbing at it with a wet cloth that smelled of horse liniment.

"That's it," the froggy little man said. "It doesn't do any good, Beatrice, unless it soaks in real good." He looked up at Lee. "Well, well, so our naughty boy is wide awake, is he?" He shook a stubby finger at Lee. "And you have been a naughty boy!"

"Who the hell are you?" said Lee, and his voice came out a rusty croak.

"My dear, you sound like I look," the froggy little man said. "I am Bud Martin, proprietor of my own sundry sundries and millinary emporium, enemy to the death of Greedy Kimble, the Mercantile King, and, to your very good fortune, a two-year medical student at Tulane College, which only happens to be the finest school of medicine in the entire South!" He pouted and preened himself for a moment. "Which establishment I

157

was forced to abandon due to my style of Universal Love."

"You fainted out downstairs," Beatrice Morgan said to Lee, as she dabbed the liniment onto his hand. The hand was dark red and swollen.

"How long—"

"Oh, do try to be original, now," the little man said. "You've been in this sweetie's sweet bed for just three or four hours." And the little man patted Lee on the shoulder. "Handsome is as handsome does," he said, absently, staring into Lee's eyes.

"Don't be distressed," he said, "I'm not spooning. Just making sure you're not badly hurt . . . Beatrice, turn up that lamp and bring it here."

When the girl brought the lamp over, Martin held the light up to Lee's eyes and then moved it back and forth.

"How many of these lamps do you see, Naughty One?"

"One," Lee said.

"Hmmm . . ." The little man turned and handed the lamp back to the girl. "Well, I do think you'll survive, though your looks are certainly spoiled for the time being."

"How is . . ?" For a moment Lee forgot the Englishman's name.

"Yes?" said Mr. Martin, looking interested in this lapse.

"Ashton."

"Oh, Mr. Ashton prefers to forgo my medical advice. I believe he disapproves of my style—"

"—of Universal Love?" said Lee, with a smile.

"Precisely," Mr. Martin said, and patted Lee on the shoulder again. "My dear," he said to Beatrice, "you appear to have better judgement than most of your sex. And now I'll leave you two together, to make any mistakes you wish . . ."

"Thank you, Doctor," said Lee, and the little man,

pleased, paused at the door to bow in a dignified fashion.

"He's nice," Beatrice said when the little man was gone.

"I guess he is," Lee said.

"He's as good as a real doctor when it comes to most things."

"I hope so," Lee said, and he smiled at the girl. It hurt his face; that Englishman had given him quite a walloping.

"He said you should just stay in bed until tomorrow." She blushed.

A blushing little whore, Lee thought.

"Well, I can be going now, I think," Lee said. "I feel pretty good. I don't usually go to fainting in saloons."

"No," she said. "No, you shouldn't go. Mrs. Chase said it would be quite all right for you to stay as long as you want."

She got up and went to a dresser and got a bottle of medicine.

"Does laudanum make you sick? I know it does some people."

Lee shook his head, and the girl carefully measured out two drops of the drug into a glass of water. When he reached out to take it, Lee could feel that his right hand was all right—stiff and sore with split knuckles, but no bones broken. As good with a gun as ever in a few days.

"Mr. Martin said you were very lucky your rib hadn't broken all the way. It might have stuck something inside."

Lee shifted on the soft bed. Sure enough, his chest was taped tight. Ashton had broken a rib on him with that punch just the way he'd thought. Or cracked it good, anyway.

The girl, Beatrice, came back to the side of the bed, picked up his hand, and began dabbing at it again with the liniment. It stung a little, and the smell reminded

159

him of the stable on his family's old farm in Parker, Indiana.

Lee slept, and he dreamed that he was there, up in the hay loft, with Puss, the cat, waiting for James to come home.

He could hear his mother talking with Bertha May as they worked in the kitchen cooking dinner for all the people that would be coming to welcome James back home.

It would be a big welcome because James was a sergeant. He became a sergeant after he got a medal at Fredericksburg. Lee had been jealous for two years, waiting to be old enough to go. The war would have to last three more years for him and George Babcock to make it. They were both thirteen, and their folks wouldn't let them go, not even as drummer boys. It was unfair, because everybody knew this was the last war there would be. And it meant that James would have this over him no matter how old he got. And just for being born a few years too late.

He rolled over onto his back in the hay, smelling the stable smells—leather, and horse shit, and liniment. He'd got up early and done all his chores. There was nothing for him to do all day now but wait and see James and watch everybody make such a fuss over him that it made you sick to see it. What for? For doing what *he* would do if anybody gave him a chance. Give those Rebs pure hell, that's what!

Puss kept trying to get away. She had kittens down in one of the stalls. Lee thought of going to look for them, but it was a waste of time. She'd just move them away again.

He thought he heard his mother calling him. Yes, she was calling him to come in. She sounded excited. James was coming down the road.

Then he was out on the road, watching for James. It was a real hot day. And there was James coming along

160

in a wagon, and everybody calling to him. Waving his hand, James was waving to them all, smiling to beat the band. And Daddy was driving the horses.

CHAPTER ELEVEN

Lee woke late the next morning. It looked almost noon. The room was bright with sunlight, and there was a bunch of fresh flowers on the table beside the bed. Wild flowers. Bluebells and eglantine.

Lee lay still awhile remembering the fight. Then he threw the covers back and sat up on the edge of the bed. He was naked, and his side hurt him whenever he took a deep breath. He stretched both hands out and flexed them, working his fingers. The knuckles were sore and swollen and cut in a couple of places where he'd hit the Englishman in the mouth and got cut on a tooth. His hands were achy, but they felt all right. And his face was sore.

He got up and walked stiffly over to the washstand and looked at his face in the mirror. It looked pretty bad, puffed up and black and blue, especially on the left side where Ashton had landed with his right.

His nose didn't seem to be broken, though. There was a bump on the bridge, but it wasn't broken.

Lee bared his teeth. They looked all right. None of them even loose. All in all, not bad, not bad for a gentleman's fight with so big a man. And a man who'd had lessons with a professional for sure.

Phipps must be real disappointed—or pleased to see them both knocking the stuffing out of each other, win or lose.

Lee turned as the door opened and saw that it was that girl, Beatrice. For a moment he looked around for something to cover himself, then he remembered what the girl was and relaxed.

She seemed shy about it, though, and turned her face aside when she came into the room.

"I've bought your clothes," she said. She had his clothes all washed and folded over her arm, and she was holding his socks, washed and rolled in a ball, in her other hand.

She put the things on the bed and turned to go.

"Are you feeling all right?" she said. She still wouldn't look right at him. A strange girl.

"Yes, I'm fine." Lee said. "It was very nice of you to take care of me last night. You were a good nurse."

"Oh, that's all right," the girl said. "That's all right. I was glad to." She went out and closed the door.

Lee started to dress, then looked around for his gun. It was in its holster, hanging on the bedpost. As he finished dressing Lee tried to remember the dream he'd had. Something about his father . . . and James. Both of them in there somewhere. Well, there was some water under the bridge. Both killed the first year of the war.

Water under the bridge.

He finished dressing, buckled on the gunbelt, and went out and downstairs. He met Rebecca Chase on the landing.

She gave him a bright smile.

"Well, hello, Mr. Lee! How are you feeling this morning?"

"Well enough," Lee said. "Thanks for the hospitality of the house."

"Oh," she said. "Don't think anything about that. I suppose you know you've become quite a famous man. Mr. Ashton was thought to have had no equals!"

"He didn't get much the worst of it," Lee said and started to go past her. She reached out and put her hand

163

on his arm.

"I keep my bargains," she said in a different voice. It made Lee angry. She was still worrying about that fancy lawman of hers.

"So do I," he said to her and went on down the stairs.

"Listen," she called down over the bannister, "there's late breakfast served in the kitchen now . . ."

That sounded good. Lee walked around the staircase to the hallway door and went down the dark hall toward the sounds of women's voices. As he walked, he worked his hands, working the stiffness out of them.

The kitchen was a big, bright room flooded with sunlight. The old Indian woman and the big-mouthed barkeep were standing at the stove frying eggs and hamsteaks. The food smelled wonderful.

The long kitchen table was packed with girls. Ten or twelve of them, anyway. Lee saw the half-breed girl and her lover, Phyllis. Beatrice Morgan was sitting at the end of the table, drinking a cup of coffee.

The girls all looked up when Lee came in. They were as brightly colored as a field of flowers, each one in a pretty wrapper, yellow or blue or green, with stripes or flowers on it. They were a nice-looking set of girls, better than most saloon women looked. Rebecca had picked some good ones.

The girls sat looking at him, and Lee felt out of place for a minute. He knew how like a home kitchen a whorehouse kitchen was for the people who worked the house. It was a place they could go and relax from business and trouble, a family place for them.

"Good morning," he said.

"Good morning," the girls said back.

The barkeep at the stove just nodded and went back to cooking his eggs. Lee thought he was still worried about having tipped Ashton's men at the bar the day before.

Silently, the girls all shifted down to make room for him beside Beatrice Morgan at the end of the table. It annoyed him a little, but he went and sat down there anyway, so the girl wouldn't be humiliated in front of her friends.

"Good morning," she said to him. "Are you hungry?"

"As a grizzly bear," Lee said.

She got up and went to the stove, and he could hear her talking to the old Indian woman and rattling around with the pans there.

"You feel all right now?" one of the girls asked him. She was a fat, round-faced girl in a yellow wrapper with ruffles on it.

"Yeah, fine," Lee said.

"My," the fat girl said, "you were sure sick as a horse after that fight . . ."

"I guess I was."

Beatrice came over to the table and brought him a cup of coffee, black. He liked cream in his coffee, but he didn't see any on the table.

"You want some cream?" she said to him.

"If you have it," he said. She went to a sideboard to fetch the pitcher for him.

All around the table, the girls were looking at him over their coffee cups.

"You sure showed that high and mighty Mr. Ashton something," the fat girl said.

"And Mickey Slawson, too," said a strong-looking girl with a squint in her eye.

The girls murmured and sipped their coffee, looking at him.

Lee was feeling like getting up and going, when Beatrice came to the table with his breakfast. There were three fried eggs on the platter, a pile of pan-fried potatoes, four biscuits, and a ham steak an inch thick. When Beatrice sat back down beside him, the other girls

165

drifted back into their own conversations, chattering and giggling, sometimes making a loud remark about some Johnny they'd had the night before and what the fool had wanted. Then they would glance sideways just to see how Lee had taken it.

Lee hadn't thought he'd be able to eat that much food, but he did, and took another buttered biscuit with his second cup of coffee, too. The Arcady fed its people well.

Beatrice sat beside him, watching out of the corner of her eye as he ate. She didn't say much. Just talked a little about how fast the summer was going and how pretty it was out in the mountains.

"You have a horse?" Lee asked her.

"No. I had one last year, but he got sick." She seemed to be thinking of the horse. "His name was Jumper," she said. She sighed. "Rebecca drives us out in the buggy sometimes to take the air . . ."

When Lee had finished, he wiped his mouth with one of the red-checkered napkins and got up.

"Thank you," he said to her. "That was a prime breakfast." He wanted to thank her again for taking care of him and having his clothes washed, but that seemed like too much to say in front of all those people. So he just said thank you again, nodded to the girls and walked out of the kitchen into the hall.

He heard the girls giggling behind him.

It was a nice sunny day outside. There was a cool breeze blowing softly through the town from the mountains to the north.

Lee was crossing the street to get to Mrs. Boltwith's, when he noticed the sign for Martin's store. He crossed that way, climbed the steps to the raised boardwalk, and walked down to the store. His side gave him a little trouble on the steps; a muscle pulled there when he climbed up them.

He bent down to peer through the glass panes in the door and saw the frog-faced little man behind his counter, talking to an old farm woman in a poke bonnet.

Lee pushed the door open to the light tinkle of its bell and walked in.

"Calico, calico, calico!" the little man was saying. "Mrs. Simmons, I don't say that fine lawn is what you need—or plain muslin either! But you just have no excuse not even trying a dimity. We are talking about a wedding, aren't we? Not plowing the north forty!"

The old farm woman didn't seem convinced.

"Oh, God, Sarah, I give up on you. If you have to have something you can cut into shirts for that old fool Ralph, then you may as well take bleached denim to start with!"

"Well, maybe I should," the old lady said. "It won't look too coarse for the bridemaids though?"

The little man waved acknowledgement to Lee. "Oh, God, Sarah, you wear me out. Of course it's going to look coarse! Your girls are going to look like three cows in overalls! But it's your decision, not mine. Don't take *my* advice! What do *I* know? I was only born and brought up in the best circles in New Orleans, that's all. I don't know a thing about proper dress and elegance. Not me!"

The old lady seemed to be wavering.

"But it would do for shirting?"

"Yes, Sarah, it would do for shirting."

The old lady sighed.

"Well, then, I'd better have it, I suppose."

The little man turned to his shelves and pulled a bolt of heavy white cloth out to cut.

"Sarah," he said. "You are the biggest fool going. That Ralph of yours is just all take and no give. It would serve that selfish man right if you just up and ran off

167

with a man who'd appreciate you!"

The notion seemed to please Sarah somewhat.

"I mean it," said Mr. Martin. And he folded and cut a length of the cloth, and folded and cut it again.

"There, that's enough even for those three fat girls of yours, dear. Why in heaven's name you don't get some of that weight off them, I don't know. No handsome boy's going to look at them twice, I can tell you that!"

"Well, they're never sick at all," the farm lady said.

"That's not all there is to life, Sarah," the little man said. "As I'm sure an experienced woman like you remembers."

The farm woman laughed a surprisingly young laugh, counted out her money, and collected the tied parcel the little man slid across his counter.

"Good day, Mr. Martin," she said, glanced shyly at Lee, and walked past him out the door.

"Well, now, what did you think of all that?" the little man asked Lee. "I suppose you thought all that was just a lot of sissy nonsense, didn't you?"

Lee didn't know what to say, so he kept his mouth shut.

"Well, let me tell you, Mr. Lee, that that sort of 'sissy nonsense' will have more to do with civilizing this wild country than that ugly gun you're wearing ever will!"

Lee smiled. "I guess you're right at that," he said.

"You bet I am," Mr. Martin said. "Now, what can I do for you? I don't sell gentlemen's clothes, but you could certainly use a handkerchief or a bandanna of some sort to compliment that blue shirt. Not a bad shirt at all, as those sort of things go . . ."

"No thanks. I wanted to thank you for your services last night and find out how much I owe you."

The little man stared up at him like an astonished bullfrog. "Will wonders never cease," he said. "A ready offer to pay for anything is a considerable rarity in my experience." He stared at Lee for a while and blinked. "Let's say the bill stands paid in full by the sound thrashing given that pompous ass of an aristo. You do know that Ashton is the nephew of the Earl of Leicester?"

"I knew he was something."

"The nephew of the Earl of Leiscester, the son of the Honorable Winslow Manning Cooke."

"My, my," said Lee, who didn't know what else to say.

"That's right. Once a very great family, some of the best people in England. And now look what they've produced! A great buffoon. Now, I can tell you, I don't give that!"—he snapped his fingers—"for the Leicesters!"

"I guess not," Lee said.

"And off he goes," the little man continued. "Off to Helena to see some licensed quack who'll fiddle with that eye until it's really injured. And I can tell you I don't like the look of that left eye myself. Cleansing, cover, and rest, that's what the eye needs! And it's never going to get it, not in this world!"

He turned away to his cloth shelves and began sorting through some material.

"A nice dark maroon," he said. "That poor great silly. A cattle baron, indeed!" He sighed. "Well, handsome is as handsome does. If the big fool doesn't know a friend when he has one . . ." He pulled out a small bolt of dark red cloth. "Here. I'll give you a yard of this for a bandanna. And do tell that child Beatrice to double hem all round. I've forgotten more about sewing than that girl ever knew!"

Lee reached for his billfold to pay for the cloth, but the little man waved it away.

"Consider it a wedding gift," he said and leaned on the counter, his chin propped in his hands. He stared at Lee without blinking, exactly like a sleepy frog.

When Lee walked up the steps to Mrs. Boltwith's he found the usual crowd there waiting for one o'clock dinner. Mrs. Boltwith's dinners—always fried chicken or pan-fried steak—were even more popular than her suppers.

The hostlers and whiskey drummers studied Lee with care as he went up the steps. That old look; a fast gun . . . fist fighter too now. Well, better to have fist fought Ashton than killed him. Especially considering what he'd done to the man's sister.

Mrs. Boltwith was squeezed in behind her little desk at the foot of the stairs. She looked up as he came in.

"Do you feel as bad as you look, Mr. Lee?" she said.

"Not nearly."

"You're lucky," she said. "And I've got a note from Mr. Walker at the bank." She handed a folded paper to Lee and watched as he opened and read it.

"My bank draft has come," Lee said to her. "Is the bank open at midday?"

"Open all day long."

Lee turned to go out and she called after him.

"Are you going to be taking a room for tonight, Mr. Lee?"

"I don't think so." And he was off down the steps, the drummers moving fast to get out of his way. He walked back up along the high boardwalk toward the bank, anxious about whether the Don had sent the full amount. It would have been like the old thief to send a short account—and a courtly note of apology along with it.

But the old man had played it straight. Walker, the banker, brought out the draft for a thousand dollars, drawn on an El Paso bank, looked it over carefully, then accepted it for deposit and withdrawals.

Walker was an odd-looking banker. He had a feed lot

170

on the edge of town, and, squat and strong, dressed more like a hand than a businessman, he seemed out of place in his oak-paneled office.

"I suppose this will do well enough," he said to Lee. "Though those damn Texas banks do go in and out of business like barbershops, the damned fools!"

It was important money for Lee; it was his wintering money. Now he wouldn't have to sell a colt off for grain and supplies.

"Mr. Walker," he said, "I have a notion to get one of the farmers around here to plant some oats and timothy on my place. Maybe some man who's short on land down here in the valley. If he'd do that, I'd go shares with him on the crop and get my horse feed out of the deal."

"Now there's strange talk for a rancher," Walker said. And his hard gray eyes gave Lee a sharp once-over. That look said, What the devil kind of fellow are you, anyway? A saloon tough, a rancher, or what?

"It's a good idea, and maybe I know a farmer'd be glad of the deal, if he could find some suitable meadow up there. Damn short growing season. It's short enough in the valley."

"Well, you get sun up there longer than you do in the valley."

"Yes," the banker said. "But I don't think that makes the difference. Anyway, I'll have Virgil go up and see you on Sunday, if you're going to be out at your place."

"Yes, I will."

"Virgil Payson. He's a nice fellow, and supposed to know his business. And I know he's looking for more growing land, so you might suit."

"All right, I appreciate it."

"Well," the banker said. "I've found that it's good business to put businessmen together. Somehow, the bank always gets something out of it in the end." He

171

gave Lee a minimum smile.

Lee left the bank with a balance in his account of fourteen hundred and seventy-three dollars. And with twenty dollars spending money in his billfold. A solid citizen, a square John, and a man with one killing, one rape, and a black and blue face to his credit.

"The wild West . . ." Rebecca Chase had said.

Wild enough.

He still felt a sharp stitch in his side while he was walking down to the livery. Two little boys walked beside him for a while, copying his walk, the way he held himself.

He didn't do anything to encourage them, and after a while they walked off. He'd had enough of that kind of stuff. He'd even liked it for a time when he was young. To have a bunch of kids hanging around, showing them how to quick draw their wooden guns. Hard to believe he was ever such an ass as to do that.

The livery was off a side street that passed behind Mrs. Boltwith's. It was run by a woman, too, a skinny spinster named McFee. Mary McFee. She had a half-wit boy named Alfred to help her with the chores and mucking out. Supposedly her husband or betrothed or whatever had been killed by Pawnees on the Platte. Though, in Lee's experience, most men supposed to have been killed by Indians had died of the pox or the runs or something unromantic of that sort.

"Great God in Zion!" said Miss McFee. "That Englishman must have put up a heller to mark an American like that!" She was referring to Lee's face.

"Yes," Lee said. And he went over to the dun's stall. The big gelding was happy to see him and whinnied and nuzzled at him.

"Handsome horse," Miss McFee said.

"Yes. What do you have for sale, ma'am?"

"You're not selling that dun!"

"No. I'm looking for a nice pinto." He patted the dun on the nose. The big horse wasn't usually so

172

friendly. "A pony for somebody else."

"Oh, I've got a bunch, all of them prime stock. I don't keep scrubs."

No, Lee thought. I'll wager you don't keep them. You sell them.

"Let's look them over then, Miss McFee."

They walked out to the corral behind the livery, squeezing past old surreys and dusty, broken-down buggies for hire. The place smelled strongly of sour old leather and fresh horse shit.

"There the beauties are," said Miss McFee. "I don't know where that half-wit Alfred's gone to. Alfred! Oh, Alfred! Abusing himself in the tack room, I suppose. If the Lord sends half-wits to hell, that poor boy is headed there on a racer!"

There were seven horses loose in the corral. Three of them were scrubs, galled cow ponies with all the run run out of them. Another was a big sturdy plowhorse, looked like some Belgian in him. There were two pintos and a pretty little mare, a light-built gray with black stockings.

"What are you asking for the young pinto?"

"Oh, that's a fine horse, best Chippewa blood in the state," Miss McFee said. "That's one in a thousand."

"How much?"

"Oh, my goodness, I couldn't let Lightning go for less than $300. Or, since you're a friend, say $275."

"That's a fair price, and I'd pay it too," Lee said, "if I was Andy Carnegie. But since I'm not, I'll offer $75 flat."

"Great God in Zion!" said Miss McFee. "You're a jokester, you are, Mr. Lee!"

And so it went back and forth for several times, until Miss McFee sacrificed Lightning at $97.50, plus an old rope halter and lead.

"Nothing else for you?" asked Miss McFee, noticing that Lee had glanced at the mare quickly, twice. "She is

173

a little beauty, isn't she? Manuela Ryan—the captain's wife up at the lumber camp?—she brought that beauty in here consigned to sale. Manuela's in an interesting condition now, and the captain won't let her ride. Won't hardly let her walk, from what I hear! You'd think a fine figure of an Irishman like that could do better that some dark little dab of a Mexican girl that don't know beans when the bag is open. But that's men for you . . ."

Lee climbed the corral fence, which made his side hurt more than a little, and went slowly up to the mare to look her over. She was a well-behaved, friendly little horse, and had obviously been a lady's pet. She came prancing shyly up to Lee and stretched out her soft muzzle to be stroked.

He slid his hand over her and found no whip weals or galls, no spavin or leg-splint. Her neat little hoofs were sound as stones.

"Two hundred dollars," he said.

"I like a man with a sense of humor," said Miss McFee.

A while later, poorer by $97.50, and by an additional $243.75 for one lady's horse, three years old, furnished with bridle rein, martingale, and a sidesaddle, slightly worn, Lee handed Miss McFee his bank draft for the full amount.

"These monies to be returned to me, Miss McFee, if either animal proves broken-winded."

Miss McFee sighed and said all right. She told Lee that Alfred would bring the dun and pinto around to Mrs. Boltwith's, ready to travel, and that he would then take a note to Beatrice Morgan at the Arcady, telling her that she now owned a fine riding mare named Belita complete with tack.

A half-hour later, Lee rode out of town, the fresh dun dancing, the pinto trotting along at the end of his lead, and Lee's side hurting like the devil. It seemed taped tight enough, but the horse's motion hurt the side anyway. Lee held the dun in and sat a little sideways in the saddle, turned to favor the broken rib.

It was a hot day, the first really hot day that Lee had seen since coming to the valley. The sun came beating down through the clear mountain air, making the brush and grasses gleam with the light. Lee felt the sting of it even under the brim of his Stetson.

He looked back, from time to time, as he rode, checking the paces of the pinto. The small horse had a nice even stride, and he stepped high. A good pony. Fair enough exchange for shooting the boy's out from under him. Fairer than that, when you consider that he'd have been within his rights shooting the boy, too.

And the horse for the girl.

Well, probably something he'd regret, doing that. She was bound to take it as a personal thing. Probably a waste of money there. Nothing wrong with the mare, though.

Once clear of the town, Lee eased his rein and let the dun find his way up the broad meadows. He turned him aside once or twice, but generally the big gelding knew his way after only a couple of trips to town. Good horse.

Summer partridge, looking ragged as chickens, flushed from the scrub as Lee went by, flying in swift angles away, then ducking down into the brush again. There was a day when, broken rib or not, Frank Leslie would have drawn and shot on them. For practice, or just for the hell of it. And probably would have hit one too.

It occurred to Lee then, as it had before, that he might be slowing up with a gun. Well, if he was, it hadn't been enough to do Mickey Slawson any good—and Slawson had been quick.

But had he been a shade off? He sure hadn't tried for Slawson's head. And that Tom Small hadn't been set

175

for a fight; too busy showing off.

And if he was a little slower than when he'd been twenty-three and killed Bob Trout and those other two men, what of it?

Settling down was to be the name of his game now.

Settling down and maybe getting married. It made him uncomfortable to think about it. He saw Rosilie smiling at him every time he really thought about it seriously. Well, it wouldn't be a girl from the valley. Not many farmers or small ranchers would want their darling daughters matched up with a shooter and brawler from God knows where. No. If he ever did make up his mind to do it—and the River Ranch was going to get damned lonely as the years went by if he didn't—he'd have to get a girl from outside. Maybe go to Helena and see about that stock-haul contract on the lumber railroad.

He'd been thinking about that just for his own horses in a few years. But it might make more sense to borrow from the bank for a five-year contract for stock cars. That way every rancher in the valley, and maybe someday every farmer too, would be hauling in his leased cars.

If Walker saw his way clear to making the loan. *And* if the railroad wasn't interested in factoring that hauling business themselves. Maybe not. Maybe not. Those people were lumber people up there, not really railroad people.

A solid businessman in a pretty valley. What would Bob Trout think of that? What would poor Holiday think of it? They'd both probably think it was funny.

He'd thrown away $243.75 on that damn mare.

He was just coming in sight of the river, late in the afternoon, when he saw the Indians. Crees, he supposed. They were fishing in the river.

There looked to be about a half-dozen all together, and a couple of them women.

Lee was considering turning the dun and riding around. A lone man with two good horses was some temptation to poor Indians. He was about to do that when he heard children's voices.

They weren't likely to be wanting trouble with their kids around. Lee aimed the dun for their camp.

There were lots of theories and advice on how to approach wild Indians, and maybe they were useful with wild Indians. But Lee hadn't seen a really wild Indian since he'd seen some naked Commanches riding out of Mexico fifteen or sixteen years ago. And that was only that one time.

Nowadays, most Indians weren't wild; they were just flat broke and out of luck.

He spurred the dun out into the shallow river rapids, hauling the reluctant pinto along behind, and booted the gelding up the opposite bank.

Four Indian men were sitting around a smoke-rack fire, smoking split salmon and trout over a broad bed of coals. One had a pistol in his belt; it looked like a Webley. Some Canadian Mountie must have gotten careless a while ago.

And the man sitting on the near end had a shotgun lying beside him. A single-barreled nothing-much, but a shotgun just the same.

Lee reined the dun over to a larch sapling and tied both horses to it. They'd circle and tangle, but it would take a while.

He nodded to the Indians. A woman was looking out at him from some kind of willow shelter they'd rigged up. She didn't seem too happy to see him. Lee smiled at her and swung down off the dun, keeping his hand away from his revolver. The children by the river didn't even look his way.

He unfastened his saddlebag, dug into it, and brought out one of Mrs. Boltwith's pies, a little the worse for wear. He had two pies in there. She had given them to him to remind Old Bupp what a pie was supposed to be about. He had two, but one was a rhubard pie, and Lee supposed the Indians would prefer the sweetness of the peach.

He took the peach pie out, unwrapped the heavy brown waxed paper she'd put around it, and set it out on the ground beside the campfire. He waved to the woman, pointed to the two little girls playing at the edge of the river, then pointed down to the pie.

Then he sat down and waited for the fish to cook.

CHAPTER TWELVE

There had been no trouble at all from Fishhook. No Fishhook riders had come over the line, and only a few dozen stray Fishhook steers had had to be chivvied back off River land.

Sandburg, Bupp, and Tom Cooke had heard about the fist fight; a cowboy named Budreaux had ridden by. And Bupp wanted to hear about every punch.

"It was just a hard fight, Bupp; let it alone."

"Just a hard fight! You call that telling a story!" Bupp hadn't thought much of the rhubarb pie, either. "Well, thanks for giving the peach pie to those Indians—if there *was* any Indians and you didn't devour all that pie yourself riding up. Peach pie just happens to be the only pie she does proper, I can tell you. And you give it away. A rhubarb pie is no pie at all without strawberries. Every cook in the world knows that . . ."

When Lee asked Sandburg how Bupp's cooking was coming along, Sandburg had considered the question carefully and said, "You still need a knife to get at them eggs."

So Lee told Bupp he'd give him the complete history of the fight with the Englishman the day Bupp cooked a good egg.

The first three days after Lee got back they'd spent

cleaning out brush down by the river crossing. It was rough work, and it played merry hell with Lee's broken rib. After the first day, working with his jaw clenched, and more sweat than usual running off him, Lee had to give up the ax work. He'd driven the team of sorrels they were using to haul and stack the heavier stuff instead. His rib didn't like that much, either, but he could do it.

He was getting so that he liked the rhythm of hard physical work, of using his hands that way. If he could keep liking that, he thought he might make a reasonable rancher some day. He thought he'd be sure to find a good market for the appaloosas over in Helena. They were a special breed, a showy-looking kind of horse as well as being strong mounts. Those rich Mine Kings over there should be happy to buy them.

And he was glad to see Sandburg being more friendly with Tom Cooke. He might not like working with an Indian, but he didn't show it anymore; they seemed to get along all right. It was one of those things that Lee had to worry about, it seemed, until it was fixed or had fixed itself. This one had fixed itself.

The pinto had pleased Tom Cooke, as why in hell shouldn't it?

Late in the afternoon on the third day, it started to look like rain, so they all came up from the river bank, Lee driving the team of sorrels home.

There was a strange horse tied at the house hitching post. Strange for a second, then Lee recognized the mare.

Beatrice Morgan had come to call.

She was sitting in the porch chair. The same chair India Ashton had used.

Sandburg and Tom Cooke raised their hats to her and rode off to the corral. But Bupp stayed to say hello.

"How are you, Miss Morgan?"

"Fine, Mr. Bupp," she said.

"Now, there's a prime little mare . . ." He climbed

off his cob to have a look. "Yes, now, there's a prime little mare."

"Thank you," she said. "Her name's Belita."

"Very nice. Oh, very nice," said Mr. Bupp.

He stroked the little mare's slim legs. "Never thrown out a splint in her life," he said. "What did she cost you?"

"She was a gift, Mr. Bupp."

"Damned nice gift, I say," said Mr. Bupp, and he glanced up at Lee and then went stumping off to the corral, leading the cob behind him.

"Good evening," Lee said to her. "It was nice of you to come see us."

"Not very respectable, I suppose," she said. She was wearing a long riding dress, a blue one, and was holding her straw hat on her lap as she sat. There was no doubt she had nice dark eyes.

"Not very respectable, but I wanted to come and thank you for her. She's too much of a gift, I know . . ." She looked down and toyed with the blue ribbon on her straw hat. "It's embarrassing to have that much of a gift . . . for just nursing you a little. That was nothing at all." She raised her eyes.

"I can tell it embarrasses you to have done it. I shouldn't have come." She stood up.

Lee climbed off the wagon and left it for one of the hands to come and get it.

"Sure, you should," he said. "I gave it to you for that smile you gave me before the fight, not for the nursing."

She blushed like a child. What in God's name was he supposed to do with her?

"Come on inside," he said, "and let's see what we have for supper."

They ate an early supper; rabbit stew and potatoes, and a dry-apple pie. Bupp put extra effort into the pie,

181

and it was quite good, but a little juicy.

"This pie is delicious, Mr. Bupp," she said.

"Call me Tim," said Mr. Bupp.

They all hadn't talked much as they ate; the rabbit stew had been good. Tom Cooke had shot the rabbits on the ridge in early morning.

When supper was over, Bupp scrubbed the dishes, and Sandburg and Tom Cooke said, "Good evening," and got up and left.

"Like to see the place before it gets dark?" Lee said to her.

"Oh, I would," she said. "My father raised horses. We had Morgan horses on our place in Illinois. People used to make jokes about Mr. Morgan raising Morgan horses."

They were walking out behind the house.

"Well, come on up to the meadow and see my young ones," Lee said. "If you like horses, you'll like them."

He led her out around the bunkhouse. He could hear Sandburg in there singing "Hop Up, My Ladies." It was a favorite song of his, and he had a nice deep voice to sing it with.

"What a pretty song," she said. "I don't think I ever heard that song."

"It's a square-dance song," Lee said. "We danced to that tune when I was a kid."

"Not us," she said. "My folks didn't let us dance at all. And my mother would only let us sing church songs in the house, except at haying . . ."

She walked along for a while without saying anything more, lifting the long skirt of her dress to keep it clear of grass.

"I suppose you think that's pretty funny—strange, I mean," she said. "For me to have been raised that way and turn out to become what I have." She looked over at him. "How I make my living . . ."

"I told you before that makes no difference to me at

all. That's not my business," Lee said.

"Yes, you're right," she said. "I only mention it all the time to keep you people from thinking about it secretly." She smiled. "As if that makes any sense at all . . ."

It was just the sort of thing that Lee didn't want to hear. If she wanted to come up, all right. There was no need for her to harp on being a whore, or talk about what he was thinking, either.

"There are the horses," he said.

The evening light was going fast. The two colts and the little filly, Lightning Bug, were playing in the long grass, galloping, rearing, kicking like lambs. They usually slept through the afternoon or wandered beside their mothers through the meadows. But in the evening, when it cooled, they became as lively as in the morning and played together, chasing each other more like puppies than young horses.

The little filly was racing ahead of the colts, kicking up her spotted behind and galloping along, her short, feathery tail cocked straight up in the air.

"What a darling," Beatrice Morgan said. "What do you call her?"

"Lightning Bug."

They watched the young horses running for a while.

"Is there something wrong with his eye?" she said, pointing at the bigger of the two colts. "He shakes his head and turns sideways when he runs."

Lee watched that colt, a tall, black-headed colt he was thinking of calling Long Tom. It ran along with no changes to its gait for a few strides. Then, just when he was about to tell her it was nothing, Lee saw the colt quickly shake its head, as if a fly was bothering it. It cantered sideways for a few dancing steps before it dug in to gallop after the others.

"Goddammit!" Lee said. "What the hell have Bupp and those two been doing not to see that!" He looked at the girl beside him. "You have a good eye for horses," he said.

"It might be nothing," the girl said. "Just a scratch from some tree branch."

Lee went down to the barn for a rope, and when he came back up, he'd brought Bupp and the other men with him and had apparently been talking to them unkindly, because Tim Bupp had nothing to say.

Lee coaxed the colt in and roped him gently, then went up the rope hand over hand, talking soothingly all the while. Then he and Bupp went over the colt carefully. It was nearly dark by then, and Tom Cooke went down and got a lantern.

The colt's left eye was scratched.

"Nothing too bad there, Mr. Lee, I promise you," Bupp said. "I'll wash it out with a little salt water tonight, and in a couple of days it'll be healed right up."

"If the colt will stand a muslin cloth drawn over the eye, I believe that will help keep it from inflaming the next day or so," Beatrice said.

"He probably won't stand it," Bupp said.

"Do it," said Lee.

"Now—"

"Do it."

"Unless you feel a patch would be better, Mr. Bupp," Beatrice said.

"Yes, I do," Bupp said. "This calls for a patch, and that's flat."

"All right," Lee said. "Let's take him down to the barn and get it done."

The colt didn't like it, but he was patient enough as Bupp washed the eye out with mild salt water and made a patch and tied it on with torn strips of cloth. Bupp was working by the light of two lanterns in a stall at the end of the barn. The main thing worrying the colt was being away from his mother and the other horses. Beatrice stood by him and soothed him, and she had torn the

184

cloth ties for Bupp. She congratulated him on the neat patch he made.

When they finished with the colt, they decided to let it loose with the others, and Tom Cooke led it back up to the meadows.

After the men went back to the bunkhouse, Lee took Beatrice up to the house. They didn't say much on the walk.

She'd intended to stay, at least for the night, for sure, or she wouldn't have come up so late. Lee supposed she'd intended to bed down with him, but he didn't feel like it. There was something uncomfortable about the whole situation for him.

"Do you want me to make us some coffee?" she said when they went into the house.

"All right; I could do with a cup."

They sat at the kitchen table after the coffee was made and didn't say much of anything. It was a quiet night, almost no wind at all, and the only noise in the kitchen was the ticking of the iron stove as it cooled and a moth's fluttering against a lantern's smoky mantle.

She cleared her throat. "You have such a pretty place up here, Mr. Lee. You must be very happy with it."

"I guess you can call me Lee," he said, "and drop the 'mister,' since you're a guest in my house."

"All right," she said.

"My first name's Frederick, but most people call me Lee."

"All right."

They sat for a little longer, until the first light of the rising moon shone in through the kitchen window. Beatrice leaned over to put the lantern out so the room was only lit by the moonlight.

After awhile, Lee stood up.

"It's time for bed," he said. "You take my bedroom; I'll bunk out in the office."

"All right," she said. "I'm sorry to have come up so

late and put you to this trouble." Her face was smooth and white in the moonlight; her eyes were shadowed and dark.

"No trouble," Lee said. He bent to light the lantern for her to take to the bedroom. "Do you have night things?"

"I'll seep in my shift," she said.

He woke to her singing the next morning. She had a sweet voice, but she sang a little off tune. She was singing "Shenandoah."

When he got his shirt and pants on, Lee went down the hall to the kitchen. Beatrice was out in the yard washing her dress and shift in a fire-blackened old wash tub. The tub was propped up on four big rocks, and she had gotten kindling and built a fire under it.

She was wrapped from neck to toe in one of the blankets, had it pinned in place somehow, and was scrubbing her dress and shift. Lee saw her stockings and underthings, too. She was singing away, a little off tune, and looked happy as a spring robin.

Seeing she was out of the house for a while, Lee stripped and washed at the kitchen pump, then went and got clean clothes in the bedroom.

She'd slept in it only the one night, but the room already smelled of a woman.

When he'd dressed and come out, Bupp was in the kitchen starting breakfast.

"You're a little late, aren't you, Tim?"

Bupp gave him a sly glance. "Better too late than too early," he said and went back to greasing the skillet.

Beatrice came in the kitchen door with her arms full of wet clothes.

"Have you a clothesline and some pins, Mr. Lee?"

"Just Lee."

"Lee?"

186

"No, I guess not. We have some light line in the barn, but I don't think we have any clothespins at all."

"How do you dry your clothes?" she said.

"Generally," Lee said, "well, generally we dry them over the porch rail."

"I'll call Tom Cooke to get you some line," Bupp said.

"No, no. I'll put these over the rail. They'll catch the sun fine there."

She hurried through the kitchen with the damp clothes, and Lee saw the slim, bare whiteness of her feet flash under the edge of the blanket.

"I'm cooking ham and eggs for breakfast," Bupp said.

"Eggs?"

"Yes, dammit, eggs. There's nothing wrong with my eggs."

"So you say. What about the colt?"

"That scratch is clearing already. It wasn't much, and it couldn't have been bothering him long, or we'd have seen him favoring it . . ."

"So you say." Now she had all the men winking at him and starting work late so he could fuck his head off, as they supposed. It annoyed him.

Then Sandburg and Tom Cooke showed up, also way late to be eating breakfast. At least they kept their faces straight and didn't favor him with any of Bupp's sass.

When they were all seated at the kitchen table, Beatrice still wrapped in her blanket, Bupp started frying the ham in a big skillet and the eggs in a smaller one. He fried them for a considerable time.

"Tim," Beatrice said.

"Yes, ma'am?"

"Would you do me a favor?"

"Well, I probably would . . ."

"You see, I like my eggs way underdone, and I would

187

appreciate it if you'd let me have mine before they're really full cooked."

"You like underdone eggs?"

"I like them next thing to raw, Tim."

"Well, if you can eat them that way, not hardly cooked at all . . ."

He slid a wide-bladed butcher knife under two of the eggs and put them on a plate for her. They were already pretty hard. Then he added a slice of the ham and two of yesterday's biscuits, warmed up, to soak in the ham's gravy.

"I'll try mine underdone too," Lee said.

Sandburg and Tom Cooke said the same thing.

"Now, come on! You can't all like them eggs raw," Bupp said.

"Serve 'em out," Sandburg said. "I'll try anything."

After breakfast, Lee went down with the men to knock out the beams of the old tool shed. They'd been spiked in wrong to start with, and water running down the posts had rotted their ends out.

They pulled what spikes and nails they could, starting on the door-end beam, then got a trace chain wrapped around it and hitched the team of sorrels to the hook. The beam came tearing out like a rotten tooth.

But the second one split, and they had to pry and hammer that one out the hard way. Lee was worried that if they got too rough they'd have the whole shed down, which, except for that run of beams, was in good shape.

The third one popped out easy, though, and it looked as though they had their method for doing it down pat.

Beatrice came down from the house to see that one go. Her clothes had dried in the morning sunshine by then, and she had her blue dress on again. She looked nice, but Lee thought he'd have to figure out a way to ask her when she intended to be heading back to town. Even though there was nothing wrong with her looks, barring, maybe, that her nose was a little big.

A whore on a ranch.

Ladylike or not, I'll find her out in the bushes with Tom Cooke if I'm not careful . . .

A dirty thing to think. He didn't believe it himself.

Though she'd sure as hell got down on her knees in front of some lumberjacks down at Rebecca's. You could bet on that. Not so much of a lady at five bucks a throw!

They got the fourth beam hooked up, cleared the chain, and Sandburg started out the sorrels. The beam groaned and then cracked free like a gunshot and flew out into the dirt.

"Now that's something like it!" yelled Bupp.

They had the beam business down pat.

"Would you like to take a ride around the ranch, Beatrice?" Lee asked her.

"Yes, yes, I would; it's so pretty. But I don't want to interrupt your work. And I do have to get back to town."

"Oh, a ride won't take long," Lee said. "The boys can finish this out."

Lee saw Bupp give Sandburg a glance at that. Well, the hell with them. If he had to worry for them, they could damn well work for him. It's what he was paying them for.

The little mare was a good goer. She could keep up with the dun quite well on level ground, and she went up and over banks and scrub like a rabbit, with Beatrice hanging on for dear life and laughing.

"I love her," she said. "She's a brave little horse." She bent and stroked the mare's sleek side.

"You look well together," Lee said. It was true enough. No reason not to tell the girl so.

Lee hadn't intended to go that far, but they stayed

out the whole afternoon, ate cold ham and biscuits and two damp pieces of Bupp's dry-apple pie. They got all the way up to the river falls.

It was near the ford where Lee had hung the cowboy, and he didn't want Beatrice seeing it or asking questions about it. So he turned off short at the rapids and found a place where they could water the horses.

Beatrice took off her high-button boots and her stockings and sat on the bank splashing her feet in the water.

Afterwards he gave her the cloth Martin had cut for him so she could dry her feet.

"My, what a pretty color," she said.

"It's for a neckerchief."

"Mr. Martin gave it to you, I'll bet," she said. "My, but that man has fine taste! Did you know he was from one of the finest families in New Orleans?"

"So I understand," Lee said. "I believe, though, that he doesn't think much of the Leicester family, the earl's family over in England . . ."

Beatrice laughed. "Yes, I know. He's always talking about that. But I think he's very fond of Mr. Ashton, has sort of a crush on him, you know?" She blushed.

"Hell, yes I know!" Lee said. "And for God's sake stop blushing, Beatrice. You're a damned saloon girl!"

"Yes." She blushed and then laughed. "I'm doing it again, I suppose."

"Yes . . ." Lee said. "Well, I think we ought to start back."

When they reached the meadows above the east ridge, she wanted to race. They rode the horses abreast, she counted to three, and off they went.

The little mare was handy and quick, and for a few strides she kept up. Then the dun began to pull ahead. Lee held him in. He didn't want to widen the gap. They thundered over the ridge at a hard gallop, the little mare just behind. They jumped a low hedge of pitch pine, threaded through some trees—the mare doing even that—and ran flat out down the wide bowl of the pasture, headed for the bunkhouse.

Tom Cooke was out by the corral and saw them coming. Lee could see that he thought for a moment there might be trouble. But a moment later, when the boy could make out their faces and knew there wasn't trouble, he called out a long, yodeling Indian yell to spur them on.

The dun was driving hard for the finish now, and Lee had the devil's own time to hold him up without the girl seeing it, but he managed it so they flew into the bunkhouse yard almost together. They were going so fast that they had to haul around the corner of the building before they could stop.

"Oh, oh," the girl called out, breathless. "You dog, you cheated! You pulled that poor big horse in!" She patted her little mare. "Never mind, Belita, we did very well!"

That night they had a very good dinner.

By the time the mare was rested, it was too late for Beatrice to get back down to Cree before dark. She asked to go, and Bupp offered to ride down with her. They needed more flour and a basket of eggs. And Lee had forgotten the horse liniment when he'd come up from town.

But Lee said no. There were Crees fishing the river, and it would be better if she rode in daylight. Bupp could go with her the next day. And so she stayed.

Tom Cooke had shot a deer, and Bupp baked a cake. That was where the last of the flour and eggs had gone. He'd baked the cake from memory, from seeing Mrs. Boltwith bake one for Chris Nasby's birthday. Old Nasby was foreman out at Bent Iron and as harsh an old man as there ever was. His cowboys had been hoping a real birthday cake would soften him up, and as it turned out it did. A cowpoker had come in the next day to thank Mrs. Boltwith personally. Said the old Tartar had broken down and cried.

This was the cake that Bupp tried to remember while he baked it.

It was just the cake part. He didn't have any cream or chocolate or vanilla for the icing. Sandburg picked him some berries. Blackberries and red raspberries were what he had.

The venison was fresh, but very good, and they had roast potatoes and carrots with it, all freighted up from town with the feed and seed.

The venison and vegetable were very good. The vegetables were a treat, not something that Lee could keep buying like that. Rather sooner than later, Bupp was going to have to start a kitchen garden.

Then came the cake.

It didn't look very good. Something had happened to the middle of it. It was sagged down. Looks were exchanged around the table, but nobody said anything. Beatrice had asked Bupp if there was anything at all she could do to help out, but he'd told her no.

Bupp sliced it for everybody, saying he didn't want it messed up. Lee took the first bite, and it was good. It was quite good. The taste wasn't exactly like cake; it was more like a big damp cookie. But it was very rich and good, especially with the berries poured over it.

Beatrice said that it was the best thing of the kind she'd ever had and that Bupp had better be sure and remember the recipe.

So there was nothing the matter with the dinner. Afterwards Sandburg brought up his checker set. His boy had been a bear at checkers, and they played by the lamplight. Tim Bupp beat them all. It was Bupp's evening.

When the men were gone to the bunkhouse, Lee and Beatrice sat awhile in the kitchen the way they had the night before. They didn't say much. Lee still felt uncomfortable about her. Just being with her in the kitchen made him restless. She was a difficult girl to figure out, and, like most women he had known, she worked at it to make the figuring more difficult.

It was hard to imagine her taking five dollars to do some of the things men liked. And that was her game, as he well knew, to make that difficult to imagine.

When they got up to go to sleep, she went to the bedroom as she had the night before. Lee went to the little office room.

He didn't know whether she wanted him to just let her come and visit and go away again like a decent girl or if she wanted him in bed.

He lay on the narrow horsehair sofa in the ranch office, watching the branches of a pine outside the window cast black, moving shadows onto the room wall. It looked like a big eagle's wing, a black wing beating slowly on the wall.

He waited a long time. Then he stopped thinking about what the girl wanted and got up and went down the hall into the bedroom.

CHAPTER THIRTEEN

She was awake. From the doorway, he saw her lying beneath the rough sheet, her arms and throat and face white, gleaming in the moonlight flooding through the bedroom windows. She was looking at him.

He went over to her without a word, reached down, and slowly pulled the sheet back. Her thin cotton shift was as white as her skin.

She lay watching him and didn't say anything.

He reached down, slipped his hand through her thick dark hair, and gripped her by the back of her neck. Then he took her by the arm with his other hand and pulled her up off the bed until she was standing there against him, barefoot and small.

When he took the material of her shift in his hands, she raised her arms like a child being undressed. He slipped the material up and off.

Then he took his hands away and looked at her.

She was almost thin, with narrow hips and slim legs. He could see the rippled outline of her ribs under the soft white skin. Her breasts were sharp pointed and heavy for her size. They sagged a little and swung slightly when she breathed. They cast shadows in the moonlight against her skin.

He reached out, took them in his hands, and squeezed gently, then harder, weighing them in his grip, tugging gently at her nipples. She swayed against him as he pulled and stroked and played with her until her long nipples were swollen and stiff. Then he put his arms around her, a hand under her buttocks, and lifted her up onto the bed.

He slid in after her, knelt over her, and put his hand over the warm thatch of dark hair at her groin. He rubbed her there until he felt her damp and wet. Then he pushed a finger into her. He left it in her for a few moments, then pulled it out, raised his hand, and held the moist finger to her lips, stroking her lips with it.

He felt her open her mouth. She licked at the wet finger gently, sucking and biting at it as delicately as a kitten.

"You like that, don't you?" he said to her softly. "You've taken some cunt, haven't you, in your time?"

She looked up at him. Dark eyes. And didn't say a word.

"I've got something else for you, little whore," he said. His cock was up and hurting him, it was so hard.

He knelt up higher, over her, took a handful of her hair, and pulled her up to it. She thrust her face up and took it, moaning, as if she were desperate, and licked and sucked at it, not caring what sounds she made.

After a few moments, he pushed her away, forcing her head back down to the pillow. She lay, panting, looking up at him.

"That's what you're good for," he said.

And she smiled up at him and shook her head, then lifted her slender arms to him and said, "Oh, my dearest . . ."

She took him in like a river.

Early in the morning they heard Bupp and the others in the kitchen, talking softly, getting their breakfast. Later they heard horses out by the corral and Bupp saying something to someone.

Then, in a few minutes, horses' hoofbeats. Then nothing at all but singing birds from time to time and the sound of wind in the trees around the house.

They fucked and made love, and made love and fucked again, and while they were lying still, resting in each other's arms, she told him how she came to whoring, what her family had been, and her life. And how ashamed she'd been of the pleasure that she'd sometimes got in whoring.

"The other girls would say they always hated it and got no pleasure at all. But I sometimes did. Sometimes, if the man was nice, or handsome, or somebody I could dream about. Then I got pleasure from it. I didn't care what they did, sometimes. Once four men took me up to a room and they made me do everything . . . and I liked it." She started to cry. "That makes me as bad as a girl can get, I guess . . ."

"Not for me," he said. "Or any other man who is a man."

But he didn't tell her about himself.

He told her some things, about where he was born and his family, and something about the horse work he'd done as a young man. He told her of hunting and riding guard, of getting into the sporting life and gambling. And he told her about Mexico and being a gunhand for an old man.

But he didn't tell her that he had killed more than thirty men face to face.

He didn't tell her his name.

They didn't eat breakfast. They took some biscuits and cold venison and went down to the corral and saddled their horses, standing the animals side by side. Beatrice knew what she was doing, but Lee checked the mare's girth just the same, to be sure she hadn't held her breath when Beatrice tightened the cinch ring.

Then they rode back up to the river and swam naked at noon in a pool. The running water made little eddies past a boulder. The water was cold as snow and the sun was hot.

They ate their venison and biscuits by the river and spent the rest of the day riding hard over the north boundary of the ranch. It was big-pine country up there, and Lee showed her the place he was planning to put in a line shack so that a small crew could cover the place better, with a man posted high on the mountain for roundups and drives when the horseherd bigged up. The line shack could come right out of that heavy timber, cut two-feet square so a little green warping wouldn't matter.

They talked about cabins and how they were best made. Beatrice described one her father had put up with nothing but an ax and an adz when he was young. The corners all stacked and fitted square, no notched logs at all.

Then they pushed the horses down into scrub country, the little mare jumping and bucketing along, with Beatrice laughing and hanging on.

They rode past the place where Lee had raped India Ashton, and Beatrice asked him what was wrong. He shrugged, and they went on by, Beatrice thinking she'd been mistaken. But he was quieter for the rest of the ride. Thinking about the Ashtons. Thinking what Rosilie would have thought of Beatrice. Probably wouldn't have liked her. Rosilie was red-headed with blue eyes. Beatrice was dark. And Rosilie was always laughing, even when something hurt her. She had had the courage of a brave lad about everything. Beatrice was a softer, sadder girl. She only laughed a lot when she was riding.

Wouldn't have liked her. Always mooning around about something, she'd have said. And she hardly has any legs at all . . . sticks, more like it . . .''

197

Rosilie had even laughed when she was dying. "That's one on us," she'd said. "But you're not getting out of a wedding that easy, Frankie, not that easy." And then she was dead. In his arms, just like in a storybook.

Oh, how he'd killed Johnny Deuce! And if he'd killed him a thousand times—a thousand *thousand* times—it wouldn't be the beginning of enough.

They rode in silence down to the west ridge, and Beatrice didn't ask him if anything was wrong.

They saw Sandburg working on the fence in the upper meadows. He waved, but they didn't stop.

At supper, Beatrice was very nice and told funny stories to them about her grandfather Zebedee, who captained a pig boat on the Mississippi. He had known Mike Fink well and said that Mike was nothing out of the ordinary in size, but was a fierce biter in a fight. Once he started to lose a fight, her grandfather said, Fink would start in biting like a bulldog. Some boatmen had got together once and bought Fink a collar and chain for his birthday. On the collar it said: *He Bites.*

Her grandfather had met Jim Bowie twice, and Bupp and Sandburg wanted to know about him. A tall, handsome man with good manners and black sideburns, her grandfather had said. A Kaintuck with New Orleans manners.

"What about his knife?" asked Bupp.

"Grandad never saw no knife on him. A businesslike gentleman," Beatrice answered.

"If you believe it," said Bupp. "That man was a devil out of hell in a fight!"

After supper—something had gone wrong with Bupp's berry pie; it tasted of salt—they all went out to the porch to drink their coffee. Tom Cooke stood at the rail.

The sun was setting over the mountains in a very fiery

way, all golds and greens and burning reds.

"The Assyrian came down like a wolf on the fold," Beatrice said, quoting from a poem.

They all joined in, except Tom Cooke: "And his chariots were painted in purple and gold."

The sunset looked just like that.

That night was as fine as the night before had been. They were very good to each other, and Lee felt more and more for the girl. It was getting to be a serious thing the more time she spent at the ranch.

In the morning, he asked her what trouble Rebecca might give her about missing work at the Arcady.

"The hell with her," Beatrice said.

Lee got back to work that day, and Beatrice worked with them, helping to load fence rails after Lee and Sandburg had cut them out and then driving the team down to the meadows. She had a natural way with horses, and the sorrels didn't make any trouble for her.

They worked hard all day because the upper pasture needed to be fenced before they could turn the mares out into it. Tom Cooke had seen mustangs near the Fishhook line, and, branded stock or not, Lee didn't want them at his mares. If there was a stallion among them, there'd be trouble with Shokan. The big appaloosa had crippled another stud the month before Lee bought him.

They got the south line finished before dark, had a cold supper with Bupp's salty berry pie, which didn't taste as bad as it had the night before, and went to bed.

Beatrice rubbed Lee's back to get the aches out, and then they started to play wrestle and so forth. They broke the bed. The side split, and the slats fell out on the floor. So they dragged the mattress onto the floor, too, and slept on it there.

Beatrice stayed up at the River Ranch for three more days and might have stayed longer. But on Friday morning, while Bupp and Sandburg were in the corral yard digging post holes, and Lee and Tom Cooke were down in the mud laying a new length of lead pipe to the trough, a man came riding up from the valley.

Beatrice had done her washing and was hanging her shift and dress out over the porch rail to dry. She'd taken to wearing one of Lee's shirts and a pair of his trousers rolled up at the cuffs and tied around the waist with a piece of cord.

She'd looked out over the valley and seen the man riding up some distance away.

She called down to the corral, and Tom Cooke climbed out of the ditch and up onto a fence rail for a look.

"Old man," he said to Lee. And Lee nodded and kept working. It might be that farmer Walker was sending up. What was the man's name? Virgil something. Payton? Something like that.

Lee climbed out of the ditch and wiped his hands on his new bandanna. Beatrice had hemmed it for him with a needle and thread he kept for sewing up the horses when they were hurt. He'd told her what Mr. Martin had said, and she'd double hemmed it.

He walked past the corral to meet the farmer coming in. An old man, somewhere in his fifties, maybe late fifties, in a rusty black suit. Neat white hair under a black slouch hat.

Lee stopped where he was and tried to think how he might get back to his gun. He'd left his gunbelt hanging on the fence when he started working down in the mud.

And it looked like that was going to kill him, because this old man was no farmer.

The old man rode closer, and when he stopped his horse about a dozen feet away, he turned it to clear his right side. The suit coat was tucked back, and the worn butt of a Colt Peacemaker curved up out of a tie-down holster. The old man's foot was out of that stirrup, hanging straight down so as not to cramp his draw.

His eyes were a pleasant brown.

"You'd be Mr. Lee," he said. He had a slow border drawl.

George Small, as sure as God made little green apples.

It felt strange to Lee. He'd thought of being killed, although never while he was gunfighting. He used to think about it afterwards. And here it was. This old man was going to kill him now. And he'd kill the others—no witnesses.

Oh, Beatrice, I did you no favor.

"That's right," he said. "And you'd be George Small."

The old man's brown eyes twinkled like a sweet grandad's. He glanced down at Lee's waist where his gun would be.

"White hair fooled you, didn't it?"

"That's right."

"Young men these days . . ." he shook his head, "just ain't raised right."

He was going for it. Lee saw the relaxation in his eyes.

"Good morning!"

The old man froze.

It was Beatrice, come down from the porch.

"My," she said, "you must have started from town real early, mister. Please to step down and have some breakfast with us."

The old man must have seen her standing up at the house, but he hadn't realized she was a woman.

And he wasn't going to kill her. The not-going-to-do-it look was in his eyes. Lee could see it.

Can't kill the woman, can't kill the rest. Can't kill Lee.

Lee took a deep breath. The morning air was sweet as

fine champagne.

"Do," he said to George Small. "Step down and have some breakfast with us."

The old man threw back his head and laughed like a boy.

"You're a tarnation fool for luck, Mr. Lee," he said. He swept his slouch hat off and made a bow in the saddle to Beatrice. "In more than one way that I can see." He smiled at Lee in a friendly fashion. "I don't have time to stop for breakfast, but perhaps if your lady will excuse us, we might talk some business."

"Oh, yes," said Beatrice, "I'm sorry. You're sure you won't have even some coffee, Mr.—"

"Small," he said. "George Small." He bowed to her again. "But I thank you kindly for the offer."

She smiled back and turned and walked away toward the house.

"If this matter is about your brother, Mr. Small," Lee said. "You're on a fool's errand. Your brother rustled some of my stock and then murdered a boy who tried to stop him."

"So I've heard, and I'm sorry to say I wasn't the least surprised," the old man said. "Tom was a rotten pup; bound to make a rotten dog. Though naturally I was a slightway curious who stopped his clock."

"If not over that then, why are you here?" Lee said.

The old man's eyes looked merrier than ever.

"Business," he said. "You have apparently offended a young lady. The young lady is rich and has engaged me to redress her injury."

He tucked his foot back in the stirrup, flipped his coattail over the butt of his revolver, and turned his horse to go.

"Mr. Lee," he said, over his shoulder. "I'll expect you in town tomorrow. Don't disappoint me, now . . ."

And off he rode, straight and easy in the saddle, and

fresh as paint.

Lee couldn't fight him. Barring that he didn't want to fight the old man, he just couldn't weather another killing. One more shooting and Tod Phipps would have to call him out. For if he didn't, and the cowboys got the notion that Phipps was afraid, his day as Marshal was done. Phipps was not the man to let that ride.

Win or lose, either way it would finish Lee in the valley. He'd be marked a cold killer.

The old man was downy. It should be possible to talk sense to him—or pay him off if it came to that.

He walked slowly back to the corral and took his gunbelt down and buckled it around his waist.

"Will he raise the hay?" Sandburg said.

"What's wrong?" said Tim Bupp.

Lee saw Tom Cooke come running from the bunkhouse. He had his old Spencer rifle. He slowed down when he saw the old man had ridden off and stood in the yard watching him go out of sight.

"What's wrong?" Sandburg said.

"Will Mr. Payson do the hay?" Beatrice said. She'd remembered the farmer's name.

"That wasn't Payson," Lee said.

He went up to the kitchen to get a cup of coffee and to have some time away from the men to think. Beatrice was making a berry pie. Bupp had said it was all right, since pies weren't serious cooking.

"Is something worrying you?" she said.

"That's Tom Small's brother."

"Oh, my God," Beatrice said. She put her hand to her mouth. "Has he put the law on you? There's a federal marshal in Helena."

"That's not his style," Lee said. "I hope you're not putting any salt in that pie . . ."

"No," she said, "I'm not." She was rolling out the dough with an old sarsparilla bottle. "Do you want me to go down to town now, Lee?"

203

"You're welcome here for as long as you like. You're about the hardest worker I've got."

She was reforming the dough, packing it into a ball, and then kneading it, squeezing it between her fingers.

"I'll go."

"Not to Rebecca's. Unless you want to."

She sighed. "No, I won't go back to Rebecca's."

"If she makes any trouble for you at all, Beatrice, tell her I said to leave you alone."

Beatrice smiled and rolled the dough out again.

"Rebecca doesn't pay much attention to what men say, except for Mr. Phipps."

"Just tell her what I said. She won't bother you."

Beatrice draped the dough down into the pie pan, crimping it around the edge with her thumb. Lee sipped his coffee and sat watching her while she got a tomato can full of raspberries from the food safe and poured them into the pan, stirring them with her finger to even them out. Then she sprinkled sugar over them.

"I never learned to make an open-top pie without it drying out," she said.

"You can come up again . . . in a while . . . when this blows over."

"Would it help if I talked to Mr. Small? He seemed like a nice old man. I'll bet he didn't know what that brother of his was up to."

She'd learn soon enough once she was back in town.

"George Small is a bad man, Beatrice. A gunhand. I suppose twice the man his kid brother ever was . . ."

She put the pie plate down, and he saw that her left hand was trembling. A nervous girl.

"But he . . ." she sounded breathless, "he could have shot you. You didn't have your gun! And he didn't!"

"Because you came down just then. He's an old-fashioned man, I suppose."

"Are you sure he's so bad? People change . . ."

Lee finished his coffee and stood up.

204

"When you put that pie in the oven, come down to the corral. We're going to pull that old pipe; I want you to drive the team."

The rest of the day was like the other days had been.

Lee stopped Bupp from talking about Small and what had happened and kept them all at the work. And that was hard enough. The water pipe had been of good quality. It was fine two-inch lead pipe. But it had been laid in thirty-foot lengths. They were more than one man—or four men and a girl—could lift, unless they wanted to be rough and lever it around and bend it, maybe break it.

Lee had an idea that it had been laid into place by a couple of drag teams from the lumber camp. It was the sort of work those people were used to doing.

So he had the men dig a dirt ramp to the new trench the pipe was to rest in, and then worked out a way to get two teams on the job, pulling together: one team to haul the pipe straight out, taking most of the weight, the other team to slew it sideways off the ramp into the trench. It was hard work. Just picking a second team from the riding stock and tacking up a harness for them took a lot of time.

If he'd had the braces, wrenches, and a man who knew pipe soldering, he might have sawed the damn pipes up into short lengths, laid them where he wanted them, and then rejoined the pieces.

If he had the braces, the wrenches, and the man.

They finally got it done late in the afternoon after two false starts that took an hour each to rerig and set up all over again. They got the pipe laid in, well supported, all the way from the pump-off pipe beneath the house, out across the yard, and down to the corral troughs.

Straight, easy flowing, and buried two feet deep. Counting digging out the ditch the day before, it was two days' work.

Lee had enjoyed every bit of it. He'd made certain of that, knowing trouble was coming. It was as if he were storing up the day, storing up the River Ranch, and Beatrice, and the men, to last him for a long while.

He'd decided to go into town and offer George Small a thousand dollars if he would give India Ashton back her money. She surely couldn't have paid him more than that, and probably a damn sight less.

It would mean selling a colt for sure, maybe the filly, Lightening Bug, to get through the winter. But it was the only way to stay in the valley as a rancher instead of as some shooter for the weeklies to come and write about, always figuring he killed the old man. That could fall out differently, too.

It would cost him the last of the Mexican money. But it might be done. The old man seemed reasonable enough.

And he'd had this good day of work and the pleasure of Beatrice being on his place. There were a lot of things not as good as all that.

After supper that night, they all sat out on the front porch and drank their coffee and ate Beatrice's berry pie.

"It's a good pie," Bupp said. "I'll say it before anyone else does. It's as good a pie as any I can make."

After the men went down to the bunkhouse, Beatrice and Lee stayed out on the porch awhile, watching the moon come up over the mountains.

After an hour, its light filled the whole valley below like silver in a cup.

They left early the next morning. Lee on his big dun, Beatrice on Belita. Beatrice was wearing her blue dress again.

"What are you going to do in town?" Lee asked her.

"I'll help Mrs. Boltwith with the maid work at her place, and maybe Mr. Martin will let me keep his stock . . ."

"Not serve his customers?"

"No," she said, reining the little mare in. "The ladies wouldn't take cloth from me."

"Beatrice . . ."

"Don't you say anything more to me," she said, "or I'll start to cry, and I know you don't like that about me." She spurred Belita and rode on ahead.

When they reached the valley at the lower river crossing, Lee had to turn back and wait until Tom Cooke came up behind them. He'd followed them all morning, with his Spencer rifle across his saddlebow. Lee looked back and saw some blackbirds rising from the scrub where the boy was following.

It took some doing to get Tom Cooke to turn around and go home, but he finally turned and went, walking his pinto out of sight into the dwarf willow.

Lee and Beatrice rode on across the river and out onto the valley grass toward Cree.

The town was quiet when they rode in, and they went to Mrs. Boltwith's first. The lady was in her kitchen, and she seemed pleased to see them together.

"Now, you two are showing a little sense!" she said. "Beatrice, Rebecca is fit to be tied. Miss High and Mighty isn't used to having a girl ride off on her like that." She glanced at Lee. "Do you know that woman tried to get Marshal Phipps to go out after her as a thief?"

"For what?" said Beatrice. "I never stole a thing in my life!"

"She said a silver bracelet."

"That makes me laugh," said Beatrice. "To hear a tale like that! She sold bracelets to me and Sally Betts and took the price out of our money every week. I bought that damn bracelet twice over!"

"What did Phipps do?" Lee asked.

"He had to go to Butte last week, or he might have come out after you. Those two are thick as thieves, and so they should be, for thieves is what they are. Silver bracelets!"

"I'm not going back to work," Beatrice said.

"Well, hallelujah!" said Mrs. Boltwith, and she glanced at Lee. "Child, that's good news. You come and work here at the hotel for me, and you'll be company, too."

Beatrice started to sniff and dab at her eyes, and Mrs. Boltwith hugged her.

"Have you got a man staying here?" Lee said to Mrs. Boltwith. "A decent-looking old man. He has white hair."

"The only old man I've got here is the minister, Mr. Pierce. And that poor man has got no hair on his head at all. Try over at Mrs. Foster's. Poor Reba'll take anything that moves and has two dollars to rub together."

Lee got up. "Well," he said, "I'll be going."

Beatrice looked at him, but she didn't say anything.

"We'll fix up your room for you, Mr. Lee," Mrs. Boltwith said. "My new maid-girl and me." She gave Beatrice a nudge with her elbow.

"Goodbye," Lee said.

Beatrice just looked at him and said nothing.

Lee went down the boardwalk to the bank. He had to wait for a farmer to finish business, and then cashed a hand draft for one thousand dollars.

Lee borrowed a piece of paper and a clerk's pen in the bank and wrote a note.

Mr. Small:

Enclosed you will find a thousand dollars

cash. I think it makes good sense for both of us, for you to take this, and go back home with it, in a peaceable fashion.

Frederick Lee

Then he put the ten one-hundred dollar bills in with the note and borrowed another piece of paper to fold it up in. The clerk sealed it for him with the bank's wax and stamp.

On the way out of the bank, Lee passed the land agent, Calthrop. The land agent nodded and passed on his way, still grudging from the way Lee had spoken to him about his loose tongue.

At Mrs. Foster's he asked for George Small.

"Mr. Small is out just now," said Mrs. Foster, who was a tiny lady with a milky-white blind eye.

"I would like to leave something for him," Lee said. "It's important that he get it personally."

The little lady bristled up like a porcupine.

"This is a respectable premises," she said. "If you leave a message for a boarder, then that boarder will get the message—unopened!" She gave Lee a hard look out of her good eye.

He handed the paper to her.

"I'm at Mrs. Boltwith's," he said. The one-eyed lady sniffed at that. "You can reach me there—if there's an answer."

Lee picked up the two horses in front of Mrs. Boltwith's and led them around to the livery.

Miss McFee wasn't there, so he handed the horses over to her half-witted hostler.

"Curry them down good and give them some grain."

The half-wit boy smiled and nodded, ducking his head again and again.

By late afternoon, Lee was thinking about going over to Mrs. Foster's to see if Small had come back and gotten the note and money. It was a lot of money just to leave somewhere.

Lee was in the hotel kitchen, drinking coffee and smoking a cigar a drummer had given him. The cigar had been made in Alabama and was supposed to be as good as the finest Havana. It tasted a little strange, though.

Mrs. Boltwith had gone out, and Lee and Beatrice were sitting in the kitchen, resting up from dinner. Beatrice still had the dishes to do.

Lee got up and opened the back door to throw the cigar out. He surprised a little boy, about ten years old, standing there with his hand raised to knock. He was a ragged kid with pinned-up overalls.

"What can I do you for sport?" Lee said. "Mrs. Boltwith's out of the house."

The little boy didn't say anything. He dug in his pocket and took out Lee's note.

Lee took it, but when he reached for some change to give the boy, the kid turned and ran off down the alley.

Lee went back to the table and sat down and opened the note.

His thousand dollars were still in there, but the bills had all been torn in half.

Something was written in pencil across the top of the paper. It said:

Young men these days just ain't raised right. I'm over at the Arcady. You come see me or I'll come see you.

Beatrice came and read it over his shoulder. She reached out and touched the torn money with her finger. Her hand was trembling.

"I suppose," she said, "I suppose you'll have to go and kill that old son-of-a-bitch, my dear . . ."

CHAPTER FOURTEEN

"I think that money is still good," Lee said. "I think Walker can exchange them for good bills at the bank, then send these to Denver and get them replaced." He folded the torn bills up and tucked them into his vest pocket.

He finished his cup of coffee and stood up.

Seeing Beatrice's face, he said, "I'll try and talk the old man out of it. It's just a lot of damned foolishness."

He left the kitchen without kissing her and walked down the hall to the stairs. Beatrice watched him from the door to the kitchen, until he turned out of sight to climb the stairs.

Lee went up to his room, sat on the bed, and shucked the old rounds out of his revolver and replaced them with fresh ammunition from a box he had bought at Kimble's. The weapon was clean, so he didn't fool with it, or oil it again. He found he did better by not fussing with the gun. He didn't even practice with it much anymore. Years ago he had practiced every day, sometimes for seven or eight hours a day, drawing and shooting whenever he could afford the cartridges.

He'd stopped doing that a while ago, however. He could draw the pistol and fire it, all in his head. And that seemed to tell him very well what he could do with it. His muscles appeared to follow his thinking.

The old man was probably still pretty handy. More

important, India Ashton had sent a lot of hate along with him. Lee wondered if the fact that he himself deserved killing for what he done would harm his shooting any. Probably not. He'd never seen a bad man die from being bad.

Of all times for Phipps to have gone to Butte, the one time he might be of use. Lee considered whether the marshal might be shy, happier to be absent from killing occasions. But it wasn't likely, not having worked for Hickok. Hickok had a nose for a frightened man, and any man who rode with him was anything but that.

Lee got up off the bed, opened his trousers, and tucked his shirt well down before buttoning them up again. He'd seen a man killed in New Mexico because his draw got caught in a loose shirttail hanging out. A silly thing to be worrying about. The look he'd seen on India Ashton's face had been a merciless look. Small was of an age to have been her father.

He strapped his gunbelt on, settled it on his hips, and left the room. He went down the stairs, back through the hall past the kitchen. He glanced in. Beatrice was washing dishes; she didn't look up at him. He went on out back to the outhouse and took a piss.

Either way it went, chances were he'd have to leave Cree. It would likely be one shooting too many for the valley people—and more than likely one too many for Tod Phipps.

Crossing the street to the Arcady, Lee saw that the afternoon light had turned to evening dusk. Some children were still playing in the street, chasing back and forth with a little yellow dog. The lamps would be lit in the saloon. Something to take care about. Shadows and shifty shooting. He didn't know why, but he sometimes fired a fraction to the left in uncertain light. Not much, maybe half an inch or an inch—just a little bit to the left. No telling why.

He went up the steps to the batwing doors. There

were people in there early, talking and laughing. No
Fishhook riders, he hoped. He pushed the doors open
and walked in.

He saw the old man right away. White hair. He was
sitting at one of the tables to the side, talking with a
drummer in a yellow suit. The old man looked to be
telling a joke. The drummer was laughing and nodding
his head. They both had beer mugs in front of them.

The old man looked up at Lee right away and nodded
in a friendly fashion as if he'd been waiting for him to
come and have a drink. Then he said something more to
the drummer, got up, and walked around the table to
stand about thirty feet from the door, looking at Lee in
an amused sort of way.

There were cowboys at the bar pretty far down. From
the quick glance he gave them, Lee didn't see any
Fishhook men, at least none that he recognized. There
were two lumberjacks playing cards on the bar, too.
One-up, or some game for drinks of that sort.

Lee started toward the old man, keeping his hand well
away from his gun. When he was close enough not to
have to yell, he said, "Mr. Small—"

The old man shook his head as if Lee were showing
bad manners and drew his gun.

He had a wonderful draw.

It was the prettiest, old-fashioned draw that Lee had
seen in years. He'd seen Bill Longley draw that way
once at a dogfight in Baton Rouge.

It was a smooth swift circle.

The hand circled back, hooking the black coat out of
the way, and going on down to the gun without a pause,
bringing it up level.

Nothing jerky or hurried about it. All smooth and
swift.

Lee shot the old man in the chest, high, and drove
him staggering back across the floor, his coattails
flapping.

But the old man's Colt had come level out of that perfect draw—and went off with a blast.

The slug struck Lee in the meat of his left shoulder and spun him hard.

That spinning saved his life, because the old man, still stumbling back, shot at him again. Lee heard the bullet go buzzing like a bee just past the front of his chest. If he'd been standing, facing front, it would have killed him.

He shot the old man low into the belly, and that put Small down on the floor, hard.

Lee jumped as fast as he could to the left, scrambling. He knew he must look a panicked fool doing it, but he was damn glad he had, because that poisonous old son-of-a-bitch cut loose again from flat on his back on the floor. Lee felt the snap and tug as the round went through the right-side flap of his buckskin vest.

From there, there was only one way to go. Lee dove for the floor—something he hadn't done in a fight for ten years.

And damned if George Small didn't fire again.

The round burned Lee across the calf as he hit the sawdust. He shot into the old man's body for the third time and killed him.

There was a long, heavy silence in the Arcady.

Nobody said a word.

Lee rolled slowly over and then climbed to his feet. He was feeling sick to his stomach from the shoulder hit. The slug had hit him hard.

He felt dizzy, and his leg hurt like fire from that graze. The old son-of-a-bitch had shot him to pieces. What a gunman he must have been when he was young and riding the Missouri border.

What a gunman.

Lee limped over to look at the old man lying on the dirty floor. He looked terrible, the way they always did: small and beaten up. He had turned on his face when he died, and his tongue was hanging out onto the dirty sawdust.

Lee limped over to a spitoon beside the bar, bent over, and vomited into it. He felt sick as a horse.

None of the people in the Arcady had anything to say.

Mr. Martin probed and took the bullet out up in Lee's room at Mrs. Boltwith's. It didn't hurt too badly, because he'd gotten up there fast, and Lee's shoulder was still fairly numb. Lee's leg stung more from the graze than the shoulder hurt.

"You," Mr. Martin said, his frog eyes bulging, "have got what the penny-dreadfuls call a minor wound. Which means it will hurt like blazes soon enough, but will not cripple you, since it impacted the bone but did not break it. But it may well *kill* you if it becomes inflamed with infectious pus." He was washing out the wound with a permanganate solution.

"This is the second time," he said dabbing at the wound with a pad of boiled cotton, "that I have had to attend you following violence. You appear to be making a habit of it."

"Sorry for the trouble," Lee said. His mouth felt dry.

"Practice for me, trouble for you," Mr. Martin said. He put a new pad in place and reached for a roll of bandage. "I will warn you that Marshal Phipps has arrived back in Cree this evening and is very angry at this affair, undoubtedly as much for reasons of *amor impropre* as legal distress. He is calling you a dangerous man."

Mr. Martin tied the bandage with a neat, small double bow. Then he cut another length of cloth, folded it into a sling, and fitted it to Lee's left arm.

"Thank you, Doctor," Lee said.

"I'm a draper, not a doctor," Mr. Martin said. But he seemed pleased all the same. "Now, I'm going to give you a reasonable dose of laudanum—nothing to interfere with respiration—and you should wake tomorrow with a very painful shoulder, but feeling better in spite of it.''

"Should he have something to eat?'' asked Beatrice, who'd been standing at the foot of the bed, wincing while Mr. Martin probed.

"A cup of sage tea or something of that sort before he goes to sleep. Nothing else tonight. Tomorrow, some soup, if he feels like it.''

Mr. Martin had brought up a big sewing basket with his medical things in it, and he started to put his instruments away and pack up.

"And the marshal may well be right about you, Mr. Lee,'' he said. "Miss Ashton has had to take poor Nigel off to Chicago.'' He concentrated on his sewing basket for a moment. "Poor Nigel . . .'' Mr. Martin sighed. "He's lost the sight of that left eye.'' He closed the basket and walked to the door. "That sad, great fool playing cattle baron. And look what comes of it.'' He closed the door behind him.

That night Beatrice got Lee his cup of tea and sat by the bed talking to him about the ranch, Tim Bupp's pies, and the feud between Mr. Martin and Kimble. She didn't mention George Small, or what people in town thought of the killing.

That night Lee dreamed of horses.

Not appaloosas, though. Cavalry horses.

All bay, and sorrel, and black.

They were running in a great herd, at night, and all of them were bridled and saddled. Running at a gallop, jostling each other as they ran.

Thundering through the night.

They had someplace to go, a place they had to be by morning. They were smarter than ordinary horses: they knew where they had to be.

There were hundreds of them. No. He was rising

216

higher now. There were thousands of them. All dark horses. He could see the dark backs surging up and over the small rises in the ground.

He couldn't see the ground because the grass was too high, and it was dark. Now he was high in the air, high over them all. Horses as far as he could see, from dark horizon to dark horizon, the land was covered with running horses.

They were running away from him, but he wanted to go with them.

When he woke, it was afternoon.

He lay a long time quitely in the bed. His shoulder hurt him; that was what had wakened him.

He thought about George Small and the shooting. About India Ashton off in Chicago with her brother, seeing doctors for his eye. He wondered if she had bothered to telegraph Cree to find out if Small had earned his money and killed him. But how would she word a telegram like that? Some message to a friend, maybe, and ask at the end of it: Any news in town? Something like that, maybe. If she bothered at all. He remembered her face, twisted in rage, then twisted in pleasure as she struggled under him. He felt himself getting hard remembering it.

Poor Small was in the right, after all; Lee'd deserved killing.

But he was here thinking about it, and Small must be in a box at the carpenters. No more sunshine for George Small. No deep breaths of mountain air. No sweets of life for him at all.

He was in the right, and now he was in a box with the lid nailed down. And that was that.

Beatrice came in to see him all through the day. Early in the evening, Mr. Martin came back up to look at the wound.

"Proud flesh and no stink, as a surgeon of my grandfather's day would have said." He pulled fresh cotton

217

bandaging out of his sewing basket, folded out a pad, and wrapped Lee's shoulder afresh.

"In those days, of course, no surgeon would have thought of even nodding to my grandfather on the street," he said. "Surgeons weren't received by any really fine family in the city. Same as barbers, exactly the same. You had one called when needed, and that was all." He finished the bandage with a neat double bow.

Mrs. Boltwith put her head in the door.

"Ah, Mr. Martin," she said. "I thought I saw you coming up. There's beefsteak and roast potatoes for supper if you're of a mind to stay."

"Well, maybe I will," he said. "Maybe I will."

"Mrs. Boltwith," Lee said. "Mr. Martin's dinner's on me. And an extra piece of pie to boot."

"Not necessary," said Mr. Martin, "but, I suppose, an acceptable recompense for an amateur physician. Where in God's name did you get that dress, Maria?"

Mrs. Boltwith seemed pleased at the notice.

"Oh, it's one of my old ones, Mr. Martin. Just an old thing from St. Louis days."

"My dear Maria," Mr. Martin said, "with all due respect to your then occupation in St. Louis, these are different days." He went nearer to examine Mrs. Boltwith's dress in detail. "And may I add that green has never been your color, whatever they might have told you in St. Louis. My God," he said, "there are ruffles on the ruffles!"

"There, you see," Mrs. Boltwith said, "that's fine work."

"I won't hear another word," Mr. Martin said. "You look like an artichoke in that thing, and if it takes an old friend to tell you so, then that's what it takes!"

Mrs. Boltwith's face got a little red when he said that, and she stepped out of the room and slammed the door lightly behind her.

"A heart of gold—and the good taste of a drunken hard-rock miner!" said Mr. Martin.

The next day Lee felt fine. It was just as Martin had said; the shoulder still hurt—gave him a real jolt if he tried to move his left arm—but otherwise he felt fine. The bullet crease on the calf of his leg had scabbed and didn't bother him at all.

He wanted to get up. When Mr. Martin came by to change the dressing, he said, "We'll leave this one on for two or three days; wound's doing well." Lee then asked him when he could get up.

"Tomorrow," Mr. Martin said. "Not before tomorrow."

Beatrice came up to visit with him when the draper left, and she brought a *Harper's Weekly* only two months old to read to him.

" 'Fishing on the Pushquohatten,' " she read, " 'is a tolerable occupation for a late summer day . . .' "

When she finished the article, Lee tried to get her to come into bed with him, but Beatrice said she was shocked just by the suggestion coming from an invalid and laughed, staying out of his reach.

Then she made him tell her about Mexico.

He told her some of it: the smoky untanned leather smell of the small towns; the look of the mountains, how dry and harsh they were; and how the quiet brown people lived up there and minded their own business.

He didn't tell her about the shootings he was in working for the old Don. He and Beatrice had had enough shooting to last them for a while.

After Beatrice went down to bed, Lee stayed up a little longer, reading *Harper's*. There was an article in there about how the South was coming-about from the damage of the war. More of the country than just the South had yet to come-about from that war, Lee thought.

He finished the article, leaned over to blow out the

lamp, and then settled himself carefully on his right side. He didn't want to injure the shoulder now, not when it was healing.

He had no dreams at all that night, or none that he remembered.

In the morning he got up and dressed.

He felt dizzy at first, just as he stood up from the bed, but it passed. When he looked for his shirt in the dresser, he saw that Beatrice had darned over the bullet hole in the shoulder so that it barely showed.

Beatrice came in while he was trying to get his boots on, and she helped him with them.

"Tod Phipps went out of town to the lumber camp last night," she said, "but he'll be back tomorrow."

"You tired of nursing me, Beatrice?"

"I was thinking I could drive you out to the ranch in a wagon today . . ."

"And get me out of town." He smiled at her. "When is Phipps due back?"

"Tomorrow afternoon, I think."

"Then I'll ride out in the morning, okay?"

She nodded and finished pushing the left boot on. She knelt there a minute looking up at him, her hand resting on the tooled leather. A lock of her long brown hair had come down while she wrestled with the boot.

Lee bent over and kissed her gently on the mouth.

"Thank you, Beatrice, for everything," he said.

Then they went down to breakfast.

Mrs. Boltwith's minister, Mr. Pierce, was down to breakfast, and so were two drummers, one with his sample case beside his chair.

Lee said good morning to them, and one of the drummers nodded back. The other two didn't say anything.

Breakfast was sausage and flapjacks and berries with honey, and for a little while, they all ate in silence.

Mrs. Boltwith came into the kitchen and went to the

stove to grind more coffee and put it on.

Then the minister, a little bald-headed man in a rusty suit, put his fork down on his plate and pushed his chair back with a scrape.

"I won't sit at this table," he said very loud. And he got up and walked out of the kitchen. One of the drummers, the one with the sample case, got up and followed him. The other drummer sat where he was and went on eating, his head bent over his plate.

"Looks like I'm costing you customers," Lee said to Mrs. Boltwith.

"To hell with them," she said, but her face was red with embarrassment.

"Tell me," Lee said to her. "What does the town think of that killing?"

"They don't mind," Beatrice said.

"Tell me," Lee said to Mrs. Boltwith.

"Oh, dear," she said, and she put the coffee on the stove. "If that George Small wasn't so old . . ."

"Yes . . ." Lee said.

"He was a murdering son-of-a-bitch!" Beatrice said.

"Yes, dear," said Mrs. Boltwith. "I'm sure he was. A Missouri man, I hear he was, probably rode with that dirty dog, Quantrell. But the people in this town have gotten so they don't like shootings all the time."

"Well, Lee's going back to the ranch tomorrow, and there won't be any more trouble," Beatrice said.

"I do think that's best," said Mrs. Boltwith, and she came over to pour them fresh coffee. She and Lee exchanged a look over Beatrice's head. It was a look from the old days for both of them, from the sporting life. It was a look of trouble.

Lee had wanted to take a walk after breakfast, maybe go back of town to the river with Beatrice, read out there, or have a picnic. Instead of doing that, though, he went back upstairs and lay down in bed for the rest of the day and read some more in *Harper's Weekly*.

He didn't go down for dinner, or for supper either.

Beatrice brought them up to him. She said the minister had stayed away for dinner, but that Mrs. Boltwith had baked rhubarb pie for supper just to draw him in, and he had come back and eaten supper for that.

That night, after she took the dishes away, Beatrice came back upstairs, got undressed, and came to bed with him. It was the sweetest night they'd had together, even with his sore shoulder.

But in the morning, he woke early, anxious to go. He was worried about the ranch and the horses. He'd been away now for three days, and Bupp and the others would be worried wondering what to do. From now on one of the men would have to come into town for the supplies and whatever. Lee would just stay the hell out of Cree for a few months. If he did that, just maybe all this would die down, and in a year or so, people wouldn't think so much of it.

And he was up early to avoid meeting Phipps. He didn't fool himself about that, either. If he fought Phipps, that was the end, win or lose. And he might damn well lose, too. His gun arm was all right; the rest of him wasn't.

And if he did win . . . well, from the smell of the town, he'd have to clear out damn fast, or they'd likely catch and hang him.

So he hurried. He roused Beatrice, kissed her awake, washed at the basin, and began dressing. She got up and helped him with his boots, and then helped him buckle his gunbelt on. Then she went downstairs to light up the stove for coffee.

The sun was just coming up when he walked into the kitchen. The house was quite. Mrs. Boltwith, drummers, minister—the whole lot still asleep.

Beatrice had the coffee on and corn cakes cooking in the pan when he came in and sat at the table.

They sat at the kitchen table without talking, drinking

222

their coffee and dunking pieces of corn cake into it. It made a good breakfast. For Lee, quiet times with Beatrice were as good as talking.

When he finished his coffee, he stood up and stretched, favoring his sore shoulder, getting the last of the bed stiffness out of his back.

"Do you want to go up with me, Beatrice?" he said. "To stay awhile, if you want."

She looked up at him. "Oh, yes. Yes, I would."

"Then go get your possibles. I guess you'll want more than that blue dress. But only bring what you can carry on Belita."

"Oh, yes," she said and jumped up and started out of the kitchen, then came back around the table to kiss him, then ran out again.

"What in the world is the matter with that child?" said Mrs. Boltwith coming into the kitchen. She was dressed in a Chinese wrapper and had a nightcap on with the strings tied underneath her chin.

"We're going up to the ranch together," Lee said.

"Are you?" said Mrs. Boltwith, giving Lee a glance. And she sniffed. "I suppose marriage wasn't mentioned in this," she said.

"No, it wasn't," said Lee.

"The more the fool you," said Mrs. Boltwith. "More coffee?"

She brought herself a cup and came and sat down.

"I suppose," she said, "that you thought that old Martin was right about my St. Louis dress the other night."

Lee had to think for a minute to remember what she was talking about. He sat down again, too, to be polite.

"No," he said. "No, I don't think he was just right on that. I think you look good in green."

"Well," said Mrs. Boltwith, with some satisfaction, "I suppose I'll take a man's opinion then on a lady's looks." Then she looked somewhat uneasy. "Still, Mr.

Martin knows fine things and good taste. He once told Miss Ashton she looked like a sofa in her purple riding suit. And, you know, she never wore that suit again."

"Oh, he's right about most things like that, I'm sure," Lee said. "But he made a mistake about that green dress of yours, I'll tell you that."

"Well, you know," said Mrs. Boltwith, "I believe you're right. The light isn't much up in these rooms at night. It's a daytime walking dress really, and that's a different color green in the daylight."

"Well," Lee said, getting up again, "I'll be getting my own stuff together." He bent over the table and kissed Mrs. Boltwith on the cheek. "And thanks for being so nice to Beatrice."

"Oh, no, you don't!" said Mrs. Boltwith. And she grabbed Lee's head and pulled it down and kissed him on the lips.

"If I was ten years younger . . ." she said.

Lee went up to his room, packed his hairbrushes and razor case in his saddlebags, picked his Stetson off the bedpost, and went out, shutting the door behind him.

Beatrice was waiting at the bottom of the stairs. She had an old carpetbag with her and some cord to tie it on the saddle with. She'd packed fast; there was a corner of some white cloth sticking out of the closure on the carpetbag.

"I'm ready," she said, breathless.

"That can't be much," Lee said, looking at the bag. "If there's more that you want to take, go get it. We'll handle it on the horses."

"No, no," she said. "This is all I need. Let's go now."

"All right," he said, seeing she was worried. "Let's go."

They walked out the door of Mrs. Boltwith's, down

the porch steps to the boardwalk, and off toward the corner where the street turned to the livery. Beatrice gave a little skip to her step to keep up with him, and Lee shortened his stride.

"Is that bag heavy for you?" he said.

"No, it's fine."

There were some people on the street now, going to work in the stores and freight offices.

Lee saw Rebecca Chase standing on the boardwalk ahead of them in front of the bank. She was talking to a man on a muddy horse. He had a beaver hat and a yellow duster on.

In the next moment, Lee saw that it was Tod Phipps.

He must have ridden hard from the camp. Ridden all night.

"Let's go back!"

"No," Lee said. "Just come on and we'll cross the street. Don't look their way."

As they walked down the boardwalk steps, Lee saw Rebecca staring at them.

They were halfway across the street when Phipps shouted after them.

"You there! *Lee*! You there, damn you!"

Lee stopped walking and turned.

Phipps had gotten off his horse. The duster was spattered with mud from his ride.

Lee heard Rebecca say: "Oh, don't, Toddy!"

"Lee! *Lee*! You're under arrest for a fatal shooting!" Phipps shouted. "You throw up your hands and come over here to me!"

People had stopped all along the street. Watching. Some man was pushing a woman into a store doorway.

"Stand away from me," Lee said to Beatrice. He shoved her away to the side.

"Small pushed that fight, Phipps! And he drew his revolver first!"

"Throw your hands up, damn you!" Phipps called.

225

He started across the street.

"I'm leaving town now, dammit!"

Still a distance away, Phipps pulled the duster back to clear the guns in his sash.

Then Rebecca screamed, "Oh. Toddy, Toddy, *don't*! He's Frank Leslie! *He's Buckskin Frank Leslie!*" She stood screaming on the boardwalk. "Oh, he'll kill you! *He'll kill you!*"

Phipps stopped about forty feet away. He stood still in the middle of the street, his duster held back from his guns, staring at Lee as if he'd never seen him before.

A man shouted something down the street.

"Forget it, Phipps!" Lee called to him. "I want no trouble with you." It was all over now. If he and Beatrice walked down these streets for fifty years, people would say: "There goes the killer and his whore."

He felt a terrible desire to draw and kill Rebecca Chase.

"Lee . . ." Phipps said. His face was white.

"I'm leaving the valley, Phipps. You have no call to fight with me . . ."

Phipps just stared at him. The poor son-of-a-bitch didn't know what to do. Everybody was looking at him.

Lee slowly turned, walked over and took Beatrice's arm, and started to walk away. His left shoulder hurt like blazes, even though he hadn't moved it, hadn't taken his arm from the sling.

"Frank Leslie!" he heard a man shout across the street. People were running, either to get away or to come see.

Maybe that decided Phipps.

Rebecca screamed.

Lee shoved Beatrice away as hard as he could and turned to his left to get further from her. He saw she'd fallen as he turned.

It all took time.

Phipp's first round burned across his ribs and knocked the wind out of him. Lee'd turned to face him.

Phipps was standing up straight, his arm outstretched, taking good aim.

Lee shot him in the belly. He heard the slug thump when it went into the man.

Phipps took a stiff step back, but kept his aim and fired. The bullet cracked past Lee's ear.

The marshal was shooting for the head.

Lee shot for his belly again, and missed him clean. It was too damn long-range shooting.

He ducked and hurt his bad shoulder. The marshal fired again. The round popped the air over Lee's head and went on back into a store window. The glass back there smashed with a loud musical sound.

Lee took a little time and shot the marshal very near where he had shot him before, straight on in the belly.

Phipps was no George Small.

He screamed like a woman and dropped his revolver and turned away. He walked stiff-legged over toward the boardwalk where Rebecca stood, holding his stomach and screaming. The second round had opened him up. There was pink and blue stuff between his fingers.

When he reached the boardwalk, Phipps sat down in the dust. He wasn't making any noise now.

"Lee!" It was Beatrice.

Lee waved her back and walked across the street.

Rebecca had run down into the street and was hovering over Phipps, moaning and screaming little screams.

When she saw Lee coming with his pistol in his hand, she flew around in front of Phipps like a desperate mother bird to get between them. When Lee got closer, she began to shriek at him, her fingers curved like claws.

He tucked his revolver under his bad arm, took her by the hair, and flung her down in the dirt. Then he stepped up to Phipps. The marshal stared up at Lee as wide-eyed as a baby. His intestines were coming out into his lap.

When he walked past Rebecca Chase, she lay still in the dirt. Her eyes were blank as slates.

Beatrice came to meet him, stumbling. He was reloading as he walked.

"Let's go," she said to him. "Let's go." Her face was white as flour.

"I have to go now and never come back."

"Yes," she said. "Let's go."

Men were standing on the boardwalks, looking at them. Soon, Lee thought, some of them will go get their shotguns. It's time to leave this town.

"Go back to Mrs. Boltwith's. I'll go get the horses and come 'round for you."

She started to say something, but he said, "Go on, do it."

She went a few steps and turned back and called to him, "You'll come for me?"

"Yes," he said. "Go on." She turned and went on across the street.

Lee watched her go, and then he walked over to the bank. People were watching him, but nobody said anything. Two men were standing over the marshal's body, and a woman was kneeling down beside Rebecca.

He climbed the steps to the bank, pushed the door open, and went in. The clerk was there standing beside the counter, and Walker was standing in the doorway to his office. They both looked at Lee in an odd way. He'd seen that look before.

They were afraid of him.

"Mr. Walker," Lee said—it occurred to him that they might think he was going to rob the bank—"I want to do some business about my ranch and give you some damaged bills to exchange."

Walker cleared his throat and said, "What business?"

228

"I've sold my ranch and my stock and transferred my bank account, too. I want that sale and transfer made right and proper."

"All right," said Mr. Walker. "I guess you better come on into the office."

Through the office windows, as Walker and his clerk drew up the papers, Lee watched what the town was doing. Some men had carried Phipps's body into the carpenter's shop. He had seen Mr. Martin and a woman bent over Rebecca where she lay in the street. Lee had not yet seen a man carrying a rifle, but he thought it wouldn't be long now.

"Well, there you are," said Mr. Walker, and he read from the paper:

" 'In consideration of the receipt of the sum of one dollar in U.S. currency, I hereby sell and transfer that entire property known as River Ranch and all its attachments, livestock, and land rights. I further do submit and assign my account in Cree Bank, as with the foregoing properties, to Miss Beatrice Morgan of this county, Cree County, Montana, on August twenty-third, eighteen-hundred and eighty-seven.' "

"Now, if you will sign, Mr. Lee, we will witness, though . . . though I must tell you . . ." Mr. Walker looked unhappy. "Well, damn it, it's a hell of a lot to give away!"

Lee signed the papers "William Franklin Leslie, also known as Frederick Lee."

"Will this stand in law?" he said.

"Yes," said Mr. Walker. "It'll stand, all right."

Outside the office window, Lee saw a store clerk walking down the boardwalk. He was carrying a double-barreled shotgun.

"Here's your copy," Mr. Walker said. "Signed and witnessed. And I'll send those damaged bills to Denver for her."

"Goodbye, Mr. Walker," Lee said, and he leaned

229

over the desk to shake hands with the banker and his clerk.

"I'll . . . I'll try and look out for her for you," Mr. Walker said. His face was red.

"I'd appreciate that," Lee said.

Lee left the bank by the back door and walked down the alley toward the livery. Two lumberjacks came walking toward him. One had a pistol in his belt. Lee could hear men calling to each other out on the main street.

"Hey, you!" One of the lumberjacks ran over to him. "Is it true the marshal was shot?"

"Yes," said Lee. "He was shot, all right."

"Hot damn," the lumberjack said. "Who did it?"

"I did."

"Oh," the lumberjack said. "You did?"

He stepped back and stood beside his friend. Lee walked away from them toward the livery.

"What do you think of that?" Lee heard the man ask his friend. "He was ribbing you," the other man said.

In the livery, Lee gave Miss McFee two dollars for grain and found, saddled the dun, and led him out. He was wondering whether he might make a stop at the ranch. Better not. They'd go there first if they got a real posse together.

He swung up on the dun and settled himself. His shoulder was hurting something fierce, and his side stung where the slug had grazed it.

He touched the dun with his spurs and headed down an alley, riding for the river bank and the way out of town.

By nightfall, he was high in the mountains on the far bank of Rifle River. He'd ridden the landline of the ranch, but he hadn't gone on in. He thought, from a rise above the west ridge, that he saw one of the appaloosas, maybe a mare, running the high meadow below him. But by then it was already getting dark and he may have been mistaken.

Bupp and Sandburg and Tom Cooke. They'd do their best for Beatrice. She was good with horses.

No future for a little dark-eyed whore riding with a killer.

The moon was coming up, rising like a slice of silver over the peaks of the Rockies. Its white light would fill the valley soon. Lee pulled the dun up on a stony ledge and sat his saddle to watch. Slowly, very slowly, as almost an hour went by, the moon rose high enough.

Its cool, bright light poured slowly down like milk running into a dark green cup, and filled the valley up.

What had Beatrice sung at River Ranch always a little off tune? She'd sung "Shenandoah," and once, "The Last Rose of Summer."

> It was the last rose of summer
> That bloomed all alone.

Lee turned his horse's head, spurred him, and rode away.

THE LEGEND CONTINUES

Doc Holliday called him "the fastest gun I ever saw . . ." He was Buckskin Frank Leslie: gambler, sportsman, pimp, and mad-dog killer—until the girl he loved was shot down in a gunfight that he had provoked.

That same night, Buckskin Frank Leslie—friend to Holliday and the Earps, sworn enemy of the Texan gunmen, Ben Thompson and Clay Allison—left town. Rode out—and was never heard of again.

Never heard of—except for odd rumours . . . legends . . .

—About a man named "Fred Lee," who tried to settle down on a ranch in Montana—only to blaze a bloody trail through the valley of the Rifle River . . . and ride away.

—And about a man named "Farris Lea . . ."

GUNSTOCK

CHAPTER ONE

Farris Lea had been waiting for an elk for two hours.

Lea was a tall, lean man, his clean-shaven face burned deep mahogany by the mountain sun. His dark hair was flecked with gray at the temples, the same shade of gray as his deep-set eyes. He was sitting high on the slope of Edge mountain—named, not for its saw-spined ridge, but for a trapper, Ephriam Edge, who'd hunted the Bitteroots half a century before.

The elk was past due. Lea had sent Tocsen scouting past the mountain shoulder to spook the bull elk down the draw and into the broad, autumn-brown meadow below.

There, with any luck at all, his Lordship, Baron the Graff Rudiger von Ulm-und-Felsbach would manage to shoot the damn thing.

Lea shifted the heavy Sharps across his lap. He shouldn't need it for backup on the elk; not this time anyway. The Baron was a squarehead pain in the ass, but he could shoot. The Sharps was for grizzly.

The big bears were thick in the Bitteroots now, just

5

before the snow came in for good. Old Abe Bridge had warned Lea about them when he'd hired him on as hunting guide. "Just two years ago, I lost a fat French banker to one of those pig-bears! And I don't damn well intend to lose another paying guest in that fashion! Understand me, Lea?"

Lea understood him. Old Abe Bridge was the sole owner and proprietor of the biggest, finest, fanciest, and most expensive resort hotel in the west. Gunstock was a luxury resort, for sure, but it wasn't set up in some civilized place like Denver or the north of California.

Gunstock, all 600 rooms, was stuck way out in the lonesome, deep in Idaho's Bitteroot mountains. The rich dudes who came by train and stagecoach from the East expected to get the Wild West served up to them on a plate. And Farris Lea, the Shoshones, and the grizzlies were expected to oblige.

Gunstock was Abe's pride and joy, a million-dollar dream that had taken every penny of the old prospector's one big lucky strike: a fortune in silver dug out of the old grubstake in Colorado.

Abe had hired Lea on almost a year before, when he'd come riding his big dun through the mountains, heading for the Pacific coast, dead broke. It happened that Abe's previous guide, a handsome halfbreed named Dark Cloud, who'd been a great favorite with the lady guests, had wound up under a pack mule after a thousand-foot fall.

Abe had noticed Lea out behind the kitchens, cutting some firewood to pay for his supper, had stopped to talk, and must have found something about Lea that he liked. He'd offered him the job on the spot, and a plum

6

job it was, if you enjoyed kissing the butts of robber barons, politicians, and the odd European nobleman out for a backwoods time.

Well, Lea hadn't enjoyed the butt-kissing and had refused to do it. He'd held onto the job anyway. The guests had enjoyed his independent air and sometimes Lea even enjoyed the hunting. And if, as it happened, he had spent some time in Chicago, and more time than that on the rougher fringes of San Francisco society, there was no need for the dudes to know that. They were happier thinking their guide was a right mountain man who wouldn't know the proper way to order a beer in a barrel house.

Well, that was fine with Lea. He'd caught on quick to the theatrical part of the job, and he acted the frontiersman like Bill Cody himself. It was a good job, all in all, and old Abe still liked him, even if his daughter didn't. Blue-eyed Sarah had cold-shouldered Lea from the start, thinking he was just some smooth-tongued drifter taking advantage of Abe. And it seemed she thought his predecessor, Dark Cloud, to have been the perfect noble savage, and Farris Lea a pretty poor substitute.

Lea had kept out of her way as much as he could, and kept doing his job as well as he could. He had not bothered to tell Sarah Bridge what old Tocsen had told him, namely, that Dark Cloud's real Blackfoot name had been "He-That-Farted," and that the halfbreed had gone in terror of the Shoshones who roamed the Bitteroots.

The Shoshones hadn't bothered Lea yet, or Gunstock. Abe had had the smarts to talk to their peace-chief, a man called Side-of-the-Hill, and had arranged some payments of food, horses, and blankets. Gunstock was a visiting place for the whites, not a settling place. And as long as that was true, and the Army kept a garrison at Salt River, the Shoshones would stay peaceable. Lea had seen them many times, shadowing his hunting party along the ridges, and the dudes had been thrilled—and a little scared—when he'd pointed them out. But the Indians never came closer.

Tocsen was a Shoshone, of what rank Lea had never found out, though his clan was Turtle, and that was maybe another reason the Shoshone didn't come in for trouble.

The old Indian had just walked into one of Lea's camps one night, settled down by the fire without a word, eaten supper—while a New England ship owner sat staring, bug-eyed—and in the morning had simply gone to work, catching and packing up the horses, striking the camp tents, and boiling the breakfast coffee.

He'd been working with Lea ever since. And he was worth his weight in whatever Lea might have chosen to name. The old man had a nose for game to beat any buffalo hunter or trapper Lea had ever known, and, unlike many Indians, he was a damn good shot.

All in all, he had a good job. And in country as pretty as the country Lea had left. But there was no use thinking about that. No use at all.

He sat up suddenly, tightening his grip on the Sharps. Something had moved down in the breaks by the mouth of the draw. Nothing. Nothing, for maybe a full minute. The chill autumn wind swept across the frost-killed grass carpeting the meadow below. Lea

8

hoped that the Baron hadn't gone to sleep on him. He'd seen more than one dude lose a shot for not being able to stay awake in a stand.

Then Lea saw it. A bull elk with a rack like a moose's slowly, slowly walking out of the brush into the open. Tocsen had done it just right, as usual. He'd moved the elk out, but hadn't spooked him. The square-headed Baron wouldn't get a finer shot at a finer animal in his life.

Lea rose to his feet in one easy motion, the barrel of the big rifle balanced across his left forearm. He shrugged off the long buffalo coat he'd draped across his shoulders, and stood alert, staring down into the valley below. He was wearing plain brown cowhide boots with low hill-country heels, dark-brown wool trousers, a wool plaid shirt, and a handsomely fringed buckskin vest, decorated with fine Indian beadwork. As the cold wind blew through the Bitteroots, the soft buckskin folded back momentarily in the breeze, and the long fringe fluttered against the worn walnut butt of a short-barreled Bisley Colt .45, worn high and forward on his right side, the butt slanting back to just above his hip.

Why the hell wasn't that German taking his shot? The elk was a hundred yards out into the meadow now. As Lea watched, it suddenly stopped, its great head lifted, swinging as it tested the air. And the same moment, Lea felt the mountain wind begin to shift direction, short gusts drafting along the mountainside, turning more and more from the north. The elk would be smelling sauerkraut in a few seconds: why didn't the son-of-a-bitch shoot?

Then came the shot. Lea froze, the butt of the Sharps halfway to his shoulder.

The big elk staggered as the brittle, echoing crack of the Mannlicher died away. The Baron had made his shot. And too damn high. As Lea watched, the bull elk recovered, stumbled, then sprang into a hard driving run toward the brush at the end of the valley. *No good,* Lea thought. *You made the wrong move, brother. You should have turned back to the draw.*

The elk was only yards from the border of the brush when the German's rifle spoke again. The big animal seemed to collapse all at once, like a huge puppet with cut strings. It fell, and rolled once, and was still. Lea sighed and lowered the hammer on the Sharps. The end of the hunt was always the saddest part.

He had taken only two steps down the mountainside when a third shot rang out, and he saw the animal jolt to the bullet's impact. The Baron apparently liked to make sure that dead was dead. That was usually a pretty good idea. It had been Lea's idea, too, once upon a time.

"That first shot was not my fault!"

The Baron had never admitted that anything was his fault during the four days Lea had been guiding him.

"Let me see that rifle," Lea said. He'd never cared for the Baron's Mannlicher. It was a neat piece, and very finely made—a match piece, actually. That was just the trouble with it. It was not a weapon for rough handling in rough country, at least not in country as rough as the Bitteroots in November. It had jammed at the breech twice already in the last few days; and once had cost the Baron one of the handsomest mountain sheep that Lea had seen since he came to Gunstock.

The Baron handed it over with a grunt. They were standing beside the elk while Tocsen butchered it out. The old Shoshone had come trotting out of the draw on

10

his little pinto just as Lea had walked down the mountain slope. "Nice driving, old man," Lea had said to him. "Yes," the old man had said, and nodded, "I push elk good." He'd swung off his pinto, drawn his knife, and gotten to work on the elk. Tocsen wasn't much for long speeches.

Lea looked the Mannlicher over carefully, keeping his ungloved hands off the beautifully polished steel. It was the sight for sure. The Baron had ridden out of the hotel stables with a fine telescopic sight on the rifle. The fine sight had lasted for two days, then a pack horse had walked over the rifle while they were striking camp by Turkey River. The sight had bent like licorice candy.

"You have a bent sight, Baron," Lea said. "The shot wasn't your fault. Matter of fact, you made a damn nice second shot there, considering." *That ought to hold the son-of-a-bitch*, Lea thought.

The Baron was a big man, with blank blue eyes and iron-gray hair, cropped close. He looked a little fat, but he wasn't; he was strong as a horse. If he'd had something of a sense of humor, and been willing to pitch in somewhat to help with the camp work—which a lot of the better dudes were happy to do—then he would have been a fair enough hunting partner. But the Baron had no sense of humor at all, and didn't appear to enjoy anything much except shooting, and he never, never lifted a finger in camp. Lea and Tocsen did all the doing, and that was that. It made for a stiff, unfriendly hunt.

"Can you fix dat?" the Baron said. He spoke English well, but he had a tough time with *th*.

"No," Lea said, "It would take a gunsmith and gunsmith's tools to get that sight-leaf straight." He punctuated that by spitting a little tobacco juice to the side.

11

The Baron muttered something in German. "What did you say?" Lea said.

"I said," said the Baron, "what de hell am I to shoot wit, now?" He looked considerably annoyed. None of the Gunstock guests liked to have anything go wrong. It seemed to make them nervous. And the Baron liked it less than most.

"You use the Martini-Henry," Lea said. The Martini was new, a nice weapon, well-balanced and easy to shoot, and it had the strongest action made. The rifle's only fault was the moderate striking power of its ammunition. You couldn't be sure of knocking a big animal down with the first shot. But that was what Lea and the Sharps were for.

The Baron made a face, and glared down at the Mannlicher as if it had personally insulted him. Lea decided to earn his money.

"It's a beautiful firearm, Baron, but it just wasn't made for these here conditions. And that's a fact." He spit a bit more tobacco juice. "I guess you Germans make about the *nicest* firearms there is." The Baron looked a little happier, and grunted.

"I will use de Martini," he said.

"You look," old Tocsen said. He was standing up beside the half-butchered elk. He'd already gutted it, and caped-out the head and rack for salting. The Baron liked to have something to show.

"Men come," the old Shoshone said. He was looking down the valley.

There were three men riding slowly down the valley toward them. They were still a good way off, and didn't seem to be in any hurry, ambling along—but coming on straight, just the same. It was the rifle shots that had fetched them, of course. The three of them, still a couple of hundred yards off, rode abreast down

12

the middle of the valley meadow, their horses stepping high through the cold, damp grass.

They didn't look good. They looked too easy, too relaxed at meeting three strangers in the middle of nowhere. Lawmen? Maybe. Lea didn't think so. There were too many of them for serving papers, too few for a posse. Besides, the Gunstock range was a long way from Boise—or from any other law-station, for that matter.

"Load that Mannlicher, Baron," Lea said. The German was somewhat familiar with trouble. He breeched a round into the Mannlicher and didn't say a word.

Lea looked around for Tocsen, but the old Shoshone wasn't there; he'd ghosted back up to the tree line. Lea saw him bend over a pack for a moment, then straighten with a double-barreled Greener in his hands —loaded with double-ought, and both hammers back.

The three men were coming in. The one riding in the middle was smiling in a friendly way. Lea reached down and eased the keeper-loop off the hammer of his Colt. If there was trouble, it was going to be trouble close-in.

"Howdy!" the middle one called. He was still smiling, a very friendly fellow.

None of the three looked like much, either for good or bad, but Lea didn't spend much time on that. Looks didn't mean much for a killer, or a good man either. The middle man was a thin fellow with a three-day beard and bright brown eyes. The man riding on his right was big and haunchy, with dirty blond hair done up in a couple of pigtails. He looked a bit like a squaw man. The third rider, off to the smiler's left, was a sallow-faced kid, maybe seventeen years old, maybe not. All of them were armed.

Lea saw this much in one fast glance, but it wasn't what interested him. What interested him was the horses.

Their horses were dead beat. Wind-broke, spur-scarred, and worn. The three of them must have roweled the animals sharp to bring them down the meadow so lively—trying to cover their condition.

Whatever their reasons, whatever their trouble, these men needed fresh horses badly.

"Say now," the smiler said, "that's what a man could call a real prime elk you fellers got there."

The sallow boy wasn't paying attention to the talk. He was looking over to the nearby tree line. Looking at Tocsen and the Greener. Looking at the horses.

It was a prime string: Lea's big dun, the Baron's fancy bay stallion, Tocsen's little pinto, and three first-class Morgan-cross pack horses. Abe outfitted with nothing but the best. Nothing else would do for Gunstock.

The sallow boy was eating those animals up with his eyes.

"I guess you fellers couldn't spare say a quarter of that elk deer, now could you? We could sure do with some prime fixin's. We'll pay gold."

"Ain't that so, Louis?" the smiling man said, real sharp, to the sallow boy. He'd seen Lea notice that hungry look at the horses. The boy turned back slowly, not worried and not hurried.

"I suppose," he said. He wore a Smith & Wesson Russian model .44, fixed for a left-hand cross draw.

"We could use some meat for sure," the big pigtailed man said. He had a soft, pleasant voice, and colorless eyes.

"Who's the dude?" the smiling man said, looking at the Baron.

The Baron's meaty face flushed up turkey red. He wasn't used to people talking down to him like that. The smiling man saw the flush, and smiled wider. "No

14

offense," he said.

While he said it, the sallow boy kneed his horse a step or two farther out to the smiler's left, out to the side.

Lea had seen it all before, a lot more times than he cared to remember. He wasn't even angry at them.

"Listen to me," he said to the smiling man. "Listen carefully. If your bad-boy there moves his horse one more step to the side, or moves his left hand at all, the old Indian is going to kill him. Then, I'll kill you and pigtail."

The smiler heard him out, but his smile got a little stiff. Lea felt, rather than saw, the sallow boy shift in his saddle.

"You're about to get killed," he told the smiling man.

"Hold it!" the smiling man said to the boy. Then he stopped smiling and stared down at Lea.

"All right," he said, glancing down at Lea's holstered Colt, then back up to his face. "All right. We're not looking for shooting." He paused, looking into Lea's eyes. "But, I'll tell you, Mister, we need those horses. We *need* them, and that's flat!"

"We sure do," the pigtailed man said.

"Now," said the middle man, and he started smiling again, "we will pay you folks a real good price for those animals . . . in gold. And I mean a real good price."

"That's right," the pigtailed man said. The sallow boy said nothing.

"Now what do you say about that?" said the smiler.

Lea smiled back at him. "Turn and ride out of this camp," he said. "And keep riding. If you don't, we'll shoot your buttons off."

The smiling man stared down at Lea for almost a full minute.

"You folks are being unreasonable," he said quietly.

"Baron," Lea said, "when I kill this man, shoot the

big one with the pigtails.''

"I vill do dat," the Baron said. "I haf kilt men before dis time!"

The smiling man was no fool. Seeing cruelty, or courage, or savage temper in Lea's face wouldn't have impressed him at all. But he saw none of those things. He saw a man considering a familiar job of work, and nothing very special, at that. It was a look the smiling man had seen before.

Even so, he might have made a play. He had considerable confidence in the boy's draw. And in himself and Squaw Murrey, too.

Something else stopped him. He'd seen this hunter before, and he was damned if he could remember where. It had been a long time ago. Years ago. But he couldn't remember who, and he couldn't remember where.

The smiling man, who was a bank robber named Thomas Deke, decided to pick a better time.

"Well, hell," he said, and leaned in the saddle to spit, "if you people want to act so damn unfriendly, then to hell with you!" And he turned his horse's head. "Come on, boys," he said to his men, "we'll leave these assholes be."

CHAPTER TWO

His men looked surprised—especially the boy, and for a moment, Lea thought the kid was going to lose his temper and open the ball on his own; but the smiling man, not smiling now, flashed the boy a cold, hard glance, and the kid slowly turned his horse and followed after the other two.

Lea stood where he was and watched them go, not bothering to spur up their tired animals now, riding away at a walk. None of the three looked back.

"Should ve kill dem?"

"No," Lea said. "We don't kill them. Not now."

It looked for a minute as though the Baron was going to argue about it. He stared after the three riders, the Mannlicher balanced in his hands. His blank blue eyes weren't so blank now.

"If they come at us again, we'll fight," Lea said. "All they've done so far is give us hard looks and offer to buy our horses."

The Baron grunted and shook his head, unconvinced. He apparently was a bloodthirsty Baron back home.

They stuck camp, Tocsen finishing the butchering of the elk, and Lea striking the tents and packing the horses. The Baron, as usual, didn't do a damn thing. He sat on a folding camp stool, the Mannlicher across his lap, and looked out down the valley, probably hoping the three drifters would come galloping back full charge.

Tocsen finished with the elk, and lugged the quartered meat and salted trophy-head over to Ranger, the one pack horse that didn't mind the smell of blood. It took him three trips for the meat alone.

The old man helped Lea pack the meat into the diamond frames. Then they set the head and cape atop the load, and braced the gunny-sacked bundle with cross lashings. Gunstock guests were mighty particular about their trophies.

Tocsen said nothing about the three horse-hungry drifters; the subject didn't seem to interest him. When the men had ridden away, he'd just eased the hammers of the Greener, and then gone back to camp to unload it and put it away. Then he'd gotten back to his butchering.

"We'll go back by High Pass," Lea said to him, and the old man nodded and finished the lashings. High Pass was an awkward way to go. It would cost at least another day getting back to Gunstock, and it was a bad way for the horses, stony and narrow, above gullies and gorges. High Pass was the place where Dark Cloud had wound up a thousand feet down a mountain and under a mule. Lea had traversed it several times, once in a bad blizzard. It was no pleasure, but with a little care it could be done. It was also a way the three drifters were unlikely to know.

"Baron, we're going back to the hotel a different way," Lea said, when they were mounted and ready to move. "It's a mountain pass I know; it shouldn't give us too much trouble this time of year."

"You do dis to avoid dos tree?" the Baron said, reining his big stallion in. That was a very testy horse, that bay. The Baron was settling down from the near fight, Lea noticed. He was pronouncing his *v's* just fine now. Only the *th's* were still giving him trouble.

"That's right," Lea said. "That's exactly the reason. I'm not paid to bring in dead guests, Herr Baron." The 'Herr Baron' should go down pretty well, Lea thought.

"I don't run from dogs like dat!" the Baron said, and he gave Lea a careful look. "It is not, is it, dat you are a coward, Mr. Lea?"

For an instant, Lea felt his temper rising, and just as quickly, he got it under control. This squarehead was used to riding people roughshod; he probably had no idea that Lea, a hired hand, might take serious offense. Why should he? For the Baron, and for people like him, real courage was the property of gentlemen, not backwoods roughnecks.

"No, Baron," Lea said, and forced a smile, "I'm no coward. And I'm not any damn fool, either." And he turned the dun's head to lead out of camp. The Baron's broad face was red as a turkey cock's as he spurred his stallion after.

Hours later, deep into afternoon, they were climbing. Snaking back and forth up the steep ridge to the mountain Abe Bridge called Saddleback. And that mountain was only a first step up the long reach to

19

Collier's Hill and High Pass.

Lea turned in his saddle to see how the Baron and the pack string were making out. No problem with the Baron; the German was a good horseman, in a stiff, cavalry sort of way. He sat his big bay stallion like a statue in a park. He noticed Lea looking back at him, and immediately looked away, pretending to admire the scenery, which was something considerable to admire. The Baron was still annoyed over being called a damn fool. A hired hand had nipped at him, and he didn't like it.

Lea looked farther back, checking old Tocsen and the string. The old man was going fine, as always, singing to himself, rocking along on that fat little pinto. Lea wondered again why the old Indian had come in to work with him. Tocsen didn't seem to care for whites very much, and Lea was under no illusion that he was an exception to that. The old man got along with him, worked with him, put up with him—and that was about all.

The pack string was stepping along, taking the slope in stride, moving up. Three good solid horses. They had to be. By next morning they'd be pacing along trails not three feet wide, spiked thick with granite shards, and edging off into clear sky blue, empty, as far as a man could see.

Ranger, Button, and Candy Cane were loaded with pack saddles, blankets, bridles, halters, stake ropes, hobbles, lash ropes, panniers, pots and pans, tarps, tools, tents, and a big chuck box full of everything from canned peaches to horse liniment. Three fine and heavy-laden horses worth killing for.

* * *

They made the ridge of Saddleback before dark, and Lea called a halt there for the night. They pulled up in a long, level clearing just past a stand of aspen. Lea and Tocsen hobbled the horses, and staked them out to graze in the clearing. It was sparse, this late in the year, and frost-burned, but it would do the animals some good, and, with a feed-bag each of grain, would carry them to Collier's Hill the next day.

The Baron, still with nothing to say to Lea, took his folding canvas camp chair up to a little rise beyond the aspens, took a fine pair of field glasses out of their case, and sat scanning the countryside below—some thirty miles of mountainside, valleys, river-breaks and forest —for sign of the three drifters. Nothing wrong with that. It was just what Lea had had in mind himself.

He took the battered little telescope—it was battered because it had taken that long fall with Dark Cloud— out of his saddle bag, and walked over to join the Baron on his little rise. The Baron rolled an eye at him, but didn't say anything.

For a few minutes, they scanned the country below them.

Finally, the Baron stood up with a grunt, and put his fine field glasses back into their case.

"Dey are not dere," he said.

"Maybe," said Lea. "Maybe they aren't."

"Vit dose horses, dey don't keep up," said the Baron, and he went off the way he usually did at a halt, to find some tree cover and piss in private.

It was likely the Baron was right. They could, of course, have kept up by letting the boy, the lightest of them, take all three horses—leading two behind him— and ride them by turn as they tired. But that would mean leaving the other two men afoot. Not likely.

So, they couldn't follow. Lea had set a stiff pace throughout the afternoon. It had wearied their own fine mounts, and the pack horses as well. The three ragged mounts under the drifters wouldn't have been able to make half the miles in half the time.

Lea closed his eyes, trying to remember, to picture the drifters, their horses. The smiler and the boy had talked Texican. Some time away from it, maybe, but Texas voices all the same. Not pigtail, though. And their rigs? The boy had forked a Brazos double, a Texas saddle, Lea was sure enough of that; but try as he might, he couldn't be certain of the other men's rigs.

It came down to pigtail. If he knew the Bitteroots, he'd know that High Pass was the long way around, picked just to weary them off the track. And sure as hell, he'd lead his partners across the Pace River breaks and through the gap to Gunstock. If that was so, all three of them would be sitting at the other end of High Pass by tomorrow's sunset, waiting.

There wasn't much chance of that, but there was enough of a chance for Lea to worry about. The Baron might still be able to show him up for a damn fool after all.

It depended on pigtail.

Lea had learned long ago that enough worry was enough. If he'd called it wrong, he'd damn sure find it out at the other end of High Pass.

Lea walked over to the campfire. Tocsen had dug a pit first, and built the fire down in it to keep the flame from showing through the mountains.

Lea grubbed in the chuck box, and came out with the last can of peaches and the bottom siftings of flour.

22

He'd use elkfat for shortening. It made for a strong-tasting pie, but he'd fed it to some mighty picky eaters, used to Europe's best, and gotten no complaints. He and Tocsen had an unspoken agreement: Tocsen cooked the meat, and Lea did the fancy fixin's. Lea'd learned to bake the camp pies and breads in the gigantic kitchens at Gunstock, where, occasionally, the head chef, a very fat and temperamental Frenchman named de la Maine, had made a face of disgust and then given Lea a word of advice.

By the time Lea had his pie dough rolled out and tucked down into the greased Dutch-oven, Tocsen grunted and rattled the tines of the big meat fork on the light iron grill that Candy Cane had been hauling over the mountains for the last four days. It was the Shoshone's announcement that the steaks were ready.

There were three thick, long slabs of prime elk loin, rubbed with cracked black pepper and butter scooped from a Gunstock storehouse crock, and studded with slivers of the little wild onions that grew along the Bitteroot streams in late autumn. All three of them lay sizzling over a raked bed of dull red aspen coals. Tocsen forked one up and slapped it down in one of the big tin platters, scooped up more butter to smear on the smoking meat, and tossed a knife and bent fork onto the plate beside it.

It was rough service, and the old Shoshone never varied it, not for Grand Dukes, not even for railroad kings. But after tasting the old man's cooking, all the dudes seemed glad enough to put up with his lack of manners. The Baron was no exception. He'd been standing by the fire, waiting, and was eager to take that first steak, bent fork and all.

Lea was finishing the peach pie. He poured the canned fruit into the pastry shell, topped it with butter, folded the top edges of the pastry over for an upper crust, and then slid the covered Dutch-oven deep under a lifted shovelful of coals. Then he picked up his own steak, scraped a little salt over it from the salt cake in the chuck box, pulled his sheath knife, and cut his first, dripping, red-centered slice, almost two inches thick, and still cooking in its own sputtering juices.

The pie was ready by moonrise. Lea took his portion, walked down through the aspens, and stood munching the sugary-tart crustiness, watching the silvery moonlight slowly flood the land beneath him. It looked too beautiful to be dangerous.

CHAPTER THREE

They were up before morning light.

Lea had taken watch with Tocsen through the night, and he stretched now, working the stiffness out of his muscles by the morning fire. He tilted the big camp pot, pouring himself another cup of coffee.

The Baron was up on time, as usual. Give the squarehead that; you didn't have to pry him out of the soogins every morning. Now, by firelight, he was doing exercises. Lea supposed he had learned to do that kind of thing at officer's school or whatever. Up, down, up, down. Turn this way, turn that way. Up, down, up, down. Now it was time for him to start touching his toes. This was the part that Tocsen liked. Lea watched, smiling, as the old Shoshone, hunkered down by the fire, stared at the big German, watching fascinated while he puffed and grunted, his hind end in the air, trying to touch his toes. It was probably the best part of Tocsen's day.

The Baron, sweating a little in his double-breasted wool outfit, stood tall, stretched out his arms, and took a deep breath. He always ended his exercises the same way. Now, Lea knew, he would have one cup of coffee, black, a half loaf of sourdough bread, and three fried eggs for breakfast. Then he would march out to the latrine ditch, do his duty, and march back. Then he would say *guten morgen,* check his rifle—the Martini-Henry today—get on his stallion, and sit, stiff-backed as a Cheyenne war chief, waiting for Lea to lead off. The Baron was a man of habit.

When Lea led out of camp, the rim of mountains to the east were just touched with red and gold along their peaks. The camp lay still in darkness.

By full dawn, they were high on the plateau, riding up through deep stands of lodgepole pine, the rising sun gleaming gold through their lofty needled tops. The day was cool and still, the wide pale sky arching high from mountain range to mountain range.

They saw mule deer below them, on a dwarf-pine swale along a ridge. A lead buck, then five, maybe six, does.

Lea looked back, and saw the Baron turned in his saddle, watching the deer below. Behind him, the pack horses climbed steadily along, loads swaying a little, heads nodding with the pace.

The Baron looked up and saw Lea watching. He gestured down at the deer, and looked a question at Lea.

Lea shook his head, and the Baron grimaced and nodded as if his suspicions had been confirmed. The German was no fool: he'd noticed the watch the night before, and he'd noticed the tension in Lea as they traveled. And now, no hunting—no rifle shots.

Lea still expected trouble from the drifters, if not by

chase then by ambush.

Lea didn't need to read the squarehead's mind to know what he was thinking. He was thinking that Lea had been a soft-headed fool after all, for not shooting the drifters down as they rode away.

Lea had *known*, as the Baron and old Tocsen must have known, that the drifters were too desperate for mounts *not* to try for the string. There'd been no doubt about it—and no doubt about the kind of men they were, either.

Lea had backed away from doing what had to be done. That dodge might very well cost them when they left High Pass.

He was afraid, and not of the three drifters. He was afraid of a name, and the reputation that went with it. *The West's Premier Gun-man.* That was what that fool Ned Buntline had written. And it might have even been true—once. He had lost too much because of that name, that gun-killer reputation. The man who'd shot down those three drifters in cold blood would have been a marked man, a man to inquire after, to question.

Lea's hands were clenched on his saddle bow; then he jerked roughly at the reins, spurred the startled sidle out of the big dun, and rode up the ridge at a run, waving reassurance to the pack train behind him as he went. He needed time to think.

He rode to the top of the ridge; from there, looking down, he could see the stands of gold-leaved frost-touched aspen. Then, at an angle by timbers fallen from an old lightning fire, he saw the crawling dots of the pack-train coming up. Four small dots in a landscape.

He swung off the dun, looped the reins around the bushy tip of a dwarf pine, and went over to a bed of pine needles lying rich and light brown in the morning sunlight. He took off his hat, lay down, and tucked the high-crowned gray Stetson under his head for a pillow.

He didn't have any more thinking to do; he realized that even as he stretched out, easing his muscles in the soft, aromatic warmth of the pine bed. It was all decided already, had been while he was riding up.

He'd hired on to guide. He'd taken the job, and that was that. The squarehead Baron was his responsibility —the same as if it was Lily Langtry herself he'd taken hunting from Gunstock. He'd signed on with old Abe Bridge to take care of Bridge's people on the hunts. And that was what he would do.

If the drifters made their try—it would be near sunset before the pack-string could make it through the pass— then so much the worse for them. And if a certain secret, a personal thing, got known because of that, then it would be known. He'd run before. He could run again.

Lea lay resting for a while, watching high, white mare's tails sailing over the Bitteroot peaks, clouding in from the west. Storm—but not tonight. Tomorrow, maybe. *By this time tomorrow,* he thought, *we'll be high on the hog up at Gunstock,* or we'll be dead.

Soon after, he heard the click and clack of the horses' hooves. The string had caught up to him.

He got up, walked over to the dun and swung aboard, turned the horse's head, and trotted to meet the string.

"We'll pull up and rest the horses at the base of the next ridge," Lea said to the Shoshone. "Cold coffee and cold elk meat, Baron; I want us up into that pass before sunset." The Baron tilted his head up to look. So did

Lea. Another ridge, laced with zig-zags of lodgepole pine, rose above them. Beyond that rose another ridge, granite, with ice and snow streaking its sheer faces. Its towering slabs shone and flashed as the morning sunlight struck the ice. Behind, and higher yet, was Collier's Hill.

It was one of the highest mountains in the range, snowcapped at all seasons, with storms of sleet in midsummer, arctic blizzards in all other seasons. Since Gunstock opened, seven dudes had tried to Swiss-climb their way to the summit. Three of them were still up there.

High Pass cut just below the shoulder of the mountain, below the worst of the storms, Lea hoped. And if it was a dangerous traverse, it was also a short one. An hour should see them over the crest of the mountain's saddle, down into the valley, and Gunstock beyond.

It was never smart to hurry in the mountains. But this time, at least so far, the mountains had let them get away with it.

They'd rested the horses at the base of Cook Stove ridge. Lea and the Baron had drunk cold coffee, and eaten cold elk and sourdough sandwiches. Then they'd gotten back on the trail. Cook Stove went pretty easily. A pack pulled loose going down the other side, and it took some hard work to recover what they could and lash it up again, but no one was hurt, and nothing lost that they couldn't spare.

The worst trouble came in the afternoon, in a field of scree midway up the long slope of Big Bump. It was higher than the first ridge had been, and rougher, a rubble of granite and ice.

The Baron's bay stallion, a shifty heller named Blixen, pulled the kind of trick Lea had been expecting since he'd seen the horse prancing around the stable yards at Gunstock. They had just entered the field of scree, picking their way slowly through the jumble of fallen ice and boulders, when suddenly, right under the hooves of the Baron's stallion, a chickeree, one of the small brown mountain squirrels, came flashing out, chattering and mad as hell. The little animal must have had some nest or burrow there.

Instantly, all hell broke loose.

The bay stallion reared in panic, misstepped, and fell over, rolling. Lea, seeing it happen from a few yards ahead, spun the dun and spurred back, ready to shoot the stallion fast if the Baron were stirrup-caught.

The Baron had been damn lucky. The stallion had hit hard on its shoulder, kicked and rolled. The Baron had been thrown almost twenty feet from the fall, in a deep bank of reddish, mineral-stained snow. The snow was a leftover drift from last year's late winter fall. It was rotten and mushy stuff, hard on the Baron's fancy blue wool suit, but pretty easy on the Baron. Nothing, bar a few scratches and bumps, hurt, but his pride. And that had been marred plenty already.

The big man had heaved himself out of the snowdrift cursing a blue streak in what sounded like very vulgar German. He'd charged up to the bay stallion, which was standing trembling from the fall, and kicked the nervous horse hard in the ass. It had taken some high kicking, but the Baron had got it done. Lea had never liked the German better.

With grim determination, the Baron remounted the

bay, said something in German to him, and moved out across the scree as if nothing had happened. The kick seemed to have done the big bay some good, because the stallion moved off as steady as a railroad train, and gave the Baron no more trouble at all.

They reached High Pass well before dark. At least before the rest of the mountains were dark. High Pass was as black as a closed woodshed, and freezing cold.

They had just cleared the last field of stones, high above Big Bump, when they saw the pass. The huge, towering gateway of black basalt loomed a thousand feet above them, and the trail up to that monstrous split in the mountain chain was wide as a fine Chicago avenue, but broken, heaped and piled by landslides and avalanches until it seemed like a road into hell.

Lea didn't stop to rest men or horses. He rode back to the string, picked a coil of long lead line off a horse pack, and spurred back to the Baron.

"Fasten this lead to Ranger's bridle, Baron," he said, "and lead him out. Tocsen'll follow up the rear and push 'em along."

For a moment, Lea thought the big German was going to argue with him. Then the Baron nodded with a grunt and took the lead rope.

When the pack string was roped up, the Baron riding lead, old Tocsen riding pusher, Lea waved them on, turned the dun's head to the pass, and trotted forward, picking a track. The closer he rode up that slanting causeway of rubble, the harder the wind blew—howling down from the massive peak above. Halfway up, it was black as night, and icy wind and sleet lashed Lea and the staggering dun. The big horse kept trying to turn back, to put his tail to the blizzard wind, but Lea

31

held him in hard, and spurred him on, scrambling over the sharp-edged scree.

Holding his hat brim down in the gusting wind, Lea turned in the saddle, straining for a look at the pack string. Nothing. Nothing but the murderous cold and white sleet on black wind. High above, he heard the mountain's distant grumble, the dangerous talking of tons of rock, weighted and rotten with snow. He turned forward again, bent his head into the gale, and spurred the big dun on. Once, a few yards farther on, he felt the horse's hooves strike a sheet of ground ice—felt the slip and slide as the dun flailed for footing, missed it—and then took hold and strove back up to solid rock.

The wind from the peak began to buffet back and forth, shifting, changing directions. Far ahead, Lea began to see a faint gray glow, a lighter shade of darkness.

Falling stones, knocked loose from the wall of rock above hissed down nearby, cracking and exploding yards away as they struck the granite shelf. Lea saw daylight, just a shimmer, a touch of blue. The wind thundered past him. The icy darkness began to fade. And the dun, picking up its head, champed the bit and sidled, then bucked and broke into a run, down the dim last yards of the pass, and out into the sunlight.

Gunstock valley lay beyond, dark green with dense pine. It stretched below for a dozen miles to the distant foothills that the huge hotel loomed over. It was sunset; the shadows streamed long across the valley floor. They would be home by moonrise. Unless pigtail knew these mountains.

*　*　*

Lea sat the tired dun just below the pass, waiting for the others to follow him out. Knowing that if they didn't, he'd be riding back in to find them.

He waited for eleven minutes, by the big old silver-backed hunter he tugged from his vest pocket.

Then Baron the Graf Rudiger von Ulm und Felsbach came riding down out of the pass.

He was leading the pack string behind him, and both the Baron and his bay stallion looked a little the worse for wear. As Lea watched, the last of the pack horses—the slab-sided Candy Cane—came skittering down the pass. Then old Tocsen showed, drumming his fat pony's sides with his moccasins, his toothless mouth wide open in some Shoshone song or other.

Lea waved his hat, not wanting to yell. They saw him and slowly worked their way down to the edge of the lumber-slash where he waited. The hotel was of native stone, but many of Gunstock's out-buildings had been cut from this timber. The slash was nearly a quarter-mile wide, littered with fallen timber and clumps of pine too small to have been worth the trouble of cutting.

Lea gave them a short rest there, giving the horses a breather. The Baron didn't have anything to say about High Pass, but he looked a little pale. That ruddy color had faded out a bit. Lea gave them an extra couple of minutes, then he swung up onto the dun.

"Get your weapons out," he said. "We'll be snaking through this fallen timber fast. I'm taking us around the south edge there. If those three made it here before us —and they could have—they'll be waiting for us along the track. Cutting over south might fox 'em."

When Lea finished, the Baron muttered something in

German, and reached down to haul the long Martini out of his saddleboot. Tocsen yawned, and reached behind him for the double-barrel Greener. He'd tied it with cord under the cantle of his saddle.

"You set?" Lea said.

The Baron grunted. The old Shoshone just looked away over the timbered slash, and yawned again.

"Then we *go!*" Lea yelled. And he spurred the dun hard, lining out through the cut timber at a wild gallop, jumping fallen logs, running full out through the scrub pine.

The Baron, the pack-train, and Tocsen came thundering after him.

He was halfway through the slash already, the dun running handy through the broken wood. Lea used his fronted Sharps to ward off branches whipping at him as he went. He wished for a Henry, or some other carbine for this work; it wasn't going to be range shooting if it came to shooting, not in this scrub. And the Sharps was a distance piece.

Lea glanced back. The Baron was coming fast, riding hard in his tall, stiff-backed fashion, and behind him, the pack string and old Tocsen churned along.

Pig tail hadn't known these mountains, after all.

Just as Lea thought it, and started to rein the dun down into the dusk-shade of the uncut pines, a shot rang through the timber. The Baron swayed in his saddle and pitched out headlong into the brush.

CHAPTER FOUR

Lea saw him fall, spun the foaming dun, and spurred him out into the timber slash again. He felt a quick rush of air past his face as he rode. The rifle's crack sounded to the left.

Lea kept the dun lined out for the patch of pine scrub where the Baron had gone down. He drove the laboring dun into the scrub, lifted his foot out of the stirrup, swung his leg over, and lit running, the pine branches whipping at him, the big Sharps balanced in his hands. A third rifle slug snapped through the scrub.

Lea tripped in the tangle and went down hard. He rolled, and was up on his feet again, running. He saw the flash of dark blue in the green of pine. The Baron. He was alive.

The big man was sitting up, his broad, meaty face dead white, the left side and sleeve of his fancy wool suit soaked black with blood. The Martini-Henry was lying across his lap.

He looked up and said something to Lea in German. Lea didn't have time for it. He'd heard a branch breaking from the left, way out. The shooter was coming in.

Lea jumped up a short staircase of splintered logs. The setting sun flashed bright gold into his eyes. In the dazzle, two hundred yards away, he saw a silhouette come leaping. It was pigtail.

Lea got ready to kill him, as he'd done many times before. He raised the Sharps slowly, letting the long heavy muzzle drift, swing, and find its way to pigtail as he came running out of the golden sunlight.

Pigtail was up on the tilted end of a big pine log, still almost two hundred yards out. Standing there, drawing a bead with some kind of lever action. A perfect target. And perfectly safe.

Lea had jammed the muzzle of the Sharps with dirt when he'd fallen. He dropped the big rifle—he'd always hated gunfighting with rifles, the God-damned things. He drew the Colt, steadied it with both hands, and tried a shot. Miss. Just too far.

Pigtail's silhouette shifted, and he fired. He was a good shot. The round smacked into the log beside Lea's hand—a spray of splinters stung his cheek.

Lea turned to try for the Baron's Martini-Henry, and saw the Baron standing tall on a rough pine stump just behind him, the Martini to his shoulder, his bloody left hand gripping the long fore-stock.

"Get down, you damn fool!"

Too late. The Baron, blood dripping from his sleeve, swayed on that uncertain footing, steadied himself, drew his bead, and fired.

The round boomed past Lea's head. He turned just in time to see pigtail—a black stick figure against the flaming setting sun—spin like a dancer and go down, pitching off the end of the log into the brush below.

"Todt!" said the Baron with great satisfaction, and he sagged, swayed, and fell forward full length on his face.

Lea holstered the colt and jumped down to help him. Then, a pleasant high-pitched boy's voice stopped him cold.

"Good shootin, for a dude."

The kid.

Lea turned slowly, and saw the boy standing near a heap of discarded pine slab, maybe twenty, twenty-five feet away.

The boy carried a Spencer carbine balanced in his right hand down by his side. His big Smith & Wesson .44 was still holstered. He hadn't even bothered to cover Lea when he came in. Very fast. Or very stupid.

He didn't look like a stupid boy.

"Looks like he's out," the boy said, glancing down at the Baron. "Out, or dyin'." He looked up at Lea with a smile. "But he sure stopped old Bobby's clock."

So the pigtail's name had been Bobby.

"Just like I'm goin' to stop yours, Dad," the boy said, still smiling.

The Spencer didn't even move. Lea saw that the boy was pistol proud, intended to kill him with the Smith & Wesson.

"Listen to me, son," Lea said. "Just turn around and walk away. And call that other friend of yours, and tell him the same."

The boy's smile widened.

"Listen to me, now, damn it! I'm trying to give you a break!"

The boy laughed aloud. "Goodbye, old man," he said.

37

Just then—only a stone's throw away to the right—the swift blast and boom of a pistol and shotgun fire mingled.

Tocsen. And the third man.

The boy didn't let it shake him. He was a very cool hand, for so young.

He went for his gun, still laughing a little.

His left hand snapped around to the butt of the .44 like a stockwhip's lash—straight across his narrow belly in a classic cross draw.

It was one of the best that Lea had ever seen. The boy was a natural gun, no doubt about it. And if he'd known to put a little curve into his reach, he might have been even as fast as John Ringo had been. The .44 was coming out in a flash of blued steel.

Lea drew and shot the boy square in the stomach.

The impact knocked him staggering back. He squeezed off a wild shot and the round went smacking into the ground past Lea's right foot. The boy tried to steady himself, to plant his feet, but they wouldn't work for him; the bullet had drilled straight through his lean belly and hit his spine and broken his back. He collapsed against a pine stump, folding up like a carpenter's rule, throwing a long angular shadow across the timber litter beside him.

He sat there, half on his side, and still he tried to bring the Smith & Wesson to bear. A game boy.

Lea shot him in the chest, going for the heart. But the boy slid sideways as he fired, and the slug slammed into the boy's chest.

The boy screamed then, like a hurt child, and the .44 flew out of his hand, forgotten. He thrashed down onto his side, turning, convulsing, trying to crawl away from

38

the agony.

The boy screamed again, trembling in spasms of agony, his face contorted, red as a wailing baby's.

Lea bent over to him and put the muzzle of the Colt behind the boy's jerking head.

Suddenly, vomit came up into Lea's mouth with a rush. It filled his mouth, bitter as gall, and spewed out. He turned aside for a moment, retching.

The air was split by the ringing blast of a shotgun. The boy's head dissolved into rags. A spray of clay-colored brains struck the pine stump with a sudden spatter. Silence. No screams. Lea vomited hard, leaning out to keep it from his trousers and boots.

Tocsen stood watching him, expressionless. Then, he reached down to his shell belt, pulled two buckshots out, and glanced down to reload the Greener.

Lea retched empty, gasped for breath, and slowly straightened up, the Colt still clutched in his hand.

"Other one," Tocsen said. "He I shoot in leg. He goes still back to get a horse from us."

Lea cleared his throat and spit. "You're doing so damn good today," he said to the old man. "Why didn't you go after him and finish him off, too."

The old man shook his head. "He too good shot with pistol. I don't follow him more. You want; you follow."

The old man looked down at the headless boy, and then at the Baron, lying flat out on his face. Lea thought the Baron was still breathing.

He knelt down beside the Baron, and gently turned the big man over. The big German was unconscious, bloody, pale as snow—and alive.

"Get that damned suit off him, and bind that

39

wound!''

The old Shoshone nodded.

"I'm going after the other one."

Lea left the old man working over the Baron's still figure. Reloading the Colt as he went, he trotted off to the right, back toward the line of untimbered trees. It would be where the horses, scared and turned loose, would gather. Where a wounded man would work his way to get them. Damn old Tocsen for not finishing him. The smiling man must have come real close with that one shot, to have made the old Shoshone get so sensible. He wasn't interested in white-man's trouble.

The Baron. The big man could die yet. He was bleeding hard. Damn those three—that boy.

Lea was trying to find the spot he'd heard that shooting from. The old Shoshone didn't lie: If he'd said he'd hit that pilgrim, then he'd hit him.

After he'd cast around in the soft dusk light for a few minutes, quartering the ground, Lea found it. A spray of darkening blood across a patch of brown pine needles. The smiling man was in trouble.

Lea moved out through the fallen timbers, moving fast past the tangles, scrap slides, and deadfalls. He had perhaps half an hour before dark to find the man. Find him, and take or kill him, and then get the Baron to Gunstock before he bled to death.

The long shadows were already fading through the timber, sinking into the soft gray before darkness fell. If the smiling man weren't where Lea thought, if he hadn't tried for a fresh horse, then Lea had lost him, and the man could wait until they tried to move the Baron out, then take his shots from hiding. Lea had to find him, and find him fast.

The blood disappeared. The man had used his bandanna, perhaps torn his shirt for a hasty bandage, anything to stop the telltale bleeding from that wounded leg. Buckshot. It must be hurting like hell.

A horse whinnied. Well ahead, a good hundred yards off at the edge of the pine woods. The smiling man was trying for a horse.

Lea began to run, angling through the tangle, headed for the horse, bulling through the scrub where he could, jumping it, skirting around it where he had to. He didn't try to be quiet about it. The time for that was past.

He pulled up short, still a stone's throw from the forest line, and stood, controlling his breathing, listening hard.

Lea put his fingers to his lips and whistled, loud and long. Instantly, he heard the shuffle and stomp as the big dun, yards away, tried to move toward him.

Lea moved that way, his Colt still in his holster. He'd never had to draw it before trouble faced him, and rarely before trouble had already started. The only damned blessing of a fast draw.

"Hey!" The voice rang through the darkening woods. "Hey, you people! Let's talk about it!"

The smiler knew his people were gone. He must have seen pigtail go down. Maybe heard the boy screaming. Now, he thought three men were coming for him.

"Hey now!"

Lea didn't answer him. Just keep moving in, carefully. It was getting darker. He circled a little to the left, watching where he put his feet on the rough, scrap covered ground. The smiling man had nothing more to say.

41

At first, seeing just the south edge, Lea thought the little clearing ahead was empty, the horses and drifter farther into the pines.

Then he saw the Baron's stallion. The big bay shifted restlessly, tied to a bent pine branch. Past him, Lea saw the dun's big sand-colored rump, dull in the fading light. The pack horses were hobbled in a bunch, just beyond. The smiling man lay behind a stump a little in front of them. The drifter was stretched along the ground, his right knee bent to ease his wounded leg.

Tocsen and the Greener had done a rare job on that leg. The drifter looked to have tried to bind it with the sleeves torn from his shirt. But it was very bad; the bone had been smashed. There was a small puddle of dark blood under the man's lower leg. A gleam of white bone between the bandages.

The smiling man wasn't smiling now. He was lying still, his face as white as milk, a long-barreled Peacemaker gripped in both hands. He was aiming in the direction Lea had been when he'd whistled.

Lea stepped out into the clearing as quietly as he could. There was a chance—just a chance—to take the man alive.

"Now, put that revolver down right there," he said quietly.

The drifter froze, his face twisted with fear.

"Just put that piece down, and you'll live," Lea said to him. The man had no choice, lying back to him, less than twenty feet away. Meat on the table.

The smiling man had guts. He dropped the Peacemaker, and then, grunting hard at the pain, he slowly struggled until he was standing awkwardly, balanced on his good leg; the other, bleeding, he held just off the

42

ground. He reached out to hold onto a bent pine branch, then looked Lea in the eye. He managed to force a smile.

"The best laid plans of mice and men . . ." he said. "Damn if I thought anybody around these days could kill that kid."

"I'll take you in," Lea said. "A doc'll look after that leg."

"Much obliged," the smiling man said. He gave Lea an odd look, staring at him hard through the gathering darkness. "I . . . " He stared harder, his eyes widening. "Oh, my God!" he said. "Great God almighty, you're *Buckskin* Frank Leslie!"

"I'm sorry, pilgrim," Lea said. "I'm sorry."

And he shot the smiling man through the heart.

CHAPTER FIVE

Sarah heard the orchestra playing the *gallop*, "Garryowen", as she came down the grand staircase. At Gunstock, the balls lasted till one. The *gallop* was always played at midnight. Herr Speyer was in good form tonight, the orchestra sounded wonderful.

Sarah had just spent a very trying half hour in the Blue Suite, trying to comfort an unhappy young Baroness who'd been soundly snubbed by Harry Van Dettler just an hour ago during supper. Harry's father owned half of upstate New York, and Harry, golden blond and six-foot-three, was a great deal too handsome for his own good—or for the good of little Swedish Baronesses.

"Ah, it is indeed my lovely hostess, Miss Sarah Bridge!" Sarah, almost at the bottom of the staircase, glanced down. Count Yuri Orloff, at the foot of the stairs, stook looking up at her. The Count was a small, neat young man, with smooth, pitch-black hair, and a rakish cavalry mustache. His almond eyes were black as well, and seemed to glitter in the bright

44

haze of candlelight.

Count Orloff, as old Abe had put it to his daughter, had the worst damn reputation in Czar Nicholas's court. And that, he added, was saying a "by-God-damn big say!" When the Count's carriage—shipped ahead of him a month in advance to Truckee, thirty miles down the mountains—when that blazoned carriage, shining with trappings of silver and gold, had thundered up the long drive to Gunstock, escorted by half a dozen bearded Cossack savages who rode their black horses like Cheyenne, Sarah, waiting on the wide granite staircase to welcome their guest, had felt an odd chill that had nothing to do with the fresh bite of the mountain wind.

To be sure, the handsome young Count had been nothing but courtesy itself. Always polite, always attentive, as if, for him, there could be no one so fascinating as a tall, slightly awkward girl, the daughter of a rough old prospector who'd struck it rich and opened a luxury hotel.

The Count paid her a great deal of attention, and he smiled. But Sarah had seen him once, from her bedroom window, when one of his horses had bucked and kicked out at him as he prepared to mount it in the stableyard below.

The Count had stepped back from the animal, smiling, and had made a little sign with his hand to the two Cossacks who stood by him. One of them, a black-bearded giant named Grigori, had walked to the horse, uncoiling from his shoulder the long-lashed braided whip the Cossacks all carried, and as Sarah watched from above, flinching, her hand over her mouth, and whipped the screaming horse until it bled

45

in streams onto the stable stones.

The news of that had gone around the great hotel in a flash, and Sarah had begged old Abe to throw the Count out of Gunstock, Cossacks, carriage, whips and all! But Abe had just shaken his head. They'd had cads and bounders and roughs at Gunstock before. And he knew —and Sarah should know—that the swells were, if anything, a wilder trade than a riverside inn's. The Count was richer than a dozen robber barons—except for Tom Larreby, maybe—and if he chose to mistreat a horse, well, it was his damn horse.

Sarah couldn't bring herself to tell her father that she was afraid of the man. Old Abe would have been amazed, and embarrassed, to think that anything or anybody could frighten a daughter of his. And Count Orloff had never done anything, never said anything to her that wasn't the pleasantest compliment.

It was what was unsaid, what was in his eyes, that frightened her.

"May I say, Miss Sarah," the Count said, "that that blue gown is a perfect compliment to your eyes."

"Thank you, Count," Sarah said, "You're most flattering." And she stepped to the bottom of the staircase and tried to go past him.

"But Miss Sarah," he said, and his slender white hand reached out to gently grip her arm. "Will you not honor me with a waltz? Just one?"

Sarah tried to pull away, but the white hand closed on her arm with a slow and dreadful power. She felt her arm numb to the wrist from that viselike grip. The Count seemed to have the strength of a man twice his size.

"My waltz?" he said.

46

Sarah turned to face him, her eyes blazing.

"Let go of my arm, damn you, or I'll hit you in the face!"

The Count's bright black eyes widened, and he grinned.

"You do not disappoint me, my dear savage," he said. And he let her go. "Another time, perhaps." He bowed. "When you know what it is that you *really* want."

Sarah turned her back and walked away across the great two-storied hall, feeling her heart pounding as she went. At the wide double doors to the ballroom, she paused to compose herself.

I won't tell father . . . I won't! That smiling bully! To put his hand on me that way! She took a deep breath, and stepped forward into the ballroom.

It was a sea of gold and crimson. More than a thousand candles—Sarah knew their cost to the penny —blazed along the walls. And the walls, covered in rich crimson velvet, seemed on fire in the light. Three-hundred couples, the men in fine black broadcloth and snowy linen, or in the uniforms of a dozen armies: all blue, or red, or white and gold. The women were moving fairylands of velvets, silks, and lace. Diamonds, rubies, and sapphires sparkled at their breasts, and ropes of pearls gleamed on white throats and shoulders as they swayed and swung around and around in the dance.

Ball night at Gunstock. Leo Drexel's pride and joy. Leo Drexel had been a scion of Philadelphia society, until some old scandal involving a handsome young groom had necessitated his removal to, as he put it, "more rustic purlieus." Whatever his oddities, Drexel had been a godsend to old Abe Bridge. It was Leo Drexel who had instructed the tough old prospector

47

exactly how to attract, entertain, and generally cater to what he called "The Great World," by which, Leo meant the rich—titled if possible, but always rich.

"A Palace in the Wilderness," he'd said to old Abe. "That's what you want to create. A palace, a resort, a spa, a gambling den"—old Abe had pricked up his ears at that—"a place to see, and to be seen. A place, above all, that's *expensive!*" Leo Drexel of Philadelphia, and Abe Bridge of Silver City and points west, had understood each other very well.

Now, Leo had his suite in the south wing, a very handsome, if somewhat sullen young Peigan Indian as "body servant," and an occupation that consisted almost entirely of giving parties—the more splendid the better—for the guests of Gunstock.

And if many of the parties ended in the small hours at the tables of the ornate little Gunstock casino overlooking the wide back terrace, and a hundred miles of moonlit mountains, so much the better.

Sarah was well aware, since she acted as her father's accountant, as well as hostess and housekeeper-in-chief, that without the casino, Gunstock would soon be bankrupt. And even the casino didn't bring in the money that it might have, thanks to old Abe's habit of giving in to the pleas of some of the casino's losers— young adventuresses, and desperate young men with grim fathers in businesses in Boston, London, and New York. Faced with these white young faces, tearful and strained, old Abe would all too often heave himself up out of his fine leather wing chair, stump across his study —decorated for him in books and animal hides by Leo Drexel—open the safe, take out the young unfortunate's losings, and return them with a pained roar. "Hear, damn it! Take the damn stuff back!"

48

This earned the old man a great deal of gratitude. But it cost Gunstock a pretty penny from time to time. A penny that huge resort could ill afford to lose.

A young man named Easterby, a second son of the Earl of March, came up to Sarah, smiling. Toby Easterby was out in the American west on his father's business— the Earl had considerable holdings in Wyoming and Idaho—and for his own pleasure. He was a short square-built young man with reddish hair. A nice young man.

"Hullo, Sarah. Good god, what a crush you have here! I've been going mad waiting for you to introduce me to that Austrian creature!"

The 'Austrian creature' was a handsome blonde woman, several years older than Toby Easterby, known as Giesela von Rhune. Sarah suspected the lady changed her name and her title whenever it suited her. Her taste in men appeared to run to older, very substantial types, all very rich, none of them second sons.

"Isn't she a little . . . well . . . a little . . ."

"Old for me?" said Toby, who regarded Sarah as more of a sister than another young lady. "Not a bit. She's just my style, Sarah." He flushed a little. "But you wouldn't understand."

The notion that, having practically run a great resort hotel and casino, catering to the fastest sets in Europe and the East, she should not understand, struck Sarah as funny.

"No, I don't suppose I do," she laughed; and took Toby Easterby in tow, threaded around the circling dancers with him, and finally located the very handsome von Rhune in animated conversation with a sixty-year-old banker—a recent widower—from Baltimore.

49

The lady was not greatly pleased to be introduced at just that moment to young Toby Easterby. She knew—as she knew about every eligible man in the room—exactly what young Easterby's prospects were, and she found the elderly, and very rich, Mr. Blalock far more attractive.

She gave Sarah a quick, cold look, smiled brilliantly upon Toby, and sent him off, happy as a clam, to get lemonade for her. Lemonade, this evening. Mr. Blalock was a teetotaler.

Sarah had just turned back to cross the wide room to the band—when Leo Drexel came up to her, tall, thin, elegant, and annoyed.

"Well, there you are!" he said. "I've been scouring this barn trying to track you down. Your impossible father is tangled in a billiards game and won't listen to a word I say! Some creature from the stables has been lurking at the back entrance whining for Abe to come and see. To come and see *what*, the creature wouldn't tell me!"

"I'll go," Sarah said.

"And what, in heaven's name, is old Speyer doing to that Meyerbeer? He's been asked to play Strauss twice, and by people who could buy and sell this place!"

Sarah left the ballroom, turned down the broad hallway, and walked toward the maze of back passageways commencing under the massive main staircase.

She went to a narrow door deep in the shadows at the end of the hall, opened it, stepped down a flight of stairs to a short hallway, and walked out into Gunstock's servants' dining room. There was no one there except one of the upstairs maids, a short, pretty little

50

turkey from the remains of supper upstairs.

The girl got to her feet when she saw Sarah, and bobbed her a curtsy.

"Can I help you, Miss Bridge?"

"No, no, Edna, go on with your supper."

Sarah went to the big closet by the door, opened it, and searched through the hanging waiters' jackets, maids' uniforms, and cooks' smocks for something to use as a wrap. Finally, she found one of Mrs. Parker's old shawls, wrapped it around her shoulders, and started out of the dining room.

"Edna, if anyone needs me, I've gone out to the stables."

"I'll tell 'em, Ma'am," the girl said, and stood waiting until Sarah had left the room to sit down again to her supper.

Sarah walked through the noise and steam and bustle of the huge kitchen, nodding and smiling to an incomprehensible remark shouted across the tumult by the immensely fat Monsieur de la Maine, head chef of Gunstock, and a testy, very talanted tyrant. No guest who came to Gunstock ever left complaining of the food. She pushed open the heavy kitchen back door.

The mountain night was as cold as spring water, and pitch dark. The moon was just visible through the thick branches of the tall ponderosas that rose from the border slopes of the back lawns. Its soft silver light barely filtered through their dense, dark foliage.

Sarah had just started down the flagstone path beside the terrace wall, when a hulking figure stepped out of the dark into her path to block her way.

She drew back, clutching the shawl to her throat.

"Who are you? What do you want?"

"Miss Bridge, ma'am?"

Sarah relaxed, feeling her heart still thumping. It was

51

only Tiny Morgan, Frank Budreau's stable hand—a huge, gentle half-wit, and the butt of Budreau's occasional, cruel practical jokes.

"Yes, Tiny? What is it?"

She saw the gigantic figure, in dark silhouette against the deeper darkness of the night, respectfully remove its hat and shuffle awkwardly at addressing the boss's daughter.

"Well, ma'am, Frank . . . he sent me to tell the boss. Tell him there's trouble, Frank said. Right down in the stables."

"What kind of trouble, Tiny?"

"Oh . . . bad!" the huge shadow said. "Shootin' trouble!"

Sarah began to be sorry that she hadn't gotten her father out of his billiards game after all. Abe had a short way with any gun play or troublemaking. She thought of going back inside to get him. But, no! She'd run enough this evening. That nasty Russian had sent her scurrying into the ballroom like a cottontail, and she was damned if she'd make a habit of scooting.

"Well, Tiny. . . what are you waiting for? Let's go see that trouble!"

She followed the stablehand's dark bulk along the great length of the terrace wall. Above them, through the closed French doors, she heard the rythmic sounds of the orchestra.

Tiny led her to the end of the terrace wall, then turned off down the path to the stables. The path led down through the gardens, and Sarah looked across the moon-bleached flowerbeds to the small fountain splashing bravely away against the looming backdrop of the Bitteroots, their snow-streaked peaks gleaming in soft starlight.

Tiny walked before her out onto the scrubbed

52

cobbles of the stableyard. Most of the rough cedar buildings were dark, but a single bright beam of lantern-light shone out across the stones from a half-open door in the carriage house.

Sarah brushed past the lumbering stablehand, and hurried toward the light. The doctor, she was thinking. If someone is hurt, surely Budreau has had the sense to send for Dr. Edwards. Edwards was a young Yale man. A fine physician, she supposed, though he seemed more interested in hunting and fishing at Gunstock than his doctoring. He had a brusque way with imagined illnesses, but his good looks kept him popular with the older ladies. He was also a *devotée* of the new English sport of *mountaineering,* and had twice tried to climb Collier's Hill.

Sarah pushed the carriage-house door wide open, and stepped into the light, inhaling the close, smoky smell of an overheated stove. Then she stood still, and the stove's heat seemed to vanish into ice.

Doctor Edwards was bending over a man stretched out unconscious on the broken old rawhide couch the coachmen used. The man's clothes were soaked with blood. It was the Baron.

"Oh, my God!"

Edwards looked up, irritated. "Come in or out, Miss Bridge, but shut the door." He bent over the injured man again. Where's your father?"

"What's *happened* here?" Sarah said, going to the couch.

"He's been shot." Edwards said. "That's what's happened."

"My fault, Miss Bridge."

Standing behind the couch, Farris Lea looked at her, his eyes steady. The rage welled up in her.

She stared at him for a moment, wordless, too angry

to speak. And he stood staring back—Tall, filthy in his trail clothes, Unshaven—and staring back at her as if . . .

"Oh! You *saddle bum!*" Her face flamed red with anger. "How *could* you have let this happen!"

She knelt beside the broken sofa.

"Doctor Edwards, just how badly is he hurt?"

Edwards muttered, busily bandaging the German's broad, grizzled chest. "Oh, he'll do. He'll do. Lost a lot of blood."

"The way it happened—" Lea began.

"I don't *care* how it happened," Sarah said through clenched teeth. Looking up, she saw the ugly old Indian that followed Lea around on the hunting trips. The old man was squatting in front of the pot-belly stove, staring into the glow of the cherry-red iron.

"I don't *care* what stupidity has caused this! But I can tell you that this may *ruin* us!" She drew a deep breath, her blue eyes sparkling with anger. "And I can tell you and that Indian of yours to get out of Gunstock—get off our land! And if you don't get out, I'll have our hands *whip* you out!"

CHAPTER SIX

Lea woke an hour before dawn, coming awake with a jolt. He'd been dreaming of the smiling man just as he'd shot him through the heart. Murder. Cold murder, and nothing else.

Someone was scratching at the door of the little cabin he lived in at Gunstock. They'd offered him a separate room in the hand's bunkhouse. He'd refused it. Coming from the stillness, the healing quiet of the mountains, the rowdy noise of twenty Gunstock cowhands would have been no pleasure at all.

He wouldn't have to worry about that anymore. He'd been ordered off the place by Abe's daughter, that bony blue-eyed bitch. And it was probably just as well. Better not even to try to explain what had happened. Leave it a hunting accident, and nobody the wiser.

No questions, then. Wasn't likely anyone'd miss those three drifters. Not soon, for sure.

The scratch on the door came again.

Lea stretched, grunting, on the narrow cot, then threw the Hudson blanket back and swung his legs to the rough puncheon floor. He reached under his pillow, snaked out a Root Sidehammer, and with the small revolver in his hand, strode naked the few steps to the door.

He reached out to slide the bar free, and stepped lightly to the side as the heavy plank door swung open. It was an odd hour for visiting, even with the Baron hurt and the whole place in a quiet uproar about it.

As the door opened, a small white hand reached in from the darkness to grip it, to keep it from opening wider. A girl's slender shape slid into the cabin.

"Oh, close the door, Farris. 'Tis cold as blue blazes outside!"

Lea frowned into the darkness, swung the door shut, and barred it.

"Edna."

He'd been screwing the little Irish maid for months—and so, probably, had a large number of the male guests at Gunstock. But he sure as hell wasn't in the mood this morning. Even as the girl leaned against him in the dark, he heard the echo of the smiling man's voice. "The best-laid plans of mice and men . . ."

"Listen, Edna, I'll be leaving pretty soon this morning."

"And don't I know that, my dear," she said, "with the whole grand place in a topsy over it. The missus is that angry about it! That poor old German."

One of her small, cold hands slid down Lea's naked side, stroked, reached to feel his cock, grip it, squeezing.

"I've got to be out of here by first light, Edna," Lea said, pushing her away gently.

"Ah, no . . . ah, no, now." The girl began to move

her hand on him. The small fingers, warmer now with the cabin's heat, curling, tugging at him.

Lea felt his cock stiffening, growing slowly fat and hard in her grip.

"There now . . . there now."

"You want it that bad, you little bitch?"

"Ah, yes . . . yes, I do, you dirty man." Her other hand was on him now, tugging, massaging, squeezing. He felt her breath hot on the bare skin of his chest.

He'd first had her behind the stable, the second month he'd been at Gunstock. The small, black-haired Irish girl had been drunk and laughing, full of whiskey from one of the late-night stable dances the Gunstock hands used to run once a month, in rough imitation of the swell's balls up at the hotel.

Edna had staggered up to him, her round, white face flushed, and announced she needed a strong man to take her out behind the stable "for a vomit, dearie."

She'd reminded Lea of the half savage, wild-haired Irish gandy-dancers he'd seen. A fierce, tough, crude little peasant girl, all overlaid—for her employers— with the meek and respectful air they expected in a parlor maid. She was the wildest and most beautiful of the dozens of little Irish girls who dusted, and mopped, cleaned and linened the endless rooms and corridors of the great hotel. Between these girls and the hardcase cowhands old Abe hired to run the Gunstock cattle, after hours tended to become a little lively.

Lea had fended off a dead-drunk cowpoke, taken the small girl by the arm, and steered her out into the winter night. He'd been a little drunk, himself. Too drunk to give a damn about the cold, or anything else. It had been weeks since he'd had a woman.

Edna had shivered in the cold; she was wearing only a shawl and a cheap spotted gingham dress. She'd stumbled over against the stable wall, thrown her shawl back out of the way, bent over, and vomited her guts out into the snow.

Lea was impatient, hot and angry, and in no mood to wait. As the girl was bent over, retching, he'd stepped up behind her, reached down to pull her long skirts up, gathered the flowing material up in one hand, and reached down again to grip the soft, cool rounds of her ass. He'd squeezed her hard, digging his fingers into the hot softness between her cheeks.

Edna had gasped with shock, had tried to straighten up, to pull away from him.

"I'm sick," she said. "I'm sick."

Lea'd paid no attention. He'd probed, shoving his fingers up between her legs, into the fat pout of fur—slid his forefinger up and deeper, until he'd felt the soft line of dampness and then dug his finger into her.

She'd cried out and tried to struggle, but Lea had gripped the back of her neck and held her hard.

He'd gotten his cock out, forced her against the stable wall, and bucked hard against her naked ass, driving his cock into her with one savage thrust. Surrounded by the snow and icy air, he'd felt the sudden wet and heat of her cunt clutch at him as she'd cried and tried to twist away.

He'd held her there, and fucked her hard, winding her long black hair in his fist to keep her still.

She'd yelled, and cursed him.

"There, now . . ."
He was up, fully hard.

"That's what it is I want." She went up on tiptoes in the dark to kiss him, licking at his lips, thrusting her wet little tongue into his mouth.

Both her hands were on him, gripping him hard.

"All right, you little bitch . . ."

Lea reached down, gathered the small girl up in the darkness, and carried her over to the bed. Then he dropped her onto the cot, held her while she squirmed impatiently, and peeled the long dress up and off her. He snapped the lacings of her cheap corset, pulled it away, and swung his leg over to straddle her, gripping her round little breasts hard enough to make her whimper. Then he bent down in the dark to kiss her deeply, getting his tongue into her, drinking from her as if the girl were a cup of sweet water.

Edna groaned, moving under his weight, her small hands rough on the hot skin of his swollen cock. He felt her thumb rubbing at the tip, smearing the heavy shaft with the slippery oil leaking from it.

"Ah, darlin' . . . me darlin' . . . I want ya . . . do me, darlin', before you'll be goin' away."

Lea slid his hands down the silky length of her thighs, soft as down over the neat smooth muscles of years of woman's work. He hooked his thumbs behind the soft bend of her knees, and forced her legs up and out, spreading her. He put his hand down in the darkness, and found her there, hairy, hot, and wet.

He smelled the faint, salty, meaty odor of her. And he pushed a finger into her.

The girl grunted. Lea heard the soft wet sounds as his finger moved in deep. He put a second finger into her and she heaved up against him on the creaking cot.

"You like it, don't you, you little whore?"

59

"Ohhh . . . oh, yes. I do like it, oh, you dirty man."

Lea took his hand away from her and hitched up higher on the cot, crouching over her in the dark. He slid his hand to the back of her neck, gripped it, and pulled her head up. He held his swollen cock with his other hand, and pressed the hot, aching tip of it against her face, rubbing it hard across her lips.

"Mmmm . . ."

He felt her breath against him. Then, the soft, warm, wetness of her tongue. He felt her lapping at the bulging tip, lapping at it like a cat. He heard the quick liquid sounds of it in the dark.

Slowly, Lea forced his cock into the girl's mouth. She tried to resist, to turn her head away, but he wouldn't let her. He shoved the swollen head of it into her mouth. He felt the wetness, the heat, the slight stinging scrape of her teeth as she struggled to take it all.

She wanted it now. She wanted all she could get.

He kept slowly driving the length of it into her, as she licked at it, sucked it like a hungry baby, making desperate, thirsty sounds in the close darkness of the cabin.

He had the head of it in her now, and some of the stiff, veined shaft. He felt her tongue moving frantically against it, the touch of her teeth.

He fed her another inch and felt her gag, her soft throat convulsing around the head of it.

"Swallow it, you little bitch."

The smiling man would get no more of this. No girl would moan, gulping on his prick.

If only he'd had sense enough to keep his mouth shut. Sense enough not to say the name . . .

Couldn't a man run far enough, or fast enough, so as

60

not to have to kill to be left alone?

The little Irish girl thrashed under him, choking, struggling, trying to breathe.

He put another inch into her. It slid right in, deep into her throat. Her throat closed around it, spasming against the wide shaft. He would kill the bitch if he wasn't careful.

Suddenly, Lea pulled away—pulling the length of cock out of the struggling girl's mouth. It was dripping.

She turned away, heaving, gasping for breath—sobbing with the need for air. With fear. Lea bent down to kiss her.

"I'm sorry, pretty girl. I'm sorry . . ."

"That's okay." He felt her soft lips against his cheek. "I know it's you that's sad, poor darlin'."

He began to stroke her breasts, calming her, soothing her, carressing her round little belly.

When she was calm, moving slightly under his hands, Lea bent over her again, and lightly kissed her nipples, sucking gently at the stiff, swollen little buttons of flesh.

She groaned with pleasure, moving restlessly under him. He smelled the sweat on her, now, felt her skin's heat through his hands.

He reached down, gripped her waist, and turned her over on her belly. She went over easily, softly, a small heap of silken flesh. He bent over to press his face against the cool round cheeks of her ass, breathing in the warm earthy smells. The odors of a healthy, sweaty, young girl—fresh from a bath to hot bed work.

He gripped one of her ass cheeks in each big hand. Squeezed them, gently pulled them apart.

Then, while she lay groaning beneath him, Lea bent

61

down again, and began to slowly, gently lick her spread crotch, licking deep into the soft, furry heat of her, running his tongue up along the hot moist crack of her ass. Licking at the neat little bud of her asshole, then down and in, to the wet, slippery folds of her cunt.

Edna gasped and pulled herself up to her knees, crouching with her head buried in the sweaty pillow, her slim back arched, her round little buttocks gleaming white in the first faint light of dawn.

He spread her ass cheeks wide, and buried his face in her, as if to eat her alive.

CHAPTER SEVEN

She was crying aloud, shoving her little butt back into his face as he worked on her. It was a pimp's trick—butt-licking. And why not? Lea had spent a lot of good years in the Life—no use letting them go to waste. All those years.

Canary, Big Nose Kate, The Yellow Cow, all those tough sweethearts from the cowtowns, and railroad whorewagons, and mine-town parlors. Ugly as sin, most of them. And damn good sports. And a damn good living, too, while it lasted.

Edna was crying, sobbing with the pleasure he was giving her. She was loving it. Shoving her ass back for more. Lea licked his finger, and slowly, carefully, worked the tip of it into the girl's ass. And then twisted it in deeper.

"Oh, Jesus!" She cried out and tried to move away.

"Shhh." He moved the finger farther into her. Slowly, gently. "I won't hurt you, beautiful."

She groaned and turned her head on the pillow. And she thrust her ass back for more.

Lea hunched up behind her, turning his finger in her tight, clenching asshole. He reached down with his other hand, gripped the taut shaft of his cock, and slowly stroked the swollen tip up against her wetness. He felt the soft, furry dampness against him.

He held it, pushed, working under his other flattened hand, the finger still moving in her ass. He felt the moist grip, the hot oil of her cunt, and drove full into her.

"Ahhhh!" Edna screamed with pleasure as the thick length rode slowly into her—shoving, driving deep into her with a rich, liquid sound, until his belly smacked softly against her soft ass, his imprisoned finger.

Lea reached under her crouching body with his other hand to grip and stroke her plump little breasts, to pull and tug at her nipples—at first gently, then harder and harder, until she moaned and murmured with the sweet pain of it.

Now, he was moving over her, faster and faster, smacking into her, his swollen, wet cock pushing deep into her, pulling out, thrusting in again. Edna buried her face in the pillow, groaning, yelping with pleasure as he fucked her, squealing mindlessly as her ass clenched around the slamming pole of his cock, the tickling, twisting finger moving in her ass.

"Ahhh!"

"You like it, Edna? You like it, little whore?"

"Ahh God . . . ahhh . . . Jesus yes . . . oh, I love it!"

Lea pulled his finger out of her, and she screamed when he did it. Then he reached down with both hands to grip her breasts, squeezing them.

She was writhing, slippery with sweat, smelling of salt and fish. Grunting like an animal as he came at her.

He crushed her breasts in his hands, threw back his head blindly, and he came. It rushed out of him, flowed out of him like a river. It burned and soothed and jerked out of his throbbing cock deep into the hot, wet, moving core of her.

Edna's thin scream echoed his gasps as she thrust her round buttocks higher, her soaked, hairly little cunt gaping wide, then clenching as she came.

He felt the firm grip, the heat and softness and swelling around him. He heard her soft whimpers, and felt the small taut body under his soften and relax. She slowly collapsed beneath him, slumping under him into a warm, slippery cushion of girl, softly murmuring her pleasure.

"Your luck isn't bad luck, Farris. 'Tis good luck that you're havin'."

"That so?"

They were lying tangled together on the narrow cot, drowsy and at ease as the gray dawn light slowly brightened in the little cabin.

Lea would have been glad of some quiet just then. Soon, he'd have to be up and going—packing his warbag and saddlebags—going out to saddle the tired dun for the ride out. He wished he could give the big horse another day's graining and stable rest, but it wasn't in the cards, not the way Abe's daughter had sounded last night.

Best to be up and away by full sunrise. No use giving Budreau a chance to sic the hands on him—to hustle him off the place.

Budreau. A bowlegged bully, and stud duck at Gunstock, at least as far as the ranch work went. And the ranch work was a big part of the Gunstock operation, for cash as well as supplies of beef and garden goods for the hotel kitchens.

Budreau hadn't liked Lea's face from the start—hadn't liked him going off hunting with the swells, for money every bit as good as Budreau got for breaking butt with the hands and the cattle.

Budreau was a stocky, bull-chested foreman, with his long-nosed foxy face, his long black hair greased into girlish waves with Macasser oil.

Lea had never seen him wearing a gun. Only a knife—a big broad-bladed Bowie with a point and edge curved like a reaping hook.

A bad one. Lea could smell them. A bad one, gone straight. At least straight enough to ramrod the Gunstock cows to old Abe's satisfaction.

"Are you asleep now, Farris?"

"No. I'm awake.

Edna turned in his arms to kiss him. "Did you hear me, then? About the hotel and all?"

"What about it?"

"Why, the old man and his daughter are to lose it, sure. And then what's to happen to us who work for them, I'd like to know?"

"Lose Gunstock? What are you talking about, Edna?"

She snuggled into his arms.

"Oh . . . I was folding in the linens on the fourth floor last night, by the green suite, you know, and I could hear 'em plain as day, plottin' and plannin' their schemes in there."

"So?"

"Well, it was that nasty old Mr. Larrabee, and that Rooshin . . . that Count what's-his-name!"

66

Lea yawned, stretched, gently untangled himself from the girl, and sat up on the side of the cot.

"Oh, don't go just yet, will ya?"

"I have to, sweetie." He reachd back to stroke her bare leg. "You're a good girl, Edna . . . a good woman."

"I'm a wicked, sinful girl, that's what I am."

He turned and bent down to kiss her. "Never think that, beautiful." Then he stood up and walked naked to the water basin near the small pot-belly stove. He bent, opened the grate, and slid another stick of hickory onto the coals, then he stood at the basin to splash his chest and face and armpits with cold water. He thought of washing his groin, then didn't. He liked the idea of riding off with the sticky love juices still drying on him. It seemed less lonely, to go off that way.

Edna lay sprawled in the sheets, watching him wash and dress. She loved to watch him naked: the long, lean body, roped with muscle, streaked in a half dozen places with the quick white lines of old scars. Scars from fighting, from knives and bullets. She'd seen scars like that on her own father and brothers.

She'd known Lea for a fighting man—a killing gentleman—the first time she'd seen him. And she'd wanted him then.

"You're well out of it. Old Larrabee and that Rooshin Count are surely goin' to steal old Bridge and his daughter blind!" she continued.

Lea sat on the edge of the cot to pull on his boots. "And how's that, Edna?"

"Why, for the silver, man. The silver!"

Lea laughed. "There's no silver in these mountains, girl. And if there was, old Abe would know it."

"That he would not! That Mr. Larrabee told the

67

Rooshin that his railroad surveyors found a fine vein of it showin' in a landslide by Little River!"

"Well, then, so what?"

"Well, Little River is on the Gunstock land, isn't it?" She sat up, tugging the sheet up to cover her breasts. "And that's why they're goin' to take the whole shebang from old man Bridge."

Lea laughed. "And what does the 'Rooshin' have to do with all this?"

Edna pouted. "You go ahead and laugh, then, you brute." She stretched up to bite his ear. "But I'm for tellin' you you're well out of this, lucky to be gone. Because that Rooshin is to make trouble for Mr. Bridge with those nasty Cossacks of his."

Lea walked over to his warbag and began rolling and stuffing his clothes into it. Woolen workstuff, mostly, and one good blue St. Louis suit which he hadn't worn for two years.

Maybe more than two years.

He was listening to Edna with only half an ear. Servant's gossip was plentiful and cheap at resorts like Gunstock. And the notion of old man Larrabee, who'd been a partner of Commodore Vanderbilt's, making common cause with that coldeyed little Russian count in any kind of business, rough or smooth, seemed mighty unlikely.

"Now, what do you say to that, Smarty?"

Lea buckled the warbag shut, and reached up to lift his saddlebags down from the wall peg where they hung.

"And what's in it all for that Russian?" he said. "I hear the man owns a couple of counties over there— and the serfs to go with 'em."

"And so he may," Edna said, and stuck out her tongue at him. "But cash money is what his Nibs *don't* have. And Larrabee said he'd give him a million in gold to do his work!"

She lay back on the pillow, thoughtful. Lea could see one small pink nipple peeping over the edge of the sheet.

"I was thinkin' maybe Mister Larrabee'd be grateful to a girl who knows how to keep her trap shut about somethin'." She glanced up at Lea.

He turned to face her, his eyes suddenly cold, and slate-hard.

"I don't know if there's anything to this bull you've told me," he said to the girl. "But if there is anything to it—if you did hear something like that—you better damn well stay away from Larrabee and the Russian, both! Either one of them would break you like a stick if you crossed them at all. Do you understand me?"

"Oh, all right," Edna said sulkily, "I was just thinkin'."

"Don't think about it—and don't do it."

"I said I wouldn't." She looked up at him through her lashes. "Do you have to be goin' now . . . right this very minute?" The sheet slid down farther from her plump breast.

"Right now," Lea said. "Right this minute."

He slung the warbag over his shoulder, picked up the saddlebags and went over to the cot to kiss her goodbye.

He bent awkwardly with the bags, hugged her warm, naked little body, and kissed her. Her tongue slid into his mouth like a snake. She smelled delicious.

"Goodbye, beautiful."

"Oh, Farris," she said. And her face screwed up like a little child as she began to weep great sentimental Irish tears. "Don't go away from me, darlin'."

But he kissed her again, picked up the big Sharps, and walked out the door.

The only man in the stables was Tiny Morgan. Lea had always gotten on well with the giant half-wit, and Morgan greeted him with a broad smile.

"Good morning, Mr. Lea."

"Good morning, Tiny. How's the dun look?"

The big man shook his head. "Oh, your horse is still a little tired, Mr. Lea. You shouldn't ride him today."

"Got to, though. Lead him out, will you, Tiny."

The big man shook his head sadly, and went to get the horse.

When he brought him out, Lea saw that the dun was fit enough, but damn sure not at his best. The big gelding stood quiet while Lea saddled him and strapped the bags behind the cantle. Lea slid the Sharps into the saddle boot.

"I rode you pretty hard, didn't I, fella?" The dun was getting old for that kind of hard riding. *He isn't the only one getting a little old for hard riding,* Lea thought.

"You'll be easy on him today, won't ya' Mr. Lea?" Tiny Morgan said. The big man loved the Gunstock horses. They never made cruel fun of him the way Budreau and the cowhands did.

"I'll be easy on him, Tiny." Lea led the dun out into the morning light. The sunshine streamed gold across the cobbles. He swung up onto the big gelding. "Bye, Tiny," he said.

"Goodbye, Mr. Lea. Good luck."

CHAPTER EIGHT

By noon, he was high in the hills to the west of Gunstock, taking the easy way this time. No ride through High Pass.

He'd seen a big grizzly in the morning, rambling and chewing through a thicket of cloudberries. Lea had automatically marked the big bear, working out its territory, its ways in and out of those steep hill slopes, as if he were still a guide with dudes to bring for the trophy.

You're lucky, bear. I won't be by this way again. He was heading for Oregon, then maybe down to California and Mexico. West. But not to San Francisco. Too many people would remember a sport named Leslie. A sport who sometimes had killed people, just to watch them kick.

Lea pulled the dun up on the steep rise of a rocky knob. The country spread out around him like a patchwork quilt. The autumn colors: browns, dull, glowing reds, bright splashes of yellow, streaks of soft pine greens were as good as a painted picture.

Maybe better.

He swung down off the dun, looped the reins to a gnarled pine stub, and loosened the girth. The dun needed the breather; he'd gone pretty good since sunup, with just a water stop at a mountain branch, and a little cooling time after that.

Lea had drunk deep of the icy water running that little branch, rinsed and filled his canteen at it, and wished he'd taken the time to get some bread and cold meat for the trail.

Lea found a flat sun-warmed seat on one of the clusters of small boulders scattered along the crest of the knob. He dug in the side pocket of his buckskin vest for the stub of a stale cigar. One thing he would miss for sure about Gunstock, besides the French cooking, and sweet Edna O'Malley, was the fancy Havanas old Abe had shipped in for the guests. They beat steamboat stogies hollow.

He could forget that now. All of it. The good hunting . . . the good times. He hoped the Baron pulled out of that bullet wound. He'd looked pretty good, considering. But Lea had seen plenty of men looking pretty good who were dead by morning. The Baron had done all right. He'd gotten a good shot at pigtail—and already hit himself. The Baron had done fine.

The sun was hot, this far up in the hills. Autumn or not, the sun came down hard when you were this high. A hot sun, and a cold wind. Mountain autumn.

Well, Oregon'd be a change. Green and rainy there, most places, he'd heard. And Idaho, and the Bitteroots, just something more to remember.

A girl shot dead in a quarrel. Dead long ago, yet alive in the heart. An old drunk horse doctor had said something like that to Lea in Kansas. The old man had been talking about his wife. "Alive in my heart," the old man had said. "Alive to me . . ."

How she would have laughed to see Frank Leslie herding dudes through the Bitteroots. "Good lord, you're worse than Bill Cody!" Alive in the heart.

There was another girl, another place, to be remembered.

A thin little whore, and a tough little town, an Appaloosa stud, and a ranch. A mountain ranch along Rifle River.

Lea stood up, and as he stood, he saw a distant flicker of motion.

He shaded his eyes and stared hard out to the east—toward Gunstock. A thousand feet down, and maybe two, three miles away, something was moving over the crest of a wooded ridge.

A voice sounded just a few feet behind him.

Lea had turned and drawn before he saw who it was.

Tocsen.

The old Shoshone stood slouched beside a wind-stunted pine, looking at Lea without much interest, his heavy-lidded old turtle's eyes still as still water.

The old son-of-a-bitch had followed Lea after all. Lea'd thought that Tocsen would drift off on his own. The old man had never given any sign he liked Lea's company, after all.

"What the hell do you want here, old man?"

The Shoshone didn't answer. He stood looking at Lea for a moment more. Then he grunted and gestured to the east. "There is two riders coming."

"Let 'em come. It's nothing to do with me . . ."

"*Is* to do. They come for you. They follow your

73

way.''

Tocsen turned and walked off down the slope of the knob, stepping along with his easy bow-legged gait, his long smoke-blackened deerskin shirt flapping almost to his knees.

Lea saw that the old man still had the Greener shotgun strapped on his back. Gunstock property, that piece, but the old man looked to have appropriated it.

Lea walked to a small ledge and looked east again, trying to see the riders. For a while, he saw nothing. That was bad news, because it could mean they were trying to come in secretly.

But why? Gunstock had nothing to do with him anymore. Not even if the Baron had died. There was no law to chase him for those dead drifters. Even if there were, they wouldn't be getting this fast a start after him.

Then he saw them—still a couple of miles out, still far down the hill.

Two men. Riding down a long meadow toward a stand of dwarf willow. A long way down the hill yet, but dead on his trail, and riding out in the open.

He heard hooves clattering behind him, and turned to look. Old Tocsen was riding up on his little paint pony, set to travel. It seemed that Lea had a trail pard, like it or not.

Tocsen kicked the paint up to the top of the knob, and sat the little pony beside Lea, watching the riders far below. Those two men seemed to be running their horses pretty hard. Moving up fast.

Tocsen sighed and farted. The old son-of-a-bitch had had the good sense to get his breakfast at the kitchens before he rode out of Gunstock. The old man was no fool, anyway you sliced it.

"Decide. We go—or we stay?"

"We stay," Lea said, before he knew he was going to say it. "We'll see what these two want."

Tocsen grunted, shook his head, and climbed down off the fat paint.

Lea walked over to the dun, and slid the Sharps out of the scabbard. He had a few of the big cartridges in his vest pockets, and he dug into his saddlebags for a few more. It might turn out to be a long day. Then he came back to the ledge, and hunkered down beside the old Indian. They would watch and wait and bask in the hot mountain sun. And in an hour or so, they'd climb down a little lower on the trail and find good places to greet the horsemen riding up.

Lea wished to God he had something to eat. His belly was kissing his backbone.

The riders made good time.

Leaving their horses reined over the knoll, Lea and Tocsen had worked a couple of hundred yards down the trail and picked their stands, Lea farther down, in a rock shadow a few steps to the side of the track; the Shoshone higher, in a tangle of fallen lodge-pole pine. Then the distant sounds, the scrape and clatter of driven horses on a stony trail, came echoing up the mountainside.

Lea stood well back into the shadow's coolness, the sleek weight of the Sharps balanced in his hand. At the bend in the track here, he could probably do as well, maybe even better, going for his first shot with the Colt, getting the Sharps into action if the second man took a run for it. He'd need the rifle in his hands for that long shot.

So, it would be the Sharps, all the way.

Now, he could hear the creak of saddle leather. He took a quick look around—back up the trail, and higher on either side, up in the rocks. Once, some deputies in New Mexico had tracked him for a shooting, tracked him high. And they'd been smart enough to send their horses up a mountain trail, making all that noise, while they circled around afoot. It had almost worked.

He didn't see Tocsen when he looked back. He didn't expect to, though why the old man was putting his hat in this ring at all was a question.

Lea saw the horse's shadow come lunging across the trail from behind the sheer side of a huge yellow boulder. The mountain light was fiercely bright, like theatre limelight.

He knew the rider. A Gunstock cowhand named Folliard. An old man, almost sixty. A stringy, tough old man. What the hell he was chasing trail for?

Then the second horse and rider came out. The horse, a broad-chested sorrel, grunted as it took the fresh stony slope after the turn.

Another Gunstock cowpoke. Edwards . . . Edwins . . . some name like that.

They had no reason on earth to be trailing him. Both cowboys were armed. Spencers in their saddle boots, pistols stuck down into those clumsy holsters cowhands used. And something more, something Lea felt about them. Something he knew, just looking at them.

They weren't looking for trouble, and not fearing it. They had about them only the natural kind of alertness any man had better have in this country.

They were looking tired. Their horses were tired.

76

They'd come far and fast in a half day's riding. Coming after him.

He let Folliard ride up to within five yards of him. Then Lea took three strides and stepped out onto the trail in front of him, cocking the Sharps as he went.

Folliard's head snapped back in surprise, and he reined his horse hard so that it reared and tried to turn away. The old cowhand gentled it, his eyes on the muzzle of the Sharps.

"You scared the poop out of me, mister!"

Lea saw the second man draw up on the trail below. He wasn't reaching for a weapon. He stared up at Lea, hands still on his reins.

"You're on my track. You tell me why."

Lea saw the old man's adam's apple bounce.

"Hell, Mr. Lea, we're just doing like we was told!"

"Say what?"

"Budreau said Mister Bridge wanted you back at Gunstock—pronto. Said we was to ask you real friendly if you would come back, you know." He reached down carefully to pat his restive horse's neck, his eyes still on the Sharps. "We sure didn't mean to spook you. We was just sent with a message. That's all."

The other cowhand came up the trail to side his buddy. Lea now recognized him, name and all. Nat Edwinson, a bald man with a bad ear.

"And they sent you two riding this hard just to invite me back to the hotel. That's what you're saying?"

"That's it," old Folliard said. "Budreau said the old man was real anxious to see you back there."

"That's what he said," Nat Edwinson chimed in. His sorrel was sweating from the climb. "He comin', Bob?"

"Hell, I don't know," old Folliard said, and they sat

their shifting horses staring down at Lea with "We-done-our-job" expressions, waiting to see what he had to say.

"That German Baron dead, is he?"

"Him? Hell, no," Nat Edwinson said. "Not that I heard."

"No, he's all right. No trouble about that that I know about," Folliard said. "And I'd sure be obliged if you'd lower the muzzle on that there Sharps."

Lea looked at them both a moment more, then he lowered the rifle.

Folliard looked relieved. "I'm obliged," he said.

Lea stood for almost a full minute, thinking, ignoring the waiting cowhands. He had never found it a good idea to backtrail—especially if he'd had a damn good reason to leave in the first place. And Abe might be needing a neck to stretch—needing it bad—if the Baron had gone and died, and there'd been real trouble about it: like maybe some talk of murder by his own hunting guide.

"What else did Budreau say to you?" He gave Folliard a hard look as he asked it.

"Mr. Lea, that's all the man said, what I told you!" The old cowpoke seemed genuinely exasperated. "Mr. Bridge is real anxious to have you come back to see him; that's all I know!"

If the Baron was dead, he and Tocsen both could be in deep trouble with Abe Bridge. Still, lying and trapping just wasn't Abe's style. If Abe had wanted Lea hanged, the old man would have come after him himself to do it; and with a dozen men to give him a hand.

Still, a man *would* be a damn fool to backtrack into

trouble, just to satisfy his curiosity.

Lea heard horses on the trail above.

He turned fast, the Sharps coming up, and saw Tocsen riding down the track on his pony, leading Lea's big dun behind him.

While Lea'd been thinking about it, the old Indian had gone to get the horses for the ride back.

The Shoshone knew a damn fool when he saw one.

CHAPTER NINE

It was a long ride back. Too long for the tired horses.

They camped at dark in a fold of the hills, just seven miles out from Gunstock. It was a dry cold camp. The north wind was bringing the breath of winter into the mountains.

Lea and the cowhands sat at a small brushwood fire, blankets around their shoulders. Lea puffed at the last inch of a cigar while the cowpokes shifted their chaws, stared at the fire, and spit into the coals every now and then.

Tocsen sat across from them, wrapped in a very dirty old Hudson's Bay blanket. The Shoshone stared into the flames, his hooded eyes unwinking.

Lea'd never known much about old Tocsen. He'd known a lot of Indians, but he'd never been fool enough to think he understood them.

Folliard was telling the story of how he'd come west, when he was young, to go farming in Oregon. The ox-train had been wintered in, and he and two other young men had gone to work for a rancher in Colorado

—started in cowboying and never stopped.

The scrub fire slowly burned lower, falling in on itself in brittle bright-red coals. The night deepened around them until the stars crowded the black sky above them like clouds of silver dust. The wind blew stronger from the north.

Lea got up from the fire, stretched the stiffness out of his joints, then walked off into the dark, carrying the Sharps. He liked to sleep back from a fire in camp. It lessened the chances of an unpleasant surprise.

He found a small hollow in the hillside above the camp, maybe fifty yards up from the fire. There was tall grass there, matted, winter-killed, and soft enough. He laid the Sharps down and, wrapped in his blanket, lay down beside it, the brim of his gray Stetson tugged down to protect his face from the wind sighing down the steep hillside.

Tomorrow would likely be an interesting day.

They rode into Gunstock well before noon.

The Russian Count and his Cossacks had met them on the way, thundering by at a gallop, looking ready enough to run them off the road.

"There's a bunch I could learn to dislike real easy," Folliard said.

"That there's the man that whipped that horse," Nat Edwinson said. "He sure is big."

Lea turned in his saddle to see the last of the Cossacks disappearing around a bend in the trail. They rode well; there was no saying they didn't. Lea'd heard about that horse-whipping, and he'd heard, too, that Tiny Morgan, the huge half-witted stablehand, had gone wild with anger when he'd seen what had been done to the animal. Lea thought it probable that the Cossack, giant though he was, had been lucky Tiny Morgan hadn't been at the stable the day he lashed that horse half to death.

Seeing the Russians had brought Edna's wild tale to mind. The Count and old man Larrabee . . . a hidden fortune in silver ore.

"You stupid son-of-a-bitch!"

Abe Bridge sat glowering in his big leather swivel chair. Across the wide desk, Lea stood, looking back at the old man, not saying a word. It wasn't the first time Lea'd been called a son-of-a-bitch. Lea'd stopped killing men because of name-calling a lot of years ago.

The old man scowled furiously at him, his gray beard wagging to emphasize every word.

"Why in Christ's name didn't you just *explain* yourself?" He shook his head impatiently. "I know, I know . . . Sarah gave you a little tongue whippin', and told you to get out. But God in heaven, man, *I* run Gunstock. You could have come and told me what those owl-hooters tried to do!"

He muttered, and dug into a desk drawer for a folded sheet of paper, tattered and trailworn. He unfolded it, and slapped it down on the desk in front of Lea.

"Take a look at that, you fool. When the Baron told me what had happened, I sent some men out to the slash to bring those bodies in. The young one was carrying this."

Lea bent over the desk to look at it. A wanted poster —for three bank robbers. Thomas Deke, a man named Murrey, and a boy. No name for the boy.

"So, why the hell didn't you come and see me before

you high-tailed out of here? Tell me that!''

"I didn't want to get mixed up in this, for a lot of people to hear about, Mr. Bridge.''

That was telling the old man straight.

And the old man took it straight.

Abe grunted and stared hard into Lea's eyes for a few moments, then reached out to pick up the wanted poster. He folded it, and stuffed it back into the cluttered desk drawer.

"I don't suppose we have to noise it around the country every time some high-grader gets out-gunned in the Bitteroots,'' he said. "The Baron's pleased enough with himself as it is.'' He leaned back in the big chair. "So, we'll let him play the hero. You just stand back and keep your mouth shut.''

"The Baron's going to be all right?''

"Hell, yes. Or so Edwards says. He's up in his suite right now, telling every damn fool dude in the place how he shot it out with three hardcase outlaws. The fool's proud as punch!'' Abe got up from behind his desk and went over to a big walnut humidor resting on a side table. "Cigar?''

"Thanks.''

Abe walked over to Lea and handed him three of the big Havanas. "Take three,'' he said. "That's for saving that German's ass.''

"He did some saving on his own. He made a fine rifle shot.''

Abe grunted and went back behind his desk. "So I've heard—so everybody's heard!'' He settled back into the big chair with a sigh. "Now, I presume you're back on the payroll. Will you please get your butt up to the penthouse suite? The Baron's been asking for you all morning. And when you're finished with that non-sense, there's a party due to go out for partridge after lunch. Take 'em, and show 'em some shootin'."

"Like this?"

Abe glanced at Lea's trail-blackened buckskins.

"Why not? The dudes expect a mountain man to smell like a horse. Now get on up there!"

Lea went up the back stairs. Abe or not, he didn't care to make an ass of himself by stomping up the grand staircase dirt-black and smoke-stained, with rifle in hand, so that the ladies coming down for the buffet lunch would have something to goggle at.

Abe was a good man. The best. He'd do his best to keep Lea's name out of the hoorah over the dead outlaws. But three dead men were three dead men. In all common sense Lea should be over the Bitteroots by now, not going up a dozen flights of stairs to be gawked at by the Baron's friends.

Two young maids came giggling down the service stairs past him, eying him as they went past with a swish of starched black skirts. They'd have heard all about it, of course. Back stairs knew front stairs, top to bottom. No secrets were kept.

Lea wondered where Edna was working. The little Irish girl would be glad to see him back.

He pushed through the heavy green door at the top of the stairs, and walked down the deeply carpeted corridor toward the penthouse. Gas lamps flickered behind their cut-glass shields on either side of the passage as he went—one of Abe's expensive luxuries. The little gas plant below the kitchen gardens had cost him a pretty penny—and stunk up the place when the wind was wrong.

84

Near the end of the corridor, a tall, paneled oak door stood ajar. Lea could hear laughter and the clink of glasses. The Baron must be feeling a damn sight better than he had in the slash timbers two evenings before.

Lea paused before the doorway, and rapped two or three times on the carved paneling. After a few moments, the door swung open, and the Baron's man, Otto, stood looking up at Lea, with a cold, faintly surprised expression on his face.

"Yes?" Otto said. He was a short, dumpy little German, with a complexion white as a corpse's. He was dressed like a corpse, too, in a neat black suit and shiny black shoes.

"Farris Lea. The Baron's expecting me."

Otto seemed to doubt it. "I don't believe—"

"Oh, get out of my way!" Lea walked through the little man, ignored his clucks and gobbles, leaned the long Sharps against the entrance hallway's velvet-covered wall, and strode on into the suite's sitting room.

A dozen people were there, gathered around the long sofa under the windows. Sunlight was streaming in, filling the room with tiger-stripes of sun and shadow. The Baron, looking pale and tired, but cheerful enough, lay propped against a pile of pillows, wrapped in a long, quilted green silk dressing gown.

They turned to look at Lea as he walked into the room.

A few of the really rich dudes were there: Señor Bibao, the Marquis of Stene, and old man Larrabee—pink, short, round and fat, with his snowy mutton-chops, looking like old Santa Claus himself. And others: Leo Drexel and Toby Easterby, and Dr. Edwards. The

Baron's sister was there, too, sitting by the sofa with a needlework sampler on her lap. Erica, her name was. A handsome woman, tall and thin. Pretty, too, with those pale, pale eyes and ash-blonde hair, almost white.

Sarah Bridge was standing by the window, looking out over the sweep of the drive to the carriage road and the mountains beyond. When Lea walked in, she turned from the window to look at him. A flash of anger showed in those blue eyes. Not too happy to see Farris Lea back again. Not after she'd ordered him off.

Lea smiled at her as if butter wouldn't melt in his mouth.

"Ah, dere he iss—my fateful guide!" The Baron's English was off a bit this morning. The burly German sat up on the sofa, holding his hand out for Lea to shake. It looked as though the Baron wanted some kind of theatrics, so Lea sighed and obliged, striding over to the sofa like any rough-but-honest mountain man, and giving the Baron's big paw a firm and manly pumping.

"What a fellow dis iss!" the Baron said, letting go of Lea's hand. "Between us, we killed dos tree quick!"

"Bravo," said the Marquis of Stene. He was sitting across the room in a chair by the fireplace, and didn't seem very impressed by the theatrics. But young Toby Easterby said, "Damn well done!" and seemed to mean it. "I just wish I'd been there, that's all."

"Well," Lea said, "old Tocsen did us some good out there."

"Modest," said the Marquis, and yawned.

"Yes," old man Larrabee said, and he nodded at Lea from across a coffee table loaded with cake and cinnamon rolls. "Yes," the old man said, nodding and smiling like Santa Claus, "good man, good man."

Lea thought for a moment Larrabee was going to offer him a cup of coffee. But no such luck. The frontiersman was here on exhibit, not as a guest. He felt a sudden hot anger against these people, these damn stupid snobs who didn't know or care who the hell they were talking to. What would they say if he told them "I'm Buckskin Frank Leslie. I've killed more than forty men, face to face, gun to gun. From Anchorage to Vera Cruz men fear my name. I've lived high in New York City, Chicago, San Franciso and Montreal. I've loved Jenny Lind, and spent one night with Lilly Langtry."

"Mr. Lea has done just what he was hired to do," said Sarah Bridge from the window. "No more, and no less."

CHAPTER TEN

Coming down from the Baron's suite, Lea took the grand staircase. He didn't give a damn what the guests thought. He came fast down the center of the wide, carpeted stairs, furious and scowling, the big buffalo gun swinging in his hand. The guests using the staircase looked up in surprise and quickly stepped aside. Except one. Count Yuri Orloff stood waiting at the bottom of the stairs.

The Count's riding clothes and high boots were mud-spattered from his gallop. Still, standing on the thick Turkish carpet, its blaze of greens and reds and patterned gold a backdrop for his slender, elegant figure, he seemed as much at home as he had thundering at the head of his band of Cossacks.

The Count smiled as Lea walked frowning down to him.

"You seem to be out of temper, hunter," he said. "Perhaps an overdose of civilization."

Lea said nothing, and would have walked on by, but the Russian reached out one small white hand, and held his arm.

They both stood still for a moment at the foot of the staircase. At the touch of the count's hand, Lea had turned to face him, his gray eyes as cold and dark as ocean ice.

For just a moment, the Russian's black eyes widened, then narrowed like a cat's when faced with sudden danger. Then he laughed.

"Yes. I think an overdose of civilization."

"Count," Lea said, "take your hand off my arm."

"Of course," Orloff said, and his hand dropped to his side as he bowed. "You must forgive me, Mr. Lea. I have become used to dealing with *softer* types of Americans." He smiled. "I'd forgotten that some of you frontiersmen are very like our Siberian hunters . . . and bandits." His smile didn't waver. "So very touchy—so proud."

Lea felt a sudden urge to hit the man, to knock that smile off his face. He had a quick vision of the small Russian lying across the stairs, snarling, bloody mouthed.

"What do you want, Count Orloff?"

"Why, only a little grouse shooting, Mr. Lea. What else should I want?" Of course. Old Abe had told him: a party to take out. The Russian stood watching him, smiling.

"All right. We'll go up the hill north of the drive. There're grouse up there about a mile and half. There's a stand of young pine they like. We'll take a spaniel up there to flush them."

"One of my men will come to carry my guns . . . if you don't mind, Mr. Lea?"

"I don't mind, Count," Lea said. He'd heard the

Count liked to have one of his Cossacks along when he went out with a gun. Probably needed a bodyguard where he came from.

Lea met them at the east end of the terrace, half an hour later.

The Count had changed to canvas trousers and a shooting jacket, and he wore them as elegantly as if he were going to dinner with the Czar. The Cossack standing behind him wasn't so neat. Lea had seen men like him all over the West, and this Russian model wasn't much different. Big, in a neat black uniform with bright brass buttons. Big, with a face that looked hacked out of oak. A pair of muddy, slanted brown eyes, a big beak of a nose, a long, dropping mustache over a slash of mouth.

A killer—a disciplined one. Lea had known cavalry NCO's like this; big, brutal Irishmen and blacks. Men treated cruelly by life, held under ferocious discipline —ready to repay cruelty with cruelty.

"This is Josef," the Count said, gesturing to the Cossack standing behind him.

"This is Pee-wee," said Lea in the same tone of voice. The springer spaniel yelped with pleasure at the sound of its name, and frisked around Lea's feet, anxious to get hunting.

"Well," the Count said, and he bent to pet the excited dog. "Shall we be going?"

"I say! I say, you chaps!"

Lea turned, and saw Toby Easterby trotting across the terrace toward them. He was wearing the odd outfit that English people seemed to think appropriate for bird shooting: a checked tweed suit, high brown shoes, and a strange fore-and-aft-hat. A deer-stalker hat, was what they called it. You couldn't tell if it was coming or going.

"I say . . . do you chaps mind, I mean would you mind awfuly if I went along?" He had a nice-looking 20-gauge double, a Purdy, Lea thought, broken across his arm.

"I mean, I don't want to be *de trop*, you know, if you fellows would rather go out alone."

"Oh, I think you're welcome enough, Mr. Easterby," Lea said. He'd hunted with the young Englishman before, and funny hat or not, the boy could shoot a scattergun.

"You don't mind, Count?" Easterby said.

"Certainly not . . ." The Count bowed. "Your company will be the greatest pleasure to us . . ."

Still, from the hard glitter in the Russian's narrow black eyes, Lea thought he'd as soon not have Toby Easterby along. He was angry about something— probably afraid the Englishman'd show him up on the grouse. Fast, difficult targets, grouse.

Lea leashed in the spaniel and moved out across the drive, up the hill. Pee-wee was the apple of the Gunstock kennelman's eye, a big liver-and-white dog, friendly as a pup, and a terror around birds. "A range like a pointer's, and a setter's flush," the kennelman said. He was pretty much right. Pee-wee (named as the runt of the litter, before he began to fill out) was a dandy bird dog. Old Abe had gotten some very handsome offers for Pee-wee; had refused every one. He'd made some good friends for Gunstock by breeding the big dog to prime bitches and then sending the pups out as presents to the grander sportsmen among

Gunstock's regular guests.

As it turned out, Count Orloff had no reason to fear comparison with Easterby's shooting. The Russian was a superb shot, one of the best men with a shotgun that Lea had ever seen. Even a better shot than Lea with a scattergun.

The Russian had made a few shots that Lea would have thought impossible. One of them, a crossed double against two grouse flying like bullets in opposite directions. It was a double kill that left Toby Easterby groaning in disbelief.

"Good God! Orloff, you just ain't human!"

The Count had smiled and passed his gun back to the Cossack for reloading.

"A lucky day for me, I think," he said.

"Luck ain't in it." Easterby said. "Is it, Lea?"

"No," Lea said, "it isn't luck. It's the best passing shooting I ever saw."

The Count didn't answer, because Pee-wee, knowing a hot gun when he hunted with one, had already charged into a fresh bank of pine scrub, his stub of a tail spinning with joy as he ran.

The Cossack handed the loaded gun back to his master, and the Count hefted the gleaming piece, watching the dog, waiting for the birds to explode out of the tangle of green.

They came fast, whirring out of the pines in a drum of wing beats, weaving through the air grass high.

Then the Count stood back, smiling, letting Easterby take his shot.

The young Englishman, unnerved by the Russian's shooting, took his first shot and his second—and missed both times.

One grouse settled. The other two were gone, at least

eighty yards out and traveling fast.

The Count stepped up, snapped the shotgun's stock to his shoulder, and killed both birds.

"Have you ever seen shooting to equal that?" Toby Easterby asked Lea as they walked toward the kennels to return Pee-wee. The Count and his Cossack had gone straight back to the hotel.

Lea whistled Pee-wee to heel, and shifted the seven brace of grouse, tied by their feet to a loop of cord, to his other hand. The kitchen would be glad to get them.

"Not with a shotgun," he said. "With that, I think he's the best I ever saw."

"Good lord, I wonder if the fellow's as fine a shot with a revolver and a rifle."

"No," Lea said. "He wouldn't be. He might be a *good* shot with a pistol or a rifle. But not the way he is with a shotgun. Each weapon takes a different hand and eye . . ."

"Well, thank heavens for that. The fellow would be insupportable!"

Lea didn't say anything. Whatever he might think about the Count, he'd learned to steer clear of the guests' quarrels.

"Fellow's always smiling, don't you know . . . as if he knew a jolly good joke, and the joke was on you."

Young Easterby left Lea at the south terrace, and went off to change. Chef de la Maine was glad enough to see the grouse when Lea took them into the kitchen.

"We can use these . . . yes," he said. "We hang them a little while . . . then we shall see." He felt the little bird breasts. "I think a pie . . ."

Lea left the kitchen and went looking for Edna. The Irish girl must have heard he'd come back that morning. Lea'd expected to see her waiting for him in the kitchen—or, if de la Maine was in a bad mood, in the servant's dining room. No luck. A girl name Sally Connell was in the dining room drinking coffee and making cow's eyes at a groom. Sykes was the groom's name; he was a tough, thin mountaineer from Tennessee.

"Sally," Lea said, "you seen Edna?"

"No, I haven't, Mr. Lea."

Sykes shook his head too. They both stared at Lea, thinking, probably, about the gunfight at the slash.

"Well, when you do see her, tell her I was asking."

They both nodded, still staring. It annoyed Lea; the Baron was supposed to be the big shooter. He didn't blame the girl for looking bug-eyed, but Sykes should have known better than to goggle.

You could never tell about women. He'd been sure Edna would be damn glad to see him back again.

It would be like the little bitch to give him the go-bye, and then to show up in his cabin as a surprise. Lea hesitated, then walked across the cobbled yard to the stables. He owed that old dun a lot.

Tiny Morgan was there, mucking out the mares' stalls, and doing the work of at least two men, judging by the pile of straw and manure heaped by the stable door. He looked up as Lea walked in, and smiled the wide, innocent smile of a child.

"Good afternoon, Mister Lea," he said. It had taken Tiny some effort to learn the difference between morning, afternoon, and evening. But once he'd done it, he found that he liked the *sound* of afternoon best. So it was afternoon, as far as Tiny was concerned, from dawn to dusk.

"Afternoon, Tiny. How's the dun doing?"

"Oh, fine, fine!" Tiny spread his massive arms to show how well, how big and fine the dun was feeling.

"He's been eatin' some mash."

Lea took a look at the dun himself, just to be sure. But Tiny had done his job well. The big horse looked rested and at ease. A few hard rides were in the old boy yet.

When he left the dun, Lea saw that Tiny was again cleaning out the mares' stalls.

"Say, Tiny!" he called. "Have you seen Miss Edna today?"

Edna was a favorite of Tiny's, because she sometimes brought him candy left over from children's parties at the hotel. A surprising number of Gunstock's guests were willing to bring their children out to the wilderness, as long as they never left the hotel grounds.

Tiny liked Edna for another reason, too. She was one of the few Irish girls who weren't frightened of the big halfwit.

"Oh, Miss Edna was here early in the afternoon." Lea knew he meant morning. "Then she went away."

Lea walked back toward his cabin. If she wasn't there, then to hell with her. He'd go to the wash-shed and buy a hot bath from Bobby Chen. God knows he needed one.

He lifted the latch on the cabin door, and eased the door open slowly, braced for the girl's rush—or a pail of water on his head! Edna, drunk, had once braced a pail of water over his door for forgetting her birthday.

Lea eased the door open, then suddenly shoved it wider and jumped inside.

A knife came out of the dark and struck him over the heart.

CHAPTER ELEVEN

Lea felt the impact, the bright, slicing pain. He knew it was a knife. And he knew he might be dead in less than half a minute.

He kicked out hard and hit something. He leaped from the doorway deeper into the cabin's shadowy darkness, then doubled into a somersault over the rough pine floor, drawing the slim Arkansas toothpick from his right boot as he came to his feet. He was alive.

He cursed the civilized manners of Gunstock. He hadn't worn his .45 to go out bird-shooting with the Russian count.

Lea stood in the close darkness, not breathing, not moving.

The man with the knife had been careful; the wooden shutter had been shut over the little cabin's one window. It was as dark as a closet in the small room.

Lea felt the warm blood running down his chest under the slashed buckskin shirt. There was no way to tell how bad it might be. The jump he'd made into the cabin had thrown the knifeman off. Lea had taken the edge instead of the point.

Lea breathed softly through his open mouth, listening.

He felt it before he heard it: the sudden warm draft of air at his back.

Lea spun, crouching low, and thrust up hard with the needle-pointed toothpick.

The knife bucked in his hand. He heard a sharp cry of surprise as the double-edged blade slid home. Lea was hit in a furious driving charge that straightened him up and slammed him across the dark room and into the opposite wall with a crash. Only a strong man would have the strength to do that.

Lea spun away from the wall, stepping into the darkness. The man drove in again.

Lea jumped back to the wall, letting his boots sound loud, and spun away again. As the man came in again, going for the sound like a bear, Lea whirled back to the wall and swung the toothpick, wanting nothing more than to nail the son-of-a-bitch to the wall.

He felt the long blade slide into meat—and into the logs beneath it.

The man bellowed and struck out with his own blade. Lea heard it slice the air over his head.

Lea's wrist was almost sprained as the man tore free.

The bastard was as strong as an ox.

No doubt about it—it was Budreau. The sweet stink of macassar oil hung in the cabin's close air.

The burly ranch foreman had waited with his big hook-bladed Bowie.

Lea'd gotten steel into Budreau twice. But the big foreman didn't seem weaker—or slower. Budreau was a professional with a knife. Lea had thought so when he'd first seen the bow-legged foreman swaggering around Gunstock, the big Bowie sheathed at his hip.

Lea didn't like the odds. He could fight with a knife, and had killed men with them, but Budreau was an expert. The cabin was dark, and Lea's home territory, otherwise Lea's guts would already be warming the floor. That fast move at the door had given Lea a break.

Budreau came at him once again. Lea caught just a glimpse of him in the shadowy light, a darker darkness moving in.

Lea moved left, then jumped out to the right. He knew it was a mistake while he was still in the air.

An instant later Lea felt the steel slice his side, graze a rib, and cut free.

Lea struck back with the toothpick, and missed. Budreau was gone, back into the dark.

Lea felt the blood pouring from his side. His whole side was burning, searing in agony. It was hard to breathe.

The next time Budreau might kill him.

Lea began edging his way along the cabin's short back wall. He tried to stifle his gasps as he breathed; he was starting to feel sick to his stomach. He could hear the soft sounds of blood dripping onto the pine floor. Budreau laughed, a soft chuckle from across the dark cabin.

He was cut up himself, maybe cut bad. Yet he laughed, laughed at the hoarse breathing, the stumbling shuffle along the wall, the dripping sounds.

Lea leaned against the wall, slid along it a step at a time. He listened for Budreau. The big man had stopped chuckling. There was no sound in the dark, no sound at all, except for his own labored breathing, the scrape and shuffle of his boots along the cabin floor.

He heard the pine creak.

The knifeman was coming.

Lea fumbled with his weapon, got the grip he wanted, and felt along the wall in front of him. The floor boards creaked again, nearer.

Lea braced his legs and reached over the cabin's window sill. He felt in the darkness, then found the shutter.

Sunlight flooded the cabin in a rush of gold and Lea saw Budreau standing frozen ten feet away, blotches of red where the toothpick had bitten him. Lea spun, whipped his arm back, and threw his knife overhand with all the strength he had.

The big man blinked in the blaze of light, saw the blade flashing toward him, and, as light on his feet as a girl, swayed out to the right to let it pass.

He moved right into it.

Lea had learned long ago that right-handed men tended to duck to the right.

The toothpick slid into Budreau's throat, the slim double-edged blade buried deep.

For an instant, the big man stood stock still, his face contorted in shock, glaring down at the knife-grip thrusting out from under his chin.

He convulsed, clawing at the dagger, staggering across the cabin's sunlit floor, spitting and gargling as he tried to breathe.

Rather than watch the man, Lea watched the knife. Gleaming, with just the slightest smear of blood across the shimmering steel, the big knife fell to the white pine floor as its master stumbled, drowning in his own blood.

Finally, Budreau lay down. He sat first, red with blood. He managed then to pull the toothpick from his throat. He sat holding it in his hand for a moment, then fell onto his side, trying to die.

Lea had had enough. He limped over to the cold stove, picked up a piece of firewood from beside it, and smashed in Budreau's head.

Otto had served the Baron ever since the death of the old Baron. The old Baron had taken Otto out of the stables and made a servant of him. Otto never knew why he'd been so favored, but he'd been grateful, and faithful, in return.

No man could say that the present Baron was in any way as good a man as his father had been.

"Take care of my boy, Otto," the old man had said.

Otto had taken care of the young Baron. Very good care, indeed.

Still, he was not really prepared to deal with this howling wilderness, filled with savages and madmen. Idaho was worse than Italy! And that was saying a great deal.

It was not enough that his master lay wounded, not by a French bullet in an honorable war, but shot in the woods by horse thieves!

And now, not yet content, the Baron must send him to this hunting guide's shack. And with a bottle of champagne! A gift for the fellow!

And what for, God alone knew. It was, after all, the Baron who had done what fighting needed to be done against those three ruffians.

Otto marched up to the cabin door carrying the

bottle of champagne in a silver bucket filled with cracked ice. It had taken him a while to find it in the maze of stables, shacks, bunkhouses and storage bins behind the main building of the huge hotel.

Otto knocked. There was no answer.

He knocked again, tapping his foot impatiently on the cabin's door-sill.

He reached out to knock once more. It was likely that this specimen of frontier trash had gone off to the hotel kitchens to eat and get drunk with his fellow servants.

But, as he knocked, Otto heard a sound inside. The fellow was home.

There was another sound behind the cabin door. The latch was lifted, and the door slowly swung open.

Then, standing right in front of him in the doorway, was the most appalling sight that Otto had ever seen. It was a man *covered* in blood, with a stick of wood—a club—in his hand.

As Otto stood, staring at this horror, the bloody man said something, swayed, and fell into his arms.

"Oh, heavens, heavens! What am I to tell *Herr Baron?*"

"Really, Otto, the Baron is hardly likely to care about a dropped bottle of champagne in these circumstances!"

"But it was *Perrier-Jouet!* The Baron chose it himself for a gift!"

Lea thought he was dreaming. An uncomfortable dream. His side hurt like hell.

He thought old Abe's snotty daughter was looking down at him. She looked sorry for him. "Oh, where is that damn doctor!" She didn't sound very ladylike.

101

"Hold on, Mister Lea—just hold on! The doctor is coming." She looked as though she were about to cry.

"Don't cry," Lea said. He knew it was no dream. He remembered it all. But for Christ's sake, the girl was looking at him as if he were dying!

Lea said to her as clearly as he could, "Listen, I'm just cut up a little. I'll be fine. Don't cry."

It must have been the wrong thing to say, because she started crying in earnest. He thought, maybe, that he was dreaming after all.

He woke hurting as much as he had hurt in a long time.

He was in a room in the hotel, he could see that, but it was night. The room's curtains were drawn and just over the foot of the bed, he saw a fire burning behind the isinglass of a Franklin stove. Old Abe's daughter was sitting on the other side of the bed, looking at him.

"Are you in pain, Mr. Lea?" She wasn't a beauty, but she did have nice blue eyes. "Mr. Lea. Are you in pain?"

"A little," Lea croaked, cleared his throat and tried again. "Just a little . . . my side."

"Yes. Your side was the worst. The wound on your chest was not quite so bad . . ." She got up from her chair, went to a basin beside the head of the bed, dipped a cloth in water, and wrung it out. "It is very late at night, Mr. Lea. Your . . . your fight took place this afternoon." She folded the cloth and reached down to put it across his forehead. It felt cool and good.

"How bad are the cuts?"

She pursed her lips. "Bad enough. But the doctor said they should heal fairly quickly."

"Not fast enough to make any difference!" It was Old Abe's voice. And it sounded cold as ice.

The old man walked into the room, and left the door open behind him. "Sarah, you get on out of here, now."

"Father, he needs someone to nurse him."

"No, he doesn't." Abe stood at the bedside, looking down into Lea's face. "I'm hanging the son-of-a-bitch in the morning."

CHAPTER TWELVE

Lea didn't think for a minute the old man was joking.

His daughter didn't either. Lea saw Sarah Bridge's face grow pale. The year before Lea had come from Montana to Gunstock, four drifters had come riding by the great hotel and its cattle ranch, and asked for a handout. They'd gotten a few day's lodging, food, and fodder for their horses. Then they'd ridden out.

They'd paused in the high pastures, long enough to steal forty head of beef.

Abe and his ranch hands were after them the next day. They caught them, too, just the other side of High Pass. Abe hanged all four in the lodge-pole pines.

No, Lea didn't think the old man was joking.

He tried to move in the soft hotel bed, but a streak of pain ran up his side that took his breath away. He glanced at the bedside table—no gun. The old man had him cold.

"Father—"

"You get out of this room right now, Sarah!"

"But—"

"Damn you, girl! Did you hear me? I said clear out of this room—*pronto!*"

Nobody argued with Abe Bridge when he looked like that.

Sarah, her face white with anger, turned without a word and went out.

When she was gone Abe stood glaring down at him. Lea hitched himself up onto his elbow. He didn't figure he had much to lose.

"What's all this talk about hanging, Abe? That pig Budreau laid for me in my own place, and attacked me!"

"Yes. And why would he do that, Lea? Except if he found out, and came to get you for it!" The old man looked ready to hit him.

Lea felt a cold, sick feeling in his guts.

"Get me? For what?"

The old man's fists were clenched, trembling.

"For choking the life out of that little girl . . . *that's* what."

"Edna?"

"As if you didn't know—you dirty son of a bitch!" Abe exploded. He reached down and caught Lea by the throat, and shook him; the strong, gnarled old miner's hands squeezing.

Lea twisted on the bed, his side, his chest in a flame of agony—clawing, trying to tear the old man's hands off his throat. The firelight was going, dimming, wavering as he fought. He saw only Abe Bridge's snarling face, shifting and rippling as if it were under dark water.

"You could have killed him!"

"By God, I *meant* to kill the son-of-a-bitch!"

"Get out of my way, both of you." The doctor's face swam out of the dark above Lea. He felt hands on his throat, the bandages at his side.

"Not bleeding again . . . no thanks to you, Mr. Bridge."

Lea forced his eyes open. The lids seemed very heavy. He saw the doctor bending over him, Sarah Bridge and old Abe standing just behind him.

"Welcome back, Lea," Dr. Edwards smiled down at him. "You've had quite a day!"

"And his last!" Abe Bridge said.

"What do you mean by that?" the doctor said.

"I mean he murdered that poor little Irish girl! That's what I mean by that!"

"The hell he did. Wasn't he riding back here with your own men last night?"

"That's right, doctor."

Edwards straightened the twisted bedsheet, folded it down, and examined the bandage over the cut on Lea's chest. "Mr. Bridge," he said, "that girl was strangled last night—and early in the night, at that."

"Then he couldn't have killed her," Sarah said, giving her father a very cold look.

"Not if he was on the trail with those ranchhands, riding in." Edwards pulled the sheet up over Lea's bandaged chest.

"I was—" Lea croaked, cleared his throat, and tried again. "I was with those men. Who found her?"

Abe pushed the doctor aside. "Listen, boy, I made a fool of myself here."

"Looks like . . ." said Sarah Bridge.

Abe glared at her. "Well, damnit, I'm responsible for

those girls! You think I'm going to let some dirty dog choke the life out of a little girl at Gunstock—and get away with it?'' He reached down and took Lea's hand. "I'm sorry I flew off the handle, there, boy, but I knew damn well you'd been stepping out with that O'Malley girl. And, well . . .''

"Stepping out . . ?'' said Sarah Bridge. This time it was Lea who got the cold look.

"Forget it,'' Lea croaked. "I understand . . .''

"Very handsome,'' Doctor Edwards said. "Now if the courtesies are over with, I'd like Mr. Lea to get some sleep. In fact, I insist on it.''

"All right.'' Abe let Sarah lead him to the door. "I suppose it was Budreau.''

Edwards looked down at Lea. "You must be in considerable pain, Mr. Lea.''

"Not much.''

"Ummm. Not much, you say?'' He turned away to the bedside table and dug into his leather bag. "Well, I think we'll prescribe a few drops of laudanum all the same.''

Lea spent the next three days and nights dreaming while awake. Edward's laudanum floated him down a river that flowed past everyone he'd known for many years. People who had died. People who had left him. Doc Holliday came walking into his dream, looking just as Lea had first seen him, in Fort Smith those many years ago.

"Frank Leslie,'' Doc had said, "I understand that you are a rare pisser indeed with a Colt. Is that so?'' His bony, wasted, ugly little face was screwed up in curiosity. Lea thought the little dentist might be looking

107

for a fight.

"I cannot tell a lie," he said to the little man, smiling. "I am indeed a considerable hand with a six-gun."

"It's a lonely life, isn't it?" Holliday said to him, peering at Lea with those watery, pale blue eyes.

"Lonely, and bitter, and foolish," Lea had said to him.

Doc had laughed and nodded. He even bought the first round of beers. The other men in the bar had been disappointed. The silence had dissolved into murmurs, then laughter, as they all went back to their drinks and their games and their girls.

"You've dreamed of me enough, Frank," Doc said to Lea. "Remember me dying in Denver? You surely don't want to dream about that." Lea saw Holliday's small, bony hand clenched around the glass of beer. The beer was cold; the glass had frost on it. They'd brought snow down from the mountains to the Denver bars.

Lea awoke, thirsty, and knew he was awake. It was bright, cold, and sunny outside.

He thought at first there was nobody else in the room, then he saw old Tocsen squatting on his haunches in the sunlight under one of the tall windows. The old man was leaning back against the wall, smoking a sloppily rolled cigarette. Lea could smell the Bull Durham. The old Shoshone turned his head to look at Lea, as if he'd expected him to be awake at just that moment.

"You want water?" he said. "You want eat?"

"Water," Lea said, and watched the old man rise to his feet and shuffle over to the nightstand. Tocsen picked up the glass from the tray and dipped it into the water pitcher. He brought it up half full. Lea rolled up onto his elbow, feeling the dull, ache in his side as he did. He reached out, took the glass, and drank. He finished it in seconds.

"Want more?"

Lea shook his head and lay back down on the pillow. He didn't feel so bad. He didn't feel sick either. Just tired. Tired right down to his bones.

Old Tocsen took back the glass and stood beside the bed, staring down at him. He didn't seem too interested.

"Women come back by and by," he said to Lea. "By and by" was a phrase the old Shoshone was fond of.

"What women?" Lea said. He was asleep before the old man could answer him.

He dreamed he was standing on the bank of Rifle River, watering the dun. The dun was young again; his hide flashed sleek in the summer sunlight. He was mouthing the water, sucking it up in great gulps.

Lea dreamed he pulled the horse away, mounted him, and rode off into the meadows. He rode a long way, which passed quickly in the dream, and came to the west ridge that rose above the ranch.

There, he reined in the dun. He didn't want to ride over the crest for fear of what he'd see. The ranch all ruined and gone, maybe. Or buned out. Or never there at all.

Then he took a deep breath and spurred the big horse through the pines, up to the crest of the ridge.

It was there.

The big cabin with its square logs, the corral and sheds and stables. And the horses. He could see the appaloosas in the high pastures, the little colts and fillies trotting after the mares, the big stud higher on the hill.

The place looked good. He was glad he'd gone up to the crest of the ridge. Now he could see it all, all the broad pastures deep in grass, green with spring. The fields, the stands of hardwood and pine, the valley stretching out below.

He saw old Bupp come walking out of the stable. The old man was lugging grain buckets out to the corral. He seemed a little more stooped than usual.

Lea wondered if the Blackfoot was around. He'd be a fully grown man by now.

Then he saw the girl. She came riding out of the trees below the cabin, across the meadow on a little dapple mare. She had on a pair of trousers and a bright red calico shirt; a floppy-brimmed straw hat sat on her head. She was leading a pack-horse hitched up with sacks and boxes from town. Looked like she knew her business.

"Good girl," Lea said to her.

He stood up in his stirrups and called down to her. "Good girl!"

But he called too loud and felt himself spinning.

He could just see the mountains looming over the valley, their peaks sparkling with spring snowfall through the distance. The girl looked tiny. He thought she turned her face up to look at him.

When he woke again it was night. Sarah Bridge was sitting in the upholstered rocker by the bed, knitting something; it looked like an afghan, black, green, and gold. She was rocking a little, her soft brown hair shining in the lamplight. Lea lay still, watching her.

When she finally looked up from her work, she seemed a little startled to find him looking at her. "You're awake, Mr. Lea."

"Yes."

"Are you in pain?" She put aside her work and came to stand beside the bed.

"No." And he wasn't. The sharp ache along his side was gone. He felt stiff, awkward, all along his body.

"You've been very ill, Mr. Lea." She was mixing some brown medicine into the water glass.

"How long?"

"Three days," she said. "Here, please drink this."

"What is it?"

"Just an iron tonic. Nothing to be afraid of." She smiled at him. "I don't think it even tastes very bad."

It seemed to Lea that there was more to Sarah Bridge than he had thought. She appeared to have been nursing him, even though she'd never much liked him. She had beautiful blue eyes. The tonic tasted terrible.

CHAPTER THIRTEEN

He woke again just before dawn.

It was still dark outside the tall windows, but the darkness had a touch of gray, a soft light to it.

Lea turned his head on the pillow to take a quiet look at Sarah Bridge. She wasn't there.

Another woman, older, slim, dressed in gray, with pale ash-blonde hair was rocking slowly in the big rocking chair, reading a book.

It was the Baron's sister, Erica. What in blue hell was she playing nurse for? As far as Lea could remember, the Baron's sister had been even more of a snob than the Baron himself. People waited on her, not the other way around.

The German woman turned a page, then looked up to see Lea watching her. She stared back at him for a moment, her pale gray eyes expressionless. Then she smiled.

"Good morning, Herr Lea." She looked down at a little gold watch pinned to the bosom of her dress. "It is just now five o'clock."

"Good morning." Lea reached out for the water on the bedside table.

"No, no." She was out of the chair. "That is my task, as your nurse. Is it not?" She reached down to put an arm behind his shoulders, lifting him as she held the glass to his lips. She was stronger than she looked.

"Since you have been so brave in helping my dear brother against those bandits—" "I thought the least I could do was to relieve Miss Bridge. The poor child was quite exhausted." She put the glass down and plumped up the pillows behind him.

Lea felt one slender hand gently stroke the back of his neck. Then she arranged her wide silken skirt and sat carefully on the side of the bed, smiling at him.

"It doesn't hurt you if I do this?"

"No," Lea said. "I'm healed up pretty well." It was strange; the Baron's snotty sister had never struck him as the ministering-angel type.

"Yes, I think you are," the German woman said. She stared at Lea, the pale eyes still. She touched her lips with the tip of her tongue. "But a bad injury, the doctor said, especially the cut along your side." A flush of color rose in her white cheeks. "To have fought in such a way. To have fought in the darkness with knives, against a brute such as that! To have cut him like that, to have stabbed him and killed him!" She flushed again, and looked down at the carpet. "It was very brave."

"Not much," Lea said. "I was plenty scared."

She looked up at him, staring with those pale, pale eyes. "I don't think so," she said. "I think you like to fight, Mr. Lea. I think you enjoy the struggle when a man pits his strength against yours, attacks you with a weapon so you must kill him or be killed yourself."

113

"The hell I do," Lea said.

But the German woman just smiled, sitting on the edge of the bed, staring into his eyes. It was as if she knew something about him.

"I have known men like you," she said softly. "Men who kill people." The pink tip of her tongue showed again, touching her lips.

"I don't make a habit of it, lady," Lea said coldly. What the hell was this bitch after?

"No?" She smiled and stood up beside the bed, smoothing the wrinkles from her long skirt. "Don't you?"

She stood, looking down at him for a moment. In the dull gold of the lamplight, he could still see a small blue vein throbbing along the slim white column of her throat.

She cleared her throat. "I think that I had better change the bandage for you. It will be one less thing to be done by Miss Bridge in the morning."

"It feels all right," Lea said. "No need to bother."

"It is not a *bother*, Mr. Lea, it is something that must be done. Please to turn over onto your other side." She reached for the bandages and scissors on the bedside table.

Lea turned over onto his right side, half expecting a twinge of pain. There was none. Just a feeling of tightness, the scratchy discomfort of a row of stitches. A few days in bed and hours of sleep had fixed him up pretty damn well.

The sheet was pulled down from his shoulder, and in a moment he felt the German woman's cool hand resting against the muscles of his back.

He didn't even have a nightshirt on, but the lady

didn't seem to give a damn. He felt her cool fingers stroke for a moment along his back, then gently begin to work at the sticking plaster at the edges of the long bandage.

There was no doubt about it; the Baron's sister was enjoying herself. Lea had known women who liked a little violence in their lives. Most like violence at a safe distance, but there'd been one or two who liked it right in their lap. Jane Canary, for one. And that Mexican girl in Monterey. But near or far, the Baron's cold, thin sister had some interest in killing. Maybe it was in her blood. Lea remembered the Baron's eyes as he'd watched the three drifters riding away when they'd first sent them out of camp. A hard bunch, the Prussians.

"This will hurt you a little, I think."

Lea felt the cool fingers tugging at the tape holding the bandage along his side. He felt them grip and tear the whole bandage free.

"Damn it!"

"I said it would hurt you." The damn woman was laughing at him! "But not too badly I hope." The cool fingers were on him again, caressing.

"It is a terrible scar . . . ugly . . . red."

The hands were not so cool now. Lea winced as a fingertip prodded at the barely healed wound, and slowly traced the long scar down along his ribs.

"And you have other scars—here." The slim hand rested warm against his side. "You have fought men before, and killed them, haven't you, Mr. Lea?" Her voice was hoarse with pleasure.

Lea knew what she wanted.

"Yes. I've killed men."

Again, he felt her fingers trace the long, inflamed

115

scar, the ladder of stitches. She swallowed. "How have you . . . done it?"

He wanted to see her. He started to turn, but her hand was at his shoulder, stopping him.

"Tell me," she said. "Just tell me." Both her hands were on him then, rubbing gently up along the wound, fingertips feathers along the scar. Her slim hands felt hot.

"I've shot them," Lea said. His own voice was hoarse now, his throat tight. As her hands worked on him, rubbing harder, digging into the muscles of his side, he felt his cock stir against the smooth sheet. However the bitch wanted it; that's how he'd give it to her. He turned his face into the pillow to smile.

"Tell me," she said. "Tell me."

"I shot a man in Montana once. I hit him in the belly."

"Yes," she said. He felt her nails dig into his skin.

"He'd fired twice at me, but it was across a street, and he was shooting for my head. He missed." One of her hands moved down across his naked hip, hot against his skin. "I shot at him and missed him. Then I shot at him again and hit him in the belly. He was turned to the side a little and the bullet tore him open." Her warm hand gripped at his hip. Lea felt the nails scratching. "He turned and tried to walk away. A lot of men do that when they're hurt bad. As if they can walk away from the pain, I guess."

Her hand was still. Lea felt something warm touching the swollen red scar. He stiffened, his cock rising hard against the sheet. He heard a soft sound, felt the quick motion along the wound.

She was licking it.

"Then . . . then his guts came out. You could see

116

them coming out with all the blood. A coil of it came out of him, sticky and blue-white in the blood. It was hanging down onto his pants."

Her hand slid down his belly and found his cock. She was squeezing, her hand moving slowly up and down under the sheet.

"I would have shot him again, but a woman was in the way. She came running out in the street and got in the way."

Lea heard the German woman moan. He felt her trembling as she bent over him. Her tongue was frantic as she licked at the scar; he felt her teeth against the stitches.

Then he turned.

"No," she said, and her hand left his swollen cock. Her face was flush, and a strand of hair had come loose and trailed across her forehead. Her mouth was wet.

She tried to stand, but he reached up and took her by the arms and held her. She tried to pull away, but he wouldn't let her go.

"I haven't finished," he said. "There's more to tell you, about how that man died."

She moaned something in German and turned her head away.

"No, no," Lea said. "I haven't finished—and you haven't, either."

He pulled her back down to the side of the bed, gripping her arms hard enough to hurt her. Then he reached up with one hand to touch the hair gathered at the back of her neck. He held her there. Then, with his other hand, he took her slender wrist—as slim as a child's—and forced her hand under the sheet to his cock. She kept her fist clenched against him there for a moment, then her hand slowly opened and her fingers curled around him.

"If I do this, will you let me go?"

The small hand gripped gently, squeezed, stroked. He looked up and saw her staring at him, her pale eyes wide.

"I haven't finished what I was telling you," Lea said.

"I don't want to hear."

"Yes, you do," Lea said. "You want to hear it all." Her smiled at her. "You want to see something, too, don't you?"

He let go of her wrist, picked up the top of the sheet, and threw it back.

She stared at him for a moment more, looking into his eyes. Then she looked down at his cock, standing red and swollen, laced with knotted veins, thrusting up out of the narrow grip of her white fingers.

"That's what you like, isn't it?"

She didn't say anything. She just sat beside him, staring down at him, at her hand.

"You like licking things," Lea said. "Then go ahead and lick that."

She shook her head without saying a word. He saw that she was starting to cry. He tightened his grip on her hair, gathering it in his fingers at the back of her neck; then, slowly, he forced her head down. She tried to twist away, to get off the edge of the bed and stand up, but Lea tightened his grip until she cried out with the pain.

The bulging red head of it touched her cheek, left a pale smear across it. Lea had both hands on her head now, guiding her. He brought her back, brought her lips down to it. She sobbed, opened her mouth, and took it.

Lea felt her teeth against it, the heat and slippery wetness of her mouth.

She still held the shaft in her hand, and now, angry and frightened, she squeezed harder. Lea felt some juice rise in it.

He held her still there, hunched over him, the nape of her neck shining like white silk in the lamplight. There was a faint dusting of hair down along the back of her slender neck.

She was trembling, breathing heavily through her nose. Lea could see the bulge of his cock in her mouth. Her pale cheek ballooned, her mouth stretched achingly wide. He felt her tongue move against him.

"Be still," Lea said to her. "And listen to me."

She groaned, struggled a moment more, and then was quiet.

"When the woman came out and got in the way," Lea said, "I walked on across the street to them. He'd already gone down. I could see him sitting in the dirt beside the boardwalk. You ever seen a pig butchered? He was sitting down in a big puddle of blood, and his guts were out into his lap. He had his arms around them, the way you'd hold a baby in your lap. I guess to keep them out of the dirt."

The German woman moaned and moved under his hands. Then he felt her tongue begin to move against the head of his cock.

"The woman came at me, to try and keep me away from him, I had to shove her aside. I walked up to him. He was already half gone; just stepping up close to him, I was walking in the blood."

Her head began to move slowly, up and down. Gulping, swallowing, she began to suck on him, her

119

hand shaking as she held him. His cock was wet now, soaked with her saliva. She was slobbering over it, gasping for breath.

"He'd been a handsome man, this one. Tried to look like Hickock, I guess. A fancy dresser—a sport with two guns, long hair, and a silk vest."

Lea bit his lip and heaved up against her. He felt it coming. They were sweating now. Her face was flush with blood, with effort, as she pulled and sucked at him as if she were starving for it.

"Oh, you bitch! Take it! Here it comes for you!" He groaned with the pleasure of it. It was coming out of him as she sucked, moaning and shaking her head as she worked on him.

"Take it the way *he* took it. He looked up at me as if I was going to help him. As if I was going to put his guts back for him. Ah, Christ!" Lea tried to hold her, to keep her from sucking so hard, so fast. It was hurting him it felt so good.

"He looked up at me with his damned long hair in his eyes, looking for some kind of help. I put the barrel against that bastard's head . . . and I cocked the piece . . . and . . . I . . . blew . . . his . . . God-damned *brains* out!"

Lea groaned through clenched teeth, heaved, and thrust up into her. And he came.

Moaning, he let it go. He let everything go. Let it flow into her mouth.

She took it—drinking, sucking, and swallowing again —and bent further to lick, and lap it up where it had run.

CHAPTER FOURTEEN

She cleaned him the way a cat cleans her kittens. He'd let go of her and lay back onto the pillows, watching her. She was very thorough.

When she was finished, he reached down and pulled her up to him, kissing her throat, and mouth, and eyes.

"You darling," he said. "You're a beauty, aren't you?"

She smiled against his chest. "A whore is what my brother would say." She turned her head to look at him. "And you were very cruel to me."

"And it's usually the other way 'round?"

"Usually," she said, and bared her teeth to nip at a fold of his skin, biting down hard.

"Ouch!"

"See." Her teethmarks were red on his skin. "I have my revenge."

Lea reached down to pull up her full skirt, sliding his hand up the slim, silk-stockinged legs.

"But not your pleasure, I think."

"Oh, yes," she said.

And a moment later, sliding his hand high up between smooth, cool, slender thighs, he felt a hot, tangled little patch of fur.

"Yes," he said.

"But play with me a little, my killer of men."

Sarah Bridge came in and woke him at noon. Dr. Edwards and Leo Drexel were with her.

Lea felt fine, almost well enough to get out of bed.

"Any reason I shouldn't get up, doctor?"

"No, you can get up now if you like, though another day in bed wouldn't hurt you." Edwards checked both wounds—the small cut on Lea's chest, the longer, stitched scar down his left side. "Damned lucky, Mr. Lea, I'll say that. Although from the looks of the scars already on you, this sort of injury appears to be fairly common for you."

Lea grunted and let him get on with his work. He was watching Sarah Bridge at the window, putting a fresh bouquet of flowers into the vase on a small table there. He had a momentary vision of her lying across the bed, as the Baron's sister had lain there just a few hours before, her skirts thrown up, her knees high, legs spread wide, gasping with pleasure while he did to her what he'd done to Erica.

She turned back from the window, smiling at him, and Lea felt suddenly embarrassed at what he'd been thinking. What the hell. She was Abe's daughter, and she'd been damn good to him while he was lying around half out of his head. There was more to this girl than her cunt.

"Good God!" Drexel was watching over the doctor's shoulder as he dressed the wound on Lea's side. "That looks dreadful!'' Drexel turned pale and looked away.

"Leo,'' Edwards said, "if you're going to be sick, leave the room.''

"I am not going to be sick, doctor,'' Drexel said with a sniff, and he walked over to the fireplace and sat down in one of the armchairs.

Edwards finished his bandaging, then fished a small bottle of tonic out of his leather bag and handed it to Lea. "Take a spoonful three times a day until it's gone.'' He closed up his bag, nodded to Sarah, and walked out.

"By God, he's in a hurry,'' Drexel said.

Sarah laughed. "Two Austrians asked him to go climbing with them this side of High Pass this afternoon. I think he was afraid he was going to miss them.''

"What Austrians?'' Drexel said.

"Those brothers—the Erlingens.''

"Oh, those two. I'm not surprised. *Mountain climbers.''* He shrugged.

"Mr. Lea,'' Sarah said. "My father . . . well, if you're feeling up to it, he'd like to see you.''

"Fine,'' Lea said, and sat up. Then he remembered his naked chest, and lay back down. "Let him come.''

Drexel laughed. "Behold, modesty.''

"Oh, Leo! Well, Mr. Lea, you see, he thought you might still be angry with him for what happened.''

"No,'' Lea said, "I'm not angry with him. It looked bad enough for any man to think I'd killed her.''

She smiled at him. "Well, I'll go and tell him to come up.'' When she was at the door, Lea called after her.

"Miss Bridge.''

"Yes?''

"I just . . . I just wanted to thank you . . . for taking care of me. It was very nice of you.''

123

"Oh, we take care of all our people at Gunstock, Mr. Lea." She smiled again, and was gone.

"I think you're outclassed, Lea," Drexel said from the armchair.

"I don't doubt it." Lea threw back the sheet, swung his feet out of the bed, and sat on the edge for a moment. He thought he'd feel a little dizzy, after being flat on his back for almost a week, but he didn't. He felt fine.

When he stood up Drexel had to catch him as he staggered and fell against the bedside table. The water glass rolled off the table's edge and onto the carpet. Drexel had moved pretty fast to get there so quickly.

"That was stupid," Drexel said. "You should have let me help you."

The giddiness had passed, but Lea had to sit back down on the bed. His side hurt like hell. All that exercise with the Baron's sister hadn't bothered it at all, but standing had seemed to tear the wound apart all over again. He glanced down at his side, at the bandage.

"No," Drexel said, "it isn't bleeding." He sighed. "Listen. If you don't mind, why don't I help you get your clothes on. Otherwise it'll take you all afternoon."

Lea knew what that "if you don't mind" was about. He was stark naked, and Leo Drexel was a sissy. But there were worse things to be than a sissy.

"I think," he said, "I saw my clothes hanging in that closet over there. But God knows what they did with my underwear."

When Lea was finally dressed and sitting down in an armchair beside the fireplace, he was damned glad to be there. They'd brought his Sunday best black suit, shirt,

124

and other clothes over from the cabin.

The side didn't hurt so badly, now, although it was still stiff and sore. But the weakness bothered him. A few years ago, a couple of cuts—even as bad as these—and he'd have been in bed maybe a day and a night, and that would have been it. He would have been up and riding by now.

Drexel sat for a moment, staring at Lea. Then he smiled.

"Uh, tell me, Mr. Lea, have you spent quite *all* your time shooting wild animals, and, I suppose, people?"

"Not quite all my time."

"Ah, yes . . . I see. You've been something of a sport, then? San Francisco, I suppose?"

"And Chicago."

Drexel nodded. "Good! I'm very happy to hear it." He looked into the fire for a few moments. "Because I believe that Gunstock—and the estimable Bridges—may be falling into some very deep difficulties indeed. Difficulties requiring quick wits, as well as a strong right arm."

Lea said nothing. He'd always found it best to let the other man talk himself out—if he was talking about trouble. He had nothing against Drexel; from what he'd heard in the kitchens and stables, the elegant sissy was a decent enough fellow, and a friend of the Bridges. Maybe he was.

"You have nothing to say?" Drexel said. "That's surprising. You surely don't believe, for example, that that very unpleasant Mr. Budreau, who—*ventilated* I think is the term—who ventilated you with his trusty Barlow knife, did so out of a murderous jealousy?" He smiled at Lea, and carefully smoothed the wrinkled sleeve of his suit coat. "Say what you will of the noble red man," he said, gazing at the rumpled cloth, frowning, "he makes a disasterous valet."

"And why," said Lea, "wouldn't Budreau have been jealous enough to have killed Edna and then come for me? He might have been with her. A couple of others were."

"Tsk, tsk. Unchivalrous, Mr. Lea. And wide of the mark." Satisfied with the sleeve at last, he looked up at Lea. "The ferocious Mr. Budreau didn't care a hoot about that young lady—or about *any* young lady." He shrugged. "Budreau was of *my* persuasion." He smiled. "Not, I hasten to add, that I know that from personal experience. Let us say, rather, that I have a nose for it." His faded blue eyes sharpened, watching Lea's face. "Did you know that? Did you know it all along?"

"No," Lea said. "Not that. But I knew it wasn't a personal matter."

"Pretty god-damned personal, I'd say! To try and cut a man's guts out! And choke a pretty girl to death!" Abe Bridge was a quiet walker, and the thick Gunstock carpets had ushered him into the room silently. Lea didn't like that kind of surprise. He'd remember from now on how softly a man could walk on fine Oriental rugs.

But Abe had heard what he'd said and Drexel was already guessing. The cat was halfway out of the bag; might as well show it clear, nose to tail.

"No, Mr. Bridge," he said. "Not personal at all." Out of the corner of his eye, he saw Drexel nod. Abe stood in the shadows of the open doorway, feet planted wide apart, as if he'd grown from the Gunstock floorboards, and glowered down at Lea with an odd look on his face.

126

"Budreau was *hired* to try for me—probably hired to kill Edna first, then clean me up too, in case she'd talked too much in bed." Lea paused for a moment, then said softly, "She had, poor baby. I should have known she wouldn't leave it alone."

Abe reached behind him to swing the door shut.

"Leave what alone?" he said.

"What indeed?" said Leo Drexel.

"Edna was cleaning a room in Mr. Larrabee's suite," Lea said. "She told me she overheard Larrabee and Count Orloff in a conversation about a silver deposit in the mountains."

"Where?" said Abe. "What silver?"

"At the railway cut, down by Little River."

"She was lying—poor girl—there is no damn silver in these mountains. And, by God, I ought to know!"

"Larrabee's surveyers told him they found some—a heavy lode of it, too—when they dynamited down there. I'd say they know their business." Lea said. "At least Larrabee believed it. He only has railroad rights there. It's your mountain."

"Damn right," Abe growled. "And he paid through the nose for those rail rights, I can tell you."

"Well, it seems, Abe," Drexel drawled, "that he's decided to improve his investment." He glanced at Lea. "By doing precisely what, Mr. Lea?"

"Edna said he'd hired the Count and his Cossacks to ruin Gunstock—probably so that you'd have no choice but to sell the whole shebang to him dirt cheap. That would leave Mr. Larrabee controlling a mountain full of silver."

Abe snorted. "Some yarn! I don't believe a word of it! These Irish girls are full of dreams and blarney. The poor girl dreamed it. That's all there is to it!''

"And they had her murdered for her Irish imagination, I suppose," Drexel said. "It won't do, Abe."

Abe turned on him. "Well? And what do you suppose Count Yuri Orloff is doing in this plot, then? The man's a *Count,* for God's sake! He owns more land than you can ride across in a week!"

"Abe, a man can own all the land in the world and still be desperate for cold, hard cash." Drexel turned to Lea. "Did the girl say how much the old man offered our fine Russian Count?"

"A million in gold," Lea said.

There was a little pause, then Abe reached out to the rocking chair, dragged it over nearer to the fire, and sat with a grunt. He looked suddenly older in the shifting light of the burning hickory logs.

"My God," he said. "Why the hell is it so dark in here? It's only afternoon! Draw those damn curtains, will you, Leo? Let's have some sunlight!" He turned to Lea. "So why did they kill her? Answer me that!"

"She went back to try and get money from them, I think," Lea said.

"Poor girl," Drexel said, pulling the velvet curtains wide. "Poor little girl."

Sunlight flooded the room.

CHAPTER FIFTEEN

Lea moved back into his cabin that night, and found Tocsen waiting there. The old Shoshone just nodded with a grunt when Lea walked in, sitting cross-legged on his smelly bedroll in front of the pot-belly stove. The old Indian had stoked the stove red-hot against the deep chill of the mountain autumn, and, having grunted his greeting to Lea, he returned to rocking slightly back and forth, muttering to himself and puffing on a cracked briar pipe he had picked out of the Gunstock dump. The big double-barreled Greener twelve-gauge was lying on the bedroll beside him. Lea had a notion the old man was playing bodyguard.

He was not unwelcome either. Lea was worn out. Just sitting on his butt talking to Abe and Drexel for a few hours while they tried to figure a checkmate to Larrabee's plan had worn him to a frazzle. The beefsteak dinner sent up from the kitchens had helped —but not enough. Lea needed a solid night's sleep; he needed it badly. A long, sweet sleep, with someone to keep watch for him while he had it. Lea didn't think for a minute that Larrabee had forgotten about him—and knew damn well that that fat old son-of-a-bitch had been told of the meeting Lea'd had with Abe and Drexel. Larrabee was the kind who made sure he was informed.

No, Larrabee wouldn't forget about Lea. That was just as well for him, because Lea had no intention of forgetting—or forgiving—old man Larrabee. The old millionaire must have thought that having a little Irish maidservant killed was nothing but a minor business inconvenience. It was a misjudgement that Larrabee wouldn't live long enough to regret.

Lea sat on the narrow cot, biting his lip against the sharp pain stabbing up along his side as he wrestled his suit-coat and shirt off. Sitting there, he noticed that someone had freshly sanded and scrubbed the cabin floor. Done a good job too. The stains were hardly noticeable. There was a soft knock on the door.

Old Tocsen was a rare one, no doubt about it. The moment the knock sounded, the old man had casually picked up the Greener, cocked the hammers and, still squatting on his bedroll, swung both barrels around to cover the cabin's only window. A rare old man, Lea thought, and smiled.

He slid his Bisley Colt out from under the cot's hard pillow and called out: "Come on in."

Sarah Bridge swung the door open and walked in, her skirts rustling, bringing a breath of cold night air in with her.

When she'd closed the door behind her, and lowered the latch, Lea slid the Colt back under the pillow. A moment later, Tocsen lowered the Greener, muttering, and eased the twin hammers.

"Mr. Lea."

Lea got up off the cot and gestured toward it. "Here, sit down."

"No thank you." She stood beside old Tocsen at the stove, warming her slender hands over the dull cherry glow. "I . . . Mr. Lea—"

"Just Lea'll do."

"Very well . . . *Lea.*"

"Your father's talked to you?"

She turned from the stove to face him, her face drawn with worry. "Yes, he has. He and Leo, both. I . . . I didn't want to believe . . ."

"That sweet old Mr. Larrabee would do such a thing?"

She flushed. "Well, I didn't *want* to think it, I suppose . . ." She glanced at him. "We . . . we could all be mistaken about this, after all."

"Could be."

"Well, we *could!* Mr. Larrabee is an old man, and a very important man too. He's *very* rich and important. He's a friend of the President! So I don't see why in the world—"

"And how do you think Larrabee got to *be* so all-fired important, Miss Bridge? Knitting mittens for the poor?"

She drew herself up. "I'm not trying to be amusing, *Mr.* Lea."

"No," Lea said, and he sat back down on the cot to pull off his boots. "There's not a damn—pardon me—thing funny about it. Ask Edna O'Malley. Ask Budreau for that matter."

She looked down at her clasped hands. "I . . . I know. I know you were fond of Edna." She looked up. "But . . . but you see, my father is riding out tomorrow.

131

He's taking six of the hands with him and riding down to Little River to see for himself about that silver that you—"

"That I say is there?" Lea pulled off one of his boots with a pained grunt.

"Yes."

Lea wrestled with his second boot. The son-of-a-bitch didn't want to come off! And his side felt as if it were on fire. With a sweep of her skirts, Sarah came to the cot, knelt, and gripping the boot, tugged it off his foot.

"Thanks."

"Mr. Lea—"

"Lea."

"*Lea*. You shouldn't even have been out of bed today."

"Let alone feeding your father that cock-an'-bull yarn?"

She stood looking down at him, her dark blue eyes steady on his. "I'm worried about him, Mis—Lea. I'm worried that he will be made to look a fool if there's no silver down at Little River."

"And you're worried he'll be killed out there if there is."

"Yes."

"Well, Abe *could* get killed out there, Miss Bridge. I offered to go with him."

Sarah began to pace in the cabin's cramped space. Old Tocsen turned his head to watch her, puffing his pipe, his heavy-lidded old eyes following her. White women were restless; that was certainly true.

"Oh, you couldn't go with him. He was right not to let you. You won't be able to ride for days."

"He has six men with him?"

"Yes."

"And the Count and those Cossacks of his are staying put?"

"Leo said there was no sign of their leaving."

"Fine. As long as Orloff's not out there, Abe will be all right."

She stopped pacing. "Yes, I suppose you're right. He has taken good men with him: Folliard, Tiny Morgan, and a man named Johnson who they say is good with a gun."

"Nothing out there to bother them," Lea said, "as long as Orloff stays at Gunstock."

"Yes. Leo's having people watch him and those men of his." She stopped pacing, glanced at him, and frowned. "Oh, Lea, I'd forgotten how ill you'd been. I'm terribly sorry! You need rest, not to be bothered with *my* worries." She went to the door. "I'll leave you, and let you sleep. Do you need anything? Do you have Dr. Edward's medicine?"

"I've got it."

"Well, then . . ." She unlatched the door, and turned, smiling. "I apologize for troubling you with all this. Good night. Good night, Tocsen."

The old Indian grunted in reply, and Sarah swung the cabin door open, went out, and shut it behind her.

A nice girl, Lea thought. And damn right to be worried about old Abe. Probably a mistake for the old man to leave Gunstock right now. Might have been better to have waited Larrabee out, handled the Russians here, on his own ground.

Lea sighed and stood up with a grunt to unbutton his trousers. Not a damn thing *he* could do about it anyway.

Abe would do what Abe would do.

"Restless Flower Eye." Tocsen said, staring into the fire in the potbelly stove.

"What?"

But the old man had nothing more to say.

Lea dreamed of Edna. "My God," he said to her in the dream, "I leave everyone dead behind me, as if I were death himself." She looked at him as if he'd gone crazy, and laughed. She was sitting up in a bed somewhere. Her breasts were bare.

"Do you know he looked at me?" she said.

"Who?" Lea said in the dream. "Who looked at you?"

"That little Rooshin," Edna said to him. "He stood underneath a tree and watched while Budreau choked the life right out of me."

"Oh, don't worry about him," Lea said to her, and she smiled and reached down to stroke her nipples. "I'll kill him. I'll kill them all. Didn't I kill Budreau? Didn't I put a knife into his throat?"

"You choked the German woman," Edna said, and pouted. "I know that well enough!"

"I couldn't help it," Lea said to her.

"He can't help anything," the smiling man said, and he walked through the room and out the door.

"Tell me what it's like to be dead, Edna," Lea said. "Do you still know you are Edna?"

"I know nothin'," Edna said to him. . . .

Lea woke early in the morning. Old Tocsen was snoring beside the potbelly stove. Lea felt better than he had since the fight with Budreau. The stitches itched along his side, but the muscles there didn't hurt. He felt

134

a little stiff, but all right.

He got up and dressed in his boots, jean trousers, a wool shirt and his buckskin vest. When he sat on the bed and stomped his boots on, Tocsen woke up and stared at him, blinking.

"Come on and let's get something to eat," Lea said. He strapped on the Bisley Colt and found his Arkansas toothpick lying on the little cane-bottom chair beside the bed.

"I keep for you. It sharp." The old Indian rolled back over on his side and began to go back to sleep.

"Thanks." Lea slid the knife down into his right boot.

He unlatched the door and stepped outside. It was a cold, clear morning. Smoke trailed across the blue sky from the towering chimneys of the hotel looming across the stable yards.

Lea walked across the cobbles to the kitchen garden, and on up the path. He was walking with his head down, thinking, and he heard boots coming down the path toward him. He looked up and saw one of Orloff's Cossacks coming down the path toward him from the kitchen. The Cossack was chewing on a chunk of bread.

Lea recognized the man, but didn't remember his name. He was a tall, bony-looking man with lank dirty-blond hair, and a full beard, like the rest of them.

The Cossack glanced down the path at Lea as he came. He had greenish eyes and his face was gray with dirt.

From that look, and the way he was walking, Lea saw that the man intended to walk him off the narrow path. The Cossack didn't have a saber, but he was carrying a big pistol in a closed holster on his belt. A Nagent, it looked like; maybe some big European pistol.

He swallowed the last of the bread and walked fast, straight toward Lea, swinging his arms. He stared into Lea's eyes, grinning at him.

Just before the Cossack reached him, just as Lea sensed the man bracing himself, lowering his shoulder for the impact, Lea side-stepped to the right, well off the path, smiled, and tipped his Stetson as the Cossack went striding past.

The Cossack turned his head to stare at Lea, and laughed. Then he walked on his way and didn't look back.

Lea went up the path to the kitchen and down past the row of salad tables, where people were already laying out the garden stuff to be cleaned and cut and arranged for lunch. He was turning into the doorway to the servants' dining room when he heard chef de la Maine calling his name.

Lea stood and waited while the big Frenchman bellied past a dozen scullions running back and forth with pots and pans—Indian girls, most of them—and came up to Lea with his flour-white hand out and a big smile on his face.

"So good!" he said, and took Lea's hand and pumped it hard. "So good!" He nodded at Lea, and winked. *"Tres bien!"* He made a slicing gesture with his free hand. "You 'av cut that Budreau well, no? For his killing la petite Edna!" He nodded again, and his tall chef's hat bobbed on his head. "You go in to the dining room, an' I will per-r-rsonally bring br-r-reakfast."

Lea smiled and nodded, took his hand back—the chef was a strong man—and went into the dining room and sat down. Three chambermaids were sitting across the table. He knew one of them, a girl named Patty Burke, but they didn't say anything to him, just stared and whispered back and forth.

After a considerable while, and Lea getting hungrier by the minute, Old Tocsen looked around the corner of the dining-room door, then shuffled in to sit beside Lea at the table. The maids had already left. Tocsen sighed and farted, then sat waiting for breakfast, muttering to himself.

De la Maine came in with a tray, smiling. The smile turned a little sour when he saw Tocsen sitting at the table. He rolled his eyes. *"Alors, la belle sauvage!"* He set the tray down before them. There was a plate of lamb-chops, each with a little white cuff of paper, curled strips of bacon, a big omelet that smelled of cheese and green herbs, and a hot cake with white icing and raisins. It all smelled wonderful.

Lea got up and shook de la Maine's hand again. It was not a small thing for the chef to cook something special for one person. Lea had eaten fine French cooking before. But not often.

Between the two of them, he and Tocsen cleared the tray. Lea ate the bacon, and the omelet, and the cake. The Shoshone ate all the lamb-chops.

CHAPTER SIXTEEN

When he finished breakfast, Lea left the old Shoshone sitting there chewing on the lamb-chop bones, and walked out through the passage under the main staircase to go to the gun-room. Tocsen had told him that Davies had taken some guests out bird-shooting while he was sick from the fight with Budreau. Lea didn't think he'd be taking many more guests out hunting from Gunstock. And Davies, who was head wrangler and a good hunter to boot, had probably handled everything all right. But it wouldn't hurt to check.

He dug in his buckskin jacket pocket for the key, and unlocked the heavy oak door.

It was a big narrow room, with a long mahogany table, covered with an oil-stained canvas tarp, running down the center, between two glass-cased walls of guns. Almost three hundred guns altogether. The room smelled of gun oil, and the cleaning table was littered with patches, rods, oil cans and bore brushes. Davies was a good hunter, but he still had something to learn about keeping a gun room. At this rate, it would be a pigpen in a week. He'd have to talk to Davies.

Lea got to work cleaning up. It was work he'd done a hundred times; work he didn't even have to think about. It left him free to think about other things. Like packing up, getting the old dun out of the stable, and making tracks the hell out of Gunstock. He'd been out and gone once—and had come back when the old man called. He'd owed Abe that much, for giving him the job. Well, he'd come back, and now he'd killed the bully who'd killed Edna.

What now? A stand-up fight against those Cossacks? Against Larrabee and his millions? No way for him to win there—even if he got lucky. Win? Kill a Russian Count . . . kill Larrabee . . . Do that, and every newspaper reporter, every peace officer in three states would be out to get him. Hell, the U.S. Army'd be sent out!

The name of *Farris Lea* wouldn't stand long under that light. It would be Buckskin Frank Leslie before you could shake a stick! They'd hunt him, they'd catch him, and they'd hang him high as Haman.

Moving on was the thing to do.

Lea leaned over the gleaming mahogany, rubbing the soft wax into the dark, shining wood with hard, forceful sweeps of his arm. The table top was dark and as reflective as dark water in the soft glow of gas lights.

So why the hell wasn't he gone already? Edwards had said the stitches needed to come out of his chest and side in about ten days, but any frontier saw-bones could pick those out of him. He could do that himself, in fact he *had* done it.

Lea put the can of wax away, pulled a clean square of chamois from the drawer, and began to polish the table, avoiding the eyes of his reflection as he slowly worked his way down the glossy length of wood. As he worked, he felt the faint tug and ache of the healing wound along his side. Cut to the muscle, Edwards had said. The chest wound wasn't so bad. Budreau had tried for the heart thère, and got a rib instead.

The table was finished. A damn good job. And Davies could damn well do it from now on . . .

Lea knew he wasn't going to leave Gunstock. Not yet.

He was staying because he wanted to stay. Not to help Abe, though that was part of it. And not to help Abe's daughter, though that was part of it too.

The real reason was what it had always been. He wanted them to know. He wanted all of them: Abe, Sarah, that Russian Count, and old man Larrabee, to know exactly who he was!

He wanted them to know the way Budreau had known, standing with that knife in his throat.

He didn't want to run anymore. He was finished with running. He had left so much behind him. There was almost nothing left of Frank Leslie.

There was a soft knock on the gun-room door. Lea stood clear of the long table. "Yes?"

"Lea?" It was Leo Drexel.

Lea slid back the bolt and slowly swung the heavy door open. Drexel stood in the doorway, slender, elegant in a fine gray suit. One eyebrow was raised.

"Being careful who knocks?" He smiled. "Very sensible, Lea." He strolled into the room and leaned against one of the gun cabinets while Lea closed the door and bolted it. "I have news. Nothing spectacular, I suppose, but interesting."

"What is it?"

"Well, you understand, in Gunstock I have my sources." He turned to examine his reflection in the gun-case glass, adjusted his cravat.

"Yes?"

"It seems that our notable Mr. Larrabee has taken *steps*. He has, in fact, sent his valet to the gardener's shed to hire a boy to ride to Salmon Station with a telegram." He stepped back so that he could view his whole reflection in the glass front of the case. "Not bad," he said, and nodded at it.

Lea didn't say anything. He stood, waiting for Drexel to tell him.

Drexel turned from the glass. He wasn't smiling anymore. "That telegram said, and I quote, 'To Henry Buskirk, Santa Fe. Send Shannon Gunstock soonest. Repeat, soonest.' "

Drexel stood staring at Lea. "Now," he said, "why that little message should strike me as ominous, I don't know, except perhaps that it is so simple. A man like Larrabee could send for an army, if he chose."

"He's a quieter man than that, I think," Lea said.

"Yes. Then who, or what, is "Shannon?"

Lea stood, thinking, looking past Drexel to the tall, heavily curtained window at the end of the room.

Lea had known a man named Shannon once. A big, thick-bellied, bearded man. Partner in a freight outfit in Colorado. Surely nothing to do with this.

The only other Shannon he'd heard of was a gunman. If it was the same fellow, he'd been in a shooting in Wyoming years ago. Killed Slim Wilson out of Cheyenne.

Lea had met Wilson once, a long time ago. If this

141

Shannon was a shooter, and the same man, then he must be very good, if the years hadn't slowed him down. That shooting in Wyoming had been a long time ago—more than ten years ago.

"What do you think, Mr. Lea?" said Drexel. He wasn't playing the fine sissy now. He looked like a worried man.

"Well, I think he's probably sent for a violent man. Probably would have, in any case, to balance off those Cossacks of Orloff's. Men like Larrabee like to have an ace in the hole."

"And this Shannon?"

"Must be an ace," Lea said, and smiled. "Wouldn't be sent for otherwise."

"Yes." Drexel frowned. "So I thought, too."

"How soon—"

"The fastest," Drexel said, speaking with the confidence of a man who's made countless travel arrangements for countless spoiled, impatient, and influencial guests, "and damn the Southern Pacific Railroad and the Idaho spur—the fastest he can travel, for Larrabee or God almighty, will get him to Gunstock in six days at the earliest."

"Only six days from New Mexico!"

Drexel smiled sadly. "That's why I damned the Idaho spur. That line was built out to Salmon Station years ago."

"But just for beef and freight—and barely once a week at that!"

"Unless someone with a great deal of influence, Mr. Lea, were to ask them to route up a special . . ." Drexel sighed. And Lea knew he was dead right. He'd be at Gunstock in six days.

When they left the gun-room, Drexel had shaken hands with him, a little mournfully, Lea thought, and left him to go out into the grand pavilion alongside the lobby. Lea turned back down the passageway under the wide staircase, stepped out into the corridor leading back to the servants' hall—and ran straight into a damn gaggle of guests.

Young girls, most of them—a girl named Maxine Budweiser, who's father was supposed to be a big brewer in the east, and four other girls Lea didn't know —all of them goggling at him, their eyes as big as saucers. The dangerous man, the *killer*, had suddenly appeared before them.

They were pretty girls—Maxine was anyway—and not one of them a day over seventeen. All of them ruffled up in muslin and taffeta or whatever. But to Lea they seemed like a herd of silly heifers, the way they stood huddled together goggling at him.

Toby Easterby—for once giving up on the older, faster ladies—was squiring the bunch of them around. Another boy, Arthur, was hovering around too.

"Good day, ladies," Lea said, and gave them his best smile and bow. Watch the sparrows scatter.

And scatter they did—in a flustered flurry of sqeaks and chirps and hasty curtsies, midway between manners and terror.

Easterby and Arthur finally herded them together and away, Easterby grinning over his shoulder to Lea as they went.

When Abe got back—*if* Abe got back—he'd probably get an earful from a few mamas about allowing bravos and butchers to patrol the halls of Gunstock, to frighten their little girls.

143

As he started down the flight of steps to the servants' hall, Lea thought of Edna for a moment.

Edna had been seventeen years old. It was a young age to die.

"Me darlin' " she'd said to him once, lying naked as a baby on him, and covered with sweat from their fucking, "Me darlin', you're damn near as good as auld Fadder McFee."

How they'd laughed.

" . . . damned near as good as Fadder McFee!" Lea started laughing now, and met Sarah Bridge coming up the stairs.

She frowned up at him, and he went down two steps more, to her level. Her blue eyes were sparkling with anger.

"If Mr. Drexel has spoken to you, Mr. Lea, I'm at a loss to know what you find funny about the matter!"

Well, Drexel wasn't keeping secrets from the lady of the house. And the lady looked mighty worried about it, as well she might.

"I wasn't laughing about the arrival of Mr. Larrabee's hoodlum, Miss Bridge." He saw the worry carved into tiny lines at the corner of her mouth and eyes. "Or about the spot your father may get into, either."

"I . . . I know."

"Orloff and his men are still here, aren't they?"

"Yes . . . yes, they are."

Her head was down, her face shadowed under the dim staircase light. Lea saw she was starting to weep.

He hesitated a moment, then put his hand on her arm.

"Listen Sarah, Abe isn't going to get hurt as long as

those Russians stay put. He must be nearly to Little River by now. It won't take him long to find the silver ore, if it's there. Then he'll be on his way back. You'll see him again in two or three days.''

"Oh, I know he'll be all right." She took out her handkerchief, dabbed at her eyes, then blew her nose. "I know you think I'm being a silly fool." She shook her head and looked up at him, trying to smile. "Abe . . . Abe would be furious if he knew I was so frightened for him! Daddy thinks he can handle anything!''

"I think he can too," Lea said, and smiled at her.

"Yes." She sniffed and put her handkerchief away. "But Mr. Larrabee and that dreadful little Russian. They . . . they're different!''

"A loftier sort of skunk, you mean?''

She giggled. "Yes, I suppose I do mean that.''

"I don't mean to make light of them," Lea said, "or to make light of the trouble your father might be in. But I'll tell you this: there is no way that Larrabee, or the Russian is going to be taking Gunstock away from you.''

She looked up into his face. "Thank you, Mr. Lea. I know that you mean it. I thank you for staying to help us." She smiled, wryly. "Particularly after I made such a cake of myself, ordering you off the place when the Baron got shot!''

Lea laughed. "Well, you weren't far wrong at that. I was the guide. I was responsible for getting him shot!''

"No." She blushed. "It wasn't your fault at all. I lost my temper, that's all.''

"Well, if you'll forgive me, I'll forgive you.''

"All right." She glanced up at him. "I forgive you.''

What a good-looking girl you are, Lea thought. Their eyes met.

"Thank you, Miss Bridge," he said. And he bent down and kissed her gently on the mouth.

CHAPTER SEVENTEEN

Her lips were cool and slightly parted. He thought, just for a moment, that she pressed her mouth against him. He felt heat, wetness. Then it was gone. She turned, brushed past him with a rustle of skirts, and went up the stairs.

That afternoon, Lea went out to the cabin and gathered up an armful of dirty clothes, his extra pair of boots, and his soap and razor. Then he went over to the Chinaman's.

It was generally supposed at Gunstock that all four of the fat, sturdy Chinese women working for old Chun in the laundry shed were his wives. Chinese were known for multiplication in that field, and each of the four certainly treated the old man with the bullying lack of respect proper to a wife. Chinese women were just as hard on the Indian girls who helped them stir the huge laundry tubs and work the big newfangled steam-mangles that Abe had had freighted in all the way from Boise.

Lea walked down the long stone flagway. The laundry shed was behind a planted row of loblolly pines, out past the kitchen gardens. He climbed the steps to the big corrugated iron door, and swung it open.

Walking into the laundry shed was a little like walking into hell—blazing hot, swirling with clouds of steam, and noisy with the hiss and whistle of the big boiler powering the mangles, and the screams and curses of Chun's four wives.

"What you need, Mr. Lea?" Chun had come out of the wall of gray like a Chinese ghost.

"Laundry. . . bath . . . shave."

Chun made an exasperated face. "Busy. . . busy. . . busy!"

"Then I'll come back tonight."

"No, no!" The old Chinaman's goatee was dripping sweat and condensed steam. "You give!" He snatched Lea's laundry bundle out from under his arm, and ducked away, back into the steam. "You come on!"

Lea followed him into the fog.

Chun led him through the steam-filled laundry, through a door, and into another room lined with long tables where Indian girls were ironing and folding from heaping baskets of fresh wash.

Then they went through another door into a small room behind the boiler. Big cast-iron washtubs stood in ranks against the wall. The little room was soaking with water condensed from the steamy air.

"Bath!" said Chun, and he pointed to the first tub in the row. Lea looked into the tub, and was relieved to see it was empty. The last bath he'd had at Chun's he'd shared with several dirty sheets. Chun walked out, taking Lea's laundry with him. Lea undressed, pulling his boots off with a grunt. He still felt the side when he did that. He stuck the toothpick point first into the dark, soaked wood beside the tub, and hung the Bisley Colt from a peg over it. They'd both need cleaning and oiling after sitting around in this steambath, but they had to be handy: a bathhouse was a very good place to surprise and kill a man.

Naked, Lea stepped into the tub and gingerly sat down in it, favoring his side. It was a big tub, but still a tight fit for a man, sitting. He lifted his left arm, and screwed his head around to see the stitches along his side. They looked ugly enough, but not infected, not inflamed. He'd come out of that lightly enough, for a knife fight.

One of Chun's wives—a very fat one—came bustling into the room. She was chattering something in Chinese to an Indian girl following along behind her, lugging two buckets of steaming water. The Indian girl, short and stocky in a soaked missionary dress, didn't seem to understand Chinese, but Mrs. Chun kept it up at a great rate.

The girl set one of the buckets down and went to Lea's tub with the other. The water was still steaming, and looked way too hot to Lea. He was opening his mouth to say something about that when the Indian girl heaved the bucket up and poured the whole thing over on him.

"Jesus!" It was scalding hot. Lea hunched forward to lift his ass up as the hot water sloshed down into the tub. It burned the wound along his side. "Some *cold* water, for Christ's sake!"

No good. Mrs. Chun gestured to the Indian girl, and

the second bucket of hot water was dumped over his head. Lea cursed and struggled to his feet, lifting one foot and then the other out of that steaming water.

"Bath!" said Mrs. Chun, with considerable satisfaction, and she stumped over and handed Lea a chunk of brown lye soap.

When he walked out into the cool afternoon air, Lea felt pretty well. Clean, freshly shaved, and with every stitch he had on or was carrying under his arm washed and line-dried over the boiler firebox. It had cost three bits—really two. One extra to the Indian girl for going to get some cold water to pour in the tub.

Neither of the cuts seemed to have been harmed from the bath. They stung a little from the hot water, even more from the soap.

It was a touch more than cool outside though. He could tell it, fresh from the laundry shed. There was an edge to the air. A winter edge—still a way off, but coming down fast enough.

He walked past the stables, waved to one of the stableboys, a kid named Turley, and turned up the path to his cabin.

The moment he took that turn, he saw Larrabee. The old man, bold as brass, was up there waiting for him.

Larrabee had seen Lea, too, and raised his hand to greet him. The little old man, plump and rosy in a fine English tweet suit, his silver mutton-chop whiskers fluffed out as dandy as you please, was roosting at his ease on one of those dude shooting-sticks—a walking cane with a handle which folded out into a skimpy seat. Old man Larrabee leaned back, lounging at his ease as if he were in a parlor rocker. He smiled at Lea as he came up.

Lea didn't smile in return. He looked back over his shoulder instead. But there was no killer there.

"What do you want, Larrabee?" Lea said, and without waiting for an answer, walked past the old man, unlatched his cabin door, and went inside. He didn't intend to talk to a millionaire with laundry under his arm. He dumped the clean clothes on his cot, noticed that old Tocsen had moved out, bedroll and all —probably back to the grain barn, where he had a little hideout over the oats.

When he went back outside, the old man was still smiling, still lounging at his ease on that shooting stick.

"Won't you invite me in, Mr. Lea?" he said. He had a pleasant voice. It sounded younger than he was.

"No," Lea said.

The little man pursed his lips.

"Mr. Lea," he said. "Just about the first thing that I learned about business—and I learned it a very long time ago—was that it is *always* a mistake to lose one's temper. And *not,* mind you, only in business, but in all the contingencies of life. It is always unwise to lose one's temper." He glanced up at Lea, his bright blue eyes twinkling like anybody's merry grandfather. "Now," he said, "I have given you some very good advice in advance of our . . . *negotiations.* I wonder if you're wise enough to take advantage of it."

"You're mistaken, Larrabee, if you think I've lost my temper with you. I don't do that with people I intend to kill."

The twinkle went out of those bright blue eyes then.

"A number of men have threatened me, Mr. Lea. Men, I might add, in every way more formidable than a

151

wandering frontier rough. One way or another, each of those men have been ... *disappointed."* Then he smiled. "I see no reason to believe you an exception."

Lea smiled back at him. "Do you have anything else to say to me, Mr. Larrabee?"

"Why, yes. I do! We have exchanged—oh, I imagine you could call them threatening snorts, or roars, if you like." He chuckled. "Now, if you can bear it, I would like to do a little business."

"What kind?"

Larrabee rocked forward on the shooting stick, balancing himself neatly with the shiny black toes of his high-button boots. "Cash business, Mr. Lea, what else?"

"How much?"

The old man nodded. "Admirably direct. And so shall I be. Mr. Lea, you are a fairly formidable fellow. You have dispatched Mr. Budreau who, as I believe the term to be, was no *lily* himself. And previous to that you, with our brave Baron, dispatched three wandering outlaws. So you are a good man in a fight. A *very* good man." He rocked back, balancing himself nicely. "As a fighting man—particularly out here, so far from the intervention of more a civilized authority—you may present an obstacle worth, oh, say, five-thousand dollars, to remove." He glanced up at Lea. "Not impressed? Oh, dear. As it happens, you do have an additional value to the opposition, you might say. The French would call it *morale*. By your presence you *stiffen* the opposition. To remove that factor would, I suppose, be worth another five-thousand dollars."

He sat, smiling up at Lea, rocking gently back and forth. He had good balance for such an old man.

He was talking about a tremendous amount of

money. And that meant that there was, beyond any doubt, silver ore in the mountain at Little River. It meant that hundreds of millions of dollars were in the balance here—a god-awful way deep into Idaho mountains, at a hotel in the middle of nowhere.

And the ten-thousand dollars? Lea didn't doubt for a minute that Larrabee meant every word. It was more money than he'd ever had in one piece in his life. Money like that would *change* his life. He could go to Canada, or Mexico—anywhere—with that much money, and perhaps buy a small ranch, and stock it too. Or he could go east, where no one would ever know who he was, buy a house somewhere, buy into a business.

The old man was offering him a new life. If he could take it.

Larrabee knew the answer before Lea said a word.

"Oh, dear," he said. And he stood up and turned to fold the handle of his shooting stick. The top of his head didn't reach Lea's shoulder. "Oh, dear."

He stood for a moment, looking up at Lea.

"I'm sorry," he said. And he turned and walked away, leaning on the stick a little where the path was rough.

Lea stood looking after him, but the little old man didn't look back.

When he was a boy, Lea had once met Bill Longley in Texas. And, years later, he'd had lunch with Jesse James and his brother in New Orleans for the Sullivan fight. Meeting those men had been like meeting Larrabee. They were all very dangerous men, but it wasn't that that made them seem similar to Lea. It was their certainty. All of them had it. That air of having always won, of having always accomplished what they'd set out to do.

Winners all. And they'd ridden a sight of men down on their way.

Of course, Longley was dead now. Jesse too. No man was bigger than death.

That's why he had meant what he'd said about killing Larrabee, though he doubted the old man had taken him very seriously. It was not just that Larrabee *deserved* killing for having Edna O'Malley murdered. How the hell had that little girl dreamed she could blackmail a man like Larrabee?

There was no other way to beat him. No other way to save Gunstock, Abe and Sarah Bridge, because he'd surely murder them too; he'd have to. No other way to save Farris Lea either.

Let him keep breathing much longer, and that old man would eat them all alive.—This Shane, or whatever his name was, would only be the first. Soon, Larrabee would have an army in Gunstock. Hell, given enough time, he'd have the *U.S.* Army in Gunstock!

And, if the old man weren't bad enough, there was that damn Russian and those eight Cossack bullies of his, who'd be pleased to cut a man's throat—or whip him to death—if the Count were to raise his little finger.

So far, the Count and his men hadn't moved. But when they did all hell was going to break loose in Idaho!

Just maybe, Lea thought, I might have bitten off a plug too tough to chew. He went back inside the cabin to grease and sharpen the Arkansas toothpick, to clean and oil the Bisley Colt.

CHAPTER EIGHTEEN

In the morning Lea went up to the gun room for cartridges. It was just dawn and the lobby of the big hotel was deserted except for a few cleaning women finishing their night's work.

Then Lea went out to the stable, called for Turley, and finally got the dun out of his stall and saddled him himself.

He rode out toward the hotel ranch, two miles north of the main building. Halfway there, he pulled the dun up at the head of a small *barranca*. The gully was lined along its sides with scrub pine and red fern, but the uneven bottom of the draw was fairly clear. The ground ran some two-hundred yards straight out from the gully's head.

Lea left the dun tied at the head of the draw, took the Sharps and Greener down with him, and scrambled down the bank to the rutted dirt at the gully's base.

He left the firearms leaning against some brush, and climbed back up to the dun to untie a gunnysack full of peachcans from the cantle and lug it down into the draw.

He practiced all morning.

First, with the shotgun. He threw the cans for straight one-on-one shooting. Then he threw two at a time, swinging left and right to fire at both. When he stopped missing at that, he threw three cans at a time, and had to hustle to get the Greener reloaded and into position for his third shot. Stopping every now and then to let the shotgun cool, Lea kept at the three-can throw, wanting a good run of hitting all three before he quit. He finally got his run after two hours shooting.

He'd never be the hand with a scatter gun that the Count was, probably not as good as old Tocsen either. But he was as good as he was going to get, and that wasn't so bad as shotgun shooting went.

Then he picked up the Sharps and went to work. Two-hundred yards wasn't enough distance to really work the buffalo-gun out, so Lea worked on very fine shooting—on hitting the peach on the paper label, instead of just hitting the can.

He fired until his arm got tired, then he cut a hasty rest from a pine branch and used that. He did some good shooting with the Sharps—especially with the rest. He worked hard, and after more than an hour he was hitting the peach on the can labels eight out of ten shots at two-hundred yards. He knew other men who shot that well with a buffalo gun—though not many—but he considered that it was fair country shooting, for a *pistolero*, anyway.

And he'd for sure shot away a sight of cartridges. He'd have to tell Sarah to reorder.

The last few shots he took with the rifle, he fired as passing shots—fired from the hip at peach cans rolling along the sides of the gully. He hit one, missed three, but not by too much. There was no telling when he might have to use the big gun close up.

There was no telling anything about gunfighting, beforehand.

It was almost midday when he finally put the big Sharps down alongside the Greener. Lea'd skipped breakfast and was feeling more than a little hungry. That was all right—hungry was a good way to shoot.

Lea had brought both his Colts. He never wore more than one pistol—the damn things weighed too much—but he always carried a spare in his war bag. Any pistol, used hard, will shoot loose, and was a long way between good gunsmiths. His second gun was the image of the first. The same manufacture lot, in fact, so Lea could be sure the steel quality and the fit were as close to identical as the people in Hartford could make them. They were both Bisleys. He liked the shape of the grip; it sat back in his hand in a nice way.

He holstered one of the Colts, taking no particular care how it went into the leather, and commenced to stroll up and down the length of the gully, tossing peach cans this way and that, and drawing and shooting them.

He missed some, at first. Then he didn't.

He shot them straight on, and thrown high in the air, and he drew and shot them shied to the side, to rattle and bounce along the gully's sides. He pitched the cans behind him too, throwing them over his shoulder, and then underhand.

After a while he didn't miss any of them.

Lea almost never practiced with handguns. It didn't seem to make much difference to his shooting. He had known very fine shootists who practiced every day.

157

He'd heard that Hickok had done that—though the times he'd seen Hickok, that handsome pimp had usually been drunk as a skunk, and had stayed that way for nearly a week. So perhaps he didn't really practice as much as all that.

Still, Lea thought, here you are practicing now, all right. The great Buckskin Frank Leslie must be running just a mite scared.

He changed guns, and worked the other Bisley the way he had the first one, being careless as he pleased about how the pistol was holstered, as long as it was in there firm enough to stay without the riding-keeper strung under the hammer. Lea'd never liked fooling with the leather—soaking it for a shrink-fit on the piece, or polishing up the insides with tallow or graphite. It didn't seem much use, since almost always a gun fight happened when a man's holster was fresh soaked with rain or spilled beer, or dusted over with sawdust or trail dust, or rockhard with cold or rag-limp with Texas heat. And always when the damn holster was twisted around under a man's ass, and him sitting arms out of a captain's chair, half under a poker table, and often with some fat blonde hooker sitting in his lap to boot!

No use wasting much time on the leather.

Lea took some snapshots at pine branches—the four-dozen peach cans (courtesy of the Gunstock dump) by now were shot to such rags that he couldn't tell a hit from a miss; the rounds were as likely to sail right through without touching. He hit with his snapshots, and then tried to work on his draw.

That was no good, as it always was no good. The harder he worked, the slower he got. He had to relax, back off trying and simply draw-an'-shoot.

Then, as if by magic, it was there again. The Colt seeming to jump up into his hand, the shot coming so fast. "Quick as bean farts," Doc had said about that draw. Holliday's own pull had been none too swift. It didn't have to be, as Doc said himself. "The poor bastards are scared stiff as pine boards, just standing up in front of me! It's the ones too drunk to be scared've got me worried!"

For the fun of it, Lea fired both Colts together, left and right, right and left. He blew a small pine in two fifty yards down the gully, twirled his guns like a kid, laughed, and put them away.

It took him a while to collect all the shot-up peach cans and put them back in the sack. Then he kicked the sack under some ferns and let it lie.

It took considerably longer to pick up his brass. There was a hell of a lot of it.

He finally had most of it up and jingling around inside his tucked-in shirt when he heard hoofbeats. He stood and listened, and heard them coming nearer.

One horse . . . coming fast.

Lea bent and kept picking up brass. He had to dig some of the cartridge cases out of the dirt where he'd stomped them in, marching up and down blazing away.

The horse came galloping on. It was pulled in and worked through the brush at the head of the gully.

Lea checked the loads in the second Bisley, slid the barrel of the .45 into his gunbelt on the left side, and stepped over to the near bank of the gully, under the cover of a shaggy little dwarf pine.

"Mr. Lea!" It was Sarah Bridge.

"Coming up!"

Lea went to pick up the Greener and Sharps, and then scrambled up through the brush to the head of the draw.

Sarah was standing in the scrub by a lathered horse. She was nearing a handsome blue riding dress, and carried a parrot-beak .38 in her belt. A nice little weapon.

Her face was white as milk.

"Mr. Lea. One of the gardener's men had seen you ride out this way. I . . . I rode after you and heard the firing—"

"I was practicing, Miss Bridge," Lea said. "Now, you'd better tell me what's the matter."

She stopped, and Lea saw her biting her lip hard. "Mr. Lea, *the Count is gone, and* his men!"

"Just now, you mean?"

She shook her head, her eyes filling with tears. "*No.* They rode out sometime last night."

"Hell's fire. Last *night?* I thought Drexel was watching them!"

Sarah Bridge looked sick, and well she might, Lea thought. She'd just received her father's death sentence.

"Leo *was* watching them! The Count caused a scene in the dining room last evening; he was drunk, and—"

"Pretending to be drunk."

She nodded miserably. "Yes. I'm afraid so."

"And he was put to bed in his suite, *drunk.* Right?"

She nodded.

"And Leo didn't bother to check on those Cossacks of his all night?"

She looked up, angry. "The stable boy was watching them!"

160

It made sense. The Russians had all bunked together in a lean-to out behind the stable. "And he saw nothing? Who was it?"

"It was Charlie Turley." She was glaring at Lea as if, somehow, this was all his fault. "And he's dead! We found him hanging from a *hook* in the tackroom." Her voice shook as she said it.

"All right," Lea said. "All right." He reached out and took her into his arms as naturally as can be. She came to him, and rested for a moment, leaning her cheek against the smooth, worn buckskin of his jacket. Lea felt her trembling against him.

"Crying?"

"No," she said. "No, I'm not."

Lea hugged her hard, then let her go.

"Lea . . ."

He turned away from her, picked up the Greener and Sharps, and kicked his way through the thick brush to the tethered dun.

He mounted and reined over to her, the rifle and shotgun balanced across his saddle-bow.

"Now, listen to me. Larrabee will figure your father dead for sure. That leaves you. Chances are he'll try for *you* sooner or later. Have you got a good woman who can stay with you—day and night?"

Sarah thought a moment. "Yes, I think so. There's a woman, Graciela, she helps de la Maine in the kitchen. She's an old friend of my father's."

"How tough is she? Can she handle a gun?"

"She's very tough, I think. She worked in saloons in the mining camps my father prospected at. I'm sure she can handle a gun. So can I!"

"All right. Get mounted. We'll talk as we go. Get her

161

out of that kitchen, give her a gun, and tell her what the hell is going on, if she doesn't know already. She's not to let you out of her sight! Day or night!"

Sarah swung up onto her mare, and Lea spurred the dun out of the scrub into the long grass, headed back up the valley to the hotel. She urged the mare up alongside him, and they rode in silence for a moment.

"And be careful of your food. You and this woman eat in the kitchen. De la Maine's no fool. He'll cook it *and* serve it to you."

"Yes. I'll do that."

"Now, when did the Russians ride out?"

"Sometime after midnight."

"Christ." Lea spurred the dun into a gallop, and Sarah urged her mare after him.

They rode together, running the horses hard, tracking side by side through the tall yellow grass. The wind was cold in their faces.

They rode into the stable yard, and Lea swung down from the dun while it was still pacing.

"Go up and ask the Baron if I can borrow that damned stallion of his! I'll need more speed than my old friend·can give me." He stroked the dun's flank for a moment, then led him into the stalls.

With the dun in his box, Lea trotted acorss the stableyard and up the path to his cabin. He pushed through the door, glanced around for Tocsen. The old man wasn't there. No saying he'd want in on this either. It was white man's business, after all.

Lea scooped up his bedroll, boxes of cartridges—his, not the hotel's—shoved his old sheepskin jacket, an extra pair of wool socks and his long-johns into his saddlebags.

Then he was out of the cabin, heading back toward the stables at a run. *After midnight,* he thought. It's a hell of a head start. A full day's start.

When he got to the stable, Sarah had already come down again. The Baron was with her, puffing from the stairs, his right arm in a sling. Toby Easterby was with him.

"So, Lea, you need my bad-behaved stud? I think you need help too? No? I come!"

The old squarehead was showing up all right.

"I'm coming along also, Mr. Lea."

"No," Lea said, "neither of you. It's not your business. No need for either of you to get killed in it. What you *can* do is keep an eye on Sarah. Watch out for her."

The old German blustered about that for a moment, but Toby Easterby nodded and said: "Very well, Mr. Lea. I promise you we'll take good care of Miss Bridge. I understand that Mr. Larrabee is the villain in the piece?"

"And those Russians!" The Baron went stamping back into the stalls to get the stud out. They heard him bellow for the stable-boy, then a sudden, embarrassed silence, as he remembered the boy's death.

"Take some of the hands, then, Lea!" Sarah said.

"Your father took the best half-dozen gun-hands he had, Sarah. What's left are pure cowpokes, not worth much in a gunfight. That's if Larrabee hasn't already got to one or two of them with some cash money . . ." Lea shook his head. "I'd better leave them be."

They heard a clatter of hooves as the Baron, handicapped by his slung arm, led the big stallion out. The big bay rolled his eyes and pranced, full of grain. *Just the way I need the big bastard, too,* Lea thought.

The Baron held the stud while Lea and Easterby got him saddled and bridled, and Lea lashed the saddlebags and rifle-boot on him.

Then Lea swung up.

The big bay lurched and shied into a buck, but Lea roweled his sides and leaned forward to hit the horse between the ears with his fist. The stud snorted and danced across the cobbles, but he didn't throw another buck.

"Goot!" the Baron called. "Dat's how you ride him!"

"Good luck, old man!"

"Lea."

Lea tipped his Stetson to them, spurred the stallion, and rode away.

CHAPTER NINETEEN

The big bay was a fast one, no doubt about that. And he had as many bad manners as the old Baron had himself. He'd break stride, buck, and shy at nothing but a windblown leaf.

Lea gathered him in every time, spurred him, hit him when he had to, and after more than two hours on the road, had the stud leveled out and running smooth.

The stallion was as strong as an ox, once he settled down. And fast. Maybe even as fast as the dun had been in its prime.

And the horse was going to have to be. Because Lea intended to drive it straight toward Little River, hitting the ridges all the way.

There was no way to catch the Russians in a stern chase; they were well mounted and they'd too damn much of a start. The most Lea could hope for was to shortcut, and come up on their ambush—because they'd sure as hell set one to catch Abe and his men riding back from that railroad cut.

As he rode, Lea laid the country out in his mind,

looking for a dead-sure place for a bushwhacking.

It depended on how far Abe had ridden back before the Russians met him. If he was a full day out of Little River, the Count's best chance would be in the wooded hills south of Smokey. If Abe hadn't gotten that far the Russians might catch him at Fork Creek.

Fork Creek was the place Lea would have picked. That little stream ran through a steep, rough valley no more that a pistol shot across. It would be turkey-shooting for the Cossack's carbines.

Lea knew Abe had taken fair-enough men with him. Abe wouldn't have hired them in the first place if they weren't first-class cowhands. The beef from Gunstock's ranch wasn't raised for the hotel alone. Gunstock beef was driven and shipped clear to Chicago. No question of Abe's men being good with cows.

And the six he'd taken with him must be able to handle guns at least well enough to pass for fighting men. Lea'd known plenty of cowpokes who liked a fight—and even a few who really knew how. Most working cowboys never had the time, or the application, to get really fine with a gun. Still, likely they'd give a good account of themselves—if the Count was foolish enough to give them a fair chance.

The Count hadn't struck Lea as that kind of a fool.

No; he'd lay his Cossacks off in an ambush of some kind, and they'd knock down Abe's men—and old Abe —just as fast as they could. Abe and six cowboys together were almost fair odds against the Count and his eight Cossacks, even with the Cossacks being professional fighting men. The odds would be *too* fair for the Count.

One way or another, the little black-eyed nobleman

166

would see those odds knocked down.

But if Lea could ride up on the Russians in time. One more gun, a professional gun, might make the difference.

Lea spurred the big bay out across a grassy flat, running the stallion full-out. Soon enough, they'd be up on the ridges, in the tanglefoot and shale slides. There wouldn't be much galloping up there.

By late afternoon, Lea was riding the ridges south toward Little River. The big stud was going steady as a steam engine.

The weather was holding, as it had held for days, clear, sunny, and getting colder. As the bay climbed the hills, Lea reached back and broke his sheepskin out of the saddlebags. The wind had an edge to it.

He thought about the Count as he rode, and he thought about the Cossacks too.

They were professionals, and they were used to big, rough, wild country. They were used to riding hard. They had military discipline, and they did what they were told. They were frontiersmen; they had been raised to fight Tartars as savage and elusive an enemy as any Comanche.

These particular men were armed with Nagent revolvers and Russian carbines—and sabers. And all this was pure bad news.

But *they* had weaknesses too.

Lea figured they might be a little lost, should something happen to that fine Count of theirs. Their sergeant—if that's what he was—that giant Grigori, didn't strike Lea as being particularly bright. Likely he wouldn't be too handy a commander with the Count dead. And sure as hell none of the rest of them seemed like officer material.

No. The way to handle those *hombres* was to surprise them—and to get a bullet into the Count!

Could be that the Cossacks might be surprised, too, at the fight the cowboys would put up. From what Lea'd heard, Cossacks weren't too used to ordinary citizens coming back at them in a fight.

And there was the rub. Because what *he* knew, the Count knew better. And that was why the Count would be doing the surprising, at Fork Creek or wherever he could, and why he was sure as hell going to bushwhack those cowboys down before they could come back hard at his men.

Lea swung off the bay, and led him over a shattered stretch of scree. The big stallion didn't seem to be tiring, but the weight off his back for a mile or two would give him a breather.

Lea stumped along through the rattling shale, the bay following quietly on a rein lead.

Lea hadn't seen any tracks. Not that they would have bothered to brush them out. Why should they? He knew where they were going, and he knew how they'd get there. They would have ridden at a good speed, but not as fast as they could, not as fast as he was taking the stallion. And they would have headed straight south, straight for Little River. Probably by map. In doing that, they would have ridden up and down half a dozen steep hills and ridges.

Far out to the west, the long great line of the Bitteroots marched down from the north. The snow on their peaks glittered in the early evening light. The snow shone farther down the jagged granite falls and buttresses than it had only a week before. Winter was blowing down from the peaks and high passes.

Lea felt it in the wind that hissed softly through rough grass along the ridge. It stung his face and his hands. He walked along a little farther, another quarter mile or so, looking always out to the south, looking for a smudge of smoke that might mean the Cossacks had stopped to make a fire for their tea, or had hunted as they rode, and stopped to stick-broil a haunch of venison.

There was nothing. Lea had not really expected it. The Russians probably did not think he'd be coming after them. It would be the Shoshones they'd be wary of. It was unlikely, though, that the Indians, whipped to a bone by the cavalry in the past few years, would want to attack a party of nine well-armed men.

After walking a last, bad stretch of shale, Lea swung up into the saddle again, picked up the big bay's head from nibbling at stray moss flowers, and spurred the stallion into a lope.

He would run the big horse until dark. At night it would be too dark to ride. The high clouds coming down on the wind would shade out the moonlight. After sunset, when darkness fell, he and the Russians both would have to step down to sleep until dawn.

Two hours after daybreak the Russians would meet Abe Bridge at Fork Creek or beyond. And, if it killed him and his horse, Lea would be there too.

In a high, saddleback dip, fifteen miles or so from the Creek, Lea staked the stallion out, hobbled him for good measure, and then rolled himself into his blankets to sleep. It was dark by then, like the inside of a stovepipe hat. The wind was blowing stronger from the north.

He decided he was a damn fool, rooted with his shoulder for some comfort as he lay, and went slowly to sleep, waking a little now and then when the wind gusted harder, or stopped.

He dreamed toward waking, and only for a while. He dreamed he was a boy again, standing in the hot white dust of the road, watching his father ride off to fight in the war. His brother was riding off too.

Even in the dream, Frank knew that was wrong. They hadn't gone together; his father had gone first, and been killed. Then his brother had gone, and been killed, too. But that had taken years, and they'd never gone away together like that.

He felt how hot the road dust was under his bare feet, and he heard his mother saying something.

His father didn't turn around to wave, but his brother did. Frank saw his face as plain as day against the bright green of the sycamores along the road.

"Wave goodbye," his mother said.

Lea woke with a grunt. He turned over and looked up into a dead black sky.

He sat up, looking to the east. There, along the distant hills, a narrow ribbon of gray edged the far horizon. The wind had died; the air was still and cold as cold water. The bay stallion bulked in the darkness, shifting a little. It was time to move out.

Lea rolled out of the soogins, stood in the darkness and stretched, working the stiffness out of his muscles and joints. His side hurt him. He reached down, picked up his gun belt, and strapped it on. Then he took a few strides out to the edge of the ridge, unbuttoned his trousers and pissed a stream out into the night. Hunger was on him. The stallion would be hungry, too, wanting grain.

Lea went to the horse, knelt to unhobble him, pulled the screw-stake out, and saddled and bridled him. The bay fought the cold bit, clenching his teeth against it, but Lea held his ear and tapped the bit against those big yellow teeth, dim in the darkness, till the horse took it.

Then he swung up into the saddle, looked back to see the dawn coming down the ridge, and kicked the bay into a trot.

Lea dug in his sheepskin pocket for a strip of jerky, chewed it down, then chased it with a long drink of water. It tasted of metal, and was cold enough to hurt his teeth.

"Cold bit, cold water," he said to the stallion, wondering if a German horse understood English.

When it grew light enough, he spurred the bay into a gallop.

At twenty minutes to eleven o'clock, by his watch, Lea rode the sweating bay along the last slope of the southern ridge. Half a mile to the west was the Fork Creek ford.

The stallion was lathered from the long run, and foam fell from the bridle chain, but he still went well, and was breathing as deeply as a sleeping child.

"Good horse," Lea said to him, and stroked it along the neck. "You're a beauty. Yes you are."

They were out of the shale, and the stallion's hooves thudded along the rough turf. To the right, the ridge fell away in a steep slope, too steep to run the bay down safely. That slope leveled out, two-hundred feet below, into a broad valley full of thick, high, yellow grass—buffalo and gamma and wild wheat.

Out there in the valley Lea saw the first sign the Russians had left. A narrow beaten track cutting through the the high grass to the west. It was interesting to see; the Cossacks traveled like Indians, in single file.

Lea kicked the bay into a lunging gallop, and he strained his eyes toward Fork Creek.

CHAPTER TWENTY

He rode along the ridge for another few hundred yards, the bright late-morning sunlight stretching his shadow ahead of them as they went. A wind was up, gusting and shifting over the ridge.

Then he saw Abe Bridge and his cowhands.

They were riding toward him, loping, bunched and alert, their rifles across their saddle-bows, up from the narrow end of the valley, away from Fork Creek.

There were seven of them. Old Abe and his half dozen. By the look of them, even at a considerable distance, they had been expecting trouble back at the ford.

And there hadn't been any. The Russians hadn't tried for them. And damned if Lea could understand why.

Unless the ford at the creek was too obvious. Abe looked to have been ready for trouble there.

Lea pulled the sweating stallion down to a walk, and lifted the big Sharps out of its scabbard. He'd wait till Abe was closer, then give him a warning shot and ride down to join him. If the Russians had made no trouble here, they damn well would make trouble somewhere else—maybe over at Smokey.

The wind blew across the ridge, and swept down into the narrowing valley. Lea watched as it combed through the thick grass there. Grass as high as a horse's shoulder.

It combed the grass back in long surging rows of yellow and green.

That's where Lea saw the Cossacks.

They'd laid their horses down in a great half-circle in the grass. The Cossacks lay beside them, their carbines in their hands. Lea saw them here and there, then lost sight of them as the restless wind blew the grass in billows back and forth.

He saw them from the ridge, lookig down, but Abe and his cowhands would see nothing. They were already riding into that great half-circle.

Lea raised the Sharps and fired.

The sound boomed across the valley. Abe and his men looked up to see Lea, outlined on the ridge above, pointing furiously down into the valley before them.

Abe Bridge was nobody's fool. It took him just a moment to recognize Lea, another moment to realize what he was warning them.

He was the least bit too late. They were just within the circle.

From the ridge, Lea saw the Cossacks and Orloff. He recognized the Count leaping up, mounting his horse. He saw them rise out of the buffalo grass and fire in one long rolling volley into the cowhands they almost surrounded.

Lea saw three of the cowboys go down hard. He reloaded the Sharps, stood in the stirrups, and tried a shot at the Count. Tried, and lost him in the drifting gunsmoke. Then he bucketed the Sharps, turned the stallion's head to the pitch of the slope, and spurred him down toward the valley below.

The side of the ridge fell away almost vertically. The stallion leaped out and down, slid, scrambled, and found his feet. It was fall or gallop down. The big bay galloped.

Lea lay back against the cantle, yanking at the straps to loose the Greener as they went. He expected the stallion to fall, and tried to shake his boots loose in the stirrups so he could kick his way clear when they went down.

The bay's tail whipped at his face as he lay back almost to the horse's rump. The Greener finally came free, and he had it in his right hand. He couldn't keep the reins; the stallion's head was too far down. He saw above him the tilting slope of the ridge; below, the narrow valley was exploding in gunfire, hazed by gunsmoke.

The stallion slipped. Lea felt his guts twist inside him as the horse began to fall. Then, with a crack of hoof on stone, a slamming blow up against Lea's back, the bay recovered.

When the stallion struck level ground, the high, hissing foliage of the grass, the jolt almost slung Lea away and out of the saddle. He almost lost the shotgun as well. Lea held on—more by luck than skill—and kept the Greener too. He heaved himself upright in the saddle, dug his boots deeper into the stirrups, and spurred the big bay on, thundering through the high grass, into the fight.

The cowboys had done all right. Three of them were

down and dead, and one of those still in the saddle hurt badly and swaying as he rode. Still, Abe was leading the remnants straight at the Cossack line in a charge.

It was the only chance they had.

As he cut across the valley toward the fight, Lea saw Abe riding down on one of the Russians, blazing away at the man with a pistol. The Cossack, up and mounted, sat his horse dead-still and sighted the old man with his carbine resting over his arm as if he were hunting. It was not the way to work against Abe Bridge.

Lea saw the old man as he bore down, the four cowhands riding hard behind him, revolvers smoking. Lea saw Abe fire twice, three, four times at the Cossack before him. And the Russian sagged in the saddle. The carbine swung out to the side as the Cossack leaned down from his horse, then slipped and fell from it.

Abe and his men came riding through.

Just as they did, another Russian, riding almost parallel to their ambush line, snap-shot with his Winchester and knocked Abe Bridge out of the saddle.

Lea hauled on the rein to bring the stallion over—he'd have to teach this brute neck-reining for sure, he thought—and raised the Greener as he and the Cossack galloped along for a moment, side by side across fifty feet of grass.

The Russian turned and saw Lea, then levered his carbine. He was a tall, black-bearded man with a bony face.

Lea shot him center with the right barrel of the Greener.

He saw the Cossack flinch, his long flap-tailed black coat fly out as the buckshot struck him. He fell back off of his running horse, hung from a stirrup for a moment, squealing in agony, and then dropped free.

Lea saw one of the cowhands fire down with his Peacemaker at a Cossack shooting from the grass. The Cossack fell sideways, kicking.

There was a volley of Winchester rounds, and one of the cowhands riding toward Lea, shouting something, was knocked out of the saddle. His horse was shot too. It stumbled and went down.

A Cossack fired at Lea from the grass. He heard the bullet in the air past his head.

Lea turned to find him, but the man had ducked away.

He turned in the saddle again, and saw a Russian riding down on him. The Cossack had a pistol in his hand. Lea saw that it was the tall, blond man who'd grinned at him on the kitchen path.

Lea spun the stallion, and fell to the side to lie along the horse's neck as the blond man shot at him. Then, Lea fired the left barrel of the Greener from under the horse's neck.

The charge hit the blond man in his face. One of his eyes hung dangling as he rode past.

Lea turned the bay again, and drove him back into the fight, looking for the Count.

As he rode in through a cloud of gunsmoke, he saw two Cossacks hacking at a wounded cowhand with their sabers. It was Folliard. The old ranny fired a shot at one of them, but missed. Folliard was slumped in the saddle, trotting along with bright blood running down his horse's side. He'd been shot in the first volley, and was bleeding to death.

The two Cossacks, wheeling away when he fired the wild shot, turned back after him now. They rode down on him and hit him with their sabers again, cutting his head, chopping at his arms. The old cowhand was dead. One of the Cossacks leaned out of his saddle, laughing, and drove his saber into the cowboy's back as he lay, doubled across his horse's saddle-bow.

Lea rode to them. The nearest Cossack turned to call to him, thinking him a Russian. Lea drew and shot him twice through the belly.

The other man pulled his saber free, wheeled his horse, and spurred it at Lea, yelling. Lea took care with this man, and aimed and shot him through the right shoulder. The Cossack dropped his saber and fell back across his horse's haunch, but the horse kept running.

As it passed Lea on the run, he leaned out and shot the Cossack again just above the hips, so the bullet would go through his bowels.

A round hit Lea then, fired from somewhere behind him. It struck him lightly just under his left arm from front to back, and knocked him half out of the saddle.

A Cossack came riding past him through the smoke, but didn't seem to see Lea, and went on his way.

Someone shot at Lea again. The bullet blew his saddle horn away with a crack. He spurred the stallion and saw a Russian running through the grass toward him. It was that big sergeant, Grigori.

Where in hell was the *Count?*

The giant Cossack stopped running, and stood to take better aim. Lea turned in the saddle to shoot him, and a cowhand jumped out of the grass and grappled with the Russian. It spoiled Lea's shot.

It was Tiny Morgan, already shot once, but paying it no heed.

The two huge men grappled and butted like bulls.

178

Lea kicked the stallion away through the grass and gunsmoke, looking for the little black-eyed Count. His side hurt as he rode, but whether it was the gunshot or the old wound opening up, he didn't know.

He rode out into the open, and saw the Count sitting on a fine roan horse, talking to two of his men, and waving his hand. He looked angry. Lea thought it must be because the fight had cost him more than he'd figured on.

The big bay was almost done. Lea felt him stagger under him, and wondered if he'd been hurt in the shooting.

One of the Russians turned and saw him. He saw the Count turn and look at him too, and shake his head. It looked as though he was smiling.

The three Russians turned as one and came at him. The Count held a pistol in his hand; the other two began to fire their Winchesters. The stallion squealed as a round burned his side, and he heaved and bucked to the right. Lea tried to keep his seat, but his left side hurt terribly and took away his strength.

The stallion bucked again, and Lea was off, pitching out into the high grass, the Bisley Colt clutched in his hand.

He hit hard, rolled, and heard the hoofbeats coming.

He scrambled to his feet, yelling from the pain along his side, and dove deeper into the grass.

The hoofbeats drove in after him. When he stopped running and turned, he saw a Cossack with bright blue eyes leaning from the saddle to shoot at him with a carbine.

Lea shot the man and saw him flinch, but then the Cossack lifted the carbine to sight again. Lea shot him through the forehead just as he fired and saw, when the man fell, that the back of his head was broken open. Lea wasn't hit. He didn't know how the man had missed him. The other Cossack shot at Lea, and he fell and rolled along the ground to duck the shot. The man rode close and fired again. Lea came to his knees and started to shoot back. Then he remembered the Colt was empty.

The Cossack saw that, and so did the Count. Lea heard the Count laugh and say something in Russian.

The Cossack pulled in his horse, and for a moment, nobody did anything. Lea thought of reloading, but the Cossack was sitting on his horse just a little way away, watching him, and there would be no time. Lea wished to God he'd put his second Colt in his belt, but he hadn't. It was with the stallion.

The Count called out something, and Lea heard a sliding sound. He looked and saw that the Cossack had drawn his saber. The Russian wheeled his horse and came at Lea very fast.

Lea ran away into the tall grass as fast as he could, limping from the pain in his side, and gasping for breath. He ran as fast as he had ever run in his life, and the hoofbeats ran behind him. He heard the Count laughing.

The Cossack was on him very suddenly; he must have seen the grass moving where Lea ran, and come riding straight to him. Lea felt the hoofbeats in the ground, heard the grass hissing to his right, looked over his shoulder and saw the bulk of the horse and the man on him, and a sun-bright curve of steel.

He stopped in his tracks, threw himself back, and rolled under the horse's hooves.

The blade hummed down in a flash of light and cut his coat-sleeve and his arm, though he didn't feel it. Then he was up on his feet with his side on fire and running the other way.

The Cossack must have wheeled his horse and cut at him backhand. Lea heard the man grunt, and felt the whiffle of the blade past the back of his neck.

Lea heard the Count laughing again. He ran a little way, stopped, and turned as the Cossack came after him. The Cossack had a wide, pockmarked face, and he looked tired and angry. He carried the saber up resting over his shoulder, and he rode down on Lea at a gallop.

Lea took a step to the left to set himself better in the tangle of tall grass, bent down and pulled the Arkansas toothpick from his right boot. He leaned back and wound up, and threw the knife overhand as if he were pitching in a baseball game.

He threw it as hard as he could, then ducked and rolled into the grass to his right. It did not seem that he would be able to get up again, no matter what happened.

He heard the Cossack grunt as he rode in, and he thought he saw him swing the saber. Then he thought he'd thrown it, because the sword came flying, spinning end over end, and fell into the grass.

Then Lea saw that the Cossack had riden past. His horse was trotting. Then it stopped and bent its head to graze.

The Cossack sat in his saddle, bent forward, for a moment. Then he swung his leg over to dismount, slid down to the ground, and then knelt down. When he did that, Lea saw the hilt of the knife sticking out of his chest, on the left side.

The Count called, and the man muttered something in Russian. Then he slowly lay back in the grass with his eyes open. Blood had soaked his black uniform.

Lea heard the Count cursing, and heard the hoofbeats coming toward him. He thought of getting up, and getting the saber the man had dropped. He could try with that.

It seemed like too much trouble.

CHAPTER TWENTY-ONE

Lea watched the Count ride to where the Cossack was sitting, dying with the knife in his chest.

The Count looked down at the man for a moment, but he didn't say anything. Lea thought of reloading the Colt, but he didn't know where it was. He'd dropped it while he was running. He got up and stood anyway.

The Count turned his horse, and rode over to Lea. He had a handsome, nickle-plated revolver in his hand.

The Count sat his big roan, looking down at Lea. The Cossack had looked tired, but the little Count didn't. He looked fresh as a daisy. His riding clothes were clean, and Lea could see a reflection of the grass in the gleaming polish of his right boot. His black eyes were bright as a child's.

"What an afternoon," he said. He looked down at Lea and pursed his lips. "Those men of Bridge's fought well . . . really well." He turned and looked out over the valley. "I don't see Grigori." He sighed. "I assumed my Grigori would live forever."

The Count glanced down at Lea, and shifted in the

saddle. Lea heard the leather creak.

"They were a surprise, those men." He smiled. "But not such a surprise as you, Mr. Lea. How on earth did you get here so quickly?"

Lea cleared his throat. "I rode the ridge south."

"Ah," the Count said. "I see. I thought of doing that, but I didn't care to outline my men there for any of your red savages to observe. Perhaps I was too cautious." He cocked the pistol.

"I wonder . . ." he said. "Are you . . . were you an army officer, perhaps? You are certainly an accomplished fighting man!"

"No," Lea said. "I'm a gunman. And I've been a pimp, and I've owned a ranch." Let the stuck-up son-of-a-bitch chew on that.

The Count laughed. "I see. A rogue! And a professional." He lifted the revolver and aimed it off-hand at Lea's head. "Well," the Count said, "as something of a rogue myself, I wish you farewell."

He looked surprised all of a sudden—astonished—as if he'd just realized something. And he screamed a short sharp scream like a girl's when she sees a rat on the kitchen floor.

He twisted in the saddle and the revolver went off. He grabbed at something at the small of his back.

Lea saw the polished wood and bright yellow fletching of a Shoshone arrow. The Count broke the shaft as he tried to pull it away. Inside him, the iron barb held fast.

Then another arrow came soaring through the air and into the Count's side. That one went in deep, almost to the feathers. Lea looked to see if the head had come poking out of him on the other side, but it hadn't.

The Count had dropped his revolver. He grabbed the fletching of the second arrow and tugged at it. And he looked down at Lea as if he was going to ask for help. The third arrow came and hit him higher. It snapped into the side of his chest, and Lea could see that the head of it must be deep into his lungs. It was a killing shot.

The Count stopped pulling at the arrow shafts. He threw back his head and screamed. The roan began to side-step, nervous at the noise. After a moment, the Count stopped screaming and tried to catch his breath, but he couldn't. He began to drown in his blood. Lea heard him gulping, gargling as he tried to breath. He was belching blood, and the smell made his horse shy and trot away with him.

Lea watched as the nervous roan trotted away, taking the Count with it. He saw the Russian, still sitting upright in the saddle, tearing with his hands at his mouth, his throat, throwing his head far, far back, trying to breath. His hands were red as paint.

"Where Greener?" Tocsen said, walking through the grass. The old man looked mighty sore. "You take."

Lea sat down to have a rest.

Tocsen stood in front of him and shook his bow angrily. He was mighty sore. "When we go," he said. "*I* take Greener. Every time!"

Tocsen searched through the grass for the shotgun. When he found it, and had walked down Lea's skittish bay for the shells to reload it, he was then ready to help Lea with Tiny Morgan. Morgan was the only Gunstock man alive, and he'd been bled out to a fare-the-well. Lea found him with the big Cossack, Grigori. The Cossack's neck was broken, and his head had been turned all the way around.

He should never have whipped a horse in Tiny's stable.

Abe Bridge was dead. That single carbine shot had taken him through the heart.

The other Gunstock hands were dead as well. Two of them had been wounded by gunfire, then finished with sabers.

Six of the Cossacks were dead, and the last two—one of them was one that Lea'd shot in the belly—were bad hurt and dying. Tocsen cut their throats. Then he scalped the other six. Lea assumed the old man intended to claim the bunch should another Shoshone ever inquire about it.

Lea had lost sight of the Count. But Tocsen had an eye for the roan. He found the horse grazing all the way back by Fork Creek, and found the Count lying there beside him. He'd ridden all that way, dead. Tocsen scalped him, then cut off his nose to make him look silly on the other side.

That night, they camped a little farther up the valley. They heated the barrel of one of the Nagent pistols and burned Tiny Morgan's leg wound closed. They had gathered the horses that were alive and not wounded. They'd shot the others. It turned out there were Lea's bay, the Count's roan, two Gunstock ponies, and six Cossack horses in fine shape.

Lea figured the Cossack horses to be Tiny Morgan's to keep—if he lived.

They sat in a circle stomped clear of grass around a bright little fire and ate horse steak. Tocsen chewed some up the way the squaws did for children and old

186

people, and Tiny ate that without a murmur. The big man had fits of crying over killing the Russian. That seemed to bother him more than having the gunshot wound burned closed.

Lea thought he was going to have to have that done for him, too. But Tocsen looked at the wound under his arm, and said no. His side was all bruised, black and purple and swollen under the stitches. No question he'd done himself harm riding, *and* in the fight. Tocsen washed the wound under his arm. He found some liquor in a Russian's canteen and poured that over it. It hurt bad enough to make Lea sick. He ate his steaks anyway, and drank a great deal of cold water from Fork Creek.

It was a cold, still night. Lea felt full of meat and cold water, and he felt a little sick. He said goodnight to Tiny Morgan, and patted the big man on the shoulder and told him he'd been very brave. Then he told Tocsen to take the damn Greener and keep it. He'd pay the hotel the price.

Then he lay down by the fire and rolled himself into his blankets. He wondered if he'd injured his side so much that it would never heal. He also wondered how to tell Sarah Bridge that her father had been killed under his eye. Under his gun. Because he'd been a little slow in figuring, and not looked as soon and as sharp as he should.

In the morning he was the first up. He was stiff as a pine board. His side and the gunshot wound under his arm hurt like boils. In spite of that, Lea felt very well. He took deep breaths of cold morning air, and he stood away from camp, pissed, and watched the gray dawn turning to sunrise in the east. Then he went out to the bodies.

No coyotes had come to them in the night. The buzzards would lead those into the valley today. Lea went to a dead Cossack first and got his Arkansas toothpick back. Then he walked to all the cowhand corpses and went through their pockets for anything that might tell of a family, anything they might like to have as a keepsake of these men. There wasn't much.

Old Folliard had a son in prison in New Mexico. Seemed to have been mixed up with Bill Bonney out there. A man named O'Reilly had a sister in Sioux City, a laundress at an Army post. A man named Peterson had been thinking of going home to farm. Then Lea collected the guns.

He couldn't find his own Colt. It was lost somewhere in there, buried out of sight in the high grass. He was glad he had the other Bisley in his saddlebag.

Finally, he went to Abe's body.

The old man lay stretched on his back, yawning, as if he were just waking from a nap on some country picnic.

Lea found a fine watch on him; "From Lil—With Love" was engraved inside the cover. And he found a bill from Boise Liquor and Sundries Supply, and a big bill from a freight outfit in Colorado.

Lea took Abe's wallet, but didn't open it, and took his fine spotted silk scarf as well. It wasn't damaged, and there was no blood on it. It was something Sarah might want to have.

Later in the morning, Lea and Tocsen dug a shallow grave, wrapped Abe Bridge in a blanket and put him into it. Then they went back to camp, hoisted Tiny Morgan up onto one of the Cossack horses, and rode away.

They'd ride the ridge back, the way Lea had come down from Gunstock. Tiny's leg and Lea's side would hold out better riding on the level rather than hauling up and down across a dozen ridges. They'd ride the same ridge Lea had—but slower. It was two full days to Gunstock.

Lea led, riding one of the Gunstock ponies. The Baron's bay needed at least another day's rest. Tiny Morgan followed. And Tocsen, muttering and singing to himself, the Greener across his saddle-bow, brought up the rear. Tocsen was riding the Count's tall roan and leading his paint pony behind him. He finished one song and started another.

By the next day, Lea was feeling better, and so was Tiny's leg. The leg was stiff, but didn't hurt so much.

They had horse steak again for breakfast. The meat tasted all right, but was giving them all the trots. Poetic justice, Lea said, but old Tocsen didn't understand jokes when they were told in English, and Tiny wasn't smart enough to understand it, although he laughed anyway when he saw that Lea would like that.

The Cossack horses gave them some trouble, too. They weren't used to being led, and started out the first day pushing and kicking to be first on trail. Tiny finally found the natural leader, a mean black gelding. When he was put up in front, the rest of the string quieted down.

Tocsen, though, was disappointed with Count Orloff's tall roan. The roan was too nervous for him, and it was always wanting to do this or that, shy here or start there. The old Shoshone wasn't used to blood horses, and he didn't like them. He beat the roan, and that just made him worse.

"Pet him," Lea said. "Make him like you, and he'll do what you want."

Making a horse *like* him was not in Tocsen's usual line. It was not in any Shoshone's usual line. It might be something that the Nez Percé did. And if that is what their spirits urged on them, he supposed they had no voice in the matter.

Tocsen got down off his high horse by noon on the second day's traveling, and climbed aboard his shambling little pinto. There had never been any question of affection between those two, but there was considerable respect on both sides.

On the morning of the third day they saw the high slate roof shining wet in the sun. It was a sight to see.

A rain shower had swept down the valley as they rode into it, and a long, fading rainbow arched out from High Pass at the valley's western edge.

Tiny was very excited, and pointed it out. He'd been told about the pot of gold as a child, and people had amused themselves with him lately, by telling him it was true. He told Lea that he'd gone to look for the gold twice, to buy a set of harnesses with bells on it, and had probably just missed finding it.

Lea didn't know what to say to the big man at first— but in order to keep him from galloping off up the valley after his pot of gold, finally said that indeed there had once *been* gold at the end of every rainbow. But that it had been taken away lately, so that people would be content to enjoy the rainbow's prettiness, rather than being greedy.

The big man was struck by this, and thought about it. He finally nodded and rode along content.

Lea worried about Tiny as if the giant were a child.

He decided it came from not having real children of his own to raise.

For his part, Tocsen acted with more respect toward Tiny Morgan than he did to Lea. He thought the big man had a spirit in his head.

They rode along the ranch boundary, past the dairy buildings, and into the west pastures. There were Jerseys in one of the fenced fields, and two teams of Belgian geldings in the other.

Then they rode past the laundry, the kitchen gardens, and into the stableyard. A party of guests were riding out as they rode in, clattering over the cobbles. It was a group of young men and women, some of them in hunting pinks. The only foxes around Gunstock were grays. They were no good to hunt, since they simply ran to the nearest slanting tree, and climbed it. Coyotes were good coursing though, and Gunstock made a considerable fuss about its hounds and rough-country coyote hunting.

The wrangler, Davies, was taking this bunch out, riding down to the kennels to pick up Chasen and the pack.

Davies stared at Lea as he rode by, but he didn't say anything.

They pulled up at the stable, and Tiny swung down stiffly to take their horses. Lea told him that Edwards would be coming out to look at his leg, and Tiny nodded, smiling. Lea had told him that Charlie Turley was dead, but as Tiny led the horses in, Lea heard him calling to the boy. He'd forgotten.

Tocsen walked away toward the cabin, muttering, the Greener over his shoulder, his rawhide sack dragging along the cobbles.

Lea walked across the stableyard to the path through the kitchen gardens. It seemed a very long walk to take. He wished to God it was longer.

De la Maine had heard he was back. He saw the massive Frenchman standing at the top of the steps to the kitchen door. Some halfbreed girls were peeping out behind him.

De la Maine looked into Lea's eyes as he came up the path, then made a face and shook his head sadly.

When Lea came up the steps, the big Frenchman sighed and shook his hand. "I will miss that so-loud Monsieur Bridge," he said. "*La petite* has heard you are here. She is coming down to the kitchens now."

Lea stood in the doorway, with nothing to say.

CHAPTER TWENTY-TWO

Sarah came into the kitchen, looked to the door and saw him standing there. She pushed her way through the crowd of kitchen help, all standing in the passageway, murmuring, turning to look at her as she strode past them. A stocky, black-haired woman was walking behind her.

"Lea."

He shoved his way through to her, took her arm, and led her into one of the small pantries beside the passage. He shut the door behind him, and heard, through the pine panels, de la Maine shouting at his people to get back to work.

"Lea?"

He turned. She stared up at him, her face white. She was wearing a high-neck dress, a soft blue color.

"He's dead, Sarah."

She gasped as if he'd hit her, and took a step back and shook her head. But she didn't say anything. She kept looking at him.

"My fault. I was just a little slow seeing them."

She didn't say a word.

"He . . . he and his men charged the Cossacks, and killed some of them. Abe was shot through the heart, riding into them."

"Oh . . . my . . . daddy," she said like a little girl. She swayed against Lea and pressed her face against his sheepskin coat, holding onto him as if she were going to fall.

She stayed that way for a little while and she didn't say anything more.

Sarah's face was still white as she sat in the library at her father's desk. She hadn't cried, and she wasn't crying now.

Lea and Leo Drexel were sitting in armchairs, facing her.

"My God, I'm sorry, Sarah. Abe was a dear friend to me," Drexel said. He tugged a fine lawn handkerchief from his sleeve and blew his nose.

"Thank you, Leo," she said. "Father died, I think, the way he would have wanted to." She glanced at Lea. "Now, the question is, what can *we* do?"

"The Count was killed, *and* all of his men?" Leo stared at Lea.

"Every damn one."

"Good God almighty." Leo dabbed at his forehead with the handkerchief. "That must have been a *battle* out there!"

"Yes, Mr. Drexel, it was."

"But then, haven't we won?" Sarah said.

"No," Lea said, "we haven't. The silver is out there. And Larrabee is still at Gunstock. We've cut off his right arm, but in a few days he'll grow another one."

"Shane, or Shannon, or whatever his name is."

"Yes, Mr. Drexel."

"And what if I tell Larrabee to get out of Gunstock tonight!" Sarah clenched her small fist and brought it down hard on the desk blotter.

"He'll go," Drexel said. "But—"

"But he'll leave some bought-and-paid-for people behind. And we don't know who they might be," Lea finished.

"Exactly," Drexel said.

"There's a simple way out of this, you know," Lea said. "I can kill the old man now. He has no one with him to stop me—not yet."

Drexel stared at him. "You're not serious?"

"As serious as taxes," Lea said.

"No . . . no, we can't do that," Sarah said, her eyes wide.

"It's the only way. I can kill him and be gone. With Larrabee dead, you'll have time to get to Boise, to make your own business arrangements about that silver. Contacts with companies that'll keep men like Larrabee from robbing you."

"No," Sarah said. "I couldn't. I couldn't do that!"

"It's impossible, Lea!" Drexel said. "Even if Sarah could countenance such a thing. You just don't understand this business! If a man like Larrabee were to be shot—murdered—at Gunstock, we'd be ruined! All the silver in the world wouldn't save us!"

"I couldn't do it anyway, Leo." She looked at Lea and tried to smile. "It . . . it is a generous thing to offer to sacrifice yourself that way, Lea. To turn yourself into a . . . a hunted killer."

"I'm sorry if I've upset you," Lea said and got up.

195

"We'll think of another way to handle Larrabee."

"Yes," she sighed, "we'll have to."

"Well, we have to decide something," Drexel said, standing up. "Among other things, we're going to miss Abe dreadfully when it comes to *managing* the hotel. We're going to need help with the suppliers for a start."

"Yes, I know," Sarah said. "I . . . I thought of sending a telegram to that young man that father liked at the Parker House. Father said he knew his business, said he was a first-class manager."

"At the Parker House? Oh, yes, you mean Henry Morganstern." He made a face. "That's all we need now, a Jew at Gunstock!"

"Father said he was very good."

"So I suppose he is," Drexel said, "if he'll come and work for less than an arm and a leg. If that insane old man hasn't had us all killed before he gets here!"

"If you will excuse me," Lea said, "I'll be getting out to my cabin. Edwards is supposed to see me out there when he finishes with Tiny." He walked to the door.

"Lea, wait!" Sarah called.

"Yes?"

"Lea, I didn't know you were hurt!"

"It's not serious."

"I . . . I would feel much better if you could stay up at the main building," she said. "They've already sent a man to kill you out in that cabin. Please stay up here at the hotel."

"Don't be a fool, man," Drexel said, as Lea hesitated. "We can't afford to lose you. It's that simple."

"All right."

"Good man." Drexel came to the door. "I'll see you settled. We'll put you into your old sick-room on the second floor. You'll feel right at home!"

Outside, in the corridor, Lea saw a short, broad-shouldered woman sitting by the door in a straight-back chair. It was the woman he'd seen with Sarah in the kitchen. She had a knitting bag on her lap. She stared at Lea and Drexel with cold brown eyes as they went by.

"Sarah's bodyguard?" Lea said as they walked down the hall.

"Oh, Mrs. Gomez. Yes, I believe she is. God knows she's savage enough. Went for de la Maine with a knife once, I believe. They had a disagreement about pastry dough."

"Listen, Drexel."

"Yes?"

"I meant what I said about Larrabee."

"Oh, I'm sure you did. As it happens, I agree with you entirely. But, really, Lea. I may call you Lea, I hope?"

"Yes."

"But really, I *don't* advise discussing cold-blooded murder in front of Sarah. She's a darling, and I love her dearly. As much, I think, as if she were my own daughter. She is a very nice and well-bred young lady. She has considerable difficulty in ordering the slaughter of lambs at Easter. Do I make my point?"

Lea laughed.

"I see I do." He led the way up a wide, carpeted staircase. "By the way, I'll have Edwards come straight to your room when he's finished with Morgan in the stables."

Drexel stopped on the stair landing and turned to face Lea. "How badly, may I ask, are you hurt? You seem

197

to move well enough."

"It hurts enough, but it's not serious."

"My God," Drexel said. "You men of action . . ." He turned to continue up the stairs.

"About Larrabee . . ."

Drexel turned, halfway up the staircase, and looked back down at Lea.

"I said, Lea, that I agreed with your *appreciation* of the situation. Larrabee is responsible for murdering one of the very few friends I have ever made in this world, and is, thereby, also responsible for hurting Sarah." He turned and continued up the stairs. "I take such things personally," he said.

Dr. Edwards came up to Lea's room a half hour later.

"You seem to be making a habit of being shot or stabbed in my bailiwick, Mr. Lea! I do wish you'd exercise a little prudence."

He stripped Lea's shift off, and examined both wounds—the old and the new. "Yes indeed—just a little prudence. I will say, though, that the shot wound might have been a good deal worse. Go and sit on the bed please."

Edwards cleaned the gunshot wound under Lea's arm, which hurt more than a little. Then he swabbed it with a disinfectant, and bandaged it lightly, wrapping the gauze ties around Lea's chest.

He took longer over the old knife wound, picking away the scabs along the puffed and inflamed stitches down Lea's side, swabbing each area as he finished.

"You have some bad bruising here, Lea. I believe you've torn some of the damaged tissue under the sutures. I've cleaned the wound, and the stitches have held, but you'd be well-advised to rest as much as you can for the next few days. You've got to give this a chance to heal, man!''

"Thank you, doctor.''

Edwards stood up, closed his bag, and picked it up. "By the way," he said. "If only half of what I hear is accurate, you seem to have been instrumental in performing some rough justice on a number of a very unpleasant people.'' He cleared his throat. "You, that Indian of yours, and Tiny Morgan seem to be the heroes of the day.'' He walked to the door. Lea saw that Edwards had his knickers and climbing shoes on.

Edwards turned at the door. "Mr. Bridge," he said, "was a very fine man. A diamond in the rough men of that sort are called, I believe.'' He walked out and closed the door behind him.

Lea was getting his shirt back on when there was a knock on the door. He got up from the bed.

"Yes?''

"Room service, sir.'' It was Leo Drexel's voice.

"Come on in.''

The door swung open, and a waiter pushed a dinner trolley into the room. Leo came in after him, and one of the bellmen came in after Leo, carrying Lea's bedroll, saddlebags.

"A good dinner—direct, I should add, from de la Maine's stove—and what is apparently the sum of your worldly goods.'' He signaled to the bellman to leave the bedroll and the rest beside the sofa. He nodded to Lea, and shooed the other men out of the room before him.

He paused at the door as Edwards had.

"Have a good night's sleep, Lea; you've earned it.''

It was only late afternoon. Early for dinner, and early for bed. Edwards must have had a word with

Leo Drexel.

But Lea wasn't sorry. He felt tired to his bones. Tired of the riding and the killing and the fear. He had thought he was a dead man sure when the Count sat smiling, looking down at him with that nickel-plated pistol in his hand.

A year ago he had thought that at Gunstock he had found at last a place to rest easy. Lea laughed and went to take the covers off his dinner.

De la Maine had sent up a small steak, green beans from the kitchen gardens, hot rolls, butter, a wedge of apple pie, and a pitcher of milk. The Frenchman was a sensible man.

Lea pulled up a chair, and dug in. As he ate, he noticed his grimy hands, smudged with dirt, and speckled black from his pistol's exploding powder. After dinner, he'd get the chambermaids to bring up a tub, and hot water.

He slept a rich, dark, deep sleep. He woke once to hear a gust of wind hum down the chimney, the tick and hiss of the dying coals in the grate. Then he slept again.

Much later, hours later, he heard a key turning in the door lock.

Then he was awake, and sliding off the bed with the Colt in his hand. There was moonlight in the room. Shining softly in through the high windows. Not much light—but enough.

Lea watched the door as the lock clicked open. There was a pause. The door was closed, and then swung in again a way. Lea ran out of patience. He crossed the room quickly and quietly, stepped to the side, swung the door open, and brought up the Colt.

Sarah Bridge stood startled in the lamplit hall, staring at him, the revolver, and his naked body. Her pale face slowly flushed pink.

"Oh . . . oh, I—"

"You could have got yourself shot, you little fool!"

Lea reached out, took her arm, and pulled her into the room.

Then, he closed the door, felt for his key where it had fallen onto the carpet, and locked the door again. He picked up the chair and wedged it under the knob.

Sarah was standing in the moonlight by the windows.

"Lea . . . I'm sorry. It was terribly stupid of me."

"Where's that damned woman who's supposed to be watching you?"

"She . . . she's asleep."

"Very useful." He found his trousers across a chair by the bed and pulled them on.

Sarah Bridge stood in the moonlight, her face turned away from him as he buttoned the trousers.

"I'm sorry," she said. "I . . . I felt lonely."

Lea walked over to her. She was wearing a rich, long-sleeved dressing gown. The lace on it was white in the moonlight. Her eyes were shadowed dark. He couldn't see what she was thinking.

"You shouldn't be here," he said.

She shook her head. "I believe you're wrong. I believe I should be here."

"What do you want, Sarah? Do you want me to comfort you for the loss of your father?"

"Yes," she said, and put her hand up against his chest. "Yes, I do."

Lea put his arms around her and held her, then

201

tightened his arms to hold her closer. She felt small and slender in his arms. But he felt her breasts against him.

He held her for a while, and he felt his cock begin to rise against the softness of the dressing gown, against her soft belly.

It was time to let her go.

He took his arms from around her. "It's time you went back to your room," he said, and his voice was hoarse.

"No," she said, "Let me stay."

She stood in front of him with the moonlight dusting her hair. When he put up his hands and touched her, she was trembling.

CHAPTER TWENTY-THREE

Lea felt for the fasteners of her long dressing gown and found them. A row of little buttons down the front.

She stood still in the moonlight, her face in shadow. Lea carefully undid the buttons, one by one. He had to kneel before her to finish unfastening the last of them. Then he stood and tugged the gown from her shoulders. It fell around her with a soft rustle of silk, and lay in the moonlight at her feet.

She had only a gauzy nightgown on now. It shone in the light from the windows.

Lea put his hand on her slim throat, and felt her quick pulse against his palm. Her skin was warm and smooth as glass.

He bent and gathered up the hem of the nightgown and, as he lifted it, Sarah raised her arms over her head like an obedient child, so that he could slip it off. He lifted it slowly. And then he let it fall to the floor.

She stood naked in moonlight. Lea had never seen any single thing as beautiful as Sarah Bridge just then. Her legs were long and slender. Long, round thighs flowed up into a sudden triangle of dark thick curls, and around into two high round buttocks, clenched and tense.

Lea walked slowly around her as she stood, trembling. The faint and delicate muscles of her slim back made the slightest shadow along her spine. Some of her dark hair, loosely coiled at the nape of her neck, had been disturbed when the nightgown was drawn off her, and dark, gleaming strands fell across her white shoulder, down her back.

When he stood in front of her again, Lea looked down at her shadowed face. Her naked breasts shook a little with her breathing. For such a slight girl, she had large breasts, shaped like rounded pears. They were shadowed. Lea reached to grip her slim shoulders and gently turned her toward the light. Her breasts trembled as he turned her, and the moonlight shone on them. The nipples were swollen.

Lea took his hands from her shoulders and put them on her breasts. He lifted them in his hands, weighing them, squeezing them with his long fingers. He took the nipples and pinched them.

She gasped.

"Am I hurting you?"

She looked up at him. He could see her eyes in the moonlight, dark, clear blue.

He gathered her breasts in his hands, and squeezed them.

"Am I hurting you?"

"No," she said. Her voice was hoarse. "You're not hurting me."

He reached down and put his hand between her legs. She tried to back away from him, but he squeezed her breast with his other hand and wouldn't let her go.

He felt the thick hair between her legs, and found a small slippery place. He held her still and stroked the place with his finger. She stood quiet and let him do it.

Still stroking her there, he took his hand from her breast and bent to take the nipple in his mouth. He sucked on it, and bit into her gently.

"Ohh-oh!" She twisted against him, pushing against him as he mouthed her breast. His finger, between her legs, found a small wet place, warmer, wetter than the rest. He twisted his finger and opened the wet place up. He drew his finger along a little slit. It was slippery.

He took his mouth off her breast and looked down, and saw that she was standing up on her toes, straining up to him. His finger was hooked inside her. Her nipple was wet from his mouth.

"Please," she said.

"Please what?"

"I don't know."

He moved his finger deeper into her, and saw that she was on her toes again, straining as he pushed the finger in. He felt something against the tip, touched it, and pushed again.

"Oh, you hurt me!"

Lea pulled his finger out of her and stepped back. She was standing alone, sweating. Her mouth was open a little. He could hear her breathing as she swayed toward him.

Lea reached down and unbuttoned his trousers. She watched him as he let them fall.

She looked down at him.

Lea stepped to her, bent, and picked her up in his arms.

He cradled her for a moment, feeling the slight, smooth, naked length of her lying across his arms, against his chest. Her head was back, her dark hair falling free. A delicate perfume rose from her—a mingled scent of violets, the sweet smell of a young girl's skin.

He carried her to the bed.

She lay still across it, half in shadow. Lea could see her eyes, her white face, shining in the darkness.

"Here," he said. He took her hand and put it on his cock. He felt her tremble. Slowly, she curled her fingers around it, held it, still staring up at him.

"That's what you need, isn't it?" he said.

"Yes, I need you," she said softly, her voice shaking.

He bent down and kissed her. He kissed Sarah Bridge as he hadn't kissed a woman in many years. He gave to her as much as he took. He felt her hand release him, and her long, slim arms came up around him and held him to her. He felt her breasts crushing against his chest. She kissed and sucked at his mouth as if she were starving.

He pulled away from her, slid down and put his hands under the backs of her knees, then lifted her long, bare legs up, spreading them wide. He smelled the faint odor of her sex.

He took his cock in his hand, pressed the swollen tip into the damp curls at her crotch, and began to thrust himself into her.

Sarah gasped, and started to struggle against him, but he reached up and took her wrists and held them down against the pillows. He found her mouth with his, and kissed her and bit at her lips, gently, until she lay still under him, panting, her breath hot in his mouth.

He felt the warm, wet, close grip of her around the head of his cock wet curls against him. Her heart was pounding; he felt it against his chest. Lea drove into her.

Sarah screamed into his mouth, twisting frantically under him. He was locked deep into her, in a wet squeezing heat that made him shake with pleasure.

She tore her mouth away from his. "Oh, please . . . don't! You're hurting—"

He pulled out of her, only a little way, and she gasped again. He let go of her wrists and reached down to grip her soft buttocks with his hands. Gathering the cool, round flesh in his fingers, he held it tightly.

He pulled his cock out of her a little farther, and felt the coolness as the air touched him.

He lifted her buttocks and drove into her again. His cock made a wet sound as it plunged into her. And the girl cried out and her long thighs thrashed against his sides. The quiet room was filled with the wet, smacking noises.

Suddenly Sarah reached up to hold him, her nails digging into his shoulders as he moved above her.

"Oh . . . *oh!*" Her slender body, drenched with sweat, twisted and bucked beneath him. "Oh, God!"

Her long, pale, slim legs thrashed, and wrapped themselves around him. Her round buttocks were bunched in his hands as he lifted her to him, driving his cock deep into her, grinding against the soft, wet cushion of her mound.

Lea felt a flood of pleasure rising from his balls, from the small of his back, an ache of pleasure so sweet that it hurt him.

Lea began to move faster in her, gasping in the agony of pleasure, driving into her harder and faster.

"Oh, please—" She clawed at his back, her white face contorted in the shadows. "Oh . . . oh, *please!*" Crying, calling like a cat, she came.

And Lea came with her. He groaned and trembled, and pumped into her until he thought it would kill him.

He still moved on her, and she moved with him. Both slippery, moving slowly, holding each other, bending his head to her, lifting her face to kiss.

"I'm so . . . glad," she whispered.

Lea lay with his full weight upon her, sliding against her with their sweat and juices. She grunted like a puppy with the pleasure of it, and reach up again to hug him.

"Sarah . . . I love you," Lea said. And was surprised to hear himself say it. It had been weary years since he'd said that—and there'd been only two girls he'd ever said it to.

One was dead—dead by his hand as sure as if he'd shot her down himself. The other was living—and happy, he hoped—a long way from Gunstock.

This girl was too young for him. Too rich, too brave, and too beautiful.

When he tried to get up, Sarah hugged him to her and wouldn't let him go. So he closed his eyes, there in the shadowed moonlight, and held her, stroking her sweat-damp hair, and pretended she was his forever.

In the morning she was gone. Gone, and left him sleeping like a boy.

He woke to the sun streaming in through the tall windows and stretched, grunting at the twinge along his side. (Dr. Edwards would have said it served him right.)

He lay there for a few moments, remembering, then yawned and stretched again, a long, luxurious stretch. To hell with the side *and* Dr. Edwards!

He had to piss. And he needed a hell of a breakfast, the best and biggest breakfast the Frenchman could make!

He threw the sheets aside, then bent to sniff at them. They smelled of sex. There were four small spots of blood on the bottom sheet. Where I hurt her, Lea thought, being such a fine stud of a fellow. He covered the place and got out of bed.

Outside, in the corridor, Lea found a straight-back chair against the wall beside the door. There was a strand of gray wool yarn on the carpet. Garciela Gomez had kept her watch after all.

Going down the east stairway, Lea passed a group of guests coming up from breakfast. They were English people, a family named Sutherland. "Good morning to you, Lea!" He'd shot mule deer with Sutherland when they'd first come. "Morning, Mr. Sutherland."

The lady and the children nodded and went on their way. "I say, Lea, what chance do you think of a bear before it snows? One of your big browns, or cinnamons?" Lea leaned against the bannister and thought a moment. "Those are shy bears, Mr. Sutherland. Might be better to go packing down to the Salmon, try for a grizzly this time of year."

The Englishman's cheeks flushed over his ginger whiskers. "Ah, so I said, so I said! But Florence won't hear of it. She's got some notion into her head about that French banker fellow that was eaten by the grizzlies! She won't hear of it! Says I may shoot anything I please, says I may shoot a blasted *camel* if I wish! But I am not to hunt one of those grizzly bears! What do you think of that?"

Lea laughed. "Well, they can be dangerous. But men with heavy rifles usually knock them over without too much trouble." He considered the problem for a moment. "Tell you what. If you should want a *real* trophy—a *hunter's* trophy—you might try High Pass for bighorn sheep. There's a ram up there with horns as big as a house. Some men have tried for him, but they haven't gotten him. It's very rough up there, you see. Damn high, and damn cold. It's hard going."

Sutherland lit up like theater limelight. "I say! You do think I might get a shot at it? if I can stand the gaff?"

"I think so. Ask Davies to take you up past Ship Rock. He'll know the place. But remember to stick close to him up there; it'll be damn cold."

"Damned if I don't do it!" Sutherland said. "But aren't you going to be guiding?"

"Not this week, Mr. Sutherland. I have to stay at the hotel the next few days. Expecting someone."

"Oh, bad luck!"

"No. Good luck to you with that ram. Davies is a very good man."

Sutherland shook Lea's hand. "Thanks for the tip, old man, though I do wish we could go up together."

"Perhaps another time," Lea said. "And remember, people shooting uphill tend to hold too low."

The Englishman smiled. "Right." And went bounding up the stairs. So, not all the guests at Gunstock knew about Abe's death, and the fight with the Cossacks. Sarah and Drexel have their work cut out keeping it even half quiet.

Lea went down the stairs to the lobby. He was

210

wondering if he'd see Sarah there, or perhaps in the kitchen, talking to de le Maine.

He met Larrabee in the lobby.

The old man came strolling across the gleaming marble flooring as Lea reached the foot of the staircase.

Larrabee was dressed like an Eastern college football player—dark, baggy, knickers, canvas shoes, and a blue, turtleneck sweater. His small paunch bulged against the wool.

"Amazing!" he said, coming up to Lea with a merry smile. "Really extraordinary! what a fellow you must be, Mr. Lea!" He stretched out a small pink hand, and took Lea's hand and shook it. "To defeat *that* man—and his *men*—in a fight is no small matter!" He gave Lea's hand another shake before letting it go. The old man couldn't have seemed more pleased at the way things had gone at Fork Creek. He also didn't seem to give a damn who heard about it now.

He was a very clever old man. Lea knew what he was doing, and admired him for it. Larrabee was telling Lea that he had no chance at all. That even the most spectacular victory was no real victory. It was in fact, only an interesting, temporary variation in a losing game.

"It will be most interesting to see how you and Shannon hit it off," the old man said, and smiled, eyes bright. He winked and went on his way.

CHAPTER TWENTY-FOUR

Jonathan Pierce Larrabee wasn't really as pleased as all that.

He was mighty angry, if truth be told. Not with the deceased Count Orloff and his blundering Cossacks. He was angry at himself.

The old man, hands tucked into his knicker pockets, was strolling downstairs to the hotel gymnasium for his routine massage and steam. He considered his errors as he went.

Am I becoming an old fool? To send that posturing medieval ass and his serfs to fight Abe Bridge and his men in their own mountains? To say nothing of Lea. What an odd hunting guide that fellow makes. If it weren't for Shane's coming, it might be interesting to have the Pinkertons look into our Mr. Lea. However, Shannon will likely make such an inquiry moot.

Difficult . . . difficult. Bridge dead, the girl alive and surrounded by friends . . . hotel guests. Not the sort of people you can murder a girl in front of. A little too important for that. A little too well connected for that.

Can't bring in a parcel of bully boys and simply take the damn place over, not with a stack of English lords and Boston Brahmins looking on. Too damned raw!

Larrabee pushed his way through the green baize door at the foot of the stairs and, smiling pleasantly, greeted the Indian boy who worked as attendant. Drexel's Nancy-boy if his information was correct. Might be something to see how the sissy stood up to a little pressure. Get Drexel, and *he* might well be able to handle the girl.

He walked into the dressing room, nodded to George Chapin, the only other man there, and began undressing. *There's one of the Boston jackasses, right there,* he thought. *Couldn't hold onto sixty miles of track, himself, so he went whining to that Jew, Brandeis.*

Chapin put on his jacket, wished Larrabee a cold good day, and walked out.

Good riddance, you fart.

Larrabee wrapped a towel around his plump, pink middle, and went to get his massage.

The boy had good hands, though God only knows where they'd been. Larrabee lay grunting softly as the young Peigan massaged the muscles along his spine, worked the stiffness from his neck. A good massage; relaxed a man, gave him time to think, put him in a good frame of mind.

The boy worked lower, at the small of the back, pressing, stroking, easing out the knots. And what to do about Morgan? A nice question. It was considerably more important than the brawls out here in Idaho, though perhaps not more important than a mountain full of silver. Morgan couldn't be fought, and he couldn't be fooled. That was the long and short of it.

213

Larrabee sighed and turned over on his back. The young Indian began to massage his chest, rubbing in easy, circular motions. J.P. Morgan's time might yet come, but it would take the government to bring him down. There was a notion! What the devil was he paying a senator *for*, if not for service to be rendered.

Better not to rush, though. Still, it was something to think about. In the meantime he'd give Morgan the debentures. It was hard to let them go, and stupid to try and keep them from him.

The Peigan had worked down his legs, and was massaging his feet, working his thumbs gently into the instep. A brisk rub at the soles of the feet was better than a foot bath any day. That doctor was a fool.

The boy finished, and stood back from the table. Larrabee grunted and sat up, tying his towel around his waist.

"Good rubdown, boy!"

The Indian didn't even smile. He just stood there, dumb as a post, as would a cigar-store Indian.

The Peigan ushered him into the steamroom, empty this early in the day, seated Larrabee in the first cabinet, closed the heavy maple double-doors, and brought another towel to wrap around his neck, to keep the rising steam out of his face.

"Only a few minutes today."

The Indian boy nodded, expressionless, and went to the wall to open the steam valve a quarter turn.

Larrabee heard the hiss and felt the warm breath against his legs.

The Peigan went to the corner of the room, picked up the mop there, and brought it back to the steam cabinet. While Larrabee watched, puzzled, he quickly pushed the mop handle through the brass grips on the cabinet doors.

"What the hell is that? What are you doing?"

Larrabee kicked hard against the heavy cabinet doors, and hurt his foot.

"You God-damned jackass! Get that damn thing out of the door!"

The Indian boy went to the steam valve and opened it a full turn.

Larrabee sat goggling at him, staring in shock, and felt what seemed for a moment to be a flood of ice-cold water rush in against his legs. It seemed for only a moment. Then the live steam began to cook his legs.

Larrabee yelled in pain and tried to stand, to struggle free of the heavy cabinet, slamming into it with his shoulders, kicking wildly at the solid doors. He screamed and heaved up and down, billows of scalding steam escaping, rolling up out of the neck of the cabinet, burning his face as he howled and kicked.

The Indian boy was gone. He was out of the steamroom, into the cool, small paneled gymnasium, and out through the green baize door. The Peigan locked it behind him, and leaned a neatly lettered sign against it. CLOSED FOR LUNCH—WILL BE OPEN AT 2 O'CLOCK. Then, he went upstairs. It was time for Mr. Drexel's lunch.

In the steamroom, Larrabee no longer screamed, or struggled. He sat still—in a hissing, roaring cloud of steam. His face was a very dark red, and his eyes and his mouth were open.

"Oh! How *could* you? How could you do such a thing!" Sarah's eyes were filled with angry tears.

215

The three of them were in the library again, and Lea was sighing at the memory of a golden breakfast—a late breakfast—in the servant's dining room. He and Sarah had eaten quietly there together, with no one else to bother them. Bacon and blueberry muffins—and kissing. That's what the breakfast had been. And now this.

Sarah sat at the desk, her face buried in her hands.

"To . . . to *murder* a man. Here! My father never would have wanted it. He never would have wanted *that!*"

Lea had his own opinion on that score, but he felt that the better part of valor, in this case, was to keep his big mouth shut. But it hurt to see Sarah so damn upset by it.

Drexel was the one who got up and went to her. He leaned over the desk and put his hand on her shoulder. She looked up as she angrily shrugged the hand away, and blushed to see that it was Drexel, not Lea.

"I'm sorry, Leo. What Lea has done is my fault."

"But *Lea* hasn't done anything, my dear."

"What?"

Drexel turned to give Lea a sardonic glance.

"Though apparently he's too much the gentleman to defend himself against a lady's accusations."

Lea didn't say a word. He just sat back in the leather-covered easy chair and took it all in.

"You see, dear, Lea didn't know a thing about this tragic affair, and didn't have a damn thing to do with it. I assure you, it's all been news to him!"

Sarah sniffed and searched for her handkerchief. She didn't look at Lea. "Then . . . then why—" She found her handkerchief, and blew her nose. "Then how did it *happen?*"

"It was my fault, I think." Drexel sighed. "I believe I spoke a little too plainly once in Hunting-moon's presence."

"Then he—"

"Yes, I'm afraid the poor boy assumed that I'd be *pleased,* that I'd be overjoyed at his barbaric demonstration of loyalty."

Leo sighed again. "The boy *is* a savage, after all."

"Dreadful," Lea said.

"Oh, yes," said Sarah. "But . . . but what can we *do?*"

"Well," Drexel said, "you may blame me for this, but I took it upon myself to send the boy away. Back to his own people. It didn't seem fair that he should be judged by *our* laws, particularly since it was I, after all, who probably put the idea into his head!"

"Nobly put," said Lea.

"Yes," Sarah said. She looked at Lea and blushed. "Yes, I think that you were right to do that. Mr. Larrabee *was* responsible for my father's death."

Drexel looked thoughtful. "I suppose," he said, "that it *is* a sort of rough justice."

"Yes," she said, "I think it is."

"No question," said Lea.

She glanced at Lea and blushed again. "I owe you an apology, Lea, I—"

"You owe me nothing, Miss Bridge."

"Oh, I think you can call her Sarah," Drexel said, with a sardonic look.

"You owe me nothing. I *would* have killed the old man if you'd let me."

"Well, well—that's all very nice, but not to the point," Drexel said. "Let us remember that we do still

217

have Mr. Larrabee on our hands."

"We'll have to say it was an accident."

"My dear Sarah, an accident of that kind could ruin Gunstock as completely as a murder might have! No, no. It won't do. However, I have had a notion."

"I don't doubt it," Lea said.

"I have had a notion. Mr. Larrabee was a very elderly man. And a man, moreover, without any immediate family—certainly no one who cared very much for him."

"But Leo—"

"No, dear, let me finish. So, I took it upon myself to inform certain guests that Mr. Larrabee had had a stroke while in the steam room. And, unfortunately, it had proved fatal."

"Considering Larrabee's condition, Leo, it's going to be a little difficult to make that bird fly, isn't it?" said Lea.

"Not at all," said Leo. "Not at all. I have consulted with our mountain-climbing physician, and have extracted from him a professional diagnosis *and* death certificate indicating a severe stroke."

"Oh, heavens."

"Now dear, don't concern yourself with these details. Leave them to me."

"And when the body goes back east?" Lea said.

Leo pursed his lips. "Well, I have telegraphed Larrabee's nephew in New York, informed him of the tragedy, and, since I had understood it to be his uncle's fondest wish, suggested that Mr. Larrabee might remain right here, at Gunstock, in the mountains he so dearly loved."

"Touching," said Lea.

"Oh, goodness."

"Goodness, dear Sarah," said Leo, "has nothing to do with it." He walked to the door. "And I'm off to make certain that our earnest young physician doesn't backslide."

"Just a minute," Lea said, and got up to go out with him. "I'll be back in a moment, Sarah."

When the library door was closed behind them, Lea said, quietly, "Well done, Mr. Drexel."

Drexel gave him a weary smile. "Yes, I think it *was* done fairly well."

"And the Indian boy?"

"Oh, I gave him enough money to buy a great many ponies, and sent him on his way. Frankly, until this matter came up, I think he considered me something of a bore."

"And the doctor?"

"The doctor, it seems, has become fond of us. Or fond of Gunstock, which amounts to the same thing. And now, Mr. Lea, having done my part in our little drama, I must inform you that, alas, your turn has come again, and perhaps, I'm sorry to say, with an added complication."

"Which is?"

"Tomorrow, a rather minor literary figure is to arrive at Gunstock for a short stay. His name is Ned Buntline, famous among *afficianados* of penny-dreadful tales of famous Western outlaws, killers, and so on. I understand he's met most of that crowd and is very familiar with them."

"And you thought his arrival might be important

to me?"

"Isn't it?"

Lea thought for a moment, then he said: "Yes, it might be damned important."

"So I was afraid. There's worse news yet."

"What?"

"A man named Shannon came into Salmon on the mail-coach yesterday afternoon."

"He'll be here tomorrow night."

"I believe he will."

"All right." Lea turned to go back into the library. "Thank you, Drexel."

"You don't have to thank me, Lea. Anyone who injured my friends—or Gunstock—would find me ready to do them any harm I could." He nodded, turned and walked off down the corridor.

Lea went back into the library. Sarah was in his arms before he could close the door behind him.

"Forgive me! Do you forgive me?"

"There's nothing to forgive, sweetheart," he said, and bent his head to kiss her hair.

"And now there'll be no trouble," she said. "Larrabee's dead. That gunman won't come. You can stay here forever."

Lea lifted her small chin with his finger, and kissed her.

"The gunman *is* coming. He'll be here tomorrow. Leo just told me."

Her face grew pale. "But he won't do anything! He'll find out that Larrabee's dead—and then there's no *reason!*"

"Unless he's already been paid to do his job."

"But even so, Larrabee's *dead!* Who would *care* whether he . . . he did his job?"

"He might care," Lea said.

CHAPTER TWENTY-FIVE

That night, she came to Lea's room again.

They had their dinner brought up, and they sat beside the fire, eating and drinking the pink champagne that de la Maine had sent up to them. They listened to the northern wind sighing through the ramparts of Gunstock.

"Lea," Sarah said to him, "am I an awful girl, to be here with you, to do the things we do, with Daddy just murdered and buried in those mountains?"

Lea reached across the table, and gently stroked her cheek. "Are you happy, Sarah?" he said.

She smiled. "Yes," she said. "I'm the happiest, I think, I've ever been."

"Then Abe would be happy for you."

"Yes," she said. "Yes, I *think* he would be." She laughed. "But he'd be happier if I was married." She blushed furiously and covered her face with her hands. "Oh, no! I'm . . . I'm *sorry!* I didn't have any *idea* I was going to say that!"

Lea sat back in his chair and laughed. "You trying to

frighten me away?''

''No.'' She put her hands down, and sat up in her chair, her face still red.

''Sarah,'' Lea said, ''I'll never be able to marry you.'' She had to be told, and the sooner, the better.

''I see,'' she said, and bit her lip, but didn't say anything more.

''No, you don't see,'' Lea said. ''It has nothing to do with you.''

''Nothing to do—''

''No. It has to do with me.''

''I don't— Are you . . . married?''

''No.''

''But then—''

''Sarah, my name's not Farris Lea.''

''I don't care! I don't care. A lot of men have changed their names out here. I don't care what you did!''

''My name—''

''I don't care!'' she interrupted him. Please—''

''I'm Frank Leslie,'' he said. ''Sometimes people called me Buckskin Frank Leslie.''

Sarah sat staring at him. ''But . . . but you're *famous*.''

Lea smiled grimly. ''That's one word for it.''

''You . . . you were with Wyatt Earp and Doc Holliday. . . and . . . and all *those* people.''

''Yes.''

She was clenching her hands together on the white tablecloth before her. The knuckles were white with tension.

She tried to smile. ''Did you rob banks or something? I wouldn't care!''

''No, I didn't rob banks. I . . . I killed people, Sarah.

223

For a living."

Sarah said nothing.

"I've killed about forty people now." It was a dreadful relief to say it, to tell it to her. "Most of them were fair fights, I think. If it *can* be fair when I gunfight with a man."

"Well," Sarah said, "you fought here, and you killed men here. Thank God you did!" She lifted her glass of champagne with a a trembling hand, and drank from it. "So, if that's all—"

"It isn't all, Sarah. I was a professional gambler, too. And a pimp—a *mack*. You know what that is?"

"Yes," she said, and blushed. "I know what that is. It's—it's being a . . . a bodyguard in a disorderly house!"

"No. It's living off the girls there. And it's going out and bringing girls into the life. And it's beating them when they want to leave."

Sarah sat looking at him, trying to smile, but she was crying. "You never did that!" she said.

"I did it for years. And I took money to frighten men, and sometimes to force those frightened men to fight me so I could shoot them to death."

"No." She shook her head. "No, you didn't."

Lea reached across the table and took her hands in his. "Dear heart," he said, "for all those years, I was as vicious a dog as any man *could* be—and I enjoyed it."

"All right, then!" She pulled her hands away. "Then why did you come here? Why are you the way you are now?"

"It happened that I loved a girl. Loved her as much as I love you, Sarah. I forced a fight on a man, just for the fun of it, and she was killed."

224

Lea got up from the table and walked to the windows. He looked out through the glass, past the bright reflections of the candles, out to the distant pines, their dark branches bending and swaying to the night wind.

"And that," he said, "finished that life for me, forever."

"Then," Sarah said from the table, "you . . . you can start a *new* life. Here at Gunstock!"

Lea came back to the table.

"Sarah, have you heard of Wes Hardin? Ben Thompson? Clay Allison? Have you heard of a man named Frank Pace?"

"Yes," she said, "I've heard of those men."

Lea stood, looking down at her. "There is not one of those men—not one—who, if he heard I was alive, and knew where to find me, wouldn't come looking to kill me." He sat back down at the table, and poured himself more champagne.

"They wouldn't find you, here. No one will know *who* you are!"

Lea smiled. "A writer named Buntline is checking into Gunstock tomorrow. He knows my face as well as I know yours. At least he did when I wore a beard and mustache. He's likely to recognize me anyway."

"All right!" She sat up straight. "Then we'll keep you hidden till he goes!"

"With Larrabee's gunman coming tomorrow as well?" He shook his head. "I've been lucky for the past year. After all, this hotel's not much of a likely spot for frontier riff-raff like me. It's only a question of time. Someone *will* recognize me, someday. And I'll have to run."

"But people love you here! We'll *protect* you!" She took her handkerchief from her reticule and blew her nose.

"And make a shooting-gallery out of your home? Out of Gunstock? No."

"If you loved me—"

He reached across the table and put his finger gently against her lips.

"*Because* I love you."

The next morning, Lea went out to the stables. He intended to stay out of the main building until Buntline had gone on his way. Damn the man for coming out to Gunstock. If Drexel weren't careful, Buntline would have the whole story out of the hotel help, and into the Eastern newspapers! Buntline was no fool.

Lea had met the writer in Hays, the year that Hickok was marshal. Buntline had been in his element then, sitting on the cool, shady, whorehouse porches, listening to buffalo-chips being thrown by every hoodlum and high-roller passing through. Listening, and writing it down as gospel. The secret of Buntline's great success with those nonsensical books of his, Lea thought, was that the man persuaded himself to believe the stuff. And so did his readers.

It made Hickok. Before Buntline, Bill had just been a well-known sport, fancy-man, and hoodlum for hire. He'd been very good with guns, of course. Bill'd always been good with guns. Those little books made Hickok —and killed him.

Lea'd seen Hickok years later, a few months before he went out to the Dakotas to get shot. He'd been a different man. Not so handsome anymore. He'd worn spectacles to order his lunch.

In just a few years, his own name had eaten him up, the way the Indians say the coyote spirit eats a man up.

Lea stayed in the stables all morning, talking to Tiny and the other men coming by. Tiny talked to him for an hour about rainbows before Lea even remembered saying what he had that started it. Tiny was dead certain that Lea'd been right. No gold at the end of any rainbow anymore.

"That's for sure," Lea'd said. "I was damn sure right on that!"

"Yes," Tiny said.

"No question," said Lea, and asked how the Russian horses were thriving, mainly to get off the subject of rainbows. "Oh, *pretty* horses!" Tiny said. They all had come to like him and know he owned them for his own. Even the big black gelding!

Lea walked back with Tiny to the gelding's stall, and nearly got an ear bitten off for his pains. The black was quick, and had snaked his sleek head out over the stall door and taken his bite. Lea'd ducked just fast enough for those big yellow teeth to meet air instead of ear.

"That son-of-a-bitch is a killer!"

"No such-a-thing," Tiny replied. "We scared him, coming along the stalls that way. Should have sung-out!" He had more to say about how the Russian needed some plain old kindness and care. It was intended to be a grass-eating horse, not meant for grain.

Lea agreed with it all, and made sure to walk to the front of the stables by the tackroom instead of back by the Russian's stall. He said so-long to Tiny, walked out of the stable, and paused to light up the stub of a cigar.

Right then, as sure as fate, Ned Buntline and two

227

other men came walking straight toward him.

Lea kept his head bent over his cigar as he lit up, and the men came right up to him.

"Say there, Bud," Buntline said to him, "you have some riding horses in there for guests?"

"Yep," Lea said, gestured with the cigar to the stable doors, and added, "Right in there." He tried for a Southern accent as he said it, and then turned and strolled away, puffing on the cigar, and taking his time.

Ned had put on considerable flesh. And what were the odds he'd recognized Lea? Slim odds, Lea thought. No beard now, no mustache—and a lot of years gone by.

Now he'd have to go hide in the laundry!

That evening, he and Sarah were in his room. She hadn't talked more about marriage, or about what he'd said the night before. She sat, seeming contented enough, in a rocking chair she'd had the maid bring in. She sat by the fire, knitting away like a Granny at what looked to be the beginnings of a wool muffler in red and green stripes.

He should get up and go to her, and say, "My sweet love, I won't be here to wear it."

Someone knocked on the door. Lea supposed that it was dinner, but he picked his Colt off the table before he went to answer it.

It wasn't dinner. It was Leo Drexel, looking pale.

"What is it, Leo?"

"Leo? Come in!" Sarah called.

"No, dear—have to run! *He's here.*"

Lea stepped out into the corridor and closed the door behind him.

"Where is he?"

"Down in the lobby," Drexel said. "I told him to get out." He grimaced. "He declined. But he'd asked for Larrabee. He was surprised to hear he was dead."

"What did you think of him?"

"My dear fellow, that is your line of work, not mine! I'd say, however, that he was . . . a serious man."

Lea smiled, "I'll bet he is." He thought for a moment. "You go on about your business, Leo. Leave him to me."

"With pleasure."

"I'll go down and see what he's got in his mind to do."

Drexel held out his hand. "Good luck."

Lea smiled, and shook his hand. "It's only a matter of business, Leo."

"Yours, thank God," Drexel said, and turned and walked off down the corridor.

The door opened behind Lea, and Sarah put her head out. She looked very pale. "Is that man here?"

"You were listening, weren't you?" Lea said, and bent down to kiss her nose. "I'll go down and see what he's up to." He walked into the room, picked up his gunbelt, dropped the Colt into the holster, and strapped the belt on. Then he went to the bedside table, took the Arkansas toothpick out of the drawer, and slipped the blade down into his boot. He went to Sarah, took her in his arms, and hugged her. "Don't worry," he said. "I think it'll be talking, not shooting, tonight. What's for dinner?"

"You're not thinking of—"

"Inviting him? No, sweet, I'm just hungry."

She forced herself to laugh. "You're a dreadful man! We're having ham and greens, hot biscuits, and a fruit compote.''

"Wonderful—real country. I'll be back up in a few minutes." And he was out the door. He knew he would be longer than a few minutes.

The Gunstock lobby was the size of a good-sized railroad station, but considerably more luxurious. It was crowded. The guests, most of them, enjoyed an evening stroll along the gleaming marble floors, the two-story pillars, the huge, nodding potted palms and rubber trees. It was an opportunity for the ladies to display their fine dresses from the house of Worth, in Paris and other finery.

Lea came down the main staircase and saw the gunman standing by a pillar near the entrance to the terrace.

He stood out from the rest like a cougar in a flock of penguins and peacocks.

He was wearing a long, fringed buckskin shirt, canvas trousers, and brown boots. He had a gunbelt around his waist.

Lea walked to the bottom of the stairs, nodded to Toby Easterby, who was squiring some handsome lady Lea didn't know, and went on across the lobby toward the terrace entrance.

Now he could see how the man wore his gun. High. High on the right side. Looked like a Peacemaker.

The man had seen him coming. He was watching him as he crossed the lobby.

Some people had stopped to look at them now. Nobody at Gunstock made much of a habit of strolling the lobby wearing guns.

Lea saw that the man had put his coat and hat down

on a chair beside a pillar. The coat was a beat-up sheepskin. Jobs must be few and far between.

Lea stepped around a group of guests talking about horse-racing at Saratoga. He walked up to the man.

"Shannon?"

"Yes," the man said.

He was a small man. Handsome, in a quiet way, with long, dark-blond hair, and blue eyes. Now that Lea was close, he could see some gray in the man's hair, some lines in his face.

"I think we have something to talk about, Shannon."

"I don't think so," the man said. He had a touch of the South to his speech.

Lea stood easy. They were just a few feet apart. The small man looked tired from traveling.

"Well," Lea said, "your man is gone. His try has gone with him. Any friends he has to follow up will be too little—and too late."

Shannon smiled a little; he seemed a decent sort of a man. "That's high-finance you're talking about Mr.—"

"Lea."

Shannon nodded. "I don't trouble myself with high finance, Mr. Lea."

"You've been paid?"

"Indeed I have." He'd stopped smiling.

"And you intend to earn that money?"

"Indeed I do."

"Cigar?" Lea dug into his jacket pocket for a cigar stub.

"No."

Lea lit his cigar, not troubling that both hands would be busy. He saw Shannon notice it, and got another grudging smile out of him.

"It seems a shame for us to be blowing holes in each other over a dead dog who wasn't worth much alive."

Shannon said nothing. Lea realized there'd be no waiting until morning with this one. No chance at all.

"Would you care to join me, and a young lady, for supper?"

Shannon laughed at Lea as if they were old friends, and shook his head. "Is she a fine looker?" he said.

"That, and a darling to boot."

"Then I'd better not," Shannon said. "She'd make me feel like a brute."

Here's a man I could like, Lea thought. *I can't turn him aside.*

The first bell rang for dinner and, throughout the huge lobby, the guests and their ladies began to drift toward the dining rooms.

"Would you care to step outside?" Lea said.

"No."

Thinks I might have people out there. Good man. I do like a careful man.

"Well now," Lea said. "That was a warning bell for dinner. They ring another one, a reminder, in about a minute, and most of these people will be out of here."

The small man nodded.

Lea walked over a few steps, to stub out his cigar in the dirt of a potted palm.

"You won't change your mind about this?" he said.

Shannon shook his head.

"Dammit, man, you likely have no chance against me!" Lea said.

The small man looked at him, then moved his head to one side, to see past Lea. Lea knew he was making certain the lobby was clear—no more people in the line

232

of fire.

The people were moving past them, talking, laughing. One or two men glanced back, looking at the two men with guns.

"Listen to me," Lea said. He supposed the man would think he was begging. "This is a fool's play! Take that old thief's money and ride! I say you'd have no chance against me, and I mean it."

Shannon said nothing. He stepped back a few paces, almost to the lobby wall. He was really quite a small man.

"Listen, dammit—my name's not Farris Lea!"

Shannon smiled at him. "I never thought it was," he said.

The second bell rang, and he drew. He was very fast.

Lea drew and shot him through the chest.

He found himself kneeling down on the cold marble. The cold green-veined marble gleamed in the lamplight. He thought he was in the gardens for a moment, kneeling on grass and roses.

"Oh, my God! *Oh, my God!*" Some woman was screaming.

His face felt like a piece of wood. A man was running to him. He heaved himself up and raised the Colt. He saw black dress shoes, not brown boots.

Toby Easterby was kneeling by him.

"Jesus Christ, man!" Toby held him by the arm. There was blood all over. The woman was still screaming.

"Get me up," he tried to say to Toby. But he didn't say anything. He couldn't feel his mouth. He put his left hand down into the blood and pushed himself up, got his feet under him.

Toby was still holding onto his arm. He pushed him away and looked for Shannon.

He swayed on his feet. If he looked too fast at something, he saw double. People were standing just a little way away, staring at him, staring at the gun in his hand.

He started to walk, just a few steps, to get out of the blood. It was on his boots. He looked over by the wall, and saw the small man there. Shannon was down.

Lea walked over there. It took some doing; his face was hurtng him terribly. He felt himself getting sick to his stomach. He took deep breaths to keep from vomiting in front of all these people.

Shannon was down, lying sprawled along the marble at the base of the wall. When Lea bent his head to look at him, he saw double. So he knelt down instead.

Shane was dead. Lea could see the blotch in the middle of the buckskin shirt where the round had hit him. His face didn't look as bad as most dead men's.

Toby was standing behind Lea, talking.

"Jesus!" he said. "Jesus, he was quick!"

Toby was a good boy. Didn't mind a little blood.

"Yes," Lea said. Now he could talk. But his voice sounded strange to him. Thick, muttering, like an animal's.

"Yes," Lea said, "that's Shannon. And he was fast on the draw."

"Let's get you up," said Toby Easterby. He took Lea by the arm again. Another man came to help him. They got Lea up. Toby took the Colt from him and put it in it's holster.

They walked him toward the grand staircase, but he shook them loose and walked on his own. He could hear the people talking, staring at him. One of the women was crying.

He could feel blood running down his face. Saw it spatter on the floor.

A man called out behind him.

"I know him! That's Frank Leslie!"

Footsteps behind him. Fat Ned Buntline was trotting along beside him.

"Frank? *Frank?*"

Lea paid no attention. Up above him, staring down from the great carpeted staircase, stood Sarah Bridge.

"Well?" Lea shouted up at her in his strange new voice. "Did you see? *Did you?*" She stared down at him as still, as white, as if she'd been carved for old Abe out of fine ivory.

He shouted up at her. "That . . . is *what I do!*"

He had said nothing more to her. He walked out to the stables, leaving blood behind him with every step. Toby Easterby walked with him and kept other people away. The Baron brought Edwards out to the stables afterward.

"I'm getting tired of patching you up, Mr. Lea."

Lea nodded. He was sitting on a stack of grain sacks while the doctor worked on him.

"This time I'm afraid I have some rather bad news for you."

"What is it," Lea muttered. His face hurt like hell.

Your opponent's bullet struck along the side of your face. Rather a bad wound. I'm afraid it's severed—or badly damaged—the trigeminal nerve. That means you will almost certainly have some permanent effect."

Lea didn't say anything.

"I think you'll have some paralysis on that side of

your face. At least a slight drooping of the side of the mouth. Perhaps of the eye on that side as well."

"My God," said Toby Easterby.

The Baron stumped over and patted Lea on the shoulder. "It will a good scar make, for certain."

"That," Dr. Edwards said, "is true enough." And he began to sew.

While he was working, Tiny Morgan came lumbering into the stable with Lea's bedroll and saddlebags.

"I got it all for you, Mr. Lea." He shook his big head sadly. It upset him to see Lea hurt.

"You are, by God, not thinking of traveling, Lea?" Edwards said.

"By God I *am,*" said Lea in that strange voice.

Edwards sighed. "Well, you *are* a fool," he said. "Hold your head still, and stop talking."

When he was finished, Edwards washed his hands in a basin of water. "Now, listen," he said. "Those stitches must come out in about ten days. And they *must* be taken out by a physician! There's some danger of tearing the nerve worse, if it isn't done very carefully. You understand?"

Lea nodded. It hurt a lot, just nodding.

Edwards dug into his bag, and took out a small, dark bottle. "Laudanum," he said. "You'll need it when that nerve recovers from the shock of the injury. One drop in a drink of water. And don't overdose. Bear the pain as long as you can."

Lea nodded again. He didn't want to hear his voice.

"Can we help you, old man?" Toby Easterby said, as Edwards was packing his bag. "I mean . . . well, there's no need for you to go!" The Baron nodded.

"Thanks," Lea said, in that thick voice. He got up

from the grain sacks to shake their hands. "But it's better for me to go." He forgot and tried to smile. It was like being hit across the face with a whip.

"You'd better take a drop of that laudanum, now," Edwards said.

"Yes," Lea said. "Thank you," he said to them again. "I have to go."

"But Sarah—" said Toby, and the Baron put a hand on his arm to stop him.

"I have to go," Lea said.

"Come," the Baron said to the others. "It's time we leave." He gestured to Tiny Morgan. "You come too."

"Good-bye, Mr. Lea," Tiny said. He was crying.

"Good-bye, Tiny," Lea said to him. "Remember those rainbows."

"We'll take good care of her for you, Lea," Toby Easterby said. "We'll see she's safe, and this business done properly."

Lea nodded, and lifted his hand, and they all walked out, Tiny Morgan last, looking back. He heard their footsteps on the cobbles.

Then he took the laudanum bottle, and scooped out a dipper of water from the water bucket, and measured a single drop into the dipper of water and drank it down. He rinsed the dipper out and hung it back on the nail. Then he put the laudanum into his saddlebag, and went back to the stall to get the old dun out and saddle him.

He got the old gelding saddled. Even that had been a job; maybe the laudanum had helped, and maybe it hadn't.

He was lashing on the bedroll when he heard her footsteps.

"Lea."

237

He turned to look at her in the dim lantern light, and she put her hand up to her face with a gasp. Then she came to him, and gently touched the bandage with her fingers.

"Don't go," she said.

"I've got to go," he said, in that slurred voice.

"Stay," she said. "Stay and rest. You don't have to see me. We'll *never* see each other. I promise. Just stay."

"No," he said.

"Please!" Her eyes widened. She leaned against him and put her arms around him. She held him as hard as she could. "I'll talk to Mr. Buntline," she said, her cheek against his chest. "He won't say anything."

"And the other people won't say anything either?" Lea said. "About me shooting that man to death in your hotel . . . in front of your guests." He shook his head. It hurt as much to do that, as it did to talk.

"Stay," she said.

He took her arms and forced her away from him, then turned back to the dun and finished tying the bedroll on.

"You don't love me," she said.

The Sharps was leaning against the stable wall. He went and got it, and slid it down into the rifle-bucket in front of the saddle. The dun looked better than he had for some time—rested, grained-up.

He led the horse out into the stableyard, and climbed into the saddle with a grunt of effort. The dun sidled a little, restless, rank from so much time in the stall.

Sarah came out of the stable, and reached up to hold his stirrup.

"Take care of the old Indian," Lea said to her. "Tocsen. Let him stay over the grain bin. He likes

238

it there.''

"You don't love me," she said.

"Too damn much," he said. And he spurred the big horse forward so that she lost her grip on the leathers and almost fell. He trotted the dun out of the yard.

On a hill to the west, Lea reined the dun in, and turned to look back at Gunstock. In the distance, under a rising moon, the great hotel sparkled with a thousand lights—at the windows, the terraces along the ballrooms, the lanterns lit along the winding paths.

It was as beautiful as a dream. One of those dreams a man remembers and tries to dream again.

He looked for a while, then he turned the dun's head and rode away.